MW01233858

Invisible Burdens

A Beautiful Deceit Novel

Jillian D. Wray

Disclaimer

This is a work of fiction. Names, characters, places, and incidents are the product of the author's imagination or are used fictitiously. Any resemblance to actual persons, living or dead, events, or locales is entirely coincidental.

COPYRIGHT 2023 ©JILLIAN D WRAY
All rights reserved.

No part of this book may be used or reproduced, stored in a
retrieval system, or transmitted in any form or by any means –
electronic, mechanical, graphic including photocopying,
recording, taping, scanning, or by any information storage
retrieval system without prior written permission of the author
except in brief excerpts embodied in critical reviews and
certain other noncommercial uses permitted by copyright law.

For further information or permissions, please contact
jillianwray2017@gmail.com

**FOR A FULL LIST OF TRIGGER WARNINGS: PLEASE EMAIL
THE ADDRESS LISTED ABOVE**

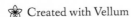 Created with Vellum

*This book is dedicated to Jessica Leigh,
for introducing me to so many things that led to the
creation of this story*

Chapter 1

Noah

"This is the worst idea I've ever heard."

Okay, maybe that's a little dramatic, but I don't love change, and adding dancers will be a *big* change, not just for us but for our tour and our entire genre of music. Without being able to gauge how our fans will react, I'm hesitant. It's definitely outside the box, and although this is what Matt, our balding tour manager, is known for, it isn't a move I would've picked.

I lean forward, planting my elbows on my knees, and pinch the bridge of my nose. Like somehow, more pressure *there* will alleviate the pressure building in my chest.

There's always pressure in my chest these days.

If it hadn't been going on for the last two years, I'd think I was having a heart attack . . . every day.

Fucking Nicole.

Our rise to fame skyrocketed almost overnight when our last album dropped. As we gained attention, I lost time to devote to my girlfriend and realized I was no longer in a place where I could handle that kind of commitment.

When I broke things off with her, she retaliated by leaking private, unflattering pictures of me, knowing how much I value my privacy.

I lean back in the uncomfortable chair and move my hand from my face to rub the burning spot on my chest. "It's always been just the four of us on stage," I argue with Matt. "We have a chemistry that works, but if you start adding people, we risk fucking that up and now is definitely *not* the time to fuck that up."

Matt's large mahogany desk sits to my left against a set of floor-to-ceiling windows, while Matt and I face each other in leather wingback chairs around a spotless glass coffee table.

"Noah, why did you hire me?" he asks in that smug tone he knows I hate as he steeples his fingers and looks down his nose at me.

I'm tempted to make rude hand gestures, but since Matt's the best concert tour director in the business, I keep my tattooed hands firmly wrapped around the coffee cup in my lap.

Even his legs are smug as he crosses one Armani clad thigh over the other, bobbing his foot impatiently and continuing to stare at me from behind his frameless, designer glasses with one brow arched. His artistic vision is second to none even if his wardrobe choices are usually atrocious.

His thinning gray hair is a testament to either poor genetics or the stress of his job. Coupled with his ruddy complexion and expanding waistline, I'd say Matt's lifestyle does not consist of hummus, vegetables, an alcohol-free mentality, or regular exercise.

I glare at Matt, angry heat creeping up my neck as I hold my unimpressed stare, refusing to give him the answer he's looking for. I'd hired him because he's fucking brilliant and sells out tours. But he already knows this and I'll be damned if he gets me to stroke his gigantic ego.

He's unfazed by my rudeness as he starts speaking again over the quiet whir of the air conditioning fan. I'm glad for the light breeze coming out of the vent because this meeting has me feeling a little clammy and panicked.

I hate the idea he's pitching, and I already know I've lost the argument. Somehow, the more famous we become, the less control we have over our image and if that bleeds into a loss of control over our music, I'll lose my fucking mind.

"You aren't just some boys making music in your mom's garage anymore, Kinkaid," he says, calling me by my last name.

I want to argue that we haven't been those "boys" in a while, but I hold my tongue because he's right.

I can't even pump gas without inciting chaos these days.

When I stay quiet, he continues dishing out what sounds like a slimy, well-rehearsed sales pitch.

"You're selling out venues multiple nights in a row. There's a *demand* for you that you've never had before. Similarly, your fans are no longer just broke college kids trying to get drunk at a cheap metalcore concert. They want a *show*. They're people willing to pay $120 a seat. They want to be *entertained,* Noah. It's your music that draws them there, but it's our *production* that's going to leave them wanting more."

I know he's right . . . again.

Doesn't mean I like it. Or that I'm ready to hand over all the control and decision making to him.

A sigh of defeat escapes my lips.

"Do we get to pick them at least?"

Matt laughs a hearty, belly laugh causing me to throw my hands in the air, almost dumping my coffee everywhere, and roll my eyes.

Still laughing he asks, "What do you know about dancers,

Noah? And I don't mean *pole* dancers. Do you know what to ask? What qualifications they need? What the actual vision is?"

No.

No.

And *hell no*, seeing as it wasn't my vision in the first place. In fact, I think it's a gigantic waste of money.

He continues, much to my chagrin.

"Do you even know what a pirouette is? No. You do not. If I let you pick the back-up dancers, they'll all be pin-up dolls with questionable dance experience. I'm not taking exotic dancers on this tour. I need *artists*. If we're lucky, you will all find them ugly with the personalities of dry-erase markers and none of you will even be tempted to look twice at them." He grins like the Cheshire cat before continuing, "But I've got a plan in case Betty Ballerina has a good sense of humor and a rack to match. I'll let you know when I've made my choices and when you're needed. Now get out, I have work to do." He uncrosses his legs, stands, and strolls to the chair behind his desk.

Looks like the guys and I are getting back up dancers whether we want them or not. We'll be the first metalcore band to share a stage with them, and it's either going to be ground-breaking or we're about to be the laughing stock of the music world just as we really start to enter it.

I resent that Matt's opinion of us is basically reduced to horny dogs with our dicks hanging out as if we can't control ourselves, but I bite my tongue and keep my mouth shut.

We may be red-blooded males, but our band is our life, not to mention our livelihood, and I'm feeling all the pressure as its founder and front man to make sure we don't squander our recent success.

Pushing out of the leather chair my ass feels glued to, I throw my parting shot over my shoulder and hope he hears me loud and clear. "I'm not getting on that stage with sequins and anything resembling Taylor Swift's pop culture."

His response is immediate, and he doesn't even bother to look up from his screen as he gives it.

"Her first twenty-two shows this year grossed over $300 million. Not only would you get on that stage with her, you'd lick the sole of Taylor's sequined, thigh-high boot if I told you to."

I grit my teeth and storm out the door, tossing my coffee cup in the trash and smiling a little when coffee splashes on his wall.

It's never been about the money for us, and we aren't going to change that now. Staying true to who we are is imperative or we'll just become another cog in the machine. This newly acquired fame is adding pressure I should have seen coming, yet somehow didn't. I think perhaps it's because I never dreamed our names would be painted all over the world with fans trying to get their hands on tickets to shows almost a year in advance.

Now that our fanbase has exploded and the demand is high, there's an expectation to turn everything I touch into gold, and I'm afraid of what the pressure will do when it's time to write new music.

Thankfully, Apex Records, our record label, has given us ten months before we need to start laying down new tracks. Our contract with them isn't great because when we signed three years ago, we were young and eager and pretty much took whatever the owner offered, but that's a problem for a different day.

I rub a hand back and forth over my sternum for the second time in twenty minutes to quell the discomfort rising behind it as I step into the elevator.

While the metal box hurtles me toward the ground floor,

there are horrible images running through my head. Bad light shows and girls in glitter shaking their asses on the stage around us not meshing with the vibe of who we are at all.

I have a feeling we're going to hate this, but worse, I fear what will happen if the fans actually like it and we let ourselves be swallowed up by the masses, losing ourselves in the process.

Another thought crashes into me. We're not exactly peaceful up on that stage. All it will take is for Sloan to get rowdy one time and the neck of his guitar is going to collide with some poor girl's head, making a mess.

People will be talking about the *production* alright.

I sigh, pulling my phone out of the pocket of my jeans to send a text to the group as I head out of the building.

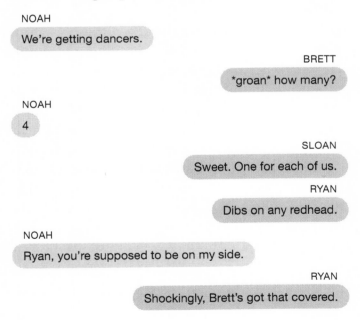

That *is* shocking. Despite my offense at Matt's earlier statement, Brett is known for his affinity for women, and I was surprised when he protested the addition of the dancers as much as I did.

> **BRETT**
> Our stage is no place for pussy . . . that's the reward for after the show.

Hmm . . . maybe we aren't much better than horny dogs.

This is where it usually devolves into an hour of pointless conversation even though the guys are most likely all sitting in the same room since we've lived together for the last five years.

We grew up together and got stupid lucky. Our parents agreed to help support us financially our first year of making music *if* we all completed college. The guys and I have natural talents we were fortunate enough to have our parents recognize, even if Brett's parents took some convincing.

It was a no-brainer.

We went to school for business, music production, and graphic design and are grateful our parents made us get those degrees in case the fickle opinions of the masses change and we have to stop making music – or at least get additional jobs to support ourselves while we continue to make music.

College wasn't for Sloan, but his parents got on board after he agreed to four years in the military. I often wonder what his deployment was like, but he doesn't bring it up. Even living with him and sharing almost every waking moment with him, I can't tell if Sloan's ever-present sense of humor means he's really that carefree or if he uses it to deflect something darker from shining through. There never seems to be a good time to ask.

I silence the chat and let them talk it out.

When I round the corner of the building, I'm met head on with a group of five girls, dressed all in black, who shriek my name and start flashing their phones in my direction.

Not being able to walk down the street without being recognized is still new to me. So new in fact, I often forget I can't do it anymore. Wanting the girls to stay quiet and not attract any more attention, I hold my hands up in mock surrender and duck back around the corner, motioning for them to come to me.

"Tell you what, I'll take selfies with all of you if you promise not to scream." I feel like I'm negotiating with terrorists as the girls immediately go silent, giving in to my demands as they surround me on all sides.

If they're true fans, they'll know the rules, but just in case, I add, "Hands to yourselves, please."

I don't like being groped by people I don't know. Hell, I don't really like being touched by people I *do* know, either. The guys are different because they're basically an extension of myself but when Nicole leaked every picture she had of me with no shirt on, and even a few riskier than that, I felt overly exposed. Not to mention, wary of trusting people.

Now, people assume I never take my shirt off because I'm still the same pudgy guy I was two years ago in those photos.

I'm happy to let them assume.

I never actually cared what I looked like in the pictures, it was the fact that I had no control over the rest of the world seeing me half-naked and asleep. The other one was of me sitting on a toilet. I actually have pants on because I was nauseated from some food poisoning and was between bouts of puking, but you can't tell and it looks like . . . well, it looks bad.

Two extremely vulnerable moments in my life made avail-

8

able to everyone in the world all because of a shitty break up I honestly tried to handle with maturity and respect.

Will fans post pictures from this tour?

Absolutely.

But at least I know it's coming. I'll be in my element, and I've given some semblance of consent by getting on that stage.

I stoop my six-foot-two self down to fit in the girls' camera frames and wait until I hear several clicks before straightening back up.

Selfies done and autographs given, I head to the parking deck where my driver is waiting and abandon any hope I had of getting another cup of coffee.

Probably better to hit the gym anyway. Something has to relieve the pressure in my chest, or I won't be around to enjoy a decades long career even if the fanbase is present to support it.

Chapter 2

Sienna

I 'm having one of those days where I question every decision I've ever made. My whole life all I've wanted to do is perform. But after sessions like today, I wonder if it's all been for nothing.

"I couldn't get anything to stick, my movements felt jerky, and I didn't trust my silks, causing me to panic not once, but twice," I vent to my best friend of fifteen years, roommate, and co-dancer, Bri Vorossi - a.k.a. the perfect female specimen.

Gorgeous, confident, smart, competitive, adventurous, and wicked - in the best of ways - to her very core. She's the type of girl you want in your corner.

She's my ride-or-die.

"Would you *chill*, Sienna? We all have bad days," she reminds me as we walk off the gym floor and head into the locker room of our training facility. "Besides, your bad days are way better than some people's best days. Remember that."

Did I mention she's also my perpetual cheerleader?

"Forget *days*. I feel like I'm having a bad *month*," I whine at our lockers.

Bri's getting ready to head home to our apartment for the night while I'm mixing electrolytes into my water bottle to get back out on the floor for at least another hour. My muscles are screaming with fatigue, but I'm determined to push through until I make this perfect.

"This is nothing a glass of wine and some couch time can't fix," Bri says, shaking her long, blonde beach waves out of her bun and running her fingers through them. "You need to rest. Overtraining is the enemy, Si. You've gotta know when to call it quits for the night."

She's probably right, but the stubborn part of myself – namely, my entire being – refuses to accept that I should walk away until this routine is better. I've always been a perfectionist, but there are things from my past that prevent me from being able to relax knowing something is half-assed. Every time I want to stop, I think about the sacrifices my dad made for me, and I suck it up and get my ass back out there. He was the one who taught me every skill can be perfected if you devote enough time and attention to it. Of course, he's also the one who showed me that devoting that much time and attention to something can ruin your life.

The end result? I struggle with finding balance.

"Besides," Bri continues as she pulls sweatpants on over her tights, "Josh offered to pick up Chinese takeout, and I know he's a pain in your ass, but free food is free food."

Bri and I live close to the dance studio because our whole lives are spent here from sun up to sun down. We were fortunate to have found a deal through Bri's brother, Josh's, best friend's dad or something.

All I know is I can afford the rent in a place where I shouldn't be able to, and I'm extremely grateful. Aerial dancers don't make much money, and right now, we're only training so we make *no* money.

Most of us hope to get a gig that will set us up long term, but those contracts don't become available too often because people rarely give those positions up. Cirque du Soleil is our biggest employer, but occasionally, we get other gigs in Vegas or Broadway shows.

To pay our bills, Bri works at a salon and I work at a local boutique when our training schedules allow it or our bank accounts demand it.

"I wish I could head home with you, but Jess said if I couldn't control that descent, she was going to pull me off the silks for a week, and I only started four months ago."

I'd been waiting over a year to start silks training. I know I have what it takes, and I don't want to lose my spot.

Bri turns and grips my shoulder. "Si, you work harder than all of us combined. You aren't going to lose your spot." I appreciate her confidence even though I don't share it. She grins wide before adding, "And if you do, then I'll boycott."

I huff out a laugh at her attempt to make me feel better.

"I'll see you at home." I hug my bestie goodbye, watching her eyes fall because she knows I'm staying, and I head back out into the gym.

The springboard-type floor is much like a gymnastics floor, and I bounce, hop, and roll my way across it to turn the music up loud and spend a minute getting more comfortable in the space alone.

During the day, I train classical ballet, modern dance, gymnastics, yoga, and now aerial dance with trapeze and silks. The combination is so erotic, and I love how the music comes alive in our bodies. The soft notes of the piano drift through the speakers and fifteen minutes in, I miss a foothold and fall six feet onto the bouncy floor, frustrated and angry.

Too angry for this music because right now I want to smash the stupid piano into a million pieces.

I need something different.

Something harder.

Something that sounds as pissed as I feel.

I hook my phone up to the speakers and scroll Spotify for one of Bri's playlists instead. I just need to clear my mind.

Bri recently got me hooked on alternative scream-o music. *Metalcore*, I think they call it? An odd choice for the five-six blonde who grew up as a pastor's kid, but once I heard it, I knew she was on to something, and I latched right on as well. There are just some scenarios in life when one needs a heavy bass line and someone beating the shit out of the drums like they're trying to exorcise a demon.

Speaking of, as soon as the bass drum kicks in, I feel it in my veins, and I jump up to grab my silks, focused, angry, and confident. When the singer whispers his lyrics it's like he's in the room with me.

Taunting me.

It's exactly what I need to up the ante and plow through this routine perfectly.

The silks caress the exposed skin of my arms and legs, and I let myself get lost in the music and the feeling, pushing all other thoughts out of my mind and focus only on the voice coming through the speakers.

Noah Kinkaid.

Lead singer of Beautiful Deceit.

His voice is one of the only ones I can identify immediately in this genre. A deadly combination of silk, sandpaper, and sex, I've never heard anyone whose voice could compare.

Whether he's singing, screaming, whispering, or just talking, he makes me want to strip out of everything and bathe in his sound.

Another Beautiful Deceit song starts, and I wind myself up higher and higher, my legs spread wide so I can roll my hips and pull up with my arms to climb higher still on the long silver swathes of silk hanging from the ceiling. When I open my eyes, I'm almost twenty feet in the air.

I exhale my nerves and commit to my descent. It feels like a free fall as Noah screams about falling into a dark abyss and the floor rushes up fast to meet my face. This time, just like I was taught, I pull my legs apart and grip the silk below my torso to slow my descent. I unravel beautifully until I'm six feet off the ground, perfectly controlled.

Elated over finally achieving the perfect decent, I spread my arms wide and swing my legs to do a couple back flips in time to the angry bass while suspended. The moves just come to me as I dance in the air, appreciating everything my body can do and every position I can achieve.

When I'm finally spent, I slide off the silks and wear my smile all the way to the locker room, just as satisfied with the mental victory as I am over the physical one.

Maybe even more so.

Grabbing my stuff, I turn to leave, almost bumping into someone and jump back startled, hand to my sports bra-covered heart.

"Sorry, Sienna. I thought you heard me come in."

"Jess! No problem. I was just lost in my thoughts." And I definitely did not hear my coach come in.

"That was good work you did out there." Her mousy brown curls bounce as she nods toward the gym.

I feel myself blush. I didn't know I had an audience and admit as much, but I'm kind of glad she saw it. That she knows I'm capable of a perfect performance.

"Oh. I, uh, didn't know anyone was watching."

She gives me a small smile. "Obviously. You perform better without the eyes on you."

Yeah, that's my problem.

Like any performing art, it can be hard to concentrate with a lot of eyes on you but *unlike* a lot of performing arts, if I mess up, an entire audience will witness me fall to my very messy death. It's much different from when I used to play music.

"I'm working on that."

I know I have to do better if I hope to do this as a career long term. An aerial dancer is no good if she can't do her best work in front of a crowd.

"Interesting music choice," Jess says. She's never been one to come across as judgmental, but I feel defensive for some reason.

"Yeah, Bri got me hooked actually," I say, like the fact that Bri likes it somehow legitimizes my music choice more so than simply liking it myself. "It really helps with my nerves. Like the energy from the music absorbs everything I'm feeling, allowing me to just sling myself around on the silk." I didn't realize it until right this moment, but it's true.

"Interesting," she repeats. "On Friday, we're doing a showcase. Nothing overly fancy but I want each aerialist to put together a three-minute routine to share with the group. Use that song. And that routine."

I must look like a deer in the headlights because she chuckles, "It's okay to be different, Sienna. The other girls may not understand the music choice, but that's the most confident and flawless I've seen you move. Pick what works for *you*. That's what the showcase is about."

I nod my head and slip my sweatshirt over my mess of red hair. Most of the girls have shorter hair so it stays out of their face and doesn't get hung up in the silks, but short hair doesn't suit my angular face, so I keep mine pulled back with a thousand bobby pins instead. I close my locker door when Jess adds, "Oh, could you let Bri know about the showcase? I didn't have a chance to tell her."

"Sure thing."

We have three days to perfect a three-minute silk routine to perform in front of all twenty-seven girls.

No pressure.

When I get home, Bri is on the couch, a glass of red wine in her hand. Unfortunately, her brother is sitting opposite her in our recliner.

It seems like he's finding more reasons to come over lately. Work must be slow. Josh is a corporate media and entertainment attorney. He has clients all over the country and is usually travelling here or there for meetings, so we don't see him much. But apparently, work has kept him home in D.C. for a while now.

I feel my face fall as I throw my bag on the floor next to Bri's and she sits up with an expectant look on her face.

"Well? How'd it go?"

I can't help but break out into a smile as I tell her about the routine, taking a seat on the couch next to her and as far away from Josh as I can get. I tell her about the music, and the run-in with Jess. Bri can't hide her excitement about the showcase.

The girl is competitive as hell and even if it's *not* a competition, she'll want to win. She's never met a challenge she didn't love.

"Can guests come?" Josh asks, sticking a forkful of lo mein in his mouth. "I haven't seen you guys perform in a while."

Josh is plenty nice. And he isn't bad looking – average maybe, but not bad. He's just been relentlessly into me for years. I thought maybe he was just into that whole *little sister's best friend* thing. Like I was the forbidden fruit and therefore interesting. Except, Bri has made it clear that she doesn't care if her brother and I hook up as long as we know we'll be in each other's lives forever because *she* will be in our lives

16

forever . . . so I'm not really forbidden . . . and he's still interested.

I've never returned Josh's feelings, but he seems to think my *no* actually means *not right now but keep trying and eventually I'll come around.*

His obsession got so bad, he threatened my ex several times – although Brad probably deserved it - and Bri finally had to have a talk with Josh to back off.

Unfortunately, it didn't work.

Mostly I just try to ignore Josh now, because Bri and her brother are close, and I don't want to put her in the middle.

"Jess didn't say for sure, but I don't think it's open to the public. It sounded like we're performing for each other and some kind of evaluation or something."

Not a total lie. But not the truth either.

After a beat, Bri grows serious and places her wine glass on the coffee table. I *hate* when Bri gets serious because her heart-to-hearts always remind me I'm a cliché with mommy issues, and it drives me batshit crazy.

"Bri, stop looking at me like that." I move to get up from the couch.

She reaches out and catches my wrist forcing me to turn back toward her.

"Si, I worry about you. You push yourself too hard. Everyone in the audience is not your mother. You *are* good enough, and no one resents you for it."

I swallow the tears that show up every time she goes down this path. I blink them down back into their ducts, willing them to behave. I swore a long time ago I wouldn't shed another tear for Lana Mariano – formerly Lana Kennedy when she was married to my dad.

I give Bri a tight smile and finger the silver K necklace at my throat. Bri and Josh both have been with me through my darkest of days. I know she comes from a good place, but no one understands the conflicting emotions I have about performing.

I need it to feel alive, but it's also the thing that kills me a little more each time.

A pang of guilt pierces my heart, and I remember I need to call my dad. He's the person who understands my struggle the most because he was there that night. Performing has always been his first love, and he's never been conflicted about doing it, even if it contributed to destroying our family . . . and even when it eventually destroyed him.

I push the thought aside. It's not like he'd answer the call anyway.

Chapter 3

Noah

"Sloan, come in a little earlier. I want you to hit that note right as Brett comes in with the bass drum. More power. And then add a pause for a half beat. I want that power to have a chance to hit before we move on in the next measure."

I pull my earbud out as I talk to the guys in the recording studio behind our house. It's not fancy, but it gets the job done when we want to lay down new tracks, try something out, or like now, prep for our tour. We have six months before it kicks off which somehow feels like both a long time and an incredibly short one.

Every day there are more requests for interviews, everyone wanting exclusives about what to expect. It's like the more we deny the requests, the more they come.

People always want what they can't have.

Our goal wasn't to build mystery, we just aren't giving interviews because there are so many details we don't know yet. However, now that we see the effect it's having, Matt has encouraged us to remain tight-lipped.

He's controlling our social media pages and releasing obscure teasers that have our fans going absolutely crazy – but I'm just as lost as the fans because even I can't fathom what the hell a silkworm has to do with this tour.

When I think about it, I have to pop another Tums.

"Yes, *mother,*" Sloan's smartass quips back.

He's definitely the class clown - or thinks he is. Everything is a joke to him. Not that he doesn't take music seriously, because he does, he's just so naturally talented he doesn't really have to try that hard to get shit right. His light brown hair flops on his head as he hammers down on the timing to get it the way I want it.

Brett, our drummer, is undoubtedly our ladies' man. He'll fuck almost any consenting female – and there are a *lot* of consenting females - especially now. In fact, our record label requires a monthly STD panel because of him. Apparently if one of us gets herpes - or something worse - and passes it on, our careers are over.

I tell him all the time I think his nose ring is ugly, and I'd rather have herpes than that thing sticking out of my face, but the girls fawn all over it, and he just laughs as he takes another chick to bed.

He's the one I worry about the most, almost always courting alcohol or a woman. Brett sometimes seems like he's trying to fill a void, but I'm not his therapist, so when he's ready to talk about it, he will.

Ryan is our level-headed bassist. Every band needs a peace-keeper, and he's ours. He's the only person who can calm my temper which tends to be connected to a short fuse these days.

If we have to give an interview, Ryan always comes with me and does most of the talking, which is weird to a lot of people since I'm the lead singer. I may make love to my audi-ence when I'm on stage, but off stage, I'm a closed book. I don't like the camera or the spotlight. Besides, Ryan is the son of a politician so he's well-versed in social etiquette and manners.

Better him than me.

Sloan, unsurprisingly, nails the timing on the next run-through and my head bobs wildly to the beat we're throwing down. We've been at it for a couple of hours and my voice is going to need a break soon so I don't strain my vocal cords.

"Sloan, that was it. Keep it just like that." I'm pretty sure Sloan has a praise kink because he beams at me and makes kissy lips, causing me to chuckle.

These guys.

Playing live is a lot different than recording. The biggest difference being no do-overs so if someone misses a measure, you'd all better be ready to improvise and pick back up at the same spot. The *best* difference though, is the energy. I love writing and recording, but there is nothing like playing in front of a live crowd no matter how big or small if the energy is right. If we can sound this good in rehearsal, it gives me high hopes that our performance in front of thirty-thousand people is going to be pretty fucking epic.

We're just finishing up the session when Matt comes in the shed-turned-studio wearing another pair of chinos and the ugliest button-down I've ever seen. Before I can say anything, Sloan pipes up.

"Hey, Matt. Bozo the clown called. He wants his shirt back, especially since he threw up on it last night."

Brett snorts. "The fuck even *is* that, man? Did you get shit on by the circus?"

Matt somehow manages to keep a straight face as he addresses the actual clowns in the room.

"Har-har. Perhaps you want to remember I'm about to make you fuckers filthy rich and what you'll learn is that when you have this kind of money," he smooths out a non-existent wrinkle before continuing, "you can wear whatever the fuck you want."

"Okay," Ryan joins the discussion. "But I think the real question is why would you *want* to wear that?" His face shows no hint of a smile which makes it even funnier, and Sloan and Brett openly guffaw, but I'm quickly losing interest in this conversation.

"Matt, what do you need?" I ask, redirecting. He doesn't usually pop in unannounced.

"I've chosen the girls you're touring with. I selected them from a showcase they put on yesterday, and I'm heading over to extend the offer of employment. I thought you'd like to meet them." He eyes Sloan and Brett warily before turning his attention back to me and Ryan. "Please keep your hyenas under control. It wasn't easy to find exactly what I needed, and I don't want any of them backing out because of those asswipes." He nods his head in the direction of my guitarist and drummer.

"Are they hot?" Brett asks, his grin stretching from ear to ear, totally unfazed by being called a hyena and an asswipe in the same breath.

Thankfully, I'm standing right behind him so I can easily reach down to smack the back of his head.

"You're not fucking the dancers, Brett. We have to spend eight months on the road with them, and no way are we risking the tour so you can get your rocks off. Besides, I thought you were against this idea?"

"Such a buzzkill," he mutters before explaining. "I *was* against it. But it seems that we're getting them whether we want them or not, so I'd at least like them to be hot since as you mentioned, we'll be looking at them for eight months."

Thankfully, Ryan steps in before I punch Brett in the throat. Since Brett doesn't do backup vocals, it'd be a safe move. I'd never break his fingers or his arms though, he's irreplaceable on the drums. The dude has unparalleled speed and can create the craziest rhythms I've ever heard.

"Brett, stop acting like there wasn't a line of pussy waiting for you after every show even *before* people actually knew who we were. No fucking the dancers. Move on," Ryan says in a bored tone.

"Yes, we'd like to meet them," I tell Matt. "And just so we're clear, if we don't click, they're gone. I respect what you do, but this tour needs to be a reflection of *us*. It's our name on that ticket. I'm not hosting four women who don't match our level of artistic passion."

Matt and that fucking smirk. "I don't think that'll be a problem."

Chapter 4

Sienna

"I don't believe this!"

Bri and I jumped around excitedly, hugging each other for ten minutets after getting the email that said our showcases were chosen for some secret project. Jess said she couldn't divulge any details but we're to find out more later today.

Once we finally calmed down, we needed to get ready quickly so we're cramped in our bathroom, both sitting on the double vanity with our feet in the sinks putting on our makeup and pinning our hair back. We were told whatever we wore yesterday for the showcase would be fine, and we would most likely need to perform our routine again, but she wasn't sure.

"I know, it's exciting, but it sounds kind of shady, right? Like, why can't they tell us what we've been chosen for? I don't think it's Cirque or a Vegas show because those are on-site auditions. I didn't even realize the showcase *was* an audition." She finishes her cherry red lipstick and smacks her lips together. "You almost ready?"

I slide my last bobby pin in my copper-red hair, keeping it

pulled back off my face, and swing my legs down onto the floor, swiping my fingers under my eyes to catch any rogue mascara.

"Yep. Let's go."

I situate my wide-necked sweatshirt and take one last look in the mirror before slipping into my Uggs and grabbing my parka off the rack by the door. It's windy and unseasonably cold today, which is crazy since it was seventy-five degrees just a few days ago. That's D.C. in the Spring for you.

When we reach the familiar two story beige building of our aerial studio, two other girls are already there. I know their names are Joslyn and Kara, but that's about it. They're both in the advanced section with Bri who waves hello at the girls as we join them.

"Anyone know what this is all about yet?" Bri asks as we approach.

"No, but there's a blacked-out Cadillac SUV out back in the alley," Kara says, causing Bri and me to exchange glances.

"Ooh maybe it's someone famous!" Bri says bouncing on the balls of her feet and rubbing her hands together. She brings excited energy to almost every situation.

"You'd be right," an unfamiliar male voice drawls from behind us. Although his tone is casual, there is an undercurrent of pride and confidence in it as well.

We all turn to see Jess and a man we don't recognize enter the gym. He's maybe forty-five or fifty with a body that resembles a sack of potatoes, whisps of salt and pepper hair hanging on as best they can, and average height. As my eyes move from his physicality to his wardrobe, I notice he's wearing a shirt that looks like maybe he *is* from Cirque du Soleil.

My palms start sweating immediately. No way is this happening for me already.

"Ladies, this is Matthew Decker. He's a tour manager for a

popular music group. Before we tell you more, we request that you all sign a non-disclosure agreement."

The four of us look at each other, our bewilderment and confusion evident in our raised brows and wide eyes.

Matthew jumps in, sensing our hesitation.

"Ladies, I assure you, this is not a contract of employment, but hopefully you'll sign those next. As of now, however, you are free to leave at any time, although I hope you don't. Because of who you'll be working with, there's a need for discretion. The NDA just assures me that even if you choose not to join us after hearing my proposition, you'll promise to stay quiet about the plans we have in place. Show business has always been – and remains – very cutthroat and I'd like to keep our tour details safe." He reaches into his briefcase as he talks and pulls out a folder.

We're all still standing on the springy gym floor but instead of moving somewhere more formal or even somewhere with seats, he pulls out clipboards with paperwork already in place. He seems anxious to get our signatures on *these* papers as soon as possible.

Intrigue outweighs any red flags - plus, we all trust Jess, and she doesn't seem sketched out - so we all sign on the dotted line.

After he's collected the documents and tucked them away, he calls to the open gym.

"Come on out, fellas."

My jaw drops as none other than all four members of Beautiful Deceit come into view.

I clutch Bri's hand, certain she and I are about to start fangirling our asses off.

"What the *actual* fuck?" she mumbles under her breath. I shrug and squeeze harder.

These guys are larger than life. They're also larger than the top of the Billboard charts right now. In fact, Bri and I tried to get tickets to their upcoming tour but every show around us was sold out already.

My eyes hungrily rove over each of them in turn, and I've forgotten how to breathe.

Bri nudges me in the side, forcing a harsh inhale, her hand still in mine as she giggles and whispers, "Kara and Joslyn have no idea who they are."

Even without my recent introduction and subsequent love of alternative metal, I would have recognized them. Their faces are everywhere and none of them are easily forgotten. Not a single one of them fades into the background.

Suddenly, I panic. If Noah opens his mouth in my presence, and I don't have the speaker as a buffer for that sinful perfection, I will either spontaneously combust or melt in a puddle on this floor.

I stand slack-jawed, staring like it's the first time I've seen snow or the ocean. Bri on the other hand, has never met a stranger. I envy her confidence in that regard, and I go completely still as she addresses the men in front of us like she's known them her whole life.

"Noah, Sloan, Ryan . . . *Brett*." She's a little breathless as she says the drummer's name. "To what do we owe this extremely unexpected pleasure?"

Sloan is the one who answers, his smile reaching all the way to his eyes. "Hey, look, Dancer Barbie knows who we are."

I can tell by the tone of his voice he doesn't mean it in a condescending way, he's just surprised to find that a classically trained ballerina knows their band. Besides, Bri actually *does* look like a barbie . . . only shorter. She has flawless skin, blonde hair, a small waist, wide green eyes, and perky boobs.

"Hey look, guitarist G.I. Joe speaks," she quips back with a wink, taking in Sloan's combat boots, cargo pants, and dog tags. She *winks* at this rock god like they're the best of friends.

"Although, I think G.I. Joe has better abs," she whispers loudly enough for all of us to hear while blatantly pretending to just tell Sloan.

I would bark out in laughter if the synapses in my brain would fire.

Sloan's hand moves to the hem of his shirt like he's about to prove her wrong when another member shoots his hand out to stop him.

Noah Kinkaid rubs his tattooed hand down his gorgeous face and my greedy eyes follow the movement like a shark watches its prey.

"I apologize for Sloan. We don't let him out often."

Holy shit, that voice.

It's even better in person.

I feel my ovaries start working like a chicken factory cranking out eggs.

How can someone sound as calm as the glassy sea, cool as a summer rain, comforting as a blanket, and as dangerous as the edge of a cliff, all at the same time? He speaks in perfect pitch and it's exquisitely rough like stubble against my inner thigh.

After years of studying music, my ear is selective, moody, and extremely judgmental and even I can't find fault. Does everyone else hear it too?

Of course, dummy, I chastise myself. *Why do you think they're number one on multiple charts with a fan base that's growing faster than fucking weeds?*

Bri giggles next to me and shrugs her shoulder. "No big deal. I've been called worse." I swear I see Brett's eyes narrow at Bri's response.

Matthew inserts himself to get us back on track as Jess finally leads the group to the side of the gym where there are tables and chairs set up for the dancers waiting for training space. No one else is here though because open training time doesn't start until one p.m.

When Noah takes the chair next to mine, I'm immediately, and acutely, aware of every move he makes. When he scratches his nose, shifts his weight, leans forward, I see it all, forgetting he can see me too and when he turns his intensely dark eyes on me, I'm pretty sure I'm going to pass out. I've never been so overwhelmed by someone's presence before.

Not like this.

I mean, yes, I've seen hot guys. There are a few who train here that are so shredded, I could use their abs as a cheese grater.

But Noah Kinkaid?

He's on a whole different level. He's a lethal combination of beauty, darkness, determination, and power. Almost like he's some kind of deity trapped inside a mortal's body, biding his time until he's set free. His face is perfect, but this feeling goes beyond his looks. It's the vibe he gives off. The untouchable ferocity lurking beneath his surface, and I feel it buzzing through every cell in my body.

He nods his head forward indicating that I should refocus my attention and says, "You might want to hear this."

Fuck. Me.

I don't want to hear it.

I only ever want to hear *him* for the rest of my life – which won't be long if I don't get my heart rate under control.

I give him a tight, embarrassed smile and turn back toward Matthew but not before I watch as Noah rubs a hand across his chest, and I have the urge to lick every single one of his tattooed fingers.

Fuck, that's distracting.

"Ladies." The start of Matthew's speech reluctantly draws my eyes toward the speaker. "The gentlemen of Beautiful

Deceit are going on tour in six months to promote their newest album. It's uncommon for bands in their genre to host dancers of any kind but I have something big planned and based on your showcases and your particular set of skills, I've chosen you to be a part of it." When he's satisfied he has our attention, he continues. "If you sign on, you'll be agreeing to travel with the band for eight months. You will have hotel accommodations and meals paid for. You will also be provided with transportation to and from all the venues. You'll find the salary to be on the last page of the contract. There are no replacements for you so short of actually dying, you'll be expected to perform. Life on the road is not for everyone, but we're hoping the salary offsets the stressful lifestyle."

We all start to tune him out as we flip through the pages of the contract in front of us while he drones on in the background until he clears his throat and regains our focus.

Well, most of our focus.

I'm sitting less than three feet from a man whose voice brings me to my knees and plays on repeat during every date with my vibrator.

Do you have any idea what it's like to sit next to the man whose voice has gotten you off more times than your ex's actual dick?

A laugh bubbles up my throat.

"Something funny?" Noah whispers in an annoyed tone as he leans forward, his scent invading my space for the first time, rendering me speechless. He smells like a crisp fall morning. Masculine but comforting like he's a blanket against the cold. Like an apple pie wrapped in leather and resting under a fragrant pine tree. I want to hibernate in its heaviness for eternity.

My thighs clench together hard, and I pray he doesn't notice. God, I wish I had jeans on and not purple fucking leggings. There will be no hiding what his voice does to me if I have to perform my routine with my legs spread wide.

"Um, no. Well, *yes*, but . . . no," I stutter, growing more embarrassed by the second. *Get it together, Sienna!*

He narrows his eyes at me, and I feel my chest rising and falling fast.

Too fast.

What's worse, I know he can see it too because his eyes are pinned to the low neckline of the tank top I had on under my sweatshirt – which came off soon after the guys entered the room because I started sweating immediately.

Matthew clears his throat and aims his annoyance in my direction as Noah leans back in his chair, taking my breath with him.

"There are a few important details I want to bring to your attention," Matt says. "First, you may not speak to *any* press at any time. No podcasts, no journalists, no reporters and your social media posts have to be approved by me before they can be posted. Second, if you miss more than three shows due to illness or other emergency, you will be removed from the tour and forfeit your remaining salary. You will have two weeks off within those eight months to spend time with family or however you choose. Consider it like R&R for the military. My company will fly you anywhere you want to go so long as you're back on time. Third, this contract also ensures you will not engage in illicit drug use, heavy intoxication, and that you will go on some form of birth control of your choosing for these eight months so we have no unexpected surprises. Lastly, and most importantly, by signing this contract, you agree to not sleep with the musicians. If you do, you will be in breach of contract and kicked off the tour, forfeiting the rest of your salary, not to mention, my company will bring suit against you for that breach of contract. As you can imagine, things have a tendency to get a little wild on the road. We're investing a lot into this tour, and it's been my experience that mixing business and pleasure never ends well. This is to protect you all as much as the band."

Matt cuts his eyes to Brett and Sloan as my eyes snap up and meet Bri's. Although, I'm pretty sure hers respond in protest whereas mine are shocked that he would make that insinuation so casually.

A few seconds later, my gaze lands on Ryan who sends a wink my way causing my cheeks to flush. I drop my eyes immediately but can't stop my traitorous orbs as they find Noah beside me.

His eyes are still dark and intense . . . and they're aimed right at me, but he's all business. I'm pretty sure he's sizing each of us up, trying to figure out if we have what it takes to represent them on stage.

If our eyes are truly the windows to our souls, then Noah's soul is as dark as the music he sings. The collar of his shirt is open, and I can just see the start of a tattoo peeking out. I quickly bring my eyes back up to his and cringe when his are still on me, hard as stone and seemingly chastising as if to say *you haven't even signed the paperwork yet and you're already eye fucking me.*

Right. Don't check the musicians out, either.

Hell, you might as well just light me on fire and tell me not to burn.

Matthew ends with, "If you need time to think about it, I understand. It's a big commitment."

But the words barely register as I sign on the bottom line of the contract, watching as the other girls do the same.

Chapter 5

Noah

"Today's the day, gentlemen!" Matt sings happily, coming into the kitchen of our house bringing a brisk March breeze with him. Thankfully, he's brought bags of breakfast as well, which helps ease the burden of dealing with him this early.

It's six a.m. and we're all just waking up, so no one says much. I'm actually surprised Brett even let Matt in the door at this hour.

"How have five months gone by already?" Ryan says, stifling a yawn as Brett tosses him a sausage biscuit.

"I agree. It's flown. Are the girls ready?" Sloan asks Matt, being serious for once.

Matt's smile indicates *yes*. He claps his hands together and I can tell he's feeling proud of himself right now.

We haven't seen or interacted with the dancers since the day we met them, but Matt assured us he was on top of their training and rehearsals. We asked if we could watch their routines since we didn't get to see them when they accepted the job offer, but Matt said he wanted us to feel them on stage instead of watching from the sidelines the first time.

Whatever.

"They're as ready as they can be after only running off your live mix recordings," he says, popping a hashbrown in his mouth. "They'll need some tweaking to get timing and spacing right with you guys on stage, but that's what the next month is for." He takes a sip of his coffee before leveling a look at me, specifically, and walking over to where I'm leaning against the door frame, too wound up to sit. "I think you're going to really like this."

"I'd better," I grumble before taking another bite of my breakfast. Part of the dry biscuit falls down the front of my shirt, but I've got so much on my mind, I just leave the crumbs on the floor at my bare feet.

I'm trying to stay open minded about all of this, but we'll only get one shot. "With such a rapid acquisition of fans, this tour will either solidify their fandom or turn them off of us for good."

Matt tries to pacify me by placing his coffee cup over his heart as if I've wounded him and puts his other hand on my shoulder even though he knows I fucking hate when touches me.

"Noah, you think I don't know how much is riding on this? It's my name on the line too, buddy. I just need you to bring that tour energy to the stage today. The girls are ready, but they're new to this. They'll feed off you guys, so I need you to show them how it's done. Can you do that?"

"Yeah, we got it," Ryan says for me as I take a deep breath and shake Matt off my shoulder. My hand immediately flies to my sternum, and I swear I'm going to rub a hole straight through to my spine before this tour is over.

"Oh yeah," Matt continues, turning his back on me, "I've

scheduled two radio interviews this week, a photo shoot, and you need to meet with wardrobe to pick out your rotation for the road. I also need your finalized set list for the first six shows and there's a charity auction I've signed you up for so you each need to find something to donate." My ears are ringing as the to-do list grows. "Now go get ready. We need to leave in thirty minutes."

"Wardrobe? Matt, we perform in jeans and t-shirts. End of story." I'm pretty sure I'm going to lose this fight too, but I have to try. It's just one more thing I'm losing control over.

"Jeans and t-shirts are fine, Noah, but they need to fit the overall aesthetic. You can't be on stage wearing a shirt for another band." His eyes drop accusatorily to the shirt I'm currently wearing.

"Why?"

"Because we want all eyes and all *thoughts* on Beautiful Deceit. You don't want one moment where the crowd's attention wanders. And trust me, whatever you're wearing, they'll be obsessed with because it will feel like a connection to you. So, if you want to hand another band all your fans, be my guest. But I don't recommend it."

I grunt under my breath. "I seriously doubt anybody cares that much about my shirt," I argue.

"Is that so?" He takes a deep breath like he's explaining something to a child who is wearing his patience thin. "Last week, you went on that popular metal podcast and declared that Raven's Wing was your favorite band. Small. Local. Absolutely *zero* following outside of D.C., and barely any following within it. Before that interview, their single on Spotify had seventy-eight plays, Noah. Twenty-four hours *after* that podcast? One hundred and twelve thousand, two hundred and eighty. People are paying attention to everything you do, everything you say, and *yes*, everything you wear."

If he was trying to stun me, he succeeded.

Forty-eight minutes later, we've all piled in the Cadillac SUV that Matt's company owns, headed to a local venue where Matt, himself, has set up our stage layout and whatever it is the girls need. We still don't have any details on where they'll be or what it'll look like because Matt has been so hush-hush about it.

My head continues to reel from the information about the podcast. I honestly can't figure out why anyone would care what I like so much. I mean, I'm super glad those guys got some love, but it's fucking terrifying to think people are putting that much stock into my words, my recommendations, my *life*. Stupidly, I thought they'd just be in it for the music. I never expected us to become their obsession.

"You could have at least dressed up for the ladies," Brett says, turning in his front seat to reach back and ruffle my hair – which he knows I can't stand.

I look down at my outfit . . . jeans and a black Henley. I don't really get into the industry standard of trench coats, studs, chokers, chains, gloves, and other shit, but that's mostly because I value simplicity.

"I did dress up," I reply dryly, pointing to the buttons at the top of my shirt.

The media have a field day making fun of my normal, "predictable" wardrobe, but I honestly couldn't care less. A fan blasted most of them a few months ago with a reel about me that went viral with the words *If it ain't broke, don't fucking fix it* (*unless you want to take it off*).

The guys gave me shit about that for a while. Not that they

don't have the same things posted about them, but I hold my cards *way* closer to my chest than they do. Not to mention that being a sex symbol is not something I ever saw myself becoming.

Brett, on the other hand, plays almost all our shows without a shirt. Even Ryan will occasionally take his off, but I'm here to fuck your soul with my voice, not my abs, and my shirt stays firmly in place.

"I don't know why you bothered to bring your A-game, Brett. It's cruel to look that good since they're off limits, bro," Sloan jokes, joining the conversation from the way back as he references Brett's light blue button down and khaki pants. If it weren't for the nose ring, the tattoo painting his neck, and his long, thick-ass hair in a messy manbun, he'd look like a frat boy.

"For eight months," Brett clarifies. "After that, they're fair game, right, Matty?" Brett loves to fuck with everyone, but Matt and I are his favorites by far.

Matt narrows his eyes. "What did I tell you about calling me that?"

"Only do it in the bedroom?" Brett suggests before a snorting laugh rips through him. Hell, even I crack a smile at that.

"You guys are giving me a migraine already," Matt says, rubbing his temple with one hand while his other stays on the wheel, but he's smiling. He knows if we didn't accept him, we wouldn't mess with him. "Alright, look, try to behave for at least the first run through. Today's going to set the tone for the next nine months."

Matt parks, and we check in with security before walking into the arena.

It steals my breath.

I don't know how long I stand in the aisle just staring, but I rotate three-hundred-and-sixty-degrees, imagining this place packed . . . for *us*.

A hand claps me on the shoulder. I can tell by the size of the mitt it's Ryan. His 6'4" frame is the only one that's noticeably taller than my 6'2".

"It's fucking surreal, isn't it?"

I nod, unable to find words.

"Okay guys, gather around," Matt calls from the stage. There are about twenty people on the platform as Ryan and I take the steps to join everyone. "Ryan, Brett, Sloan, Noah," he says pointing to each of us in turn. "This is your crew. I don't expect you to memorize all their names today but by the end of the eight months, you'd better know them, their families, and their favorite fucking food because these are the men and women who will keep you running flawlessly. They will know your set as intimately as you do. I've been on tours where the stars of the show thought they were better than their support team so let me be the first to tell you, you aren't. Treat them like family because they have the power to make your life hell."

Noted.

We all respectfully nod at the group of people in front of us. We haven't even played one show yet, and I can already see how all this power and attention could go straight to someone's head. For all the shit I give Matt, I do appreciate his mentality here. We can't run a tour this big without the expertise and dedication of these people who are also sacrificing eight months of their lives away from their friends and families to help us pull this off.

I make a note to start learning names as soon as possible.

"Noah, you're going with Tasha." He points to a woman whose skin is the color of mocha. Her hair is short, spiky, and platinum and her lipstick is purple, matching her shirt. "She's going to mic you up and run through your soundcheck." Matt's

38

voice cuts through my assessing gaze. "Also, her husband is your head of security on this tour so keep your hands to yourself."

"*Jesus*, Matt. I think you have me confused with Brett." I throw my arms wide, palms up as if saying *what the hell, man?* "I'm trying to remember her name, not figure out how to get her naked."

Matt ignores me as I go off with Tasha who's chewing gum like she's an extra in Grease and smiling as she does it. Well, at least that's one name down because Tasha is pretty unforgettable, especially after this encounter.

It takes about an hour to get the four of us in place, mics set, and sound check done.

"That'll go faster every time you do it, but an hour to start isn't bad," Matt says into his mic which comes through our earpieces. "Okay, hold tight. I'm going to bring the dancers out and get them situated."

Right on cue, the four girls we'd met a few months ago come out from stage left. The short blonde is clearly the ringleader. She's holding the redhead's hand again, and I wonder if maybe Matt didn't have to be worried about them being into us at all . . '. but then I remember the heat in the redhead's stare the day she signed on for this.

Behind them are the other two dancers. One is brunette and the other is blonde with purple highlights.

All the girls are attractive and have toned, athletic bodies. I wasn't aware prancing around in ballet slippers gave someone that much definition.

The girls eye us on the stage, each one wearing a different combination of *holy shit, oh shit,* and *who gives a shit,* but it's the redhead that catches my eye. She looks nervous as hell. She also looks like she might throw up.

We only have four weeks, so she'd better get over that *fast.*

Now that I'm getting a closer look, the blonde up front is definitely wearing an *eat shit* grin. I swear that girl is a ball-buster. I'd love to see her go head-to-head with Brett or Sloan.

The girls nod at Matt who is out in front of us on the catwalk as they stand under long strands of fabric hanging from the ceiling which I can already see myself tripping over. Then Matt waves to us and says into the mic, "Ready, boys?"

A chorus of "ready" comes through my earpiece, and Matt tells us to start with the prelude. I don't play guitar in all the songs, but I do for this part because I told Matt I didn't want a lull on the stage where I'm just standing there.

When the first note rings out, all four girls jump up and grab a hold of the silk streamers and flip upside down. Their legs open wide so they look like a T.

What the fuck?

They twist, reaching up in between their legs and pull their torsos up and repeat, climbing higher on the fabric.

When Matt said *backup dancers,* I envisioned them in our space on the stage, doing coordinated hip-hop type moves. Not *this.*

I trip over my chords, lost in their movements, until I stop playing altogether.

"Kinky, what are you doing up there, man?" Ryan's voice breaks my concentration, and I realize everyone's eyes are on me. I also groan at his use of my nickname. Life with these guys is a bitch when your last name is Kinkaid. Why my family couldn't spell it with a "c" like everyone else, I'll never know.

"Sorry." I shake my head. "Would have been nice to have had a heads up about the acrobats." I give Matt a pointed look. "Let's start from the top."

I watch Matt's lips curl into a smile. He likes that he's shocked me.

Asshole.

"I'm glad you like it," he says, correctly gauging my reaction.

One measure in, and I can tell this is going to be cool as fuck.

"Now, I need you to focus. You're going to burn our girls out if we have to restart every three minutes. From this point on, you play like it's a live show. You get off track, find your way back without stopping and restarting. I need to see where the problem points are."

We restart and the girls hop up on the silks again and spread their legs wide.

Jesus, that's distracting.

They all have on black leggings and tank tops but the way they roll their bodies through that fabric has me fighting to keep my mind on track.

Get your head in the game, Kinkaid. Don't blow this.

It gets a little easier once we make it through the prelude and start the first song. I love this album, and I get lost in the lyrics easily, tuning out the girls around me.

Until I see a quick flash of red and hear a thud.

Chapter 6

Sienna

"Ow! Fuck!" I yell, my ribs connecting with the stage. There's a black foam pad under each of our silks but it doesn't offer much protection when you fall from eight feet, although, I'm more embarrassed than hurt.

Everyone has to stop because of me, and we're only on the third song.

"Sorry," I offer sincerely through my wince of embarrassment. I don't know why but I direct my apology to Noah as I stand up and brush myself off. It's not like I can look him in the eye right now, but the words are aimed in his direction.

Bri rushes over to me. "Si, you okay?"

"Yeah, it's that damn roll into the split I keep struggling with. I don't stop myself in time, and then I'm at the end of my silks with not enough material to catch myself," I explain.

She looks over at Matt. "Can we do that part again? This transition is tricky for us, and we need to make sure we have it."

She's so sweet. It's not tricky for *us*. It's tricky for *me*. Doubt creeps in, and I wonder, for the hundredth time, why I'm here.

Bri can read me like a book and guesses my thoughts with one look at my crestfallen face.

"Sienna, don't go there. You can do this."

"Let's hope so," Noah bites out under his breath loud enough for me to hear. Lucky me, my silks are the closest to him on stage.

"Thanks, *dick*. Not helping. Besides, you totally missed your part earlier so don't act like you're perfect." Bri snaps at him which elicits a series of chuckling "OooOohhs" from Noah's bandmates as they hold their fists up to their mouths like the immature middle schoolers they are.

I don't tell her the reason I fell was because I was completely mesmerized by Noah basically making out with his microphone as his lips brushed its surface repeatedly. I've listened to this album on repeat for five months straight. Every day at practice and every night running through the routines in my head again. Which means I've become intimately familiar with his voice through headphones and studio speakers. From my spot on the stage though, I can hear his raw voice and *Oh. My. Damn.*

He's singing about stripping away his insecurities like he would strip his lover, and it was like my silks just disappeared. Nothing existed but the crack of his voice as he hit a note that apparently, is directly connected to my vagina.

This is going to be a long-ass nine months. Especially because we'll be rehearsing with the guys almost every day for the next four weeks.

"Sienna, honey, are you okay?" Matt asks, raising his voice over the guys.

"Yeah, sorry about that. It won't happen again."

Matt nods reassuringly and calls for a fifteen-minute break. Noah storms off the stage, muttering to Ryan, clearly pissed at my mistake.

Bri, Kara, and Joslyn all surround me offering support as we grab our waters and shake out our arms on the side of the stage.

"It's unfair that he's so fucking hot if he's going to be such an ass," Joslyn says, stretching her hamstrings.

I don't know why I stick up for Noah, but I guess a part of me understands it.

This tour is a huge deal for them, and he doesn't want someone messing it up. From what we've been told, our presence was all Matt's idea, and the band is still hesitant. Not to mention, this is my first big break too. I want to make sure I put my best foot forward so I don't screw up any future opportunities.

"He just wants to make sure it's perfect," I throw out nonchalantly.

"I've never seen a scream-o band where all the members are so hot though," Kara adds, echoing Jos's statement. "Like aren't most musicians either a little scrawny, with long, greasy hair, and squirrely eyes or overweight from too much booze and an out-of-control beard they think looks cool but actually doesn't?"

Bri barks out a laugh. "*Hello* stereotypes."

"What?" Kara shrugs unapologetically. "Tell me I'm wrong."

She isn't. Not really. And people can get pissed all they want about stereotypes, but they're usually rooted in the truth.

These guys, however, are jacked with lean muscle. The muscles in their forearms flex as they play their respective instruments, causing the veins to stand out in their flawless flesh. Who knew veins were such a turn on?

Noah's shoulders are broader than I picture most musicians' to be. His t-shirt is baggy at his waist, and no one actually knows what it looks like underneath. All we could find as we searched the hell out of them online were some old sketchy pictures, and he doesn't seem to have that same physique anymore, but that's purely speculation, even though the difference is noticeable in his face and arms.

Matt calls that it's time to get back to work and now we're giggling like a pack of rabid schoolgirls as we walk back to our places on stage, murmuring about the bodies of the men in front of us. My heart is thrumming so hard, I feel it in my stomach, and it's making me a little queasy.

We have to do the third song again, and I'm determined to get it right. I blow out a strong exhale and feel Bri's hand on my back.

"Try to relax. Imagine it's just you up there. You know this routine, and you know your silks. Act like you're making love to them. Nothing matters except the feel of where they are on your body."

I know she's serious and she's trying to help but a bark of laughter erupts from my throat anyway. To my utter mortification, it's followed by several more, and I'm drawing attention to myself. Bri's expression is clearly asking what is wrong with me, so I lower my voice and explain.

"Bri, that's a terrible analogy. I haven't gotten laid in like three years. I'm not even sure I remember how."

"Well, that explains your moodiness and inability to concentrate," she teases, as if she didn't know I haven't slept with anyone since Douchebag Brad and I broke up.

Brad decided that we weren't meant to be together once he realized I was serious about pursuing a career as an aerial dancer. I believe his exact words were, *"That's a childish dream. Not to mention, how are you going to actually contribute to your marriage for pennies on the dollar? Or do they pay you in funnel cakes and cotton candy?"*

Ugh. I was pretty sure Josh was going to send Brad to the hospital for that one.

The memory is enough to spark motivated anger, and I

execute the previously missed move perfectly this time, not concentrating on anything but where my body is in the silk, just like Bri said.

Perfecting the move with passion and fury, I pull myself up higher and unroll as the fabric caresses my skin like a waterfall on the way down. Looping the fabric around my right ankle and wrist in the fall, I end gracefully with my left leg pointed down toward the floor, and my right leg and arm in a vertical line above me, still suspended, just like I'm supposed to. The only negative is that in this position, my crotch is basically making googly eyes at Noah.

He turns his head and opens his mouth to say something, but nothing comes out. Clearing his throat – which shouldn't be sexy but definitely is – he rasps out, "Was that better, Matt?"

Oddly, he still sounds pissed even though I nailed it.

Using anger as a motivator is exhausting, and I feel both physically and emotionally drained.

Thankfully, we get a break for song four as we have a floor routine, only needing the silks at the very end.

"Yes," Matt answers in my earpiece, "Keep going."

As one could imagine, performing the dances with the guys on stage is a completely different experience from their music being piped in through speakers. But what one can't imagine is the energy on that stage. Noah's passion for his music crackles all around us like an electrical storm about to get way out of control.

Several times today, my eyes have wandered to the other guys, and I've noticed how even *they* look awestruck as he belts out the lyrics bringing one hundred percent every time. Noah, himself, has caught my eyes on him more than I'd like to admit, but I can't seem to tear them away.

As we work through another song, I'm getting closer to the

eye of the storm – literally - and have nothing on which to ground myself.

Matt steps closer to the stage looking like a kid in a candy store – bright, wide eyes, hands clasped together, lips slightly parted in devious wonder - as Noah nears the chorus, totally focused.

Practicing this part without the band present didn't feel so awkward, but after the morning I've had, I say a prayer that Matt told Noah what to expect as Noah launches into a line about needing her hands on him.

Just like we rehearsed, I do a full straddle to the floor directly behind Noah - his glorious jean-clad ass in my face - and shoot my hands between his legs, bending at the elbow so my fingers are splayed over his crotch as if I'm shielding the goods from everyone. I hold my breath during the entire move, excruciatingly careful to not actually touch him. I know he doesn't appreciate the contact quite like his bandmates. Not to mention, this close to his sweaty body, I have no doubt I would draw his smell deep into my lungs and I fear its perfection would render me useless for the rest of this practice.

This provocative move landed on me because again, I'm closest to him on the stage. The other girls are in a suggestive pose with each other since all the other guys have instruments in the way but Noah isn't holding anything except the mic stand during this part.

I pull my hands back down as quickly as they shot up and continue on with the routine pulling my legs together before doing a straddle roll, my crotch now flashing Brett in order to get out from behind Noah. I stand up, throwing my arms out wide, and jerk violently from side to side in time with Ryan's bass. The whole part only takes ten beats but it's enough.

Eventually, I hear Matt yell, "Stop!"

I look around, praying it wasn't me that fucked up this time.

"Kinkaid, you have to sing. That *is* what people are paying for, after all," Matt says sarcastically.

Brett pipes up from the drums. "How come I don't get a chick grabbing between my legs? I hate being the only one who has to sit down," he grumbles.

Ryan joins the mayhem, "I thought I called dibs on the redhead!"

What?

When Noah finally finds his voice, his nostrils are flared. "I'm not a sex doll, Matt. You should have cleared this with me. Give her a different move that doesn't involve my dick."

While I'm recovering from hearing Noah reference his own glorious parts, Sloan starts cracking up from across the stage. "Dude, are you *serious* right now? That was fucking hot. Thank God this guitar is in front of me because I have a massive boner."

When Noah pinches his brows and looks over at Sloan in disgust, Sloan clears his throat, "For *her* man, for *her*. That move looked good is all I'm saying."

Noah's eyes only darken as Sloan tries to clarify, but he doesn't say anything else.

Matt holds his hands up in a *See? I'm a genius* gesture which loses some of its merit because he has on another puke green shirt with yellow polka dots.

"Look, Noah, sex sells. People have never seen you so much as kiss a girlfriend in public. I get it. PDA isn't your thing. But trust me on this. Even a *hint* that you might fuck her backstage," he nods his head in my direction causing my cheeks to flame, "will drive your audience *insane*."

I see Noah's jaw clench. He's clearly uncomfortable with this so I find some courage and whisper so only he can hear me. "I promise I won't actually touch you."

If it's possible, his jaw gets even tighter.

He looks straight ahead at Matt. "Are there any other surprises we should know about?"

Matt sighs loudly, conveying his disappointment at having to give everything away, "At one point, Brianna, the dancer in the back by Brett is going to land in a split just above his bass drum before hoisting herself back up into the rafters."

"Fuck, yes," Brett says as he winks at Bri. "You can spread those beautiful legs for me—"

"That's enough, Brett," Noah snaps. "Matt, what the fuck? I have a hard enough time reigning them in as it is, and you want to prance untouchable pussy in their face all night?"

Sloan pipes up next, "Noah, *relax man.* Yes, the girls are beautiful, but they also seem to be having fun – or would be if you'd tone it down. They're just doing their job and I gotta say, I think it adds something cool with them up here."

"That's because you think with your dick," Noah fires off more harshly than necessary.

"Noah," Ryan growls in warning. Noah's eyes snap to the huge bassist who glares at him, and some understanding passes between them because Noah closes his eyes and audibly exhales, pushing the heel of his hand into his chest while we all wait.

"Fine. Let's do this." He looks right at me, pinning me in place with the fire behind his eyes. "Make sure your hand doesn't connect."

The sarcasm is out before I can stop myself.

"Yes, sir."

My sardonic smile is dripping and right now I loathe him and want nothing to do with his crotch. Didn't I already tell him I wouldn't touch him? I mean, other than ogling a little because *hellooo, famous people,* I've kept my fangirling reigned in pretty tightly considering this man's face and voice.

I console myself by thinking maybe he doesn't want me to

49

touch him because he has a small dick, and he doesn't want anyone to know he's packing a toothpick in those jeans.

At least not wanting to fuck him won't be the challenge I thought it would be.

The rest of practice goes fine although the tension on stage is so thick you could chew it. Eventually, I lose track of everyone around me and force myself to stay in the routine. We only make it through half the set though due to stopping to tweak placements and timing based on the live version of the songs compared to how they were recorded, but it feels like a good start.

At the end of the day, each of the guys – minus Noah – come around to shake our hands and are welcoming and complimentary of our performance.

Sloan comes over and drapes a lazy arm around my sweaty shoulders like he's known me his whole life and is not currently a mega celebrity I'm interacting with for only the second time today.

"Sorry about Kinky," he says, rolling his eyes. I'm still trying to catch my breath from rehearsal, but Sloan is able to talk normally even though he's drenched after working hard as well. "He puts a lot of pressure on himself and then takes it out on everyone else. Hopefully he'll lighten up once we're on the road."

"Sounds like a great trait," I respond drily with a tight smile.

Sloan throws his head back and laughs, his minty breath blowing across my face.

"Don't let his dumb ass get to you. You looked great up there. He was probably just pissed from having a hard-on all afternoon." With that, he walks off, still laughing.

Great, now I'm back to thinking about Noah's crotch. The

one I'm supposed to drag my nails across on stage without actually touching.

I groan and follow Bri and the other girls to the exit.

"I need the hot tub," I whine, feeling the soreness of the day creeping into my tired muscles.

"I need my vibrator," Kara says, pulling a genuine laugh out of me.

"I second that," Joslyn says.

We all look at Bri waiting for her response which shocks none of us.

"Forget the vibrator. I'm fucking the drummer before this is over." She pushes the door to the studio open and we catch a glimpse of the guys' taillights as their SUV turns the corner. Bri shimmies her boobs in the car's direction and makes her voice low and seductive. "I'm coming for you, big boy," she rasps.

We all break out in a fit of giggles, and I feel the lightest I have all day.

Chapter 7

Noah

Matt has arranged for promotional photos to be taken this morning which normally would be exciting, but I'm exhausted. We've been going nonstop with rehearsal from six a.m to nine p.m. and somehow, I still got booked on three podcasts which is cool, but man, they take forever. I feel like I'm coming down with the flu which isn't good so close to the tour kickoff and the guys have been pumping me full of Airborne and Vitamin C.

The tour officially starts three weeks from today which Matt says is the best time to ramp up the social media posts and advertising, so here we are, in an abandoned warehouse in front of spray-painted walls with a camera crew and whole host of others running around to ensure everything goes smoothly.

Matt somehow got the aerial silks – I learned they're called – hung up for this shoot. I can hardly wait to see what kind of torture he has planned for me today.

It's getting harder to not stare at all the spread legs and arched backs around me and spending the evening in the company of my hand isn't providing the same kind of relief that it used to.

The guys have even started commenting on my surly exterior which I'm trying to control, but it's a form of self-defense because Matt did *not* choose women I find . . . how did he put it? Oh yeah, *ugly with the personalities of dry-erase markers.*

The redhead's skills aren't quite as flawless as the others, but her determination is more visible. When I sneak glances at her, she's usually looking at me causing me to look away quickly, so I haven't had a chance to study her, but she seems to be facing some kind of demon on that stage.

I shake my head to clear my brain.

It doesn't work.

When I'm finally able to focus my attention back on the present, I see someone approaching me with scissors. All my muscles tighten in my jeans and black Metallica t-shirt – because old habits die hard - and the sharp objects cause me to bristle.

Jayne, our "wardrobe officer" – whatever the fuck that is – stalks toward me, the red lights behind me glinting off the blades in her hand.

I take a step back and arch an eyebrow in question.

"I need to make slashes in your t-shirt for the next picture," she states matter-of-factly.

"This is one of my favorite shirts. You're not taking scissors to it," I argue.

My dad and I went to this concert a couple of years ago when I could go out and not get harassed all to hell. We had a fucking blast. So, no, she can't slice my shit up for some picture.

Everyone wants to paint me as being difficult but I'm only pushing back because I feel like I'm losing control.

Of the band.

Of our music.

Of this tour.

Of myself.

I know Matt is supposed to be the best in the business, but we weren't consulted on *anything*. Matt's excuse was, and-I-quote, *"Your job is to make the music. My job is to promote it in a way that brings people to your shows so you can make money which allows you to make more music."*

It was hard to argue with that logic but every control issue I've ever had is coming to the surface.

Sensing my argument coming, Matt rushes over to explain the slashes won't be revealing . . . *just enough to give the illusion that they can catch a glimpse, Noah.* Trying to appease Matt and keep Jayne on my good side, I kindly ask the woman who manages my clothes to grab a plain black t-shirt from her magic stash and cut that one up and I'll put it on.

Why my skin is so fucking intriguing to everyone, I have no idea.

Jayne nods and scurries off toward the large black trunks lined against the far wall, with Matt right behind her.

While she's gone, the dancers arrive, and I flick my eyes to Sloan whose mouth is hanging open.

The girls are in skin-colored tights and black, high-waisted underwear basically, with black tube-tops on.

I'm in the middle of wondering how that isn't going to fall off when they get tangled in their silks when I realize it's all one piece of skin-colored material in the middle, up on the neck, and down the arms, and the black just covers the good parts.

The redhead, Sienna, eyes me warily. I'll admit, I was an asshole to her at our first rehearsal a week ago, and I never apologized. It'll be a long time on the road with this tension between us, so I walk over to her and try to make it right.

As soon as I'm in her vicinity, her vanilla scented lotion

smacks me square in the face and before I can stop myself, I wonder if she *tastes* like vanilla too.

This was a mistake, but I'm already committed so I try only breathing out of my mouth while I talk to her.

"Sienna, right?" I ask, already knowing damn well that's her name. I've gotten almost all the crew's names memorized in a week.

She nods, giving me a lukewarm smile and then averts her gaze, making me feel like an even bigger asshole. She's probably waiting for me to be a prick again.

"Look, I'm sorry about that first day," I start, shocked I can remember words. Up close, I can see the freckles dotting her cheeks. Her eyes are a bluish green, like they can't make up their mind which color they want to be, but instead of blending the colors together, there's a thin ring of green around her pupil and blue swallows the rest of her iris. I clear my throat and finish my apology. "I've got a lot riding on this tour," I try to explain.

She faces me fully, and I continue my perusal, taking her in. She's in full photo makeup which rims those blue-green eyes in charcoal. Her lashes are long and painted black, her nose is straight and curves up slightly at the end. Her lips . . . *fuck me.* Her lips are full and smooth and her tongue darts out nervously to wet them before pulling her bottom lip between her teeth.

"Like I don't?" she fires back, letting go of her lip, her brow creasing in bewilderment, catching me off guard.

"What?" I've already forgotten what we were talking about.

"You said *you* have a lot riding on this tour, as if I don't. I will literally be falling from the ceiling every night. A mistake could cost me my life so if I mess up, trust me, it isn't because I don't care or am trying to make you look bad. Besides, if I fuck this up, the chances of me getting another job as an aerial dancer are slim to none because if I fall, it'll make national news thanks to your fame."

I hadn't thought about it like that. I also am not prepared for the extreme dislike I feel at the thought of another band having my dancer. Which is crazy because this tour is only eight months long and then of course she'll move on to her next job.

I offer her a nod of understanding and then lamely repeat myself. "I'm sorry."

She thaws slightly at my apology, her expression less angry and more exasperated.

"Apology accepted. Shall we?" She points to Jayne who is approaching with my newly slashed, plain black t-shirt clearly wanting to be done with this interaction.

I grab my new t-shirt and head to the bathroom to change.

When I rejoin the group, Matt places everyone where he wants us backed up against the exposed brick. Ryan is next to me with his left elbow on my right shoulder and his right ankle crossed over his left. I'm instructed to keep my feet slightly wider than shoulder width apart with my hands - left hand over the back of my right hand – relaxed in front of my zipper. Brett and Sloan are on the outside of Ryan and me. A couple shots are taken like that of just the four of us before they bring the girls in.

The first few are with the dancers entwined in their silks in some kind of contortionist pose above us. I have to work hard to keep my breathing even when I see the positions these women are capable of.

I try to keep my thoughts professional but *damn*. Sienna's back is arched, and she's grabbing her ankles while holding on to her silks, suspended in the air, knees wide.

But it's the next photo that nearly undoes me. It seems Matt has unofficially paired each of us with one of the dancers for certain moments in the set, photo ops etc . . . and wouldn't you know it, the redhead with the luscious lips has my name on her.

He positions Sienna in a straddle on the floor in front of me this time, facing me in her black and nude outfit, legs wide, her right hand reaching up so that her fingers are about level with my belt but her torso is leaning over to the side, her eyes cast down at the floor. The other three women are in similar poses with the rest of the guys. Brett places his hand on the back of Bri's head, his fingers threaded in her hair, urging her closer while Matt eggs it on.

Sex sells.

Naturally, Sloan follows suit and decides to get creative with a pose of his own and makes his dancer stand up. He grabs her ankle and stares at her in challenge as he brings her foot to rest on his shoulder. She doesn't even bat an eyelash at the position. He loops his guitar strap over her back, trapping them both in it. She's pressed up against him, his arm around her, his hand resting on the neck of his instrument which is resting on her ass. The grin on his face is a mile wide.

Without making the conscious decision to do so, I place my index finger under Sienna's chin and tip her head back to make her look up at me. I'm unaware of how long we stay like that as the shoot goes on around us.

"Guys, this is fucking gold," Matt beams. "For the next take, I want all of you to improvise again." He looks right at me silently telling me to do more of *this.*

I'm not currently breathing, but he seems less concerned with my ability to draw a deep breath than he is with capturing this energy on camera.

When the photographer yells *"switch"* indicating that it's time to change poses, I'm at a loss. I make music which is *audibly* pleasing. I don't know the first thing about *visual* art. I was only touching her because I wanted to read the thoughts in her eyes. Sensing my hesitation, Sienna stands up and takes charge.

"I have an idea. Trust me," she whispers just to me. Then loudly, to the crowd around us, she asks, "Does anyone have a knife?"

I feel my eyebrows shoot to my hairline which causes her to actually giggle. I hate the way I feel it in my stomach.

"I'm not going to stab you with it," she says playfully, rolling her eyes. "Your most popular single off this album is *Vicious*. I just had an idea that plays on that," she says loud enough for everyone to hear. Then she quiets her voice again so only *I* can hear. "It also requires minimal touching, but I think it'll satisfy Matt," she says shyly, as if now that she's said it out loud, she regrets having this idea at all.

I have to admit, I'm intrigued.

Someone brings a plastic butcher knife to her . . . like the kind that comes with a Halloween costume. I don't even want to know where they got this or why they have it, so I don't ask questions.

"Ok, turn sideways so our profiles are to the camera," she commands me, and if I'm not mistaken, there's a slight quiver to her voice. She takes a quick breath and with her eyes everywhere but on mine, she finishes her instructions. "Hold your mic in your left hand and grab my throat with your right."

"*What?*"

Did I just hear her correctly?

"Grab my throat, Noah," she repeats, although I'm not sure if it's the massive surge in *my* lust I'm feeling, or *her* lust I'm *hearing* as I reach my hand around her slender neck. She wraps the knife in both hands behind her back and looks at me with parted lips and a challenging defiance.

I squeeze my fingers a little harder to get them to stop trembling, and I damn near lose it when I feel her push into my hand. My arm is outstretched so there are about three feet between us.

According to my swelling dick, that's too much space.

"Oh, I like this," Matt says from the side lines. "Noah, lean in like you're trying to intimidate her." I close the gap between us and really have to look down to maintain eye contact. She's at least seven inches shorter than me. "Yes," he hisses. "Now, inhale her. Dip your head down to her neck."

Fuck. My. Life.

I hear her breathing hitch as I bring my face closer. The strangled whimper she lets out shoots straight to my already aching cock.

After the longest ten minutes of my life, Matt finally calls a wrap on the photo shoot.

Thank God.

I have to get out of here. I have a new pressure building, and it's in the opposite direction of my chest this time. I'm now convinced my cause of death will either be from a heart attack *or* an erection lasting more than four hours.

Jury's out on which it'll be.

Back at the house, the guys are still going on about the shoot.

"Did you see her leg? It was *over* my fucking *shoulder*. I'm not a short guy! I bet she could have gotten her ankle over Ryan's shoulder too," Sloan says in awe, grabbing a beer out of the fridge.

I'm trying hard not to think about the redhead with the sinful lips or the determination I see in her eyes to be perfect every day at rehearsal. It's taking a lot of effort to maintain this professionalism when I know she's going to be between my legs at some point almost every night, shooting her hand up toward my dick with desire in her eyes, wearing next to nothing.

I have to remind myself she's playing a role.

She's acting.

Even if she wasn't, it doesn't matter. Not only did she sign the contact Matt had drawn up, but I've got so much going on right now that girls are barely on the radar, and nothing is more important than this tour.

Yeah, Kinkaid, keep telling yourself that.

Chapter 8

Sienna

The arena is already two-thirds full of attendees even though opening night doesn't start for another hour. I keep taking peeks from backstage, but I shouldn't.

My stomach is in shreds. It feels like I'm water in a barrel onboard a ship in a stormy sea. Rolling over the waves in one nauseating movement after another.

Bri pulls me away from the backstage curtain. "Si, take deep breaths. You've got this. It's just us and the guys. And remember, the lights are on us, so we won't really be able to see out into the arena. Here." Laying in her outstretched palm is a little white pill.

Imodium.

"Thanks." I swallow the pill and chase it with water from the bottle in my hand.

I work on taking deep breaths like Bri instructed, pulling air deep into my constricted lungs. The scent of the opening band's lingering smoke from their pyrotechnics check fills my nose, robbing me of the fresh breath I was hoping for.

"Just us and the guys," Bri repeats. "Another practice. Just keep your focus on your silks," she coaches.

I'm pretty sure I have everything under control . . . until the guys come backstage an hour later.

Holy flaming shit balls of fire.

Noah has eyeliner on, making his already dark eyes as black as a sunless, starless galaxy. His hair is freshly cut on the sides, the longer section on the top falling across his forehead and left eye, and I have a sudden, maddening urge to run my hand through it.

This is *not* what he's looked like the last four weeks. It seems all the guys have kicked their appearance up a notch in preparation for opening night.

I look at Bri whose lust is clearly written on her face as well.

Guys in eyeliner have never really appealed to me. Call me traditional, old fashioned, hypocritical, whatever, but I've always felt makeup was a woman's domain. Except, Noah Kinkaid wears eyeliner better than any woman I've ever known.

Brett is already shirtless, his shorts hanging low on his hips, and Bri wastes no time letting him know she approves by running a manicured finger across his skin just above his waistband.

"Looking good, drummer boy," she teases playfully, but I know her tells, and she's so turned on she's practically vibrating.

Brett's trying to keep his cool, but I see his cock twitch in his thin gym shorts. The hard set of his jaw tells me he's weighing the risks of fucking Bri somewhere backstage before the show, and the look on her face tells me she would be down for it.

A little closer to the stage, Kara and Joslyn are also trying to play it cool while chatting with a couple members of the opening act who've just finished up. Everyone seems excited but also like they're able to take it in stride and continue interacting in a normal fashion.

Me?

I'm trying unsuccessfully to drag my eyes away from Noah and focus on lowering my heart rate before my innards become *outards*.

When the lights go out in the arena, signaling it's our turn to take the stage, all my attempts to get my breathing in check go to hell, and I start hyperventilating. I know we still have five minutes before we go on, but it's not enough time.

Sensing my eyes on him, Noah looks up and his eyes flash with what is most likely annoyance at my obvious panic. He taps Bri on the shoulder and nods his head in my direction before picking up his guitar and walking out on stage in the dark to the deafening roar of the crowd.

Bri squeezes my hand. "Deep breaths, Sienna. This is what we've always dreamed of."

When I shoot her a quizzical look, she clarifies.

"Being an aerial dancer for a living. Actually getting a gig that will support us financially."

Oh, right. I nod in agreement as she continues talking.

"If this goes well, we could be hired for other tours or maybe asked to come back on the road with these guys again in the future."

She can tell she's starting to freak me out by pointing out how my entire future is riding on this performance, so she tries to backtrack, but it's too late. "Look, this is one show out of one hundred and eight. You'll have plenty of chances to get it right. Just start with tonight, okay?"

"Yeah, okay." I'm glad I was able to find my voice.

Just then, Matt comes over to us, his glee written all over his face. "Okay ladies, lights are about to go up." He's yelling at us because the crowd outside the curtain has gotten louder. "Take your places and knock 'em dead."

Bri holds my hand as we enter stage left.

The first thing that hits me is the noise. The roar that twenty-nine thousand people can make in an enclosed space is earsplitting. The thick black curtain I was behind did more to conceal the noise than I realized.

Bri and I are on the same side of the stage although she is farther on the outside than I am for the first few songs, so she drops my hand as she takes hold of her silks and I keep walking toward Noah.

The lights haven't come up yet, but I can see his outline moving in front of me in the dim glow of the lights on the floor, there to guide my steps.

Even though my hands are trembling, his presence calms me which I don't have enough time to sort through. Noah has been *anything* but a calming presence during practice. He's too fucking sexy to be calming. Not to mention his temper is always simmering just below the surface making him intimidating as hell.

Just another practice.

I grip my silks in my hands with my head bowed just like I'm supposed to. I'm in the middle of a deep breath that gets caught in my throat when all of a sudden, the lights come on in one blinding second and the opening chord of Noah's prelude is struck.

I'm not sure how it's possible, but the cheers of the crowd get even louder. I can feel the vibrations of all their voices in my bones, and I'm pretty sure the stage is shaking. The red lights and the fog machine whir to life behind us, and I hear my cue to grab my silks and begin my ascent. My palms are sweaty as hell, and I feel the material want to slip right through my fingers. There's chalk on the stage behind me but I'm out of time to get any.

I blow out a breath, say a quick prayer, and jump up into my first footlock. I will myself to look only at the swathe of silk in front of me as I climb higher, before spreading my legs into a split and rotating my body forward. When the four of us dancers are suspended with our legs wide, and backs arched, you'd think someone started a fire. It's so loud I can barely hear Noah even through all the speakers.

I guess we're a hit then. Good news for Matt and the guys for sure.

Although, I'm not even sure the crowd notices us. The guys command all the attention.

I wasn't prepared for this.

I make it through the first song without issue and am glad to have the first four minutes under my belt.

The energy in here is unlike anything I've ever felt. It has a pulse of its own, and it thumps rhythmically in time with my heartbeat.

I begin to relax and settle in to the rhythm of the show once song three is over, and I make it mistake-free through the descent that's previously given me issue.

In song four, as I'm in a straddle behind Noah, my hands crossed, and fingers splayed in front of his crotch, Ryan kicks his bass riff into high gear, and I witness my first thong being thrown on stage. Thankfully, it lands to my right, and I have to roll left to move on with the dance, but I almost miss a step in the routine because I'm laughing in disbelief.

I *do* miss a step when a woman in the front row flashes her actual boobs at Noah.

I just saw a stranger's nipples.

The lights up here are really bright, and I can't see far into the crowd, but I can see the mob of people up front who have abandoned their seats and are pressed against the railing on the floor to create a perimeter around the stage. It's then that it really hits me. Some people would do *anything* to be this close to these guys and how lucky I am for this opportunity.

It isn't until we're over halfway through the show I encounter my first issue. In song eight, there's a brief violin solo. It's always been a prerecorded version played in the background, even for our live rehearsals, making me think they hired this part out. But now, out of nowhere, Noah pulls a violin off a stand near Brett's drums and my vision goes fuzzy.

As a little girl, I loved playing the violin. I started lessons when I was seven and played until . . . well, the point is, I stopped playing. Now isn't the time to think about it.

I'm not sure if I stop moving or if my feet carry me through the steps I've rehearsed a thousand times, but my eyes never leave Noah.

His tattooed hands pick up the bow and drag it across the strings to create the most hauntingly beautiful violin solo I've ever heard. It's the same, yet different, from the recorded version, and it somehow fits perfectly with the lyrics he was screaming only a moment ago, creating the most perfect balance of turmoil and peace, which is exactly what the scene in front of me looks like as the indelicate ink on his hands collides with the fragile instrument he's holding.

I had no idea he played.

The song is about a woman who is part monster. *Ha, appropriate* - it's like he wrote it based on my life – and the eerie lullaby sound draws me closer to him on stage, the rest of the arena fading into nothing.

I realize I've stopped dancing and am brought back to the present when Noah is suddenly in front of me. He finishes the solo, replaces the violin and walks back to the mic stand that I'm next to.

Oh shit. When he stopped playing, it was like I was dropped back into reality with no warning and I can't get my bearings.

I look around wildly, completely lost and unsure where I should pick back up and the panic begins increasing the pace of my already rapid, shallow breaths. Trying to listen to where we are in the song is useless. All I can hear is that violin solo on repeat in my head. Catching my eyes, Noah's flash angry and then soften when he sees the turmoil in my own.

Mic in hand, he never misses a beat, but I can see the confusion in his features about what's gotten into me. I'm afraid I'm going to pass out just as he reaches his hand toward me, palm up. My eyes go wide and he nods his head ever so slightly encouraging me to take his hand.

As I place my trembling hand in his, the crowd loses their minds and the noise along with the reality of where I am slams into me causing me to exhale harshly. The heat of a thousand bolts of lightning shoot up my arm at the contact of Noah's skin under my fingertips. *I'm touching him.*

He pulls me in close to his body, connecting us from chest to thighs, and holds the microphone out to the side so his words aren't picked up. To the crowd, it looks like he might kiss me.

"Keep it together," he whispers, his words floating across my lips in a hot breath. "Two songs left. Look over my shoulder at Kara and pick up where she is." His voice is a combination of commanding and some other nameless emotion. My eyes snap up to Kara like he said, and I nod my head.

I whisper *sorry* as my cheeks flame. I expect him to let me go but he holds on a second longer. I'm about to get lost in him again when I feel him push me away in time to the music.

Acting.

He's improvising to save me from fucking this whole set up. I'm equal parts mortified and grateful as I spin back to my silks and fall in line with the other girls, wishing this night was over already.

Two things I learned in that moment: Noah Kinkaid is no longer the soft boy from those old pictures online, and he most certainly is packing a helluva lot more than a toothpick below his belt. *Damn it.*

Chapter 9

Noah

My arms are spread wide as I hype the crowd to give it up for the band. The guys were seriously on fire tonight and the whole place knows it. I just stand and nod my head in agreement with the incessant cheers, trying to soak it all in.

Every episode of heart burn and pressure I've felt has become worth it in this moment even though I have a sneaking suspicion my symptoms are about to get worse. There's no way, after the reviews of this show come out, there won't be more demands on our time, but I'm thankful it was a success and the crowd seems to be as into the dancers as they are to us, which is a huge relief.

Seven pairs of panties litter the stage as well as a pair of dude's briefs - thats's a first. The show was almost flawless.

Almost.

I need to check in with Sienna and find out what the hell happened and make sure it doesn't happen again. Touching her was damn distracting, but I knew one of us had to hold it together.

Although, as much as I don't want to admit it, it appears Matt was right . . . again. The crowd ate that unplanned, intimate interaction right the fuck up. It was impossible to miss the rise in cheers as I brought her closer.

And Matt lets me know it as soon as I get backstage.

"I don't know what the hell that was, but you're doing more of it," he says enthusiastically, assuming I know what he's talking about.

Luckily, I do.

"Matty, could we just enjoy the first show's success before committing to any changes?" I ask lightly.

In response, Matt holds up his phone and starts scrolling our social media notifications.

"Noah, you've been tagged in over twelve *thousand* posts just from tonight. Most of which are your fanbase, guys and girls alike, talking about the chemistry on that stage. Several comments include statements like," he scrolls and stops on one in particular before reading, *"untouchable Noah Kinkaid finally makes contact."*

I roll my eyes.

"Why is everyone so obsessed with the fact that I'm not a manwhore?" I muse out loud as I unclip my mic receiver from the back of my jeans and head to the water cooler in our dressing room.

My sweat-soaked shirt is clinging to my body, and I crave nothing more than a shower, but first, I need to find Sienna. If she can't handle this, I need to know immediately.

However, Matt has other plans, and he holds up two hands to stop me from moving toward the exit and the buses outside.

"Because you've made it a *thing* by never doing it. You're a mystery and your fans want to know more. They have dreams of being the one to break down your walls."

My walls? I don't have walls. I just don't find it necessary to flaunt my personal life in front of the public.

"Musically," Matt continues, "you're one of the most talented players on the field, Noah. This album is a testament to that. But people want to feel like they know you and you've always been a closed book."

I swear he looks like he's about to get off talking about this.

"Then, it sounds like it's important to keep the mystery alive," I argue sarcastically, watching as his face crumples in frustration. "So, no, I'm not going to do more touching on stage. It's fucking distracting, and if you'll excuse me, I need to go see why it had to happen tonight." I try to push past his outstretched hands. He knows enough not to touch more than my shoulder, but he moves to stand in my way.

"Noah," he says seriously, causing me to pause. "The girls are already on their bus. If you don't want to draw attention to this, although I beg you to reconsider, then you can't be seen getting on that bus with them. With *her*. You need to wait until we get to the hotel to sort this out or everyone is going to be talking about your new relationship and lose focus on the tour."

Shit.

I hadn't thought about that.

But wait.

"Didn't you just say I should do more touching on stage? If people thought I was in a relationship, wouldn't that help your case?"

"*No*," he says emphatically. I'm confused as hell, so I'm thankful when he sheds some light on this bullshit. "Your fan base wants you single. But they also want glimpses of what it would be like to be with you. To imagine your hands on them. Sienna is a placeholder for all the women who want to fuck you. She's not a threat on stage because it's business. And it's hot as hell. But the minute they think you two are a couple, they'll hate her and won't want to watch you interact on stage because she'll be the reminder that they can't have you."

The *fuck?*

"But they *can't* have me regardless of Sienna's presence on stage," I point out, unsure why I'm arguing in this pointless discussion.

"But we want them to think they *can.*"

My brain hurts.

"Okay. So, you want me to touch her on stage and ignore her off of it?" I ask, trying to figure this out.

"Exactly," he confirms with a grin on his face that disappears quickly when I answer.

"No. She's meant to fade into the background." *Not to mention she's a human and I'm not into using people.* "As our dancer, her role is to stay in the shadows. She freaked out tonight, and I had to pull her back in. I'm not turning this tour into the Noah and Sienna Show. There will be no changes to the choreography. Tonight was a one-time thing. Thanks for the heads up about the bus. Now, if you'll excuse me, I'm going to head to mine. Alone."

Sometimes we sleep on the busses as we travel. Sometimes we have to take a plane and our busses meet us at the venue the next night. But I made it clear that on the first night of this tour, we get hotel rooms. And no back-to-back concerts for the first week. That shit is miserable, and it takes its toll. We all need a good night's sleep and to be able to unpack what the hell just happened on that stage.

The guys beat me out of the building, and it's total chaos out here. I'm surrounded by security who are actually having to work to hold back several female fans.

Also, is Brett signing an *ass?*

This is unreal. We've never experienced anything like this before.

"No-ah! No-ah!"

My name becomes a chant so I throw a hand up in a small wave of acknowledgement, and it gets *loud*. A million cell phones are held high as I sign a few things thrust in my face. I notice security is collecting shit being thrown at them as well. Signs, gifts, clothes, and lots of what I'm guessing are phone numbers, email addresses, and OnlyFans account names.

It's hard to do normal things in this environment after talking to Matt. I'm now hyperaware my usual movements will be dissected and played on repeat or become reels viewed thousands of times. Actions like wetting my dry lips, blinking, or blowing out a breath become important because with this many cell phones clicking away, every millisecond will be caught. The middle of my blink will make me look high. In the wrong hands, that gets sold and stories will begin circulating about my drug addiction that doesn't actually exist. My tongue on my lips will cause speculation about what other talents my tongue may hold.

I understand it comes with the fame, but sometimes I just want to know how fans liked the show without having a million phones catching the interaction. It would be really interesting to get to know some of these people and find out how long they've followed our music or how they first heard about our band, but there are simply too many of them and people make it impossible to just have a conversation.

I've only walked three feet when a hand gropes my thigh, tugging on my jeans. I jerk backward out of their grasp but there are so many bodies pressed against the barricade, I have no way to know whose hand it was. As I pull away, there are suddenly more hands at my back. Sensing my rising claustrophobia, I feel Romeo press into me from behind, literally shielding me with his 6'5" frame. Tasha's husband is quiet and intimidating as hell, but he also has a wicked sense of humor. He's quickly becoming one of my favorite people on this tour.

"I got you, Noah. Head for the bus," he says in my ear as his arms shoot out to box me in and bat away all the hands hoping to connect.

It takes the rest of the guys forty minutes before they're able to board the bus even though it's only parked fifty meters from the arena door. Unlike me, they eat this shit up.

"Holy *shit*, that was nuts," Sloan says, collapsing onto the couch, wearing a grin a mile wide. "I was signing a t-shirt and swear I got a hand job at the same time."

"Some guy actually tore my shirt," Ryan says as he climbs aboard and wiping his brow before holding up the torn fabric for us to see.

"A chick got close enough to lick my chest," Brett says.

"That's what you get for walking out of the arena shirtless, dipshit," Sloan laughs.

"That wasn't a complaint, bro," Brett clarifies even as he moves to the sink to wet a paper towel and drag it across his skin.

Although the desire to do so is probably high right now, no one brings girls onto the bus. Ever. We need a space to be ourselves, and this is it. That's the rule we all agreed on when we bought the old, shitty RV we used during our first self-paid, self-promoted tour, and it's carried over. I'm extremely grateful for that rule right now as I relax with the guys, not worried about cell phones, strangers, or having to entertain.

Girls in the hotel rooms, fine, but no overnights.

Girls backstage, fine.

Dressing rooms, fine.

But no girls on the bus, and no girls at home. At least until it's serious – which no one is interested in right now.

"Kinky, you fucking nailed it tonight, man. Hell, those notes you cracked even turned *me* on," Brett says, tossing his paper towel and grabbing a beer out of the mini fridge before joining Sloan on the couch.

"Everything turns you on, Brett," Ryan says as he slips his own wet shirt off and grabs a fresh one out of the small closet. "But I have to agree with him, Kink. The vocals were *on* tonight. I'm pretty sure I saw one lady's O-face when you dropped an octave during that last chorus of Virtuous."

My chest swells.

I want nothing more than to make these guys proud. We've all busted our asses to get here.

Sometimes I feel like I have more pressure riding on me as the guy up front. It's not true of course, the performance belongs to all of us, but it's my voice that gets carried over the speakers. It's me that has to engage the crowd and keep the energy up.

"Same to you fuckers." I raise my bottle of water in the air, toasting my bandmates and brothers. "Helluva kick off to the tour."

We spend the ride to the hotel dissecting the show, the crowd, the dancers, and our own performances. Thankfully, the guys don't say anything about the little stunt Sienna and I pulled, and I won't bring it up without knowing the entire story.

Whatever she was experiencing was deeply personal. Even as lost as I was in the music, I could see the pain reflected in her glassy eyes, almost like she was in a trance, as I pulled my bow across the beloved strings of my custom violin. I was so glad when it finally came back from the repair shop in Italy. The timing was close and I was afraid I wouldn't have it back in time for our first performance.

The cold water in my glass works to soothe my vocal cords

and since we'll be on the bus for at least an hour, I set about making my cup of tea with honey and lemon. A strained throat is dangerous and takes forever to recover. So when I go into vocal rest shortly after we get going, the guys don't push me to talk more.

When the bus pulls up to the hotel in Baltimore an hour later, it has to go to the back door because there is another mob out front. I can't help but wonder how our fans even know we're staying here. It's not like the reservations are made under our names. Hell, even I didn't know where we were staying until we pulled up.

I sound like a broken record in my own head, but *damn* this is so different from the last five years.

We're ushered through the door quickly and taken up several floors via the service elevator. Two whole floors belong to ourselves and our traveling crew. The crew is one level below us and the girls are in the other penthouse suite right next door.

Despite the spacious accommodations, I'm starting to feel the claws of claustrophobia digging in. I've lost the ability to just go for a run or even hit the hotel gym without an entourage. Hell, I can't even take the car and hit a McDonald's drive thru.

Before the tour kicked off, the fanbase was growing but without the buses, dancers, and security, we could sometimes still blend in as long as we didn't travel together. Now, there's not a snowball's chance in hell.

It's disorienting.

The ping of the elevator tells us we've arrived on our floor, and while I'm dying for a shower and to crash in one of the four bedroom suites, I need to talk to Sienna.

Ryan goes straight for the mini bar, pouring out a small measure of scotch as is his nightly routine. Meanwhile, Brett and Sloan are getting wound up all over again, excited at our new level of travel and they head off to claim rooms. I'm tempted to join Ryan at the mini bar, but I have trouble finding the *off* switch, and I reserve alcohol for the rarest of occasions. Besides, it usually only serves to make my anxiety worse.

Ryan, however, has one - only one - every night before bed. Sometimes, I think he would be better suited in a world of financial advisors, CEOs, or academics. His level of classiness and maturity far exceeds the rest of ours.

Brett and Sloan are already reemerging in swim trunks, huge grins spread across their faces.

"Come on, Kinky. You in?"

These two always need a couple hours to unwind after a show and after tonight's response from the crowd, they may need until sunrise. Energy courses through them, causing Brett to bounce on the balls of his feet. I swear they're both related to the Energizer Bunny.

"Yeah, I might meet you down there in a few. I'm going to check in with the girls and make sure everyone's doing okay after that show."

It's not a complete lie.

"Oh, bring the girls down with you!" Brett says, as he whips me with his towel on his way to the door.

"That's a recipe for disaster, Brett." I can't help but laugh as I shake my head. "If they go down to the pool, it'll be of their own free will. I'm sure as hell not inviting them. Besides, isn't the pool going to be swarming with people?"

"Nah, Matty called ahead and had it reserved. It's just for us tonight. Well, us and the girls and crew," Sloan says before following Brett out the door. Before it slams shut, I hear him yell, "Tell Ry, too!"

Ryan got a phone call a few minutes ago and disappeared somewhere to answer it privately. He, like me, doesn't flash his business all over the place, even with us. But I still know who he's talking to, and if Brett ever finds out, he's going to lose his goddamn mind.

Ten minutes later, I'm knocking on the dancers' suite at the other end of the hall, forgetting all about Ryan's troubles and walking face-first into my own.

Chapter 10

Sienna

"**S**ienna, it's for you!" Joslyn calls to me from the doorway.

This is by far the swankiest place I've ever stayed. Four bedrooms connect to a shared living room and full kitchen. It's a shame we're only spending one night here because this place is nicer than mine and Bri's apartment.

The furniture is plush and expensive. A soft, grey microfiber couch called my name as I passed through the living room to pick a bedroom beyond. At home, we have hand-me-downs and furniture Bri and I found in consignment stores. This bedroom has a matching bedroom suit and long, flowing, white curtains against the large windows. The number of pillows on the bed is in the double digits, and I wanted to take a flying leap and land in them all.

I even made a mental note to start writing down interior decorating tips, because I suck at that, and these places always have the most peaceful, sexy, luxurious vibes.

Soon after picking a room, I stripped out of my body suit

and was just getting ready to step in the shower when I heard the knock and Jos's subsequent call.

"Coming!" I yell back, wrapping a white hotel towel around myself. It feels good to finally have my body suit out of my ass and my head free of bobby-pins. As I walk to the door, one hand grips my towel while the other fluffs my strawberry blonde hair, rubbing my sensitive scalp. Probably Jayne coming to collect our costumes.

When I round the corner into the living room and see Noah in the doorway, I pull up short. My mouth is dry, and I blink several times trying to freeze this image in my mind.

His hair is a mess, salt stains stand out against his black shirt from dried sweat, he's got his hands in the pockets of his jeans, and his eyeliner is almost completely gone. He looks tired and wired all at the same time.

How exactly am I supposed to ever get used to seeing him like this? Seeing him at all, really?

"Oh, uh, I was just about to grab a shower." I throw my thumb over my shoulder indicating the direction of the bathroom. "Give me a second, and I'll change." His eyes scan my body and freeze me in place.

After sharing that stage with him, I'm back to square one.

I had been mesmerized by the band before tonight, especially by *him*. But now? I have butterflies in his presence all over again. Whatever familiarity we had acquired after practicing for the last month together is gone, and I'm back to being totally starstruck.

Noah Kinkaid is a fucking force on that stage and how he isn't hugely egotistical and pompous, I'll never know. When he sings, it's like he's calling out all my emotions and demanding that I feel all of his as well.

"No need, this will only take a second." His eyes trail back up my body, leaving fire in their wake. His gaze is so intense, I have look away even as I break out in another sweat.

"Uh, Noah? I can't talk to you while I'm in a towel." *Because there's a good chance I'm going to climb your body like it's the tree of life.* "Especially if this is about tonight. Just give me a second."

I'm thankful I could form words as I turn toward my room, rushing off. He doesn't stop me this time. Instead, I hear his voice float through the open space and say to the girls, "Sloan and Brett are headed down to the pool if you guys want to join them. Apparently, it's been reserved so we have it all to ourselves if you want to unwind." He sounds hesitant for some reason.

When he stops speaking there are several squeals before doors slam shut– the girls getting changed, no doubt.

Does that mean Noah and I will be alone in the suite?

Oh boy, this isn't good for my cardiac health.

He's probably going to tell me I'm fired and doesn't want to have to do it in front of everyone. I slip on some cotton shorts and an old NASA t-shirt before heading back out to get kicked off the tour. No need to look sexy for this moment. I leave my hair down with all its untamed kinks from the bobby pins. Perhaps I'll be able to hide behind it if I start to cry.

Gathering all my courage, I walk back out into the living room and take a seat on the arm of the couch. A few seconds later, Bri, Kara, and Joslyn all traipse out in barely-there bikinis with towels slung over their shoulders. Bri kisses the top of my head. "Come down to the pool for a few minutes before your shower."

And then they're gone leaving Noah and I alone.

Every estrogen-based cell in my body perks its head up. Especially the ones located near my lady parts causing me to suppress a groan.

"What happened tonight?" he asks, diving right in, his perfect voice wrapping around me like his hand on my throat a few weeks ago. Its usual smoothness has a hint of gravel from singing his heart out and his tone is slightly deeper. No doubt a result of tired vocal cords. His voice is calm but curious.

When I don't answer immediately, he says my name and the inflection tells me he's asking again.

"Sienna?"

Goddamn. "You really do have the most beautiful voice I've ever heard."

Shit. That is *not* what I meant to say. The mental, emotional, and physical fatigue of tonight's performance has erased my ability to think words without saying them.

I hope he doesn't think that was some lame ass attempt to keep my job. I'm not trying to butter him up. It's just such a hard truth that apparently, I had to say it. It's already out there so there's no point in backtracking, so I let the compliment hang between us.

"Thank you," he says, walking over to the chair opposite me and matching my position on its arm. "You guys did an incredible job as well. Right up until I lost you." His eyes peer up at me through long, thick, black lashes because even though he's still taller than me while he's seated, his head is angled down toward his hands resting in his lap but his eyes are angled up at me. I almost come on the spot. "What happened, Sienna?"

I take a deep breath and start to speak but then close my mouth. He deserves the truth, but I haven't talked about it in years. Maybe skirting around the edge will suffice.

"I . . . didn't expect . . . didn't know you play the violin," I say lamely. "I was caught off guard. You didn't do that part in practice." *Great, it sounds like I'm blaming him for my reaction.*

He doesn't buy it anyway.

Noah Kinkaid is more observant than I realized.

"Me playing the violin got you so off-track on a routine you've done a million times that you almost ruined the set?" he asks, not unkindly.

"Um . . . yeah." I can't bring my eyes to meet his for fear of what he'll see there. "I'm sorry about that. If you're here to tell me you don't want me on the tour moving forward, I understand."

"What? Sienna, I'm not kicking you off the tour because of one mistake. I just want to know what happened up there. The look on your face . . . " he trails off, clearly not knowing how to finish.

Standing up, he walks over to the wall of windows overlooking the city. I find it easier to talk to him when his broad back is to me.

But only a little.

"I was just shocked is all. It's a big adjustment, and I'm not always so great in front of large groups of people," I admit.

He laughs, but it's strained. "Why the hell did you sign on for this then? Are you going to make it the rest of the tour? I'm not sure it's worth your sanity." He fires his questions at me, and his last statement is almost dripping with disdain. Something tells me he can relate to that last sentence.

"Don't worry about me. I'm fine," I snap. "It won't happen again. Now that I know to expect it, I won't be caught off guard."

He turns away from the windows and moves closer to where I'm still sitting on the arm of the chair, my arms wrapped around myself.

Shit. His presence in my personal space quickly becomes overwhelming when I think about the thousands of women who would literally chop off body parts to be this close to him. The man who emptied his soul on that stage but won't let anyone see or touch his skin. The man who touched *me* on that stage tonight in front of everyone to ground me after panic threatened to have me fleeing.

"But I want to know why it set you off in the first place," he admits quietly.

Do I tell him? Do I share one of my most intimate secrets with this untouchable rockstar who doesn't know me and who most likely is just making sure I don't cause him and the band to look bad for the next eight months?

No. Of course not.

"It's nothing. Forget it. I said I'm fine, and I am. It won't be an issue," I assure him.

I can tell he's assessing the truth in my statement even though I refuse to meet his eyes. Sensing he's not going to get anything else out of me, he comes too close and pauses briefly before placing two fingers under my chin, forcing my head up. My skin is on fire where he's touching me. A shiver makes my shoulders quake when I look at him.

A ghost of a smile moves over his mouth before he turns serious again and addresses me one last time.

"We all have demons, Sienna. I don't know what about that violin made one of yours come out, but eight months is a long time to suffer in silence."

With that, he drops his hand and walks out of the suite. I let out the breath I didn't know I'd been holding as my hands shake in my lap.

A minute later, the opening line of Barbie Girl by Aqua alerts me to a text from Bri.

BRI

Get out of your head. It's going to be okay.
Come down to the pool.

. . .

I sit for another minute, willing the worst night of my life back into its little black box and decide that stewing by myself won't actually help anything. I trod back into my room, dig out my swimsuit and prepare to spend the next hour or so in the company of my best friend and the world's hottest musicians.

"There she is!" Bri shouts from Brett's shoulders, her blonde ponytail dark from the water and clinging to her back. She looks elated at her current position, and Brett looks like a wolf who's waiting for the perfect time to spin her around to the front of his shoulders and bury his face deep in her pussy.

I've walked in on a game of chicken. Joslyn is on Sloan's shoulders and Kara is playing referee.

I laugh at the sight. Apparently, exhaustion doesn't touch these five. Disappointment creases my brow when I survey the room for Noah and come up empty.

"Come join us! You can take my spot," Jos says, but as she tries to climb down off of Sloan's shoulders, he puts her thighs in a vice grip.

"Not so fast. I want a re-match," he says, making her laugh.

A voice startles me from the doorway. "Besides, I'll give her a ride," Ryan says playfully as he wags his eyebrows suggestively, causing my stomach to flip. Ryan is built like a tank. I'm sure any ride he gives is one I'd never forget.

I let Ryan pull me toward the pool as he whispers, "I do *love* redheads," and winks at me causing my knees to grow weak. Not all men can pull off a wink. A lot of times it's creepier than it is sexy, but Ryan and Sloan both have the sexy-wink ability.

Once I'm in the heated pool, getting lost in the moment is easy. The girls' squeals echo loudly around the indoor pool deck. The smell of chlorine is overwhelming but rather than being on sensory overload, it's nice to just soak it all in.

I suck at this game, but it's fun just to be so carefree around these wildly famous, talented, men. When they're without Noah, there is an air of playfulness they keep concealed in his presence, and I frown at the realization.

His words come back to me just as Bri knocks me off Ryan's shoulders and my body smacks the water.

We all have demons, Sienna.

I wonder what Noah's are and if they're even remotely as fucked up as my own.

As I'm pulling myself up Ryan's back like a mountain climber, determined to take Bri down this time, the pool door opens again and Ryan swivels to see who it is, turning me with him. His movement is so fast, I plant my hands on his head to keep my balance as he wraps his large hands to the insides of my thighs.

Noah's eyes find mine quickly and his shoulders visibly tense, but he doesn't say anything. Perhaps he feels like he's watching the unraveling of his tour on the first night by the lack of professionalism happening in this pool.

"Kinky! Get in! We can do two on two teams!" Sloan says happily even though his excitement is watered down now compared to the last twenty minutes. He's still bouncing up and down though, tossing Jos around on his shoulders, her head lolling like a ragdoll.

"Yeah," Ryan starts, "Kara needs a partner."

Something about those words doesn't sit well with me which is ridiculous. Noah Kinkaid has made it abundantly clear he belongs to no one but his bandmates. Even if Kara does get to sit on his shoulders, that's a dumb reason to be upset.

Fuck. *Am I upset?*

Hell, I doubt he's even getting in because that would mean taking his shirt off, which he doesn't do - *ever* - according to news outlets and social media. They speculate that he's horribly scarred. *We all have demons, Sienna.*

It's as I'm replaying his words for the second time tonight that I see him cross his arms in front of himself, grab a fistful of black t-shirt in each hand, and start lifting. Whoops of joy go up from the guys in the pool, but the girls and I are stunned into total silence.

We're about to see Noah Kinkaid's actual flesh. Somehow this feels like a bigger deal than being on stage with him.

As his shirt slowly rises, I have to adjust how I'm sitting, the pressure building between my legs is making my current position uncomfortable.

Noah isn't scarred.

He's fucking *beautiful.*

And ripped. Smooth, flawless, tanned skin coats his torso, including his very defined abs. He has a tattoo of a lion on his right pec facing off against a tiger on his left pec and I've never been a bigger fan of large cats than I am right now. I can see the full sleeve of tattoos down his right arm and *Jesus take the wheel,* he has a tattoo on his hip, dipping below the waistband of his swin trunks. It looks like the top of a tree, but I can't tell and my brain is shorting out.

The collective gasps from us girls can easily be heard thanks to the echoes around the indoor pool.

Brett groans. "Don't make his head any bigger than it is, ladies."

Bri fires back quickly. "We can't even see his head . . . maybe once his shorts are wet." Her dirty humor never disappoints, but her delivery is too breathless for it to really pack a punch this time. Brett's green eyes flare in warning right before he dunks her. The move is playful but when she comes up for air, his voice isn't.

"Kinky's got enough people worrying about his dick. Why don't you pick someone else?"

While Bri and Brett keep fighting-slash-flirting, I'm stuck contemplating why anyone would want to hide that body away.

"*Oh, fuck me.*" I'm pretty sure I only say it in my head until Ryan cranes his neck to look up at me.

"Nope. That's off limits, remember?" he says, chuckling at his own joke.

"What?" I ask, mortified he heard me. Trying to cover up my mistake, I press on. "Oh, no, I just meant now I'm going to get clobbered by Kara. She's the strongest out of all of us."

His narrowed eyes and confident smirk tells me he sees right through my lie, and I'm reminded that I still lack the ability to think words without them spewing out of my mouth.

Meanwhile, Noah moves to the steps of the pool. Each of his movements more graceful than the last. His abs flex with each step like they stay permanently contracted. He has on navy swim trunks that stop high on his muscular thighs. The divots by his hips point to the holy grail, and when he dips under the water and comes back up dripping and running a hand through his hair, I can't hide my response as I clench my thighs together . . . *hard* . . . *forgetting* that Ryan's head is between them.

He taps my right thigh. "You want to loosen up there, sweetheart? I'm on your team. Choking me out isn't good for our chances of winning."

"Oh, shit. I'm so sorry."

He huffs out a laugh and moves to the center of the pool as Kara climbs on Noah's shoulders with a lustful look of wonder I suddenly want to smack off her face. When Noah reaches up to secure her in place - by holding on to her knees, thankfully - his eyes stay locked on mine and a feral growl escapes from my throat.

All the guys in the band are attractive. It just seems that Noah Kinkaid is my particular brand of heroine.

Me and the rest of the female population.

Ugh.

Suddenly, I've lost interest in the game. If I quit, then they can't play two-on-two and maybe Noah will give it up. If he insists on continuing to play then at least I can finally go grab my shower, and I don't have to watch his perfect, tattooed hands rest possessively on Kara.

Before I can say I'm out, Ryan taps my thighs with both hands.

I'm clenching again.

When I release my pressure, he calls over to Noah. "Kink, let's trade. Sienna's gonna snap my dainty neck. Why don't you two pair up and let me have a go with Kara?" Looking right at her, he asks innocently, "You won't try to sever my head with your thighs, will you, KareBear?"

She looks wistfully at Ryan, loving the attention, then down at Noah, like she's torn.

Noah shrugs. "I won't take it personally."

Without warning, Ryan dumps me backward into the water and lets go of my legs so I can float away. In the background, the other four are already playing, and Bri's laughter fills my heart as she and Joslyn basically hug each other as they try to throw the other off balance.

I approach Noah cautiously.

My heart is in my throat, and my throat is in my stomach, and my stomach feels like it's about to make an appearance in the pool.

"You don't have to do this," I say as if he needs my permission to back out of the game.

He doesn't take his eyes off me, nor does he answer verbally. He just squats down so I can put one foot on his thigh before swinging my other leg over his shoulder. He holds out his hand like he did on stage and the butterflies beat themselves violently against my ribcage.

Once I'm in place, he takes his time running his left hand up my thigh into position and then follows suit with the right. It's almost as if he's savoring the feel of my skin, but I can't see his face from here to read his eyes. Perhaps he's going so slowly because he knows this is a terrible idea. My reaction to his movements is completely out of my control as my hips push forward, my body subconsciously urging his hands higher on my legs.

And by *higher,* I obviously mean between them.

All the air is forcefully expelled from my lungs at his touch.

"Finally!" Brett shouts. "Let's do this! Best out of ten! We call dibs on Kinky and Si!"

Despite being in the cool water, I wonder if Noah can feel the heat from my core on the back of his neck. Thank God he dips down every now and then and won't be able to tell if the wet spot is from me or the pool.

His broad shoulders create a comfortable couch as well as a sturdy base, and we end up winning five of the ten matches. One went to Brett and Bri, two went to each of the other teams.

When Noah removes his hands from my legs for the last time and helps me off his shoulders, the loss of contact feels like a hole has been punched through me.

"Good game," he says, holding out his hand as that voice of perfection floats around me.

I place my trembling hand in his as I feel my cheeks flush. "You too."

He puts that dark, soulful gaze on me once more and whispers, "Get some sleep."

Not likely.

That night, my dreams are filled with smashed violins and snapped bows. My mother's angry voice yelling in the background as I cower in a corner of our home library with my hands over my ears. It didn't matter that I was seventeen. In that moment, I felt seven as I listened to my parent's marriage disintegrate, and I lost the first love of my life.

My violin.

Chapter 11

Noah

T he first month of the tour couldn't have gone better. We're finding a rhythm and really working as a team, including the girls. I often think back to that first night and how stupid it was to put everybody in the pool with next to no clothes on and expect people to not fuck each other - mostly Brett - but surprisingly, everyone's played by the rules and there haven't been any more pool parties.

The girls are low-drama and overall, a nice addition to the vibe we carry when it's just the four of us guys.

Tonight, we're in Dallas with the biggest audience yet.

I'm backstage running through the normal chain of pre-show events when I see the girls come out of their dressing room in another almost see-through one piece.

This one is new.

It's still skin colored over the arms and legs but instead of being solid across their chests and between their legs like underwear, it's meant to look like straps all over their bodies and it's hot as fuck.

I have to hand it to Matt. The girls have really been a

crowd-pleaser. All the posts, news coverage, and podcast reviews about the tour agree it was a bold move and worked out really well.

I'm doing a mic check with Tasha when I see a tall, lanky guy I don't recognize in a three-piece, gray suit enter backstage wearing the requisite lanyard telling me he's allowed back here even though he's not familiar to me. Without missing a beat, he walks up behind Sienna and throws his arms around her waist pulling her into himself. I try to stay objective since they clearly know each other, but I bristle anyway.

She's never mentioned a boyfriend.

She and I have been cordial since that first night, but she still hasn't told me what happened on stage. It's not in my nature to pry, and she seems keen to avoid being alone with me, which is probably for the best. True to her word, she hasn't had any more episodes since that first show. In fact, she's gotten much more confident and comfortable over the last few weeks. I can see it in the way she moves.

And I spend a lot of time watching her move.

More time than I should, considering the amount of shit I give the guys about keeping their dicks in their pants. But it's hard to follow my own advice when I can still feel her on the back of my neck. Even the chlorine and the multiple dips underwater couldn't mask her scent of arousal so close to my face. It's a miracle I didn't fuck her on the tile pool deck. I'm long overdue as it is.

At this point though, the girls are half our show. It's clear this performance wouldn't be the same without them, so it's only natural I would get a little possessive about this douche bag with his arms around Sienna.

It's such a good lie, I almost believe it myself.

I think briefly about intervening, but she looks happy to see him, so I ignore it and finish my mic check, hackles still raised.

Ten minutes later, the guy *still* has his arm around her waist, and if the way she's leaning away and angling her back to him is any indication, she's starting to get uncomfortable. And if she's uncomfortable, then I'm pissed off.

I march over to their little circle, Sienna and Douche are on one side with Bri and Joslyn on the other, and I stop right in front of the plump-lipped, redheaded beauty, not bothering to address anyone else. A bright side to occasionally being an ass - this rude gesture won't seem out of character at all.

"I need your help for a second."

Her face lights up, and my heart stops. Literally stops. There is nothing like Sienna's smile. Those fucking lips frame her perfectly straight, white teeth. And she doesn't just jump right into a smile, it slowly parts her lips seductively, like she's about to share a secret you'd give your dying breath to hear. The move demands all my attention.

It's also making me hard.

"Sure! Of course!" She turns to Douche Bag and slips out of his grasp. "I'll be back in a few."

That's when he finally notices me standing there, and I see the stars in his eyes as he puts a hand out. Like an asshole, I draw up to my full height, towering over him by two or three inches.

"Oh man, Noah Kinkaid, I'm a huge fan. I can't believe my sister is on tour with you."

I grasp his hand, relieved. But then again, that was a weird way to touch your sister.

"Sienna is your sister?" I ask for clarification, feeling my brows pinch together.

He laughs and his eyes flit to Sienna with pure desire in them. "Oh, no. *Bri* is my sister. Sienna is –"

Bri cuts him off. "Josh, do not embarrass yourself by

finishing that sentence. Sienna is *my* best friend. End. Of. Story."

Josh just chuckles at his sister. "You'll see. One day she'll say yes to me."

Unlikely, pal.

"Enjoy the show, Josh." I squeeze his hand a little harder than necessary before dropping it. "Sienna, I need you to help me re-mic. There's too much feedback in this one."

It's a lame reason to request her presence since Tash always works out any mic problems, but Sienna doesn't question me. When she nods her head and turns to walk down the hall toward the staging area, I place my hand at the small of her back as if I touch her like this all the time. I feel her steps falter, but she recovers quickly. I'm playing with fire and being irrationally selfish, but I want that asshole to see my hand on her. I can't hide my smile when she doesn't shake it off and allows me to lead her away.

We disappear around the corner, and her relief is written all over her face as she holds out shaking hands, waiting for me to hand her the mic clipped to the back of my belt. I stop her trembling hands with my own, causing her to look up at me in question.

Can she feel what's passing between us right now? The heat where our hands are connected? What would it feel like if our lips were to touch? *Fuck. I need to stop this train of thought immediately.*

"Mic's fine," I choke out. "You looked uncomfortable, and he wasn't letting go. I thought you could use an out," I explain, trying to act as nonchalantly as possible about the fact I want to break that guy's teeth.

She winces. "I was that obvious?"

"Only to someone who was paying attention."

I'm suddenly and overwhelmingly tempted to suck her

small gasp of realization into my mouth. *That's right, Si, I was paying attention.* Hell, I'm always paying attention.

Color paints her cheeks so boldly I can see it through her stage makeup.

"Thank you," she whispers, giving me a small smile. "Josh seems to think we're in love and I'm just playing hard to get,." She pauses before adding, "But if that's the case, then I've been playing hard to get for more than ten years."

I feel my inner caveman rising to the surface wanting to pound my chest with my fists and eat the still-beating heart of anyone who approaches this woman without her consent.

"He's harmless, and he's really nice," she adds quickly, sensing the storm brewing within me. "He just isn't for me."

She doesn't owe me an explanation, but I'll take any words she wants to give me. I'm not sure when I got this desperate to be near her.

I suppose I knew I was in trouble when I saw her thighs framing Ryan's face in that game of chicken and all I saw after that was red.

"Let me know if he gives you any trouble," I say before I have time to think about how possessive it sounds.

"I've known Josh a long time. He'd never hurt me," she says, trying to reassure me.

Spoiler alert: it doesn't work.

When the lights go down and the crowd roars to life, all I can think about is that asshole sitting out there somewhere with his eyes glued to Sienna's form as she rolls and writhes in her silks. It makes me scream harder, play harder, and do something really fucking stupid.

Because apparently, I'm the dog that needs to piss on his territory.

Occasionally, we change the order of the songs and do different ones from the previous albums just so we don't get bored. The choreography stays the same for the girls though, because otherwise, that would be too many moving parts.

Tonight, what has secretly become my favorite song on the tour – the one where Sienna's hands shoot between my legs driving the crowd absolutely wild – is played last. Unable to get rid of the image of that guy's hands on my dancer, I decide to play dirty.

Right on beat, Sienna drops into her straddle behind me but when her hands shoot between my legs, still careful not to touch me, I catch her overlapped wrists in my free hand and hold them against myself as I thrust my hips forward. I put more passion into that line of the song than I ever thought I could give. My voice cracks and sounds like an erotic whimper even to my own ears.

I only have a second before I know she has to roll away so I slide her hands down the front of my jeans, knowing she can feel my swelling cock twitching in appreciation. Before I can think about the fact that maybe I just did that against her will, she curls her fingers, trying to sink them farther into my jeans, and I feel the wicked smile spread across my face when she squeezes gently.

Somehow, we both manage to execute the rest of the song perfectly, and I'm elated at her response.

Which is not good at all.

Immediately after the show, I raise my hand to knock on the door of the girls' dressing room to apologize to Sienna but pause when I realize I can hear what they're saying.

"I almost fell the fuck off the stage, Sienna!" one of the girls exclaims. I can only tell Joslyn apart from the others because although her voice is feminine, it's raspy, letting me know that wasn't Jos.

"Did you know he was going to do that?" another one asks.

"Could you feel his dick?" *Ah, there's Joslyn.*

I'm dying for Sienna's answer, but she evades the question.

"Oh my god, guys, he was *acting*. He's performing. He knows the crowd goes insane when he interacts with us, and this was our biggest show yet. I bet the idea came to him on the fly to get everyone all fired up since it was the last song."

That *should* have been the reason I did it.

Thankfully, she doesn't seem upset about it. Instead, she sounds almost giddy, a high-pitched laugh coming out after her words. I turn to leave, satisfied I didn't upset her, when I see Douche Bag Extraordinaire approaching the girls' dressing room. Normally, I'm not so judgmental, but this dude in his loafers is rubbing me the wrong fucking way.

I have to work hard to reign it in when he stops outside their dressing room door.

Oh, hell no.

He's wearing a dopey grin and looks like he might be drunk. Or at the very least, heavily buzzed. I can tell his eyes won't focus because he's blinking rapidly and trying to squint.

"Dude, that was fucking *epic*." I'm about to nod and give my thanks because I really do appreciate our fans - even this guy - until he opens his mouth again. "Wasn't crazy about my girl rubbing your dick though. I've had wet dreams for *years* about her grabbing me like that . . . along with other things, if you know what I mean," he openly admits in his alcohol-induced state.

Before I can respond like a toddler and tell him that it's my tour and I can do whatever the fuck I want, the girls' door flies open, and Sienna runs right into me.

Literally, because she's looking over her shoulder and talking to one of the other dancers.

"Oh, shit!" Her head snaps around to see who she hit. I've got both hands on her upper arms to steady her, and I take in her short blue strapless dress. Her hair rolls in messy waves around her shoulders, and her makeup looks fresh even though she still has the slight sheen of sweat on her face, neck, and . . . *stop fucking looking at her lips, Kinkaid.*

My mouth goes dry, and I can't swallow. It feels like I'm choking.

If she bends over everyone will see her ass . . . not like they don't during the shows, but somehow that's different. The heels she's wearing accentuate her calves and quads, and she looks stunning.

Bri comes out and flings her arms around her brother before exclaiming, "We're going to an exclusive club tonight!" she squeals. "Do you want to come?" she asks Josh.

I look down at Sienna, who's still in my grip, and reluctantly let her go. Reading my expression, Sienna explains. "Matt came by and told us it's time to be seen so we're going to some hot VIP spot downtown to *keep the buzz alive.*" She uses air quotes and shrugs like she doesn't care one way or the other about going, but Bri, Joslyn, and Kara are dancing with excitement.

I've got a new line running through my head I really need to sit in silence with for a couple of hours, but no way in hell am I letting Sienna go anywhere with McHandsy over here.

Especially in public . . . even if it's a "private", "exclusive" kind of public.

"Sounds good. Let me grab the guys." I give Sienna a long look before turning away from her.

It can't be just me that feels this pull, can it?

Ryan meets me halfway down the corridor between

dressing rooms and delivers the same news I just heard from the girls. "Hey, looks like we have to make an appearance at a club called Firebird's tonight." He holds out a garment bag indicating I need to shower and change.

I grab the bag and nod. "I just heard. Do me a favor?"

"Sure, man, what's up?" Ryan asks. He's the only one I'd ask this favor of because he's the only one who won't give me absolute shit even though he'll know why I'm asking.

"Bri's brother is here. Apparently, he's had the hots for Sienna for a while, but he makes her uncomfortable. Run interference while I get ready, will ya?"

He gives me a knowing grin but says nothing. "Yeah, Kink, no problem."

I clap him on the back. "Thanks, man."

Chapter 12

Sienna

The heat of the stage can be overwhelming sometimes, but every time we do a show, I get a little more used to it. The lights themselves make the stage about eighty degrees, then add in the fog which I swear traps all the heat, *plus* you have eight people moving around and creating energy themselves, and by the time it's all said and done, that stage feels like Death Valley at noon . . . in July.

So, when we step into Firebird's and get blasted with cold air and darkness, it's so refreshing, I could almost cry.

The light is so low my eyes have to adjust to make sure it's actually on at all. There are candles scattered on all the table-tops and end tables. Some people are eating, others are sipping cocktails and lounging on the loveseats and plush, wide chairs.

Music is being piped in overhead, but it's so quiet, I can't tell what's playing. It's just enough to create a hum in the back-ground and encourage the flow of conversation.

My eyes rove around the large, open room, and they widen with recognition. Everyone here is famous. *Everyone.* People I wouldn't imagine meeting in my wildest dreams are scattered throughout the room, but I won't meet them tonight either.

We were all instructed before we got here that this is where the massively famous go to get out without having to be "on". There is a strict no-phones policy here, and if you're caught with one, you're not allowed back. Ever. It's one of the most exclusive spots in the States.

The push for the band to come here tonight was all about the press they got outside just before we entered. Apparently, this place is invite-only, and Matt got word about the invitation this afternoon. Showing up here is like claiming your place on the throne of entertainment.

Security ushers us through the doorway quickly and allows the hostess to take over as Romeo, Tim, and Juan blend into the background with all the other bodyguards. The hostess can't hide her furrowed brow fast enough, and I know she's wondering who the hell the girls and I are.

She doesn't have to wonder long.

A large frame strides right in-between Bri and me and approaches the hostess.

Now she makes the connection.

"Seating for nine, please," Ryan says to her before swinging his head over his shoulder and addressing Jos and Kara who are right in front of me. "We don't care if it's a table or the low chairs, right?"

We all shake our heads because when Ryan Battle asks a question, you give an answer.

"Sure, Mr. Battle, right this way."

Ryan follows her like this is the most normal thing in the world. Although he's more familiar with fame than I am, I know this level of status is new even for him.

With all the subtlety of a car alarm, I blurt to no in particular, "Where's Noah?"

I can't explain the panic in my voice which is much too loud for this atmosphere. It isn't like someone forgot the lead singer and left him behind, but everything was a whirlwind, and he left to change, and then we were on the bus, and now he isn't with Ryan.

Neither are the other two, but somehow that doesn't upset me.

I feel an arm slide around my waist and the familiar scent of a Gucci cologne hits my nose causing me to stiffen.

Not Noah.

Josh may be Bri's brother, but she *knows* he never leaves me alone when we're together. I'm not mad she invited him along because they're close, but I wish he would take a hint.

Before I can shrug him off or get out of his hold, I feel his hand leave my side even as his fingers seem to dig in for traction. I hear him huff. "What the hell?"

Turning around to see what's going on, I come face to face with the perfect, mouth-watering, pissed-off expression of Noah Kinkaid. He lowers his voice to a whisper and places his lips next to my ear, answering my question.

"I'm right here."

Stunned into a relieved silence, I feel my shoulders relax, and I nod my head.

Yes.

Okay.

Thank you.

I'm not sure what I'm trying to tell him with that nod, but I know, somehow, he understands.

My eyes scan him from head to toe, and I take in the tailored black suit he's wearing. With a black button-down underneath, he looks every bit the untouchable musician he is. He seems just as comfortable in this suit as he does his jeans and t-shirt, and I marvel at his complexity. He's not just a pretty face with an orgasm-inducing voice.

Josh starts to protest when Noah cuts him off with a finger in his face and a low, stern voice that leaves no room for argument.

"This is a place to relax and unwind. A place for those of us constantly in the spotlight to relax and unwind for a night. *You* shouldn't even be here, but because you are, don't forget you represent Beautiful Deceit. I won't have you making us look like assholes."

"Chill, man," Josh whines, holding his hands up in mock surrender. "Si and I go way back. How does my arm around her make *you* look like an asshole?" Josh asks as he flags down a waitress.

"Because she doesn't want it there," Noah replies coldly with no hint of remorse.

Josh momentarily looks hurt, and his expression pisses me off. Does he think I've been kidding for the last twelve years I've told him no?

Bri flashes an embarrassed look at her brother as she takes her turn putting her index finger in his face.

"Do *not* fuck this up for me, Joshua Vorossi. And leave Sienna alone for Christ's sake!" she hisses.

Josh folds his arms across his chest and slumps down on the couch. He's pouting like a toddler but wisely, he keeps his mouth shut. Pain and embarassment are easily recognizable in his eyes when he flicks his gaze toward me.

After the initial drama is over, we all settle into the evening. The guys start a conversation about a new song Noah's working on, the girls are talking about a new Netflix special they want to watch, and Josh is looking around the room in order to avoid making eye contact with me and pissing Noah off even more.

I'm watching Noah's Adam's apple bob as he takes a sip of

whatever clear liquid is in his highball glass. I opted for a vodka martini because it's the easiest and tastiest way to catch a buzz. Another perk being that I'll only have to drink one which means I won't wake up hung over and bloated from any sugary mixers.

After a couple of minutes, Noah looks at me across the table. I have to admit, I was disappointed when he didn't sit next to me. I'm like a girl on the school bus hoping the only seat left when my crush walks on, is next to me.

It wasn't, which left Noah the opportunity to take the open seat across from me.

He looks around the group, seemingly hyperaware that everyone is engaged in discussion, before returning his eyes to me and nodding his head toward the crowded bar.

I'm not completely sure I'm reading this right, but what the hell do I have to lose? If I'm wrong, I'll just tell him I wanted another drink.

Tapping Bri on the thigh, I tell her I'm going to grab another martini and ask if she or the girls want anything.

Josh looks up immediately. "Oh, I do. I'll come with you." My heart sinks until Bri reaches over and pushes him back down onto the couch.

"I'm not going to tell you again, Josh. Leave. Her. *Alone.* Look, we are so glad we got to see you while you're here for work, but you have to back off."

"I just need a refill, Bri. *Damn.* Why is everyone on my case all of a sudden?"

"Because you're *up her ass* all of a sudden," Bri says, starting to get angry.

"Twelve years is sudden?" Josh says with a crestfallen look and a pain pierces my heart.

He and Bri were both there for me when things got bad with my parents and then again when my dad went into a spiral. Not to mention, Josh was the one who talked to his friend's dad about getting our apartment so I could train with Bri. Lord knows I wouldn't be where I am today with the both of them.

I've always known Josh had a boyhood crush on me, but I stupidly never realized it seems to be much more than that.

Trying to soften the blow, I grab Josh's glass from the low table it's sitting on. "Josh, I'll get you a refill. When I get back, you and I can catch up, okay?"

His eyes light up causing me to regret the offer and resent my empathetic nature. I just can't stand to see people hurting. I read a quote one time, and I don't know who said it, but it was *don't set yourself on fire to keep others warm.* It's stuck with me ever since because that's the exact description of what I do.

Turning toward the bar, I put my back to the group and quickly get lost in the crowd that's milling about. This place filled up fast after we got here and there are no more tables or couches available so people are filling in around the bar, standing, relaxing, laughing.

My eyes start scanning for Noah immediately, but I spot the busty brunette that's stopped him en route to the bar first. I don't think anything of it until she reaches out to bat playfully at his chest, and I see him pull back.

Some think his reaction is odd. In truth, there may have been a time early on, when I did too, but after spending this short time with them on the road, I get it now.

People are grabbing at him *constantly.* Grabbing for all of them actually. They don't know these people. Or where their hands have been. It's like just because the guys are famous, it gives everyone the right to grope them and get a piece of them, personal space be damned.

In a split second, I've made a decision. It's probably a

terrible one, but he was there for me when Josh was in my personal space uninvited. Perhaps I can return the favor.

I almost back out until she reaches for him again, this time, managing to make brief contact, and I see him try to hide his grimace. Due to the clientele here, his conversation partner is no doubt famous herself and therefore, he's not blatantly throwing her off, but I can tell his smile is strained, his discomfort shining through. It's obvious . . . *to someone who's paying attention.*

I approach from behind his conversation partner, so she doesn't see me coming as I insert myself right in between them, ignoring her completely, my back in her face.

My rationale is that at least I'm a known quantity, so if someone's going to be in his personal space, I'm gambling he'd rather it be me. Especially considering his stunt earlier when he basically used my hand to fist his dick. *Not that I'm complaining, simply strengthening the me vs. her argument.*

Is it a bitch move? *Yes.*

Do I give a shit? *Not after my last martini.*

The smirk he fails to hide as I enter his orbit tells me I made the right choice *and* that he knows what I'm doing.

"I thought you should know the wolves at the table are getting restless and want their drinks. Help me? I can't carry them all." I give a small wave toward the bar, still ignoring the handsy celebrity trying to pet him.

I can't help my own smirk when I hear Noah say to the woman over my shoulder, "Nice to meet you. Just let our manager know if you want those tickets."

I feel him behind me as we make our way to the bar. If he were to reach his hand out and touch my back, I think I might die.

The crowd parts in the middle like a 90's haircut as we make our way through it and whispers go up as Noah passes. A few guys reach out to shake his hand, which he takes, graciously.

When we get to the sleek, black marble bar top, the male bartender eyes me appreciatively but not disrespectfully. I still have my stage makeup on even though I changed clothes, so my eyes are unusually dark, my fake eyelashes are still in place, and my usual pink lip gloss is absent in favor of the deep crimson stain I wear for the show.

"What can I get for you, Miss?" His smile is disarmingly bright. He probably doubles as a male model.

Behind the bar is a wall of glass shelves. A lot of bars have mirrors behind those shelves to reflect light and make the space seem bigger, but not here. The walls are paneled in dark wood. The contrast with the glass shelves is actually quite beautiful and elegant. The shelves go up about fifteen feet on the wall, holding all their reserve bottles in view. It's an impressive collection, clearly designed to cater to those with deep pockets and impeccable tastes.

I'd never really thought of Dallas as a celebrity hotspot, but I guess I will from now on.

I place my order for Josh and Kara's drinks, deciding to abandon my own, when I feel Noah step so closely behind me he pushes me slightly forward into the bar. The pressure of him at my back sends my thoughts down a rabbit hole of debauchery. Not to mention, Noah's sweat smells like sex and pine. He braces his left hand on the marble bar top just outside my left elbow and leans around my right side, caging me in.

It's not particularly loud in here but he acts like he's having trouble hearing the bartender as he leans in even further, his chest now fully pressed against my back. After placing his own order for a scotch – weird, because that is definitely *not* what was in his glass – he straightens up but stays close.

I am almost certainly reading too much into his proximity,

but my brain – as well as other parts – has officially boarded the Noah Kinkaid train, and I plan to ride this baby anywhere it goes. Fully clothed of course, because I don't want to jeopardize my job.

A member of another band comes over to congratulate Noah on the success of the tour and Noah introduces me. The man – who reminds me of Machine Gun Kelly – actually licks his lips while he undresses me with his eyes. Although it's behavior I would've expected from a rockstar three months ago, it catches me off guard now, since no one in Beautiful Deceit treats us as anything other than artistic equals, despite their humor and the sexual undercurrents that accompany the eight of us everywhere.

Instinctively, I lean back a little to create space between us, momentarily forgetting that Noah is right behind me, and I inhale sharply when my ass lands right between his powerful thighs. Almost immediately, I feel his hand on my hip to still me and keep me from backing up any further. It's so crowded where we are that no one can see him touching me, and he leaves it there as he talks to the man in front of us, stealing my breath and kicking my desire into overdrive.

Thankfully – or not – the bartender returns with our drinks a few moments later, Noah says goodbye to the other guy, and I give a small smile before reaching for our order.

Desire is pouring off me like a faucet on full blast, and I know my cheeks are flushed with embarrassment. A touch so small, and given for my benefit, shouldn't make my heartbeat in my throat.

But it did.

It does.

It is.

We're just a month into this and I'm slipping down a dangerous path of need for a man I can't have. A man so closed off, who's to say he'd be interested even if he *was* an option?

I have to get out of here. I can't pretend with Josh tonight. I can't watch more women interact with Noah and try their chances.

I need to spend a minute with myself and flush out these fantasies so I can get back to work and enjoy the next seven months.

I apologize and tell the girls and Josh goodnight, making up a story about being exhausted and just needing some alone time – not a total lie.

When I say goodnight to the guys, I see Noah's eyes darken as he flicks a glance at Josh. I think he's checking to see if Josh is going to follow me now that he knows Josh's advances are unwanted. I say a silent thank you to him and turn to leave.

Security walks me back to the hotel, alone, which is only a few blocks down the street. It's impossible to decide if I made the right decision or if I regret not spending every second I can inside the silent, raging storm that is Noah Kinkaid.

Chapter 13

Noah

I think about that night at the bar in Dallas a lot, especially Sienna's vanilla scent, but also the way she felt as I pushed against her at the bar. How she recoiled from others but pressed herself into me for safety. The way her hip felt under my hand.

God, I wanted to wrap my arms around her and bury my face in her neck – as well as a few other places - that night.

But I didn't. And I haven't. Hell, I've barely seen her at all except on stage since then.

Over the five weeks since that night, the schedule has picked up and kept me busier than I've ever been. Thankfully, the fans are responding with incredible love for the tour, but it's caused me to think about what comes next, robbing me of some of the joy of the current moment. Like now, when I should be sleeping.

The clock on the nightstand tells me it's two a.m.

Despite my anxiety, I've never had trouble sleeping, but the past few nights, the pressure on my chest has been too tight for me to breathe evenly, causing sleep to evade me. Matt's already pulled me aside once, asking if I need something.

Something.

My tour manager offered me drugs like it was nothing. Just another service he offers.

I declined.

I'll quit music before I get involved with that even though I'm so stressed I can no longer hear the music, which terrifies me. I can *always* hear the music. The song that had called to me the night we were in Dallas, left soon afterward, and I can't remember its sound.

Hell, I can't even remember what city we're in right now.

Albuquerque?

Salt Lake City?

Scottsdale?

Realizing I won't be falling asleep anytime soon, I grab my violin and leave the hotel suite. We're sharing the top floor of penthouse suites with the girls again and it almost provides a small level of comfort to know our group is all together, sequestered away from the world up here. Especially as the crowds become more intense both in size and energy.

When we got off the elevator earlier, I passed a small alcove at the end of our hallway that's far enough away that my playing won't wake anyone. Even though the notes in my mind are silent, perhaps my fingers can find the sound I need.

The large set of windows just inside the door catches my eye, and I feel the pull to stand in front of them before going in search of the prized spot down the hall. The thousands of blinking lights from the city scape below twinkle as if to tell me they don't sleep either and a reminder I'm not alone.

But even with a full staff of security, the girls right down the hall, an entire crew on the floor below us, and my best friends asleep in this same suite, I *do* feel alone, and I didn't expect that.

I had no idea that fame was so fucking isolating.

It comes and goes but there are so many faces, so many people who know my story, my face, my voice, where I went to school, and the name of my first dog . . . and I don't know *any* of them. It's disorienting.

Perhaps it's always been this way but I'm only noticing it now because the music that normally occupies my brain and keeps me company is absent for the first time in a decade.

Besides, there's only so many cities you can see from penthouse views before they all start to run together. Only so many white couches, white curtains, white counters and stock photos of art before the emptiness begins to creep in and each suite feels more like a prison cell than a luxurious retreat.

And yes, I know how fucked up that sounds. I'm extremely grateful for our success and to not have to slum it in the busted RV. But also, there was no way to mentally prepare for the dramatic change in our day to day lives.

I *need* to find the music. I need to handle this better. I need to regain control before it eats me alive.

Despite our heavy metal sounds, I find solace and most of my creativity in the violin. It's the most underrated instrument in my opinion. I don't need anything but the instrument, my bow, and a notepad and pen in case I come across something I like, although, at this point, I'm just hoping to come across anything at all.

Leaving the view at the windows, I grab my stuff and quietly exit the suite. It doesn't take long to get settled in the alcove and begin the search for the sound I need.

Thirty minutes later, I've still got nothing. My teeth clench so hard it's making my jaw sore as frustration rises to the surface. The pressure in my chest threatens to pull me under, and I drop my head in my hands, my violin nestled in my lap.

Faintly in the distance, I hear the telltale squeak of a door being opened. In my peripheral vision, I see a quick flash of light at the other end of the hallway and notice a figure floating toward me.

Only when she gets closer do I recognize Sienna's unruly, long red hair. She's wearing black pajama shorts and an over-sized shirt that says *Bite Me*. She has no makeup on and she's fucking breathtaking.

Christ, I am not strong enough for this right now.

Before she gets too close, I try shifting in my seat, placing the heel of my hand against myself. *Lay the fuck down, you traitor.*

The past few weeks, Sienna and I have mutually and respectfully tried avoiding each other. Whatever was present between us the night Bri's brother was in town had to get shut down or we would risk losing everything. We never had a conversation about it, but the side glances I gave Sienna and the sad smiles she gave me in return let me know we were on the same page.

As she gets closer, I can see her eyes are rimmed in red like she's been crying and my chest pinches again.

"Sienna? Are you okay?" I don't bother to hide the worry in my voice. This stolen moment at the witching hour is ours alone.

"Yeah. I just couldn't sleep," she lies.

"Did I wake you?" I play along.

"No. I never fell asleep."

That makes two of us then.

She nods at the violin in my hands. "What are you working on? I only heard a few notes, but it was beautiful . . . haunted," she clarifies, "but beautiful."

Something about the time of night or this place, or the stress of it all makes me give her an honest answer.

"I can't get it right. I can't even hear it anymore." I blow out a harsh sigh. "I can *always* hear it, but it's been silent in my head for a couple of weeks now and quite honestly, it scares the shit out of me." I haven't even told this to the guys. Although, they'd be supportive, I'm our main songwriter, both lyrics and music. They count on me to give them something to work with, and I haven't been able to bring myself to tell them I've got nothing.

Sienna tentatively reaches her hand out and at first, I think she's going to place her small hand on my arm, which I wouldn't mind. But she's pointing to my instrument.

My baby. My most prized possession.

"I totally understand if the answer is no," she starts, her voice shaking almost like she's afraid I'll say *yes*. "But I could show you what I heard?"

I'm transported back two months ago, to the first night of the tour and the reaction she had to seeing me play the violin. Something about it upset her, but she never said what.

"You play?" I ask, dumbfounded.

"A little," she says shyly. "But it's been a while."

No one touches my violin. Not even the guys. But something tells me this might break the spell and get her to open up to me. Plus, I could really use the help.

I slowly hold it out to her trying not to cringe as she takes it from my hands, watching mesmerized, as she cradles it. The love in her eyes is accompanied by sadness and fear.

I pass her my bow and notice her hand is trembling. Needing this to play out, I wrap my hand around hers to try and encourage her and steady her tremors.

She swallows hard before tucking the chin rest in place, her posture perfect. She doesn't know it, but this moment is more intimate to me than sex. It feels like she's holding my erratically beating heart in her hands. I don't like when people touch me, but they do . . . but *no one* has laid a hand on my violin except the man who custom made it for me. Hence the repair shop in Italy.

I fidget nervously, waiting with bated breath for her to drag the bow across the strings. Will it give in to her?

Can it tell it's not my hands caressing the fingerboard?

She closes her eyes and wets her lips, taking a ragged inhale. She brings her bow hand up with perfect form and plays the first few notes I played around with, causing goosebumps to erupt on my flesh. Her notes are flawless despite her still trembling hand, which seems to get steadier the longer she plays.

Her playing gets louder as she carries on, obviously lost to the music.

She's fucking amazing.

I can feel her anger and resentment and longing in every note. This is so much more than what I played.

So much *better.*

I pick up my pen to write this down, but I can't keep up as her bow hand flies back and forth.

She's been playing for about three minutes, when I realize I'm on the edge of the chair. My ass literally hanging off the cushion as I listen to her bleed all over this hallway.

Something moves down the hall catching my attention and I'm dangerously close to threatening anyone who interrupts this moment. I don't want anyone to see Sienna like this. So broken, open, and vulnerable. A protective instinct kicks in that I've only ever felt toward my bandmates.

As the person gets closer, I'm prepared to hold up a hand to stop their progress when I recognize Bri, who seems to appreciate the full significance of the moment . . . more so, even, than me. She eyes my violin in Sienna's arms, and her hand flies over her mouth, eyes wide and misty.

But why?

Without me having to say anything, Bri doesn't come any closer. She shakes her head, eyes wide in disbelief.

I need the rest of this story.

Bri turns silently and goes back down the hall, leaving Sienna and I alone once more. After another minute or ten – I've completely lost track of time – Sienna pulls one final, heart-stopping note across the strings. Then I watch as her body wracks with silent sobs as she unsuccessfully tries to hold her tears back.

"Sienna." Her name is a whisper on my lips. "That was fucking incredible. What could make you shut that talent away?" I tread carefully not wanting to push her, but also desperately wanting to free her from whatever this is.

She swipes at her tears frantically as she begins to apologize. "I'm sorry. It's just . . . it's been . . . a while."

My violin is my favorite part of myself, so I understand being overwhelmed with emotion when playing, but this is more than that. This is a darkness she's buried deeply, and I'm witnessing it trying to claw its way out of her soul.

I slide the rest of the way off my chair and land on my knees in front of her, gently pulling my violin from her hands and placing it on the now vacant seat behind me.

"Sienna," I say her name stronger this time, burrowing myself between her knees and encouraging her to look at me. Her eyes look like broken shards of blue-green glass. All the cracks she's tried to repair over the years are splintering before me. "Talk to me." I hold my hands out to her. A silent request to let me offer her comfort.

She stares at them for a beat, and for a second, I think she isn't going to take them but slowly she reaches forward and places her hands in mine.

That same electricity that's been present every time we've touched crackles between us despite the sadness of the moment.

"Are you sure you want to hear all of this?" she asks with a small humorless laugh.

"I'm sure."

"God, you aren't going to write a song about it, are you?" she teases, making the pressure in my chest lighten a little.

I take the opportunity to tease back. "I make no promises."

She takes a deep breath and steels herself for the story she's about to share for what I'm certain is the first time in a very long while.

"Okay, well, I started violin lessons when I was seven. My dad actually played with the New York Philharmonic for a while, and we always bonded over music. The violin and I clicked right away which is insane because grown adults have a hard time with it, and here I was, my hands too small to reach between notes without having to slide my whole hand up the fingerboard. But it just felt right, ya know?"

Yeah, I do know. I don't want to interrupt though, so I just nod my agreement.

"Anyway," she continues, "My dad started spending a lot of time with me, giving me lessons, singing my praises, bragging about me to all his orchestra friends. He was even able to get me a spot playing with them a couple of times which was a lot of fun."

I can't help but notice how her eyes dance as she remembers this part of the story.

"By the time I was twelve, I was pretty much able to sight read anything, and play it perfectly the first time through. I could also play a song perfectly with no sheet music after only

hearing it once. It's just the language my mind speaks, I guess."
As she talks, she stares at where our hands are connected as if
she's drawing strength from me. "My dad signed me up for a
talent competition where the grand prize was $5,000. He was
certain I could win – and I did – but the competition was on
my parents' anniversary." Her face falls, and it takes her a
second before she can speak again. "My mom was always
fiercely protective of my dad . . . even from me. She resented
that I took up so much of his time and attention and when he
spent their anniversary with me at this talent show, my mom
flew off the rails. It was the first episode, but it just got worse
over time.

"One night, when I was seventeen, my dad came home
all excited to tell me I'd been offered a full spot in the
orchestra if I wanted it. That he and I could travel together
for a year or two before I did college, playing all over the
world."

She stops talking but her breathing increases, and I can tell
this is the painful part, so I just sit patiently and wait with her.
My knees are aching, and my feet are numb, but I don't care.

"Of course I said yes, but later that night, my mom barged
into my room, took my violin off its stand and smashed it into a
thousand pieces right in front of my eyes."

Ouch.

"She screamed I wasn't as good as everyone thought I was,
and she didn't want my dad's reputation tarnished because of
my poor playing. She said I was given the offer to play just
because he was my dad."

Her voice trails off, and her eyes look faraway like she's
watching the scene unfold in her mind's eye.

"You *are* that good, Sienna."

I've only heard a small portion of her talent tonight, but it
was enough to know the truth in my words.

"I haven't picked up a violin since that night. Not until just now," she confesses on a whisper.

The impact of that statement lands square in the middle of my chest. She's let that talent lie dormant for . . . *wait*, "How old are you?"

"Twenty-four."

"My God. You haven't touched a violin in *seven* years and you were able to play *that* just now?"

She shrugs like it's no big deal. Like her talent is no big deal.

"I know it's probably stupid to most people. Hell, my ex-boyfriend told me I was being an idiot and should have just bought another violin, but it wasn't the violin – although that hurt too. It was that my own mother was so insecure and jealous, she couldn't be happy for me. Or proud of me. After that, she only saw me as a threat. My parents divorced six months later, and my mom made sure I knew it was my fault. I just couldn't bring myself to pick up another violin for fear that I'd ruin something else. My mom didn't even talk to me for two years because I wanted to live with my dad, and she acted like she was all heartbroken but--" her voice cracks, threatening more tears, "she didn't even like me anyway."

She lowers her eyes like she's ashamed of how she feels and before I can overthink it or change my mind, I place my free hand under her chin to raise her head and cup her cheek, wiping away her quiet tears with my thumb.

I smile when I hear her breathing falter and I damn near explode in my sweatpants when those pouty lips part on a sigh.

Jesus, Noah. Get it together, you insensitive bastard.

Reluctantly, I pull my hand back and my fingertips are fucking tingling. Exhaustion spreads across her features like telling that story took every ounce of effort she had to give.

"What about your dad?" I ask, selfishly pushing for more. "Are you still close?"

Her face goes blank as she withdraws from me and retreats somewhere in her mind. Eventually, she closes her eyes and says, "He started drinking shortly after the divorce. He needed my mom because he was a brilliant musician, but he was shit at being an adult. Eventually, he blamed me for their breakup as well and we only speak every few weeks. He's living in a halfway house outside of Lexington, Kentucky. Oddly, my mom texts me occasionally now. It's like she can finally stand to talk to me knowing my relationship with my father is ruined."

"That's so fucked up, Si. None of their issues are your fault." I tell her, having to clear my throat when the first part comes out as a whisper. In this moment, I'm extremely thankful for the sane, stable parents I have.

"Sorry to unload my baggage on you like that." She looks at me through her lashes and sits upright as a shiver makes her shoulders shake.

"Sienna, I'm a songwriter. Pain, heartbreak, *baggage* . . . that's *my* language. You don't have to be sorry for talking to me."

She swallows hard, and I quickly realize I'm barreling down that same dangerous path as a few weeks ago except instead of preparing to make a U-turn, I'm gaining speed right toward the edge of the cliff.

As if she can sense I'm about to do something stupid, she finds strength I don't have and says, "I'd better try to get some sleep." I can't tell which emotion is in her voice for sure, but it doesn't sound like embarrassment, thank God. I want her to talk to me.

I'm starting to think maybe I *need* it.

She uncurls herself from the chair and everything in me wants to hug her, hold her, offer her some kind of comfort. But

121

if she lets me hold her, I'm pretty sure I'd never stop, so I let her stand without interference, offering only my words as comfort.

"Sienna? Anytime you want to talk . . . or play," I wave a hand toward my precious violin, "Just let me know, okay? I think we could be really good together."

She flashes me the most genuine smile I've seen from her yet and my heart falters as I wonder if she heard the double entendre.

Chapter 14

Sienna

No way I'm going back to sleep after that - which is a shame because we have another show tonight, the rule enforcing no back-to-back shows long gone. At least it's in the same city, and we aren't on the bus tonight.

I'm oscillating wildly back and forth between *I can't believe I shared that part of myself with Noah-freaking-Kinkaid,* and *I can't believe he listened and didn't run away screaming.* I haven't been comfortable enough to share that story with anyone since Brad-the-asshole.

I ended up assuming everyone's reaction would be just like his. Life has taught me people have the inability to offer sympathy if your brand of *fucked-up* doesn't exactly match their own.

To people without my insecurities, my story seems like no big deal. *You're an adult. Just get over it.*

But that's just it, isn't it?

If someone *doesn't have* my insecurities, they wouldn't know what it's like to be resented by both of their parents for finding the thing they're best at and love most in the world. The

123

people who created them out of their love for each other were so insecure they had no room left for the child and regretted having to share each other with another human . . . even one they made themselves. It's a hard pill to swallow and an even harder truth to accept.

When I get back to the suite, I trod to the kitchen to make a cup of tea and process what the fuck just happened, but a shadow on the couch stops me in my tracks.

My heart resumes beating when Bri slowly stands and follows me into the kitchen.

"Si . . . " she starts, but she sounds off.

"Bri? Everything alright?" It's three-thirty in the morning, and she should be asleep. Then again, so should I.

"Si, I saw you," she says with an almost mystic quality to her voice that makes me chuckle. It's amazing how much lighter I feel after sharing that story with Noah. Like somehow the whole event lost a little of its power over me by shedding light on it. With him.

"Saw me *what*?" I ask, scrunching up my nose. God, she didn't catch me with my vibrator or something, did she? "Spit it out, Bri. You're freaking me out."

"I heard the music when I woke up to pee. I came into the hall, and I saw you playing."

"Oh, that."

I busy myself with opening the tea bag and heating the water. I'm not sure why this is more awkward to talk about than the time Bri told me she tried anal with that guy from the studio . . . but it is.

"I don't know what came over me," I admit, realizing she's waiting for an explanation. "He was struggling with a part, and it just came to me. I guess I could have written it down, but I needed him to hear it. To feel it. To know it's what he was looking for," I try to explain.

Bri is not musically inclined other than moving her body to it, so I trip over my tongue in my explanation. "It was like his violin was a Siren calling me down the hall. I couldn't deny it."

"I'm proud of you, Si. You've punished yourself for way too long."

Bri was furious when I couldn't bring myself to touch another violin. She went through all the stages of grief right alongside me when I lost the courage to play.

"It's not like it's just gone from my life now," I tell her before she gets her hopes up. I'm going to deal with that night for the rest of my life.

"But you talked about it. You opened up. You haven't done that in a long time." Sensing me shutting down and having hit my limit for this discussion, she plops onto the barstool behind me and changes the subject. "Okay I get it. Let's talk about how the hell Noah looks so fucking delicious at two-thirty in the morning wearing a white t-shirt and sweatpants. If you hadn't been having your breakthrough moment, I'm pretty sure I would have taken a flying leap right into his lap, his no-touching rule be damned." She starts fanning her face with her hand, and I can't help but laugh.

"I was in such a trance with the music, I honestly didn't notice."

It's shocking, but true.

I still get starstruck around the guys, Noah in particular, but tonight it was just the music and my fingers on that bow. "Paint me a picture," I ask her as I settle onto the barstool next to her with a mug of tea.

"I didn't get too close for fear I would interrupt you, but I could see the outline of his tattoos through his shirt and his hair had that sexy I-just-woke-up-and-ran-my-skilled-fingers-through-my-locks look. It was *really* working for him," she whines, almost out of breath as she says it. "Honestly," she continues, placing her forearms on the counter and leaning in like she's going to tell me a secret, "He can fuck my shit up day *or* night. In fact, he could destroy my world, and I'd be like, 'So, does next week work for you as well?'"

I can't hold back my snort as I burst into laughter even though the other girls are sleeping.

This. This is why Bri is my best friend. The girl can turn a phrase like no one I know, and she can make me laugh in the most emotionally tumultuous times. As I'm trying to get myself under control, she keeps talking, making me lose it all over again.

"I was about to tell the man to just punch me in the pussy and give me some damn relief already. The way he was watching you . . . *geezus.*" She fans herself with one hand while dramatically turning sideways and clutching the back of her chair.

Through my giggles, I groan and tell her about how he cupped my cheek and wiped my tears with his thumb, and she slips off her stool and proceeds to act like she's melting into the floor, making me lose my absolute shit.

We stay up until five, discussing everything from the tour to the guys to her brother to food to how miserable it is having our periods while spreading our legs wide open for thirty thousand people. At one point, I'm laughing so hard, my tears have returned but this time it feels so good.

I remember Noah telling me we all have demons. Although not completely eradicated, I feel like tonight they loosened their hold enough for me to be able to draw a deep breath for the first time in a long time.

I'm not sure how I can ever repay him for that, but I know I want to try.

During our interaction tonight, it wasn't like I was sleep-walking - I remember seeing Noah and talking to him - but for those few stolen moments, I felt like I was actually looking at *him*. Not his pretty face. Not his delicious body. Not his *skilled fingers*.

Just him.

Past the lights. Past the fans, and the tour bus, and the record deal, and the screaming girls.

I just saw *him*. And what I saw made my heart break.

When I finally crawl into bed, I manage to sleep for about two hours before my alarm goes off telling me it's time to face the day. I feel bad for the hair and makeup crew – they really have their work cut out for them. I can already tell my eyes are swollen from the tears and lack of sleep.

I can't help but smile though as I stretch my arms overhead and touch my cheek, remembering Noah's fingers there.

Will our interactions be weird today?

Best to let him take the lead, I decide, swinging my legs over the bed. I change into leggings and a tank top and go in search of coffee and the hotel gym with Tim, one of the security guards assigned to the four of us dancers, hot on my heels.

I'm not really recognizable and I protest the need for security because all he does is draw attention, but I was informed his presence is non-negotiable and decided the argument wasn't worth it.

When I get to the small hotel gym, there's a large group of restless women - and a few men - standing outside, gawking through the glass window panes in the doors.

I guess one of the guys beat me here.

My heart skips a beat hoping for more alone time with Noah, even if there are a thousand onlookers.

Tim boxes me in on the sides with his arms as he pushes me through the crowd.

"Move aside, please. Excuse us. Step back." His deep voice cuts through the crowd over my shoulder.

The crowd parts but I can see the questions dancing in their eyes.

Who is she? Why does she get to go in? Should we ask for her autograph too?

It's still overwhelming, so I just keep my eyes straight ahead and paste a small smile on my face, aware there are on phones capturing every movement I make these days.

Once we're in the gym, a wave of guilt washes over me. What if those people just want to get their workout in while they're on vacation? But a quick glance at the sight in front of me, and I realize Sloan and Brett wouldn't stand a chance against the salivating mob outside the door, so it's best to make the masses wait.

Both guys are bare-chested as drops of sweat roll down their pecs making my mouth water. I don't know how long they've been here, but they're currently on the floor, toe to toe, as they do sit ups while tossing a heavy medicine ball back and forth. Every grunt reminds me they work hard to look as good as they do, and I, for one, fully support it.

Without breaking his rhythm, Sloan huffs out, "Morning, Sienna."

"Morning, guys." I fight a yawn, but it sneaks out anyway.

"Late night?" Brett asks, accusatorily, but I'm pretty sure he's joking.

Either way, I provide a safe answer. "Just couldn't sleep."

"Interesting," he says as he tosses the ball back to Sloan. When I don't reply, he continues, "Kinky said the same thing this morning. He looked like he'd been hit by a Mack Truck. You wouldn't know why that is, would you?" He has a half-smile on his face, waiting for me to admit we were together.

Not doing it.

"Huh," I huff. "Must be something about this place."

Speaking of his band mate, my eyes dance around the area for the other two members of Beautiful Deceit as I walk over to the stand with the free weights, but I come up empty.

Sloan laughs knowingly before saying, "Ryan and Noah left for an interview with a radio station already. They won't be back for a few hours."

I don't try to deny I was looking for Noah because the more I deny it, the more guilty it would make me sound. Instead, I simply say, "Okay," and get down to work.

The performances themselves are a workout for sure, but staying strong enough to manage the silks requires accessory work as well, so here I am.

Not even fifteen minutes later, Bri, Jos, Kara, and our other bodyguard, Jose, barrel into the gym.

Brett's eyes go wide as he takes in Bri's sports bra and spandex booty shorts. He falters on the cable machine giving Sloan an opening to throw the medicine ball – which he's still using – right at Brett's stomach.

"*Oomph,*" Brett grunts when the twenty-pound ball connects with his flesh. "What the hell, man?"

Sloan gives him a wicked grin. "Quit checking out my woman."

Brett rolls his eyes and pulls down on the handles again, every ab and muscle in his back flexing in unison. "If you remember correctly, *dick*, these women are off-limits and therefore, she's not *your* woman . . . so I can check any of them out that I want."

I would say Brett is teasing, but he looks pissed.

He doesn't look any *less* pissed when Sloan quips back with a wink, "We'll see."

The grin on Bri's face is humongous as she eats this shit up. Totally down for a bandmate rivalry over her, or possibly even a threesome, she taunts Sloan.

"You have your work cut out for you, Sloan. I've always had a thing for drummers." She turns her sex-kitten attention to Brett and holds his dark stare without batting an eyelash. "I find the aggression they take out on the drums translates beautifully to their power in bed."

Sloan barks his laughter, his workout finally interrupted. He's clearly enjoying Brett's reaction, which right now, is pure, angry lust. I'm not even sure he's breathing. His pupils have dilated so the entirety of his irises are black, his jaw is set, and his nostrils are flared.

He recovers after a few seconds, shakes his head, and says flatly, "I'm sure it'd be a good time, but I can't jeopardize the tour like that."

The next second, he snaps his fingers and points toward the door.

One of the security guards pushes off the wall he's leaning against and heads out of the door first, creating a walkway for the broody drummer as screeches from the waiting fans infiltrate the small room.

Another security guard quickly follows behind to box people out like Tim did for me, before the door closes, he turns and levels a gaze at Sloan. "Do *not* attempt to leave this gym until one of us gets back. Tim's the only one here, and he'll need help ushering you out when you're ready." And then he's gone, swallowed by the sea of fans.

"What the fuck was that?" Bri asks. We all know she's referring to Brett's sudden serious tone and abrupt departure and not the instructions directed at Sloan – who appears totally unconcerned about the rowdy mob, I might add.

Sloan lays out the cold hard truth in a bored tone. "Brett has the hots for you, but it's driving him crazy that he can't stick it in."

Jos and I clap our hands over our mouths, but our snorts and giggles slip out anyway.

Bri shrugs a shoulder, appearing unsurprised by the revelation. "What Matty doesn't know can't hurt me."

"While I'm sorely tempted to agree, because Brett's been a pain in the ass the last couple of weeks, and he *needs* to get fucking laid, none of us are going to risk it," Sloan explains calmly. "You guys have added way more to this show than we all thought you would, no offense. It's not just about Matt's rules anymore. We have a good thing going and fucking each other would make it messy. Catching feelings would make it worse."

I don't miss the way his eyes float to me for the last half of that speech.

Chapter 15

Noah

When Ryan and I get back from the interview, Matt and a woman I don't recognize are in our hotel suite. She's average height with her hair cut so short it's actually buzzed in the back. She's wearing tortoise shell glasses, a black, knee-length skirt, and . . . *what the hell?* Covering her torso is a throwback Beautiful Deceit shirt from our first tour. I didn't even think we'd sold a single one of those. The uneasy feeling I've had since the radio station doubles in intensity.

I'm sure Brett or Sloan let Matt and this woman in, but I'm irritated they're here. Our privacy has dwindled to next to nothing and after the chaos at the radio station this morning, I'm not sure our current security staff is going to be enough.

I'm still a little jittery even though Romeo stopped that woman before she could reach me, and Ryan inserted himself between she and I just in case Romeo wasn't successful.

Extreme mental illness always makes me sad, and if I'm honest, a little uncomfortable, but it's part of the reason I keep my private life private. Because there *are* people struggling in the world and although I'm sure running at me with her hands full of her bared tits, screaming that she's carrying my child is okay in her reality . . . it sure as shit isn't in mine.

The woman wouldn't take her eyes off me even when Ryan stepped in front of me as a shield. No, she couldn't see anything or anyone but me as she recited things I've said during interviews and podcasts verbatim, making my skin crawl.

I'm so thankful Ryan was there and was selfless enough to throw himself in her path to buy Romeo some time to intervene, but it's also another example of what Sloan and Brett don't understand.

That's the difference between them and me in this band. Yes, people go crazy for them too, but people hear my naked soul on that stage and think they know me. The connection to our fans is stronger with me than it is with the other guys because I'm the one engaging the fans every night for two hours.

I take a deep breath and quickly look around the suite feeling my panic continue to rise at the presence of an unknown person in my personal space until my eyes find Romeo leaning against the back wall. He nods, reassuring me everything's okay, and I'm able to bring my focus back to Matt and the mystery woman.

"Welcome back, fellas," he nods at us. "I hear you had quite the eventful outing. Noah, I'm glad you made it out unscathed." *I'm not so sure I did.* "I'd like to announce that the 'kick off' portion of your tour is officially over. The first two months have come and gone and you're in the swing of things, so to speak. For the rest of the shows, you just have to settle in, find that energy, and exploit the hell out of it."

Matt and his newest – and fugliest shirt yet – continue to inform us, well, *me,* that I've continued to get more requests for podcasts, radio shows, etc . . . and he's brought this woman on to be my personal assistant for the remainder of the tour as well as help with a few of the day-to-day tour operations. My schedule is getting to be too much for him to keep track of while keeping eyes on the tour as a whole.

I fucking hate change, but maybe this means Matt can stay in the background now. Every time my eyes wander to Sienna, I'm worried he's going to see it and start lecturing me.

Sloan grumbles in the background before walking over to the counter and grabbing a banana.

"In my next life, I'm going to be the lead singer. Noah keeps getting all the good shit."

I know he means it as a joke, but this tour is a walk in the park for him. There are a quarter of the demands on Sloan's time that there are on mine. Show up, play guitar, do whatever the fuck you want until you have to show up again.

Feeling jumpy and restless, I bring my hand up to count on my fingers for show as I make my next points.

"There are two things wrong with that statement, Sloan. The first is you can't sing. The second is you seem to think having someone dictate every second of my waking hours is 'the good shit' and you'd be wrong." I try my hardest, but I can't keep my voice even and I end up barking at him. At least I keep the rest of my thoughts to myself.

If you want the "good shit" so badly, then why haven't you offered to do a single fucking interview, brought me one line of music, or responded to any of the emails about our merchandise orders?

He stops eating his banana mid-bite and narrows his eyes at me. "What's gotten in to you, Kink? It was just a joke."

I scrub a hand down my face and feel everyone's eyes on me.

Before I can formulate an answer or an apology, Matt tries to diffuse the tension.

"Noah's under a lot of pressure as the front man." He holds his hands up when he sees Brett and Sloan both bristle. "Not that you guys aren't. It's just different. And that difference is why I've brought Callista," he gestures to the young woman with him, "on as Noah's assistant." Turning to face me, he adds, "She's going to keep up with your calendar. She's also going to field all the requests for appearances and interviews and research which ones will get you the most exposure and positive feedback. She's going to help write responses to some of the questions you get asked the most to take the pressure off having to answer on the fly."

I had finally calmed down enough to sit on the arm of the couch, but his explanation has me jumping back up. Yes, I'm stressed, but I'm stressed because I feel like I'm losing control.

Allowing Callista to make all those choices means I'm giving up even more.

I sound like a whining child even to my own ears. *You can't have it both ways, Kinkaid,* I remind myself. Fame comes with a price. This is it.

The lack of privacy.

Demands on your time.

Welcome to the lifestyle of the rich and famous, asshole.

"Don't waste your time," I tell Callista as calmly as I can. "I won't use your responses. They aren't genuine. They aren't *me.*" I look around the room at the guys, "Aren't *us.* You and I just met. You don't know how I'd answer. You don't know what publications, podcasts, and stations mean the most to us as a band. So, with all due respect, I could use the help managing my schedule, but I'm not relinquishing control of our entire public appearance."

When I look at her face, what I see unnerves me. She has a penetrating, calculating gaze, like she's sizing me up. I can see the cunning almost-smirk she's wearing like she's in on some secret that I don't know.

I push the thought aside and decide I'm losing my mind.

Matt turns to face the young woman. "Callista, meet the men of Beautiful Deceit."

She doesn't look older than any of us. Ryan is the oldest at twenty-nine. Brett is twenty-seven, and Sloan and I are both twenty-six. In fact, she looks *younger* than us but none of us are stupid enough to ask her.

The guys all nod hello, and as she takes them in, I study her. Something about her makes me think I've seen her before but nothing's ringing a bell. Maybe she just has one of those faces. Especially in her glasses and punk attire, it's likely that I've seen thousands of women who resemble her. Nonetheless, my Spidey-senses are tingling.

Perhaps she's just trying to show her support with that old shirt, or impress us, or *something*, but the look on her face is making it feel a lot like she's a wolf in sheep's clothing. In fact, when she smiles at me, I'm pretty sure I see fangs.

Yep, losing it.

My fingers keep flexing at my sides, and I can't stand still. This introduction has gone on long enough.

Matt seems to feel the same way.

"I've got about a million phone calls to make for the upcoming tour stops," Matt says. "If you boys need anything, reach out to Callista. And just so you know, I'm putting feelers out for a European tour. The response to it, like everything else, has been overwhelming. Hence, the extra help."

The guys and I all share a glance. A European tour is news to us. I didn't even realize that was on the table as a possibility.

This is a lot to take in. *Good . . .* but *a lot*, and I feel the room start spinning as all the blood rushes from my head to pool in my chest, creating the familiar pressure behind my sternum.

"Matt, before you go, can you call downstairs and reserve one of the conference rooms on the fifth floor? I need to try out some lyrics."

I would call downstairs myself, but the last time I tried to make a call and order room service, the chick on the other end of the line wouldn't stop shrieking long enough for me to place my order. I wanted to hang up, but I'm constantly aware of what one pissed off fan can achieve and didn't want to risk being *that* guy. So, what should've taken ten seconds ended up taking ten minutes, and I don't have the time, or the patience, to waste today.

I need to practice what I heard Sienna play last night.

Fuck, was that only last night? It feels like I've lived six lives between then and now.

Matt looks at Callista and nods his head, "She can take care of that for you."

I barely hold back my grunt of disapproval.

"Fine. Just get me a room."

I stride past them and head to my suite for my notebook and violin case, knowing I'm being rude. Somehow it doesn't bother me with Callista like it did with the room service girl.

Callista is here for the duration, she's going to see the good, the bad, and the ugly. The fan on the phone will most likely only ever have that one interaction with me, which means it needed to be good.

When I come back out two minutes later, Matt is gone and Callista looks me over, a small smile playing at the corners of her mouth. "It's all done. You have conference room seven. I'll walk you down."

"That won't be necessary. I have security for that." I don't know what it is about her, but I don't want to be alone in her company.

As soon as I get down to the conference room, I'm sending Matt an email asking him to replace her.

"I don't mind," she argues sweetly. "Besides, we should probably take a minute to get to know each other since you've already made it quite clear I don't know you well enough to do my job. Although, I do think you'd be impressed with the amount of knowledge I do have."

Doubtful.

"The only thing Matt knows is my name, and where to send my paychecks. You don't need anything more than that either." The lie tastes bitter as it rolls out of my mouth. I don't love who I'm becoming.

Ryan interrupts in an effort to save face, like always, when he senses my short fuse has been lit.

"What our dear Noah means is he's in artist creation mode right now. He'll be happy to answer your questions, but his musical genius is showing, and he needs to go clean himself up. Best to let Romeo take him down."

I nod at Ryan in thanks as I head for the door, grateful he has my back and glad I know his secret and can help him in return for all the favors he does for me.

He's been talking to Brett's little sister for a year and although he says nothing's happened – mostly because they don't live anywhere close to each other – I know he wants it to. Emma's ten years younger than Ryan – which means she's only been legal about a year and a half - and Brett is crazy protective over his sister. He would most likely flip his absolute shit if he knew how often Ryan and Emma talk. I'm not sure the band would survive it.

The flip side is that Ryan also reads me like a book and has been able to tell I'm into Sienna since opening night of the tour

. . . in the pool. He saw the jealousy flash in my eyes when I saw her on his shoulders, and I'm convinced he's known ever since. But if anyone understands forbidden love, it's Ry. So, I know he won't rat me out.

Brett grabs my forearm on my way out the door and causes me to stop. He wiggles two fingers in a *come here* motion, so I lean forward to hear him whisper in my ear, "She look familiar to you?" He nods his head subtly in Callista's direction.

I nod my own head once in agreement, and reply low enough that no one else can hear. "Yeah, but I don't know from where and I definitely feel like something's off. What's up with the shirt?"

"I don't know, but I swear I've seen her before," he says which does nothing to ease my discomfort.

"I've gotta run, but ask Sloan and Ry. Text me if they can place her." Brett nods as he turns his attention back to Callista and the guys and I head out the door with Romeo in tow.

"Hey, I need to swing by the dancer's suite before we go down."

Romeo eyes me quizzically but just nods.

When I knock on the door to the girls' penthouse, Kara answers, but she's on the phone. She waves me in and points down a hallway, correctly assuming I'm here to see Sienna. A knot forms in my stomach at the thought that maybe I'm not acting as nonchalantly toward her as I think I am.

Romeo waits just inside the door and Kara goes back to her conversation and digging around in the fridge. It's after two, but after the clusterfuck of that meeting upstairs, I'm not hungry even though I haven't eaten yet today.

"Sienna?" I whisper loudly. I don't know why I whisper. I'm allowed to be here. I clear my throat and try again. "Sienna?"

I see her head poke out from behind the door at the end of

the hallway. "Noah! Hi!" Her eyebrows shoot to her forehead in surprise to find me in her suite, and her voice is too high-pitched.

"You okay?" I ask. It seems like I ask her that a lot.

"What? Oh, um, yeah, I'm fine." She swallows hard telling me I'm walking in on something she doesn't want me to see.

"Is now a bad time?" I slow my movements, but I can't stop walking toward her. When she's in front of me everything else fades to the background. The incident at that radio station, the stress of new management, fuck, my stress in *general* . . . it all fades away.

I can tell she's trying hard not to, but her eyes scan my body. I'm suddenly, and acutely, aware of every place my t-shirt is clinging to me because her eyes linger at those spots warming my skin under her gaze. It makes me want to just take the damn thing off if she'll keep looking at me like this.

I've always kept my body in shape for *me* because it makes *me* feel better – *your body is a temple* and all of that – but for the first time, I'm proud of it because it's eliciting this reaction in *her*.

"Oh, no. I just wasn't expecting you." Her eyes snap back up to mine. "I mean, Sloan told me this morning you had an interview, so I just didn't expect to see you until tonight, that's all," she says in a rush.

Sienna flustered and hyperaware is my new favorite thing. I'm already playing with fire, but when I'm this close to the flame, the heat dissolves the pressure in my chest, and it feels so good. Almost like I'm not breathing through a coffee stirrer for once.

"Why are you hiding behind the door?" I ask, truly curious but also wanting to keep her talking.

She looks down at her hidden body and then meets my eyes again.

"Jayne dropped off our new outfits for the show tonight, and I'm having a bit of trouble getting it on," she admits, causing her cheeks to turn a healthy shade of pink.

"Looks like my timing was perfect then. Can I give you a hand?" I didn't think her eyes could get any wider, but I was wrong, and it makes me chuckle. "I'm gonna see it on stage tonight anyway," I say, trying to convince her to let me help.

I hear Joslyn's raspy voice yell from down the hall, "How the hell do they expect us to get in this thing? I swear it was the guys who designed this death trap!"

Sienna grimaces, causing me to smile harder. So hard, my cheeks might split.

I take another step toward her and apply light pressure to the door. When she doesn't stop me, I push it open further.

An exhale forces itself out of me, emptying my lungs at the sight, leaving me so dizzy, I have to put a hand on the door frame to steady myself.

"Holy *shit*."

It's a whisper that wasn't supposed to escape at all. Before the blood circulates back to my brain from its current southerly position, to tell me what a bad fucking idea this is, my hand reaches out to trace the black sequins across her collarbone.

Her eyelids flutter shut as if she's trying to fight it and I can feel her stomach contract as she shudders beneath my touch, bringing me dangerously close to the edge of my sanity – which I already don't have a great grasp on.

"I heard you weren't a big fan of sequins," she says, lust permeating every word as she bites her luscious bottom lip with her eyes still closed.

"That was before I knew sequins could look like this," I admit with an equal amount of lust in my own voice.

This is a work of fucking art. The headlining album for this tour is titled "V". Not only is it our fifth album to drop, but every song starts with the letter "V".

Victorious.

Vindicated.

Vicious.

You get the picture.

This outfit is the same nude bodysuit she's worn before, except a black, sequined "V" starts at her left shoulder, covers her left breast, trails down over her pussy, and back up the other side. She's currently holding her naked, right boob in her hand because she can't get her arm in the other sleeve.

I exhale another harsh, ragged breath, still seeing stars.

"Turn around," I instruct, my voice too husky for my own damn good.

I step fully into her room and close the door behind me just as warning bells going off like bomb sirens in World War II.

I sweep her red hair off her back and put it over her left shoulder. When I take in the back of the costume, my heart rate spikes again. It's a V on the back as well. The nude body suit is opaque thank God, because otherwise her entire ass would be exposed and I'm not okay with that.

"*Fuck.*"

I don't realize I've said anything out loud until she says, "What?"

"Uh, nothing," I say lamely. Trying to focus on the task at hand, I pull gently on the arm of the one piece to create room for her and help guide her right hand into the sleeve. She shrugs once and the suit falls into place.

Turning to face me, she holds her arms out and says, "Well, what do you think?" There is actual hesitancy in her voice like there's a chance I might not like it.

I can't have that.

"Sienna, that is hands-down *the* hottest thing I've ever seen. I might actually fuck up the lyrics tonight."

Her shoulders relax, and she breaks out into a smile of her own. She swats at my chest playfully but immediately pulls her hand back. "I'm sorry."

I grab her hand and put it back where it was, noting how all the pressure is gone as her fingers splay across my pec.

"It seems I'm not such a big fan of personal space when it comes to you."

I'm horrifically close to crashing my lips against hers in an effort to find out if she tastes like vanilla or just smells like it. Either way, my mouth is watering right as her door swings open.

Bri is standing on the threshold in a matching costume. Although she's attractive, the sight stirs nothing in me. She sees Sienna's hand on my chest which causes Si to drop it immediately, taking my breath with it.

"Oh shit! Sorry to interrupt! I'll just . . . go . . . " she throws a thumb over her shoulder, backs out of the room and pulls the door closed.

Sienna takes a step back and seems to remember that whatever she and I were about to do is a hard *no*. She crosses her arms over her chest and pulls her lower lip between her teeth again.

Fuck me. Those lips . . . I swear to God.

"What, um, what did you swing by for?" she asks.

Fuck if I know. I can't tear my eyes away from her lips.

"Noah?"

I groan. I can't help it. Hearing my name come out of those lips has me wanting to do very stupid things. Things that could fuck this whole dream up. Sure, musicians fuck people on their crew all the time. Some even fuck their dancers. But Matt's stories of how it usually goes to shit in the end and wreaks havoc on a tour were enough to keep me in line.

But now? Now I'm tempted to say *to hell with it.*

"Earth to Noah?" she tries again.

Before I can tell her I need her help with the violin piece, I hear nails on a chalkboard.

"Ladies!" Callista calls in a high-pitched voice from the living room. "Let's meet! I want to run over tonight's lineup and ensure you have everything you need. I'll be working with Matt from now on."

Suddenly, that pressure is back in full force.

"Who's that?" Sienna asks, looking up at me.

"Callista. The new assistant tour manager."

"What happened to Matt?" she asks.

"He's still around but we're gaining so much momentum, he can't keep up. She's been hired as an extra set of hands . . . and my personal assistant," I can't stop myself from rolling my eyes. "But I'm not a fan so far. It could just be my overall aversion to change though, so don't let my opinion sway you."

"Goody," she says before flashing me a sarcastic smile and walking for the door.

Finally remembering what I came to ask her, I catch her wrist to ask for her help right as she trips over a high-heel on her floor and slams her body into mine. She's touching me from her chest to her toes. Wrapping my arms around her to steady her, I can't help but notice how *good* she feels pressed against me. Solid and grounding, yet soft and comforting. My traitorous cock swells with approval.

"Shit! Sorry! Noah, are you okay?" she asks, genuinely worried.

Of course I'm okay. She weighs like a hundred and ten pounds and is seven inches shorter than me. She could literally jump up and down on my chest and not hurt me at all . . . or she could bounce up and down on my . . .

"Yeah, I'm good," I answer hoarsely. I'm good except for the rapidly growing boner I'm sporting. I clear my throat and plow ahead, "I need help with that violin piece if you're up for it. That's what I came by to ask."

She swallows hard. "Oh, um, yeah, sure," she stammers. "Let me see what Callista wants, and then I'll change."

I tell her I'll meet her down in conference room seven and try to leave the suite without creating a scene, but Callista seems hellbent against that idea.

"Mr. Kinkaid. What are you doing in here?" she asks accusatorily.

I clench my jaw and bite back the words I want to throw at her. Damn. Where is Ryan when I need him?

"Working," I answer shortly. I owe her nothing.

She purses her thin lips in disapproval. "Do I need to remind you of the contract they signed?" she asks.

If she was attacking just me, it would be a non-issue. But when I see her sharp gaze hone in on Sienna, whose face is bright red at being called out over something we aren't even doing, I snap.

"Only if I need to remind you that *you* work for *me,* and I don't answer to you."

I see her visibly recoil in shock before a slow, malicious grin paints her face. "Maybe you don't. But they do." She nods her head toward the girls who have gathered in the living room.

Unfortunately, I can't argue with her.

The dancers were hired by the tour company Matt works for even though they are paid from the tour's proceeds. If I piss Callista off, maybe she can let them go – although I'm pretty sure Matt would have an aneurysm at this point. But if I fire Matt's company for anything other than failure to deliver services – which they haven't done – then I'm in fucking breach of contract and the whole tour goes up in smoke.

Christ, this is a nightmare already and no one's even sleeping with anyone.

When Callista makes her underhanded threat, Bri, the blonde bomb goes off, resetting the whole tone.

"First of all, lady, who the fuck even are you, and how'd you get in here? Second of all, Noah's working on new music with my extremely talented friend, and for you to insinuate that anything else is going on is total bullshit. She'll file defamation and harassment charges so fast it'll make your head spin. So, let's back up and start with why you're in our hotel suite and go from there."

I hear Romeo cough a laugh into his hand by the door.

Just to back Bri up, remove Callista from her high horse, and restore the balance of power, I look right at Sienna. "Conference room seven. Go change. I'll see you in a minute," I command, and walk out the door, mentally high-fiving Dancer Barbie.

Chapter 16

Sienna

I've been mentally laughing about Bri going batshit on Callista for the last hour. I guess Josh being an attorney does have *some* perks. Mostly, that he teaches Bri all the terms, and she's pretty good with the threats.

I have to hand it to Callista though, she recovered quickly and took her heaping dose of humility fairly well. Once Noah was gone, she was slightly more bearable, but our interaction was brief since I left after her terrible introduction and assured her I had everything I needed before racing off to meet Noah.

Half an hour into playing, Noah and I solidify the start to a new song he says is "hanging just on the periphery of his conscious mind and is *almost* available" to him. I can tell he's frustrated he can't figure the whole thing out right now, but he's still smiling at our progress. When he smiles like that, it's hard to concentrate on anything, and I'm so glad I can play the violin solely from muscle memory, even if the notes change.

After wracking his brilliant mind and coming up short, he thrust his violin in my arms and asked me to play around with various chords to see if I can coax the rest of the song out of him. Hell, he could have wanted me to sit around and practice chewing bricks, and I would have been ecstatic to try.

"We're so close, but I just can't tell what it needs," he says for the eighth time, running his fingers through his hair. It's impossible to miss the way his tattooed biceps flex with the movement, making my mouth water. If he wasn't so goddamned sexy, I'd feel bad for staring but it honestly can't be helped. His black t-shirt hugs him in all the right places even though the high cut of his crew-neck is keeping the base of his throat hidden from me. His stone-washed jeans are familiar but do nothing to lessen his appearance as they outline his muscular thighs.

It takes me far too long to realize I'm staring at the denim-covered zipper of those same jeans before I tear my eyes from his body and place the violin on the cushioned chair next to me, clearing my throat.

"Why don't we try something to help free up some brain space?" I suggest, avoiding his eyes.

"What exactly did you have in mind?" God help me, his voice just dropped dangerously low. I've gone from having overactive salivary glands to dry-mouth, so I lick my lips and watch his eyes darken as they follow the path of my tongue.

"I, um, was thinking like yoga or meditation?" I don't know why it comes out as a question until I place my hands on my thighs and realize they're sweating, my nervousness, lust, and uncertainty seeping through the pores in my palms. The tension between Noah and I is becoming almost too much to handle.

"Yoga and meditation, huh?" he asks, barely above a whis-per. "Yeah, we could try that."

I reach for my phone, thankful to have something useful to

do with my hands as I enter my passcode and search for the app I want.

"Okay, let's just do a simple meditation first. Yoga would require more space, but I do think you should try it sometime," I ramble, while filtering through the exercises lasting ten minutes or less. "Beach, mountains or jungle?" I ask.

"Jungle, definitely," comes his reply, and I'm not shocked he chose the option that would allow the most concealment and ability to get away from people.

I select a stress relieving track with background sounds one might hear in the jungle and move to sit on the floor, patting the space next to me. "Come here."

He does as I ask, no hesitation.

Sitting with his knees tucked under him, he has to splay them wide because his hips are tight, causing his left knee to rest against my right one.

So much for concentrating.

But this is about him, not me, so I force my body to stay still, and press play.

Throughout the meditation, we're instructed to focus on our breathing – mine's erratic, thanks for pointing that out – and we change positions a few times. By the end, we're facing each other with our legs crisscrossed and our hands clasped in our laps. As the meditation winds down, I sneak a peek at Noah whose brows aren't pinched for once. His shoulders are relaxed, and his breathing is actually deep, even, and slow.

Not wanting to ruin his moment, I stay motionless, allowing myself a chance to breathe in the deep, rich hints of coffee and leather emanating off his flawless skin.

"Why have I never done that before?" he asks, eyes still closed.

I stop quietly inhaling him and feel my face break out into a smile.

"Most people don't slow down enough to ever give it a try." My nose should be ashamed of her whoreish self, but Noah is a delight to all the senses. I can only imagine he tastes as sinfully perfect as he looks and smells.

"That was really nice. I felt in control for the first time in a while. Peaceful, almost."

I cock my head to the side, absorbing his words.

"Do you feel like you're out of control?" I ask.

"Not out of it, just losing it," he admits.

Without thinking, I reach forward to grab his hand to offer comfort. As soon as I touch him, the buzz that's been humming in the air around us passes through our skin. When his eyes snap to mine, I know he feels it, too.

"I wish I could offer you more," I confess quietly, hoping he reads between the lines. I wish I could be whatever he needs in order for his anxiety to leave and never come back.

His lips break into a small half-smile. "Between the violin, your kindness, and now introducing me to meditation, you've given me a lot." He moves slightly closer as he speaks, and I don't know how to respond. I don't trust myself right now. Every part of my being is focused on not crossing a line.

Suddenly, the legs of the chair beside me are very interesting, and I set about visually inspecting them while the heat of my blush creeps up my face.

"Sienna," Noah says, trying to get my attention. "*Sienna*, look at me."

"I can't, Noah."

"Why?" he demands, his voice stronger now than it has been all morning.

"Because I'll lose my job. Which means I'll lose my salary. Which means I'll have to go back to an empty apartment because Bri will still be on the road with you. And I'll have to

150

start over, and I'm not sure there's anywhere to go but down from here." The truth spills from my mouth as if he'd just dosed me with a truth serum. I seem incapable of keeping my thoughts - or my hands - to myself around him.

Latching on to the first sentence, he repeats my words as a question as if he doesn't understand what I'm saying.

"You'll lose your job if you look at me?"

I make the mistake of falling for it. I look at him to give him my best *you know what I mean* look, but his confident smirk and dark eyes lock me in place. "That's better," he whispers.

"Noah." I exhale his name as a plea, but I'm not sure it's a plea to keep going or to stop.

"I like it when you say my name." His eye contact game is *strong,* and I'm losing myself in his onyx eyes. "No one is in here but us," he points out in a tone I could swear was made just for me. "I wouldn't let them fire you anyway. You're as much a part of this show as I am."

"That's incredibly kind, but we both know it isn't true." His right hand moves to my cheek while he braces himself with his left hand on the floor just to the left of my knee.

Breathing in Noah Kinkaid is like taking a hit of pure cocaine. Energizing, terrifying, all-consuming, and life changing. If he brings his lips to mine, I will never be the same.

"Just once," he pleads, his breath brushing across my lips.

He doesn't come any closer, and I can tell he's waiting for my consent. I've never wanted anything in my life more than I want to feel Noah's lips against mine and savor his flavor. But stopping at one kiss would be impossible.

I already want more.

A lot more.

I back up slightly and cover his hand with my own but don't pull it away from my cheek. Steeling myself for making what is probably the biggest mistake of my life, I opt for honesty again.

"I don't think I can do just," I swallow hard mid-sentence because he moves back into my space, "once." In fact, I already know that kissing Noah will be the end of my peace of mind. The kiss would be destined to play on a loop in my head for the rest of my life. Having him once, and only once, would leave me starved and delirious, unable to cope with the loss.

"What do you suggest we do about this then?" he asks, his breath still floating across my lips. I try to drink in the air that was just expelled from his lungs.

"About what?" I ask, high from his proximity. My eyes want to roam everywhere and have my hands follow, but I can't look away from his face.

Unsurprisingly, he purses his lips and says, "You're telling me I'm the only one feeling something here?" He looks down at my hands, which have fallen back into my lap, before grabbing them and placing them on his chest, giving me an excuse to look down and take in the broad expanse of muscle beneath my greedy fingers. The familiar zing of pure fire races up my arms causing me to whimper loudly. "That's what I thought," he says with a level of smoldering confidence that would bring me to my knees if I weren't already sitting down.

"Noah, you're not something in my system I can expel with a kiss," I try to explain even though I know I'm failing to explain well. Without being aware of it, I've come to sit up on my knees, my shaking hands cupping his neck on both sides before running across his shoulders and back down over his chest.

"Then what am I? Or better yet, what do you want me to be?"

I want you to be a lazy Sunday morning with sex before

breakfast and coffee on a porch swing. I want you to be bite marks, ass slaps, and discreet touches under the table in public. I want you to be happy. I want you to be mine.

Shit. Fuck. Fuckitty, fuck, fuck. fuck.

"I don't know," I lie quickly, because I sure as hell can't tell him *those* thoughts.

"Yes, you do. Let me know when you're ready to admit it. But for now, you have to stop touching me like that or else I'm going to take something else you're not ready to give me." He stills my hands and gently removes them from his body. "Thanks for the session." He kisses the top of my head as he stands, grabs his violin, knocks twice on the door to alert Romeo he's ready to go, and disappears from conference room seven upending my entire world without ever pressing his sinful lips to mine. *I am the dumbest woman alive . . . I also happen to be royally fucked.*

I don't see him again before it's time to go on stage.

During the concert, Noah doesn't miss a single word of the lyrics like he said he might, due to our costumes, but he does spend an abnormal amount of time looking in my direction.

Early on, it catches me off guard and almost causes me to miss a foothold in my silks when I look down and see him staring up at me, his perfect voice filling my ears as if he's singing his filthy words only for me.

He's never broken eye contact with the crowd to look *up* at me before. To watch me spin and twirl and stretch into a split above him. Because of his attention, every movement transforms from purely art to a physical outlet for my growing desire for him.

I'm trying hard to focus, but I'm lost in thought of our afternoon. The feel of his chest beneath my hands, his hand on my face, the heat emanating from his skin. His words. *What do you want me to be? Let me know when you're ready to admit it.*

After letting go of my silks with one hand and not feeling my weight catch in my foot, I throw my hand back up and refocus, not even caring about the stupid grin on my face.

A quick glance around the stage tells me that these new outfits have all the guys fucked up, not just Noah. And having them fucked up, fucks *us* up in the best way possible.

When Bri comes down into her split, hovering just above Brett's bass drum, he's late coming back in because he's busy tracing the dip of the V in her outfit with his drumstick. The crowd goes so crazy I don't think they even notice he was behind for a couple of beats.

At one point, I look over at Sloan - who I've seen interact with the crowd, pick up panties off the stage, place them on the neck of his guitar, and blow a kiss to their owner all without missing a single note - and even *he* has his eyes closed in an effort to focus on the music as Joslyn arches into a wide saddle position above him. Nothing but the thin strip of sequins covering her crotch which is mere inches from his head.

When the guys finally come backstage after the show, they all have clenched jaws and look like they could snap any minute with the tension surging through their tightly wound bodies. Drenched in sweat and looking exhausted from their outpouring of energy for this crowd, they don't stop to chat but motion for security to let them right out the back door in a single file line.

Usually, at least one of them congratulates us on a good

show. Or jokes about our asses hanging out. Or *something*. But it's radio silence from all of them.

Which actually kind of hurts.

"Do you think this is what it's like on most tours? The band doesn't even acknowledge the dancers as if we don't leave our hearts out on that stage, too?" I ask, frustrated and angry at the lack of communication after giving that performance my all.

Not to mention the stark contrast between mine and Noah's interaction earlier today and whatever this is right now.

"Probably," Bri agrees unfazed, before looping her arm through mine and turning us toward the dressing rooms. "Let's get out of these body suits. My ass-crack hasn't been able to breathe for three hours. Plus, I'd love a real shower before we get on the bus."

Ugh. The bus.

It's nice. Don't get me wrong. It's a traveling hotel room. But I'm starting to miss my own bed. And being on my own schedule. I'm so grateful for this opportunity, but I'm also really looking forward to our first week off.

Just one more week. I haven't decided what I'm going to do with my time off yet, but I'm thinking maybe Matt will fly me to a beach somewhere . . . or maybe I'd rather go to the jungle.

Before my brain can run away with scenarios that can't happen, I refocus on the task at hand.

When Bri and I come out of the dressing room twenty minutes later and head for the exit, the other girls are flirting with a couple of guys from the opening act. It's been nice travelling with Jos and Kara. They've been incredibly supportive, and they're low drama. Like Bri and me, they've been best friends for a while and we naturally pair off so there isn't any weird group of three with one girl left out.

My cotton joggers and baggy off-the-shoulder tee feel like heaven as we step outside into the air that still has a remnant of chill in it even though it's rapidly approaching late spring. That's Phoenix for you.

I'm so tired I could probably lay down on the pavement and be asleep in eight seconds flat, even with the masses surrounding both busses. I stifle a yawn as I feel Bri bristle next to me and my eyes follow hers to find Brett fully French kissing a fan lined up outside the guys' bus.

Tongue and all.

"Gross. He doesn't know anything about her. What if she has mouth herpes?" I say, trying to heal Bri's obvious wound at this sight with humor. Anyone can see the chemistry between her and Brett. Both on stage and off. Brett follows her every move with his hungry eyes whenever she's in his vicinity. He makes jokes when the other guys flirt with her, but he always ends up brooding and uncharacteristically moody after those interactions.

"What?" she says, snapping back to the moment. "Oh, yeah. Gross. *Whatever*." She shrugs, but I know she's bothered by it. I'm sure Brett's fucked plenty of groupies on this tour already – after all, that is his reputation, but it's the first time we've actually witnessed him being physical with one.

It hits differently.

"Come on, babe. Let's go veg and watch a movie," I try to pull her toward our waiting bus that also has a gathering outside of it.

Mostly guys.

Sorry fellas, random hookups aren't my thing, and my girl over here clearly has the hots for someone else.

My internal dialogue is interrupted when I hear Bri mutter, "Two can play this game." I watch as she pulls her phone from her back pocket and turns on the video.

"What are you doing?" I ask.

"You never know when you might need a little leverage,"

she says vindictively. I know she'd never sell it or hurt Brett with it. She probably just wants to torture him a little.

I also know better than to try and talk her out of it. Bri can be impulsive and carefree, but she also holds a grudge like a son of a bitch. Add in her love of a good challenge and she's a force to be reckoned with.

After she puts her phone away, she laughs too loudly at something one of the fans outside our bus says, and I see Brett's head swing in our direction briefly before he clenches his jaw, grabs the hand of the girl he was just kissing and puts her in the back of an Escalade parked behind their tour bus.

My heart sinks a little when the rest of the guys – including Noah, another girl, and Callista pile in as well.

Maybe Noah isn't that untouchable after all.

Callista boarded our bus looking awfully chipper at two a.m., quietly announcing that everyone – and by "everyone", she meant her, the guys, and their groupies - were back, and we were pulling out. Thankfully, she didn't stay long once she confirmed we were all on board. My heart sank as the realization that she must be riding on the guys' bus smacked me square in the face.

I hate her a little more for her proximity to them . . . to *him*.

The late departure worked out well for Bri and her boy toy though, who gathered his things in a sleep deprived state and left the bus with a huge smile on his face. They were kind enough to go to the room at the back of the bus and shut the door instead of doing it in Bri's bunk, but these flimsy walls aren't soundproof. Needless to say, between the noise and the knowledge that Noah was out with others, I didn't sleep at all.

To make matters worse, I just woke up to a text message from my mother.

LANA

> I heard about your recent employment. Greg's daughter loves Beautiful Deceit. Could you get me 3 tickets? And maybe backstage passes?

It's like she has less than zero awareness of the fact that I'm a human with feelings. I don't know how she found out about me touring with Beautiful Deceit, but of course she would only want to come watch me perform if it could promote *her* in some way.

It also cuts really deeply that she would use me - her own daughter - to gain favor with someone else's since she's never given two shits about the state of our relationship.

But the thing about parents is that no matter how much they hurt you, the desire to please them and earn their approval never really goes away.

For me, at least.

We have a huge show in L.A. at the end of this week - where my mom and her boyfriend, Greg, live. They've been together for three years, and I've never met him.

The dancers and crew each get eight tickets and backstage passes for the tour. We can choose which shows we want them for and can request all eight at once or spread them out for family and friends across the country. I haven't used any of mine yet, and because I'm a glutton for punishment, I text my mother back.

. . .

SIENNA

Sure. I'll leave them at will call.

Before we get to L.A. though, we're stopping in San Diego, which I'm pretty excited about. I've never been to most of the places we're touring, but I've always wanted to see this part of the country. I'd really hoped to go sightseeing, but it doesn't sound like we'll have much time.

I've actually always wanted to try surfing out here, but it sounds like that, too, will have to wait.

It's nine a.m. when our buses stop to refuel, and I desperately need to stretch my legs and move around. Bri's still asleep, so I grab Joslyn, and we head into the little gas station/café in search of coffee and breakfast.

I don't even look toward the guys' bus because, right or wrong, I'm pissed that Noah got in that car with those girls and Callista.

Don't come at me all sexy, like, "Don't you feel this too?" and then go off with some other chick for the night.

I'll admit, the lines have gotten a little blurry, and I need to take a step back. Not just because my paycheck is on the line but because I've become fiercely proud of this tour and the vision we've brought to life and jeopardizing it over lust isn't worth it.

When I pull the door to the café open, I immediately hear Noah's angry – yet still perfect - voice.

"I can order my own goddamn breakfast for fuck's sake! You want to help me? Get the *fuck* out of my face. How about that?"

He's barely holding on.

Despite my messy emotions toward him, I can't leave him like this. I don't know what I can offer but I have to try something before someone pulls out their phone and starts recording. Thankfully, the only other people in here right now are the cashier and a cook, but that could change at any second.

I take off at a sprint across the convenience store and into the café, searching wildly until my eyes land on Noah who is about one-point-five seconds from turning over the table behind him while Callista tries to calm his temper by holding up her hands and approaching him.

Is that how you'd calm a pissed off lion, lady?

Back. Away.

"Noah," she says in a tone so patronizing I briefly think about letting him unleash on her until I remember we're in public and that wouldn't be good. "I know you *can*, but you need to let me do these things. I can't stop an entire mob of fans and if you insist on getting off the bus without security –"

I can't listen to this anymore.

"Noah!" I yell, totally interrupting her just as Ryan rushes through the door to the café with Jos. I guess she went out for backup when I raced toward the scene unfolding in front of us.

I may be pissed about last night, but my reaction to Noah's social life isn't his problem, and he's starting to tear at the seams - which anyone with eyes should be able to see, yet can't for some reason.

When his eyes slam into mine, I halt my approach. He needs space, and the ability to make his own choices, so I give him the power to choose his next move, hoping it helps him regain control.

"I heard a new piece I'd like to show you. I could use some input if you're up for it?" Perhaps I can tempt him with music.

He glances back at Callista, daring her to speak, before

striding up to me, slinging an arm over my shoulders, breakfast completely forgotten.

I slide my arm around his waist, the gesture meant to be protective, not sexual, but the ever-present electricity in the touch is unmistakable. Although that part has become familiar, the possessiveness I feel is new. And strong.

I've got you, I silently will him to understand.

As we hit the parking lot, my mind pulls up the scene in Twilight where Edward drapes a lazy arm across Bella's shoulders in the parking lot at school, saying he's breaking all the rules now. Somehow, it feels on point even though the contract never said we couldn't *touch* each other. Hell, I touch the man on stage a few nights a week . . . but this feels different.

Somehow defiant.

Before we get on the bus, Noah looks over his shoulder at Ryan who's followed us out, and I swear he's a mind reader. "I'm breaking the rule."

I guess the guys are huge Twilight fans because Ryan warns, "Noah, think about this." Like, quoting that movie is somehow normal, and he knows what comes next.

Walking closer to the bus, I can't help myself.

"Team Edward, or Team Jacob?"

Noah looks at me like a second head just appeared out of my neck. "What?" he asks, his brow still wrinkled with the stress of his interaction.

"Back there, I was thinking about a scene from the movie Twilight, just as you quoted it almost perfectly," I explain, trying to get him to fess up to being a closet Twilighter.

His face remains blank. "I have no idea what you're talking about."

Mmm hmm, sure.

Twelve seconds later, I find out he was serious. Us being on the exact same page was just a freaky coincidence. Noah is breaking some *actual* rule.

"Uh, Kink?" Sloan starts as I board the bus behind Noah. "Have you lost your mind?" he asks pointing to me. "You know the rule."

"I know it. And I'm breaking it before I break Callista's face."

A door down the bus's narrow hallway opens and Brett comes out wearing . . . nothing. He makes it a step into the small living room before he realizes I'm there, and everyone else realizes his junk is hanging out.

Simultaneously, Noah throws his hand over my eyes – like I've never seen a guy's dick and balls before – and Brett yells, "What the fuck? Why is there a chick on this bus? I thought we had a rule!"

Sloan answers calmly from his recliner, "Looks like Kinky's decided the rules don't apply to him anymore."

Thankfully, I hear heavy feet on the stairs of the bus, and I know Ryan's just come on board.

"Noah, she can't be on here, man. I've got things calmed down with Callista, but you're riding the edge of a very sharp knife, my friend. What's going on?"

I can hear the concern in Ryan's voice, and I realize the other guys haven't noticed the level of stress and pressure Noah's under. His patience has grown thinner every day. He's shorter with the crew backstage. And he just went the fuck off on Callista for not being able to order his own food.

"This is different. It's work. She's helping me with a song on the violin," he says but I can hear the remorse and embarrassment in his voice, and his eyes won't meet any of his bandmates' faces.

Noah's taken his hand off my eyes, and I see Brett's found a pair of workout shorts. While everyone takes a breath, I tread carefully, but offer a solution to satisfy all parties.

"Look, I don't want any contention. I'm happy to get off the bus. I totally respect the no-girls-allowed bro fort, but the girls' bus doesn't have that rule. Noah, why don't you ride with us for a little while, and we can work on that piece?" Just to lighten the mood I add, "That way Brett can take his clothes off again since he's obviously allergic to wearing any."

Noah thinks about it for a second while his eyes bore into mine. "Yeah, sure," he finally answers, nodding without even cracking a smile at my joke. He grabs his violin from somewhere in the back and follows me to my bus. We see Callista coming out of the café with bags of food, and she watches Noah climb on board after me. Smartly, she doesn't say anything but the warning in her eyes is clear even from this distance.

But it does remind me . . . Callista's a girl.

"Didn't Callista get on your bus last night? Hasn't she been riding with you guys all morning?"

His jaw is tense. "No. She tried but we put our foot down, claiming invasion of privacy since we're a bunch of guys. I emailed Matt to try and have Callista replaced but he said she knows people in high places, and she has to stay. Brett and Ryan both think she looks familiar, like we know her from somewhere, but none of us can place her."

We climb on board the bus, and Kara looks up, surprised to see Noah in our space.

"Oh! Hey, Noah," she says, peering over the edge of her laptop.

Noah exhales and gives her a smile. "Hey, Kara. I meant to tell you, that re-entry on stage you did a couple shows ago, for Vindictive . . . I really liked that."

She gives him a huge smile in return. "Thanks! I choreographed that move on my own. I was surprised when Matt gave me the green light, but I thought it would look really cool dropping in right as Ryan's bass solo started."

He nods and turns back to me. "Where do you want to do this?"

Our bus is set up like the guys'. A living room with a table, couch, and two recliners is what you see first. In the middle is the small kitchen. It's got a sink, mini fridge, small counter and storage. Next to that, bunks are tucked into the walls with what look like accordion-style curtains that close, giving you some semblance of privacy. Across from the kitchen is a full bath with shower. In the way back is a half bath and another lounge area without the kitchen table. Ours is pretty sparse because we use that space for stretching.

"Let's head to the back, but we'll have to wake Bri up."

I open the door to the back room of the bus to wake my bestie up, knowing she's an absolute bear when she gets woken up by loud noises – like movies, a radio, or a violin five feet from her head. Selfishly, I'm hoping that seeing Noah's face first will soften the blow.

"Why don't you stand in front of me?" I ask as I pull him forward and hide behind him before rocking Bri's shoulder. Fuck he smells good. "Rise and shine, Gorgeous," I say sweetly.

"Fuck off," comes her muffled reply. She doesn't even open her eyes.

I see Noah's shoulders shake with laughter as the bus starts moving. He mouths, "Can I?" and I wave my hand.

Be my guest.

Noah squats low and puts his mouth right next to Bri's ear and starts to whisper in that fucking voice of his. My God, he isn't even trying to be sexy, and it's just his natural speaking voice . . . but, *damn.*

"Good morning, Bri. I need you to wake up for me. I want–"

164

"What the fuck? I'm awake," Bri's eyes pop open only to realize Noah's face is an inch from her own. She gets a goofy grin across her face and arches her back to stretch like she's in a boudoir shoot. "Oh, hello, Noah. I thought I was dreaming. Did you know you sound like a porn star? Not one of the ones with the ridiculously deep voice though . . . no, your voice is like . . . perfect," she purrs, swinging her legs over the side of the couch and rubbing her face. "Also, could you teach that trick to Brett? I'd pay a lot of money to have him that close to my face whispering dirty shit."

"That was dirty?" Noah asks, with his elbow draped on the arm of the couch, clearly amused.

"It ended up there in my mind," Bri says unapologetically, laughing before going to join the other girls up front. "Have fun with whatever it is you're planning to do and let me know if you need a third." She winks and kisses my cheek before moving along.

Noah chuckles at her boldness, and it warms my heart. He seems to be over whatever happened in that café which is good. I motion for us to get started when I realize I don't actually have anything to show him on the violin, I was just trying to distract him before he exploded.

As we get settled, my phone pings.

What now?

JOSH V

I'm going to be in San Diego for work and I see the Beautiful Deceit tour will be passing through.

JOSH V

Can I take you out to dinner?

JOSH V

We never really got to catch up last time.

. . .

I *hate* being rude and hurting people's feelings. Sometimes it feels like every interaction I have is viewed through the lens of seventeen-year-old me when my heart was demolished by the selfish words and actions of my mother, and I'm afraid I've become overly sensitive to how I respond to others, careful not to leave them feeling the same way.

But honestly, this is getting so old.

Chapter 17

Noah

I can't help but notice the shadow that falls across Sienna's face as she reads her text messages. The storm brewing on her features has me concerned.

As my heartrate has chilled the fuck out, and the steady rumble of the bus along the highway reminds me of the life I'm living, I'm insanely embarrassed by my outburst when we stopped. I'm also grateful Sienna was able to get me in check. Until now, that feat has only been accomplished by Ryan.

I want to try and explain myself but whatever just came through Sienna's phone tells me now is not the time to make it about me, yet somehow, I manage to do it anyway.

"Is everything okay?" I ask, wondering when we'll have been friends long enough for it to not feel like prying, and she'll just start opening up to me on her own.

Her frustrated exhale tells me *no* even as her beautiful lips say, "Yeah, it's just been a weird morning." She rubs the back of her neck with her free hand as she takes a seat on the small couch recently vacated by her best friend. Bri shut the door on her way out and I'm enjoying the intimacy of the small space.

It's funny how a sixteen hundred square foot hotel suite can make me feel claustrophobic even when it's just me and the guys but a forty-eight square foot room inside a moving box feels too big when it's just me and her.

She's in sweatpants and a gray, lightweight sweatshirt she's trying to disappear inside of right now as she pulls the long sleeves over her hands.

I'm about to ask if she wants to talk about it when she adds absentmindedly, "It probably didn't help that I didn't sleep at all last night." Her eyes widen before they close altogether, and she makes a face like she shouldn't have said that, but I've already caught on to both the statement and the facial expression.

"Why couldn't you sleep?"

She cuts her eyes to me as I take a seat on the couch next to her.

"Look, I don't like the games women play where they make you guess what's on their mind," she starts, making me wonder where this is going. "So, I'd love to tell you the truth, but the truth is embarrassing, not to mention pointless, so I'm not playing games, I'm just not going to tell you."

For some reason, that cuts deep.

"Okay, but was it something I did?" My need to know is more powerful than my ability to respect her desire to not tell me. I don't love that about myself right now, but I'm barely hanging on at the end of my rope as it is. I also recognize it's pretty narcissistic of me to think that what I do affects her at all, but here we are. After our afternoon in the conference room before the show yesterday, I'm more confident we affect each other in the same ways.

I let the question stand.

She narrows her eyes at me. "Noah, could you just let it go, please?"

I honestly wish I could, but the blush creeping up her neck has me too curious.

"What if we take turns asking each other questions. Like Truth or Dare, but Truth is the only option," I say, desperate to learn more about her. Specifically, why she couldn't sleep and what's bothering her now.

She huffs out a laugh. "That's just called a conversation."

"Okay, yeah. Let's have one of those." I feel myself smile despite sounding like an absolute idiot.

As she's mulling it over, my cellphone rings in my pocket. Matt.

Silence.

It rings again.

I hit *end.*

When it rings a third time, I answer the call. "I'm in the middle of something. What do you want?"

Matt's smug-ass voice comes over the line. "You'd better not be in the middle of your backup dancer, Kinkaid. Callista told me you lost your shit on her and disappeared with Sienna. What's going on?"

Matt took the company jet on to San Diego ahead of us, leaving Callista to travel with us and the road crew. I should've anticipated she'd tattle.

I flash my eyes to Sienna who's typing on her own phone trying to give me privacy in the eight-by-six room.

"What's going on is you didn't clear a staffing change with me, and I don't like your assistant. At all. She won't get off my back and this morning she tried to tell me I couldn't get off the fucking bus and order my own food like I was a goddamned second grader on a fucking field trip and my permission slip wasn't signed." I leave out the details about the creepy vibes she gives me because Matt doesn't care about how she makes me feel. He cares about her keeping this tour together.

169

"She's got to let go of my leash, Matt, or I'm going to end up strangling her with it."

At my words, Sienna looks up from her phone and places her hand reassuringly on my back before pausing. I nod, letting her know, again, that it's okay for her to touch me. The slow circles she's making give me something to focus on as she hears my one-sided answers, missing the bullshit Matt is feeding me through this receiver.

"Yeah, I hear you." *Pause.* "Fine." *Pause.* "Working on a new song." *Pause.* "No." *Pause.* "Abso-fucking-lutely not. I will cancel the rest of this tour myself." *Pause.* "Fuck your contract."

I hang up the phone and shake my head at Sienna like I don't want to talk about it. She doesn't need to know that Matt is choosing to support Callista and is warning me against being alone with Sienna. I'm still fuming when Sienna gets on her knees behind me on the couch. I swear she's trying to kill me until I feel her hands start kneading my shoulders. They're surprisingly strong for someone so small but then I remember that she uses them daily to literally hold on for her life.

A groan escapes as she works closer to my neck.

"What if we play a game like Truth or Dare, but Truth is the only option?" she asks, pulling a smile from me despite my conversation with Matt.

"Sounds like it could be fun," I tease. "And like someone really smart invented it. Do you want to ask first or answer first?" I let my head drop forward as she expertly works the tension out of my shoulders. If I'm not careful, that tension is going to start pooling somewhere else with much more visible results.

"I'll answer. You sound like you need a distraction, something to hit the pressure release valve."

I start to turn my head and wag my eyebrows at her, but she catches herself first.

Laughing, she says, "God, I just meant you need to blow off some steam." She laughs harder. I could listen to it all day. "Wait, that wasn't any better, was it?"

"Nope."

"Okay, moving on," she says as she moves to a new spot on my shoulder blade.

"Oh *shiiiiitttt,*" I hiss. "That hurts so good."

"*Hurts So Good.* That should be the name of your next album," she laughs.

"Can't be. It's already the name of my sex tape," I throw back without thinking, as if I'm talking shit with the guys.

"Jesus *Christ,* Noah. Don't talk about your sex tape while I'm rubbing your back," she says with another breathy little laugh.

"Why not?" I want to hear her say it. I want to know I may be stressed out and losing my mind but I'm not wrong about what I feel happening between us.

"Not answering," she says immediately.

"Isn't that the point of this game? You said you'd answer first. That's my question." I'm not really fighting fairly, but I was wound tightly before Matt called and Sienna's right. I need her to hit the pressure release valve. "Why can't I talk about my sex tape – which is hypothetical by the way – while you're rubbing my back?"

She lets out a loud sigh, letting me know she isn't happy I cornered her into answering. "Because now I'm going to think about it."

I enjoy her honesty. She's digging her elbow into my upper shoulder making black dots appear in my vision, and I'm not sure if I'm really that tight or if this is payback, but either way, I like it.

"And you don't want to think about it?" I ask, prodding for more, fully willing to get burned by the fire I'm playing with.

"Nu-uh. My turn. I answered your question," she says, rolling back and forth over a particularly sore spot.

"*Fuck, woman,*" I choke out, fairly confident I'm going to lose consciousness just as she eases off.

"Wimp," she teases.

I have to stop myself from reaching behind me and grabbing her, flipping us over, pinning her beneath me on this couch, and teaching her a lesson. *Shit.* Even though I haven't touched her, the vision has already taken hold, and I'm in more trouble now than I've ever been.

She moves the heels of her hands to the muscles on my side, just under my shoulder blade.

"Hmm," she says thoughtfully. "I was going to ask why you actually flipped your lid on Callista, but I heard your explanation to Matt, so I've got to change my question." She pauses and the suspense is killing me although I'm pretty sure I know what she's going to ask.

Why don't I ever take my shirt off or let people touch me.

But she surprises me when she asks, "Where did you go last night?"

I immediately think what a waste the question is. "I didn't go anywhere last night."

"Don't lie to me, Kinkaid." To make herself appear more threatening, she bears down on another knot in my back, causing me to chuckle.

Vindictive little minx. *I've got a song about you,* I think to myself and smile at how much the lyrics fit her.

"I'm not lying. I didn't go anywhere after the show last night," I say again.

"I saw you get in the car with the guys, those *hoes,* and Callista," she says, the jealousy in her voice catching me off guard.

"Sienna, I didn't go anywhere last night. I hopped in the car because my favorite guitar pick fell out of my pocket earlier. It was the same vehicle they used to drive us to the door before the show because the fans had made walking impossible, so I knew it had to still be in the backseat. Ryan was already climbing in behind me, so I just got out on the other side. I was exhausted and hanging out with groupies isn't really my thing."

I feel her hands go still on my back.

When she speaks, her voice is small. "You mean, I could have slept peacefully the entire night?"

"Does that mean you *didn't* sleep peacefully because you thought I was out with someone?" I counter gently, not wanting to spook her off this conversation.

Trying to buy herself time, she says, "You answer me, first."

My answer tumbles out faster than my heart is beating. "Yes, you could have slept peacefully. I was no more than twenty feet from you the whole night. Your turn."

Blowing out a sigh, she says, "Also, yes. I didn't sleep because I thought you were out with them." Her hands leave my body at her admission, and she comes around to sit next to me again, drawing her right heel into her right thigh, playing with her hands in her lap. "My turn," she says, still looking down as she asks the million-dollar questions. "Why don't you let anyone touch you or see you without your shirt on?"

"I let *you* touch me," I argue, reaching for her hand and placing it on my thigh to prove my point . . . as if that were necessary after the massage she just gave me.

"You know what I mean," she says as she starts to trace small shapes on my jeans, distracting me.

I launch into the explanation which really isn't that mysterious at all.

"I end *every* show feeling raw and overexposed. It's impossible for me to sing on that stage and not feel every emotion the crowd brought in the door with them plus every emotion I had while I wrote this album."

She's nodding her head like she understands and after hearing her play the violin – which I'm supposed to be doing right now – I don't doubt that she does.

I continue, knowing she's listening intently to every word, not realizing how much I needed to explain this to her.

"I know the guys feel it too, but there's just something intimate about using my voice as my instrument. It pulls me closer to the crowd whereas the drums, guitars, and bass all act as a physical barrier or shield against them. The other guys have something to hide behind. I don't. I pour my soul out on that stage every night leaving me emotionally, spiritually, and mentally naked. I couldn't handle being physically naked as well." I pause and smile when I see the compassion in her eyes. I had planned to stop there. I most certainly did not plan on divulging the ugly details of mine and Nicole's breakup, but I guess I am now. I want Sienna to know everything.

I explain that three years ago, the guys and I had just been signed to our record label, and I wanted to be able to focus solely on the band. Plus, I felt I didn't have enough time to devote to Nicole, who accused me of just wanting to be free for, and-I-quote, "road pussy". It was definitely a turning point, and her comment allowed me to see she didn't really know me at all. When she realized I wasn't going to change my mind, she spread those unflattering pictures of me all over the internet as payback for something I didn't even do, leaving me open to the judgements and harassing comments from people who don't know me.

"She claimed to love me, but if that's how she treated me when I tried to be honest with her, I figure it's not safe to let my guard down around anyone anymore."

Sienna's angry, shocked look soothes like a balm.

"Noah, I'm so sorry. I had no idea. What a *bitch*."

I smile at her protectiveness and continue answering her earlier question. "As for not letting people touch me," I let out a laugh. "A lot of people actually think I'm an asshole for that, but tell me, how many people do you know who enjoy being manhandled by complete strangers? I don't mind shaking hands and meeting fans. Hell, I actually really like that, but people can't ever just leave it there. It's an arm around the waist for a selfie, but then their arm slips, and they're touching my ass. Or they're leaning in for a picture and their lips 'accidentally' brush my neck. Or they've got my shirt bunched in their hands, trying to get a hand on the bare skin beneath it. Somehow, because I'm famous now, that's no longer considered sexual harassment, and I no longer get personal space. It's like our bodies now belong to the public."

She gasps at the real-life examples I give her even though those are the tame ones, and she tries to pull her hand back, but I catch it and keep it in mine this time. "Again, that doesn't apply to you."

She looks sad and lost in thought as this conversation got heavy and serious, fast. But I'm not after her pity, so I change the subject. "Who was your text from?" I ask, silently begging her to be open with me like I just was with her.

"Which one?" she asks, even though I assume all three dings I heard were from the same person.

"All of them?" I half answer, half ask.

"I heard from my mom this morning. She wants tickets to the show in L.A. The ones I got after we came back here were from Josh."

"Let me see your phone," I demand, without having a firm plan. Understandably, she looks uncomfortable. "I won't send anything without letting you read it first. You can choose to erase it if you want," I reassure her.

She hands it over, albeit a little reluctantly. The first thing I notice is her wallpaper is a shot of the two of us. She's in her silks above me, and I'm screaming my ass off into the mic, leaning forward, clutching it with both hands while my eyes are screwed shut. It's a cool picture.

SIENNA

Actually, I lost a bet with Noah and now I have to spend the day taking surfing lessons when we get to San Diego.

I hand her the phone and watch as she reads it, her eyes going wide. I could have typed any excuse, but childishly, I want him to know it's *me* she's hanging out with.

"How'd you know I wanted to learn to surf?" she asks bewildered.

"I didn't. It's what I want to do so I thought I could kill two birds with one stone and give you an out." I eye her, a little taken aback. "You want to learn to surf?"

"Yeah, ever since I was little," she answers, her eyes bright.

"Let's do it!"

This is the most excited I've been in a while. Music is my life, and it's been a minute since I've pursued anything outside of it. It's not like I'll have a chance to build on the skill, but a morning of private surf lessons could be cool as shit. Her smile fades just as her eyes fall.

"What's wrong?" Her sudden mood change has me confused and a little crestfallen.

"I hate having to lie, even if we *do* end up going, which would be awesome." She flops forward so her forehead lands on my shoulder, the move feeling familiar like she's done it a million times. "I just wish he'd take my no as *no*."

I pull her phone back out of her hand, happy to let her stay on my shoulder, and start typing something else, laughing as I tell her, "I'm happy to make a bet that you'll lose so it's not a lie." And because I'm an idiot with no self-control, I add, "But the result of losing would be a lot more creative than surf lessons."

SIENNA

I'm not interested in you like that. Please accept my no as a no.

Before I hand her phone back to her, I send myself her contact so she has my number and I have hers. Then I go back to the other feed and pull up the message I typed but didn't send and hand it back to her, laughing as she shrieks.

"Noah! That's so mean!"

"It's not mean, baby. It's the truth."

I freeze as soon as the words are out of my mouth.

Shit.

Did I just call her *baby*?

It just flew right out there like I call her that all the time. Maybe she didn't hear . . . no, she definitely heard it.

"Sorry, I . . . " I trail off because I don't know how to finish that sentence.

She shrugs with a small smile and tucks her hair behind her ear. "No big deal. I'll fantasize about that for the rest of my life."

I can't tell if she's kidding or not.

Chapter 18

Sienna

Hearing the word *baby* come out of Noah's mouth, and having it directed at me, was the hottest thing I've ever experienced. Of course, our interactions during the show are hot too, but it's scripted.

This?

This was an absolute accident. And my heart is totally melting because of it, but now we're touching, and talking, and I'm dangerously close to throwing all the money back at him and sucking his face like my next breath can only come from his lungs.

After spending every day of the last two months on the road with these guys, you'd think I'd have lost the stars in my eyes but if anything, they've only gotten bigger and although life on the road is hard, I'm glad we have six more months together.

I realize I'm still staring at Noah's lips when he clears his throat.

Time to get to work.

"So, I think we're supposed to be playing the violin," I say, sitting all the way up and trying to give him some space.

"The violin, right," he echoes, clearly as lost as I am.

"May I?"

I hold my hands out for his violin laying on the pillow behind him and God help me, I'm going to have to improvise hard because I have nothing planned.

My only option is to play what I feel.

I close my eyes and let my mind wander, dropping into a minor scale to convey my turmoil over being so close to him but unable to have him. I think about the way he sounds on stage. The way he caresses the microphone, engages with the audience. The way his voice sounds through the speakers. The way his sweat makes his shirt cling to his body. The way I know what's underneath, and how much I want to see it again. The way his body moves in time to the beat as he purges his soul every night. The way his body *would* move if he were to empty himself inside of me . . .

Fuck.

Playing my thoughts and emotions sounded like a great idea, except I forgot I was playing for another musician. One whose primary language is music. Which means he knows everything I was thinking while I played.

I basically just gave him a blow job with this bow and these strings.

How do I know?

His pupils are dilated, his nostrils are flaring, there's sweat on his forehead, his breaths are shallow, and he's hard as a rock in his jeans.

"Sienna," he whispers my name, knowingly, placing the heel of his hand over his erection trying to either hide it or apply pressure to relieve the pain.

"Noah," I reply in warning, but he's already got his fingers laced through my hair as his palm rests on the back of my head.

"If you don't want me to do this, now would be a good time to say so, but I'm *begging* you to let me kiss you." He's so close I can feel his lips moving against my own as he speaks.

He somehow understands my tortured squeak means *yes,* and I justify it in my head by saying that it's technically not breaking the contract. Kissing me isn't the same as fucking me . . . but in the middle of kissing me, he leans over, scoops me up by my ass and plants me in his lap with my knees on either side of him. He deepens the kiss, effectively making me not give two shits about the contract.

Without any prompting, I start rocking back and forth slowly, seeking friction and giving in to the need to be closer to him. He doesn't disappoint as he arches his hips up, his cock straining hard against his jeans. I roll over him again in my sweatpants and the groan he gives me in response is the most decadent sound I've ever heard in my entire life.

I grind harder wishing like hell there was nothing between us.

He grabs a fistful of my hair by the roots and tugs gently at the same time he uses his teeth to nip my neck at the sensitive spot just behind my ear. His other hand is on my hip helping to add pressure by pushing me down onto himself.

"Ahh . . . fuck," he moans.

We're like a pair of horny teenagers, and I love it.

"Can you get off like this?" he asks, breathlessly.

"Definitely," I answer between pants.

He pulls back and gives me a wicked grin. "Then do it."

His voice. *Oh fuck, his voice.*

He briefly lets go of me to make a grab for my sweatshirt. I help him pull it off and then reach for his t-shirt. Forgetting all about his earlier stories, I'm crazy with lust and can only think about getting my hands on his warm skin. Licking my way from his neck to . . . as far as he'll let me. I'm frantically pulling at his shirt when I hear his low laugh.

"Been thinking about this a while, have you?" he taunts, as he slips his shirt over his head, revealing the most incredible torso I haven't seen since that night in the pool a lifetime ago.

Definitely too long ago. How have I survived?

"About as long as you have," I fire back, my fingers flexing into his pecs before mapping out his entire upper body. The ridges of his abs, the breadth of his shoulders, the bulk in his biceps, the tautness of his stomach, the indentions at his hips. Unable to stop myself, I pepper kisses to the wild cats inked in his skin.

"Holy Mother of God," I whimper, unable to stop myself when he flexes beneath my lips.

He laughs again, and I swear I start to come just from the sound. I pick up my speed, really grinding on his lap, afraid I'm going to make the whole bus star rocking when he reaches up and caresses the skin between my breasts, his fingers shaking.

"Stop holding back, Sienna. I want to hear you come, and I want to know it's for me." He pinches my exposed nipple between his thumb and index finger while he trails his tongue up my neck, sending me over the edge.

"Oh shit . . . yes . . . fuck . . . *Noah* . . . "

After that, it's a series of moans and grunts and whimpers as I ride out the first orgasm I haven't given myself in over three years . . . all from a man's jean-clad lap, bare chest, and that fucking voice.

"You're really good at that," I say awkwardly, still perched on his lap, my hair in my face, trying to catch my breath, unable to look at the perfect face of the rockstar I just rode like a jockey at the Kentucky Derby.

"Imagine what I could do *without* pants," he jokes, bringing his hands up to rub my back.

"I'm not sure I can handle it," I say honestly. I can feel the outline of him through his jeans.

"I'd go slow," he assures me, running a finger just under my waistband. "Well," he clarifies, "maybe gentle is the word I want. I'm not sure how slow I could stand to go."

As I recover, he grinds into me slightly, and I realize he's gotten no relief. Dipping my head to catch his eyes, I lean forward and pull his bottom lip between my teeth as my hands find the button on his jeans.

I pull back slightly. "This okay?" I ask. Because of his feelings of constantly having his space and privacy invaded, his consent is insanely important to me even if he has to repeat it two hundred times.

"Yes. You have permission to do it all, Sienna."

Oh, well, alrighty then.

I climb off his lap and slide to my knees in front of the small couch, my fingers poised to slip his pants and boxers down. Just as he lifts his hips, there's a knock on the door.

Motherfucker.

"Someone better be fucking dying out there," I yell through gritted teeth.

Bri's amused voice whisper-yells back, "Did you not notice the bus has stopped? Callista's on her way over here so you guys better suit up fast."

"Shit." We get our clothes in place, and I direct Noah to the far wall of the bus. "Just start writing notes down. Callista won't know if they're right or not, we just need something on paper." I start pulling the bow across the strings. Not the same song as before. That was just for Noah.

Long, deep notes ring out in the small space. Slowly at first as if playing at a slower speed will calm my heartrate. I close my eyes and just begin to feel the music. I'm trying to keep the tune in line with the album we're touring for so it would make sense as a prelude or interlude, and my current turmoil makes for an excellent melody.

Callista practically bursts through the door right as Noah says, "Sienna, play that last part again."

"Don't you know how to knock?" I ask Callista, rudely. She'd better be glad Bri gave us warning because if I'd had Noah's dick out and she'd seen it? I'd have to gouge the bitch's eyes out and set her memory on fire.

Whoa. That was strong.

It seems now that we've acknowledged this thing between us, there is no pretending I'm indifferent to Noah Kinkaid. Truthfully, I never was.

"Sienna," Noah's voice calls my attention back to him. "Eyes on me. Play that last part again." I don't think he's putting on a show for Callista, I think he's actually on to something, so I try to remember where I was.

Callista opens her mouth, but Noah holds up a hand to silence her. "Not yet." Eyes still on me, he says, "Sienna, *play.* This is what was missing. The song we started at the hotel. This is it." I close my eyes and pull his bow back across the strings. "Switch to C minor, speed up to sixteenth notes for the first measure, until you get to the F, then add in a half note rest."

I do as he asks and he starts firing off more instructions.

"Yes, that's it. Keep playing that," he says before racing past Callista and yells to the front of the bus, "Bri!"

"Yeah?" she responds immediately.

"Can you grab the guys and get them in here right now, please?" He kneels in front of me on the floor, with one foot planted so he can write on his thigh. Okay, I want you to drop to A minor and just see where it takes you."

I do as he asks when I feel the bus shake.

"Kinky, what's up man?" Brett comes in the little room first, followed by Ryan.

"You good, Kink?" Ryan asks.

"Yeah, yeah. Listen to this. Where's Sloan?"

"I'm back here!" he yells from the front of the bus.

"Sloan, get in here. Callista, give us a minute, we'll be out in a few," Noah says, pulling Sloan in by the shoulder and shutting the door in Callista's face. "Listen to this. Sienna, can you start over?"

Playing the violin is much easier to me than dancing, so I have no problem starting where he wants me to and playing it back for the guys. I close my eyes and let my body take over.

"Brett, can you tap out a beat for this? Nothing too overpowering, this part belongs to the bass. Ryan, this is all you. Something hard and dangerous. Sloan –"

"Already on it. This is sick."

I open my eyes and see Noah has his phone out. He's not just recording the sound, he's videoing me, to make sure he has the notes right.

Ten intense minutes later, Noah opens the door, the guys file out and I stifle a chuckle at Callista who was kicked out of the boys' club and doesn't look happy about it.

Turning to me, Noah says, "If we get this down, would you record this with us?"

"Record it? Noah, I couldn't. It's yours. I'll sign whatever you want saying you have the rights to the song or whatever." I only just picked a violin back up and although it's physically easy to create the sound, emotionally it's a whole different story.

"Si," Noah says, using my nickname. "I can't play that," he says, pointing to the instrument still in my hands. "I can't hit those notes that fast. There's a reason my prelude is slow.

Everything is a half note because it takes me that long to figure out where my fingers are going next. I do most of my creation on that violin, but I only speed it up once I have a guitar in my hands."

"You can learn though. I can teach you," I offer, feeling weird having him beg me in front of an audience.

"I can't learn fast enough. I want to record it when we get to L.A., before we all leave for our first week off."

"Can I think about it?" I ask, suddenly feeling overwhelmed with the show in San Diego and the short time we have before arriving in L.A., plus, the tickets for my mom – and possibly seeing her. Add on having to respond to Josh's text, and of course the fact that I just got on my knees for America's hottest rockstar and was dangerously close to losing my job, and suddenly, I'm feeling like I could use a shot of tequila – or six.

And now, Noah wants me to face my biggest demons . . . in the city where they live.

Noah nods, "Yeah, of course."

Callista has made her way back to where Noah and I are standing. She has a sarcastic frown on her face and her hand is planted on a pale pink skirt with skulls splashed across it. "Well, if I can speak, finally," she looks accusatorily between Noah and me, "I wanted to let you know we're stopping for lunch, in case anyone wants to go in and order their own food," she snaps at Noah which makes me want to punch her in the mouth.

I didn't realize we'd been on the road for so long already. It's only felt like an hour. Our tour buses are stocked with snacks and drinks which means we don't really have to stop for food, but they do require gas stops occasionally which gives us the chance to see past these walls.

Before I can think about what I'm doing, and what it might

cost me, I open my mouth, unsure if I'm about to help Noah or make the situation worse.

I step in front of him like a shield even though he's much taller than me and can easily see over my head as I address Callista.

"You will never know what it's like to not be able to pop into a grocery store without being harassed," I begin, defending Noah as well as the rest of the band. "There will be days when Noah and the guys want to order their own food, just to know they can. And there will be days when they'll need someone else to grab it because they're too exhausted, too busy, or because it's too crowded and their presence will incite a riot. So, instead of being a patronizing bitch, why don't you just *ask him* what he needs right now?"

I shock myself with my outburst. I'm usually so concerned with hurting people's feelings, and I guess I still am, I'm just more concerned about Noah's feelings than I am about Callista's.

"*Day-um*, Sienna's got claws. Maybe you should add her to your chest piece, huh, Kinky? *Rawr*." Brett jokes, referencing Noah's tattoos. I can't suppress my giggle when he waves his fingers through the air like paws. "This place is packed, and Sloan's already been spotted," Brett says, growing a little more serious. "I'm also pretty sure they're about to start chanting your name and stripping, so Romeo's grabbing our order, what do you want?"

Noah places his order with Brett, then turns back to Callista, "Was there anything else?"

"Yes," she says with a faux sweetness that tastes bitter on my tongue. "When we get to San Diego, you have two radio shows in the morning, a meet and greet at noon, and the arena requests that you're inside by three because they're anticipating a large turnout and don't want the anyone stuck in traffic."

186

"Ryan will do the first two, send Brett and Sloan for the meet and greet. I'll be in the stadium by three."

Noah has to attend the VIP meet and greet an hour before the show for the radio contest winners and package ticket holders. The add-ons – like this one – don't guarantee which band members will be present because it's last minute.

"And what exactly will you be doing the rest of the time?"

Without missing a beat, Noah says, "Surfing," before he grabs his violin and bow, grins at me, and walks up front to get off the bus.

Callista takes her time following his lead. If she's not on their bus, I don't know who she's riding with, but I feel bad for whoever it is. She turns her cat-like eyes on me. We have to be about the same age, and I can't help but wonder how she got to be Matt's "right-hand" so young. The petty side of me thinks she slept her way there. The cynical side says she's probably a relative he had to offer a job to. But the rational side knows it has to be more than that because I didn't get the feeling Matt would entrust this tour to just anyone.

"Don't ever speak to me like that again, or you'll find yourself unemployed," Callista threatens.

It packs a punch because I don't want to leave Noah and the guys. I'm about to apologize when Noah's back in a flash.

"Threaten my dancer again, and we'll see who ends up unemployed, Callista. Now, get off the bus."

For a second, I think she's going to spit in his face, but instead, she runs her eyes down his frame and back up again, smirking, before walking off the bus like she knows something we don't.

Chapter 19

Noah

"**M**att, you've got to tell me why Callista has to be here." I've got my cell phone on speaker so the guys can hear this conversation as well. "She's pissing me off and she's threatening to fire the dancers every day. And if by having her *handle* my schedule, you meant pack it as full as she can, then yeah, she's doing that. I want her gone. *We* want her gone."

After the lunch stop, I hopped back on the bus with the guys and immediately called Matt. The whole time I talk to him though, I'm unnerved by how much I want to be on Sienna's bus.

That's new.

I've never not wanted to be with the guys. They're my brothers and my best friends. We spend a lot of time together, but somehow it never gets old.

"I can't do that," Matt says solemnly with a tone that tells me maybe he wishes he could.

Strange, since he's done nothing but sing Callista's praises.

"Why the fuck not? Shouldn't we get a say about who's on

our team?" I argue.

I hear Matt's hand slap his forehead before he exhales harshly. "Look, she's Cal Richardson's daughter, Noah."

Cal Richardson.

The owner of Apex Records. *Son of a bitch.* That makes her Callista Richardson. If Matt had told me her last name at the start, we could have placed her sooner, and I could have worked harder to avoid her. The guys and I share a glance telling me we're all recalling the same memory.

Callista was in the studio one day early on when we were recording our first album with Apex. She kept trying to make suggestions about changing the key we were in, adding verses, and other shit we weren't interested in doing. I couldn't figure out why her dad let her interfere so much. She was a know-it-all brat back then, and it seems her disposition hasn't changed much in the time since.

Although we're grateful to Cal and Apex for taking a chance on us, we've already outgrown the label. We signed a six-year contract that was great at the time, but unfortunately, we'll be underpaid for the next three albums if our success continues in this vein.

Cal is decent enough, but I'm certainly not jazzed about working with a second Richardson.

"Apparently," Matt continues, drawing me back into the conversation, "she just graduated with a master's degree in entertainment management from UCLA and this position could make her career," Matt says before dropping his voice and adding, "Plus, she's a huge fan."

I fucking knew it.

"This is a major issue for us, Matt. Talk about a conflict of interest." I huff, feeling my anger rising once more.

I'm acutely aware of when my temper changes the mood in the bus because Ryan and Sloan glance at me with matching expressions of worry. Ryan assesses me, ready to intervene if needed, and Sloan is gauging my reaction trying to figure out how pissed he should be, too. I don't know when it happened, but I'm the guy everyone walks on eggshells around, and I fucking hate it.

Matt's unapologetic voice rings in my ear, "I wish I could help you out, Noah, but my hands are tied. I had hoped she'd fit in a little better, but it seems Daddy's money and her penchant for metal music are a deadly combination. Just try to keep your distance and play nice. I've gotta run. I'll see you in L.A."

Matt hangs up the phone, leaving me in stunned silence.

Try to keep my distance. That's his advice? He gave the woman twenty-four hour access to me for the next six months! How the hell am I supposed to keep my fucking distance?

"Well, that's a couple of questions answered at least," Ryan says in his usual voice of reason.

"We were pricks to her in the beginning," Sloan says. "I'm surprised she wanted anything to do with us."

"Shit," Brett says with wide eyes as he recalls another memory. "Do you guys remember that demo Cal played for us last Christmas?"

"No," the rest of us answer in confused unison.

"Yes, you do. The one that was terrible? We said it was too whiny and fell flat. We basically raked it over the coals and said it was the reason women didn't belong in metal," he says, offering more detail to jog our memories - while simultaneously reminding us of the pricks we used to be.

"Oh yeah!" Sloan laughs, right before his face loses its color. "Oh, shit. That was her demo, wasn't it?"

"Yep," Brett confirms.

"Okay, but surely Cal wouldn't use our harsh words verbatim? And if he did, I'm pretty confident he wouldn't tell her it was us that said it, right?" I can hear the hope in my voice.

"Noah," Ryan looks at me, pushing his glasses up the bridge of his nose. He looks just like Clark Kent when he wears his glasses - which isn't often - and it's always hard to take him seriously when he has them on. "Have you *met* Cal Richardson?"

Touché.

Cal isn't known for his cuddly qualities. He's knowledgeable, but he isn't one to pull punches.

"So what do we do?" I ask, totally at a loss.

It's Ryan who speaks again. "We have to assume she's here because we're the biggest band in our genre - and definitely at our label. Matt was right, working with us could make her career. Plus, we were easy access for her. Her attitude reminds me a lot of her father, but she hasn't been sexually inappropriate or legally inappropriate. It's probably safe to assume she either doesn't remember the review of that demo, or she wasn't told it was us who reviewed it. For now, we should watch what we say around her, but let her do her job. Matt and the board at LNV still have override control."

I grunt and throw my phone on the couch across from me, watching as it bounces off and falls to the floor. For a second, I hope it's broken so no one can reach me but that thought is quickly followed by a reminder that if my phone is broken, I can't get any of Sienna's texts.

Hell, she may not even realize she has my number.

With two hours to go before we reach San Diego, I'm feeling antsy and wish we were there already. This tour has been a fucking whirlwind. Between things escalating with Sienna, this bullshit with Callista, and the natural pressure of rising to fame so quickly, the only moments I've had to pause and enjoy this insanity is on the bus with guys as we unwind after each show.

But even that time is strained with Ryan constantly worrying about me, plus keeping his own secrets. On top of that, Brett's been acting weird and moody the last couple of days as well - worse than usual. I had hoped him getting laid last night would've helped but it seems to have had the opposite effect. The only one seemingly unfazed is Sloan. I guess when you've been deployed, it takes some pretty major shit to rile you up. He's also more used to having no personal space after his four years in the Army.

I scoop my phone off the floor, sit back down on the couch next to Sloan, and fire off a text to Sienna as Brett and Ryan head to the back of the bus for the PlayStation console no doubt.

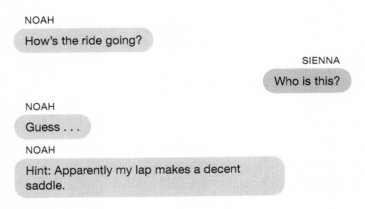

My phone rings a second later, and I know a stupid smile hits my face because it gains Sloan's attention.

"Whoever it is, she must be hot," he says, mocking me.

I should just tell him. I don't keep anything from the guys.

But not yet. I want to figure out what the fuck it is first. No need to get them involved if it's over before it even starts.

I throw an empty La Croix can at Sloan. Ryan's toxic trait

is drinking fifty of these damn things a day so there's always one within reach.

"She is. But you're nosey as fuck, so I'm not going to take the call."

"When the hell have you had time to start talking to someone?" He eyes me. I can see his gears turning, and I can tell the exact moment it clicks.

So much for keeping it a secret.

"Unless, you didn't just start *talking* to her . . . you just started *texting* her."

Yep, here we go.

I'm waiting for him to lay it on thick, but he just shrugs and says, "I hope you know what you're doing. The girls have grown on me, and I don't want anyone to get kicked off the tour. And if you hit that, you'd better be prepared for Brett's wrath. He's been holding out because of the threat of the contract."

I pull back like he slapped me.

"Where'd that serious response come from? I thought for sure you were going to lecture me and then tell me to ask her to send naked pictures," I tell him, silencing her second call. I'll text her I can't talk because these assholes are all ears when it comes to the good stuff.

He shrugs, "Yeah, well, that would be fucking awesome, but I'm pretty sure you would gouge my eyes out if I see Sienna's tits." He cuts his eyes to the back of the bus where Brett and Ryan are yelling at the TV. Looking back at me, he says, "You and Brett have different mentalities on sharing."

"You're right." Once he stops that train of thought, I look down at my phone which is buzzing in my hand for the third time.

My stomach clenches and I feel loopy like a middle schooler who just got a note from his crush. I try to brush the feeling aside and fire off a text.

. . .

NOAH

I can't take the call on the bus. The guys are always listening.

SIENNA

What did you want to discuss?

Shit. What *do* I want to discuss? I just want to talk to her. I didn't really have a plan. I just go with the first thing I want to know. The first thing I always want to know.

NOAH

Are you okay?

Sienna's bubbles pop up like she's replying.

Then they go away.

Then they come back.

When they stop for a second time, I head to the back of the bus to call her back because . . . *fuck this*.

"Hey, guys, I need this space for a few minutes." Brett and Ryan are playing Call of Duty as I enter the little lounge at the back of the bus. Although the buses have the same layout, ours looks more like a frat house whereas the girls' is clearly the space of organized minimalists.

Brett grunts but doesn't move. Ryan says nothing and his eyes don't leave the screen. It's like I'm not even here so I walk over and unplug the gaming system.

A beautiful chorus of *"What the fuck, man!"* and *"No, you did not just do that!"* rings out, making me laugh.

"Get your asses out of here, I need to make a phone call."

Brett punches me in the shoulder on his way out. Ryan recovers faster. "This have anything to do with Callista?"

"No."

Brett's head pokes back in the doorway. "Oooh, must be a girl."

Looking at Ryan, dopey grin still in place, I nod my head toward Brett. "Do me a favor and keep him away from this door?"

Ryan slaps Brett playfully in the head as he answers me, "Sure, Kink."

Sienna answers nervously on the first ring.

"Noah," she says hesitantly, like we're going to get caught even though we're allowed to talk on the phone. The slow smile I hear in her voice makes my stomach drop.

"Sienna," I say, teasing her and matching her tone. "I asked if you were okay. You didn't answer me which leads me to believe that you are *not* okay. Talk to me."

I could lie and tell myself I need her to be at her best for the tour, but deep down, I know it's more than that and with everything else going on, I wouldn't be able to stand it if I were the source of her stress.

"I'm not sure what I am," she answers honestly. Before I have a chance to probe farther, I hear her muffled, whispered voice, like she put a hand over the receiver before coming back on the line. "But maybe don't put in writing that I dry-humped my first orgasm in three years off you. I really need this job, and I respect the hell out of this tour so maybe we could pretend that part didn't happen?"

Considering the fact I'm hard just from thinking about it, that's unlikely.

"Wait, did you say three years?" No way I heard that right.

"Mm hmm. I've . . . shit . . . can we please just forget we did that?" she asks.

There are so many things I want to ask her, but instead, I point out the obvious.

"You're mostly naked and writhing on me or in front of me every couple of nights, Si. I don't think I'll forget what you felt like grinding on my lap anytime soon."

"Noah, I don't know what came over me. I really don't want to jeopardize anything." The panic in her voice makes me sad.

"Sienna, relax. I won't let you lose your job. I just don't want you to regret what we did."

She huffs out a quiet laugh. "I shamelessly rode the hottest rockstar in the world in the back of a tour bus on the way to our next show. Not a lot to regret about that."

I swallow my hurt.

Is that why she made out with me? Because of my current status?

Fuck. I thought she'd felt what I'd felt.

A connection through the music.

Something deeper than stardom.

Maybe I read her all wrong. It wouldn't surprise me if the stress of the tour was messing with my perception of this. It's certainly getting harder to differentiate between reality and this bubble of fame. Flashbacks of all the lies Nicole ever told me come rushing to the forefront of my mind.

My tone betrays my emotions and my words come out more harshly than I intend. "Being that rockstar comes with a price. Plus, that status could change overnight, so I'd find different criteria for what gets you off."

She's silent for a second, and I consider hanging up but somehow that doesn't feel right.

"Noah, that's not what I meant at all, and I'm sorry that's how it came out." Her words are shaky and the hurt in them is evident even to my ears.

This is exactly what I didn't want to do. This is also why we were told not to get involved with the dancers or the crew.

I run a hand through my hair trying to figure out how to fix this fragile thing between us, but it's Sienna who finds her words first.

"I don't make out with guys I'm not in a relationship with. I've never had a one-night stand. I've had sex with exactly one guy so far in my life. I have a ton of mommy issues and baggage, and I just meant that I regret a lot of things in my life, Noah, but those moments with you in the back of this bus, are not on that list."

Her admission makes me feel better, and I hold on to the two things I want to know more about. "Could we back up to the part where you haven't had an orgasm for three years and have only had sex with one dude?"

This makes her laugh. "Of course, that's the only part you heard, Kinkaid."

"I heard it all, Sienna. And we all have baggage. It just comes in various shapes and sizes and looks different for everyone."

"What does yours look like?" she asks, growing serious.

"I've told you most of it. Besides, right now, I'd rather hear more about how you want to get off next time. Are you an up-against-the-wall kind of girl? Or do you prefer the bed? Do you want me to pull your hair and bite your neck? Or spank your ass until it's red?"

My cock has started the countdown at T minus ten when Sienna laughs breathlessly, "Do you always speak in song lyrics?"

I hadn't even realized my words rhymed and right now I

don't care.

"I'll speak whatever language you want me to, just answer the fucking questions."

I'm desperate to know what she likes. What she wants. How she wants it. It's never been clearer to me than it is right now that I will stop at nothing until I have her. Even if it means risking everything.

Her voice is quiet when she speaks. "I don't really know. I've never had sex against a wall. No one's ever pulled my hair, bitten me, or . . . the other thing."

"Slapped your ass?" I ask, feeling the lightest I have in days, despite the one appendage that's growing heavier with every second of this conversation.

"Noah," Sienna exhales into the phone. I know she wants to explore this as much as I do, but her fear is weighing her down. I understand that all too well.

Before I can tell her more and make an attempt at phone sex – because I will take *anything* she'll give me right now – my phone beeps to tell me I have another incoming call.

Callista.

As much as I want to ignore the call, I know it's better for everyone if I just answer it.

"Sienna, hold on one second, Callista's calling me. I'll make it quick. Don't hang up."

I switch lines.

"Callista," I say by way of greeting. It comes out short and in light of everything I've recently learned, I try to soften my tone. "What can I do for you?"

"Noah," she says in a clipped tone. "I just wanted to let you know the organizer of the meet and greet has requested you specifically. He's threatening to cancel and tell the radio station that you refused to show up, which won't look good since it's a meet and greet at the adolescent cancer center."

Shit.

"Tell him I'll be there. Anything else?"

"Yeah, I've booked another photo shoot for updated promo photos for your next single."

"Callista, we don't have a single ready to release."

Because I still can't hear the music . . . unless I'm around Sienna.

"Then you'd better get on that, fast. Apex Records wants to drop one within the next six weeks to start building hype for the next album. You can play it during your encore to gauge fan reaction."

Six weeks? Has she lost her mind?

My temper is rising at an alarming rate and this time I'm afraid I'm going to need more than just some meditation to calm my ass down.

"Look, I appreciate that you're the owner's daughter but you're here in a capacity to help manage our tour. Leave the record producing to me and your father. Our contract states we don't have to release a single for another eight months."

I know because there is a running countdown widget on my phone's home screen that serves as a constant reminder I've got a lot of work to do on the song Sienna and I started and not a lot of time in which to get it done.

"About that," she starts, and I feel my stomach lurch to my throat. "Daddy dearest just got busted with his mistress for the last time. My mother has threatened to take him for everything. To make it a less messy affair for everyone, he negotiated that he'll step down and hand Apex Records over to me, give my mother one lump sum, and then run off with his barely-legal dream-girl. Obviously, my mother took the deal. There's no love lost there."

I'm still processing when she says, "I'm your new boss, Kinkaid."

Chapter 20

Sienna

Noah never comes back on the line.

In the meantime, Josh sends a follow-up text, forcing a response from me since I never sent any of the responses that Noah typed.

JOSH

So . . . dinner?

SIENNA

Josh, that's really sweet. But I've actually started seeing someone.

JOSH

On the road?

In the four weeks since I last saw you?

How does that work?

His rapid fire responses make me regret the lie immediately. *This is why you always tell the truth, dummy.*

I texted the lie before I had a chance to really think it through. The only time Josh has ever left me alone was when I was with Brad. Granted, he harassed the shit out of Brad – and for good reason – but still, he left me alone. His probing questions anger me though because I can't answer them.

I don't know how it would work, because it's not actually happening. I plug my phone in to charge, leaving him without a response, and go hang out with the girls who are playing some kind of card game up in the front of the bus.

"So, what did you and Mr. Kinkaid get into back there?" Joslyn asks in a teasing tone. I've kept to myself the past hour, and I know they're all dying for details.

My actions with Noah could have significant ramifications for all the girls because our performance depends on all four of us, and we're a solid unit. I feel selfish for crossing a line with him and risking everything for everyone.

"Well, let's see." When I start talking, the girls immediately fall still and silent. "First, I gave him a shoulder massage, then he kissed me, then I rode him like a cowgirl at the rodeo. I was just about to get his pants off when Bri warned us that Callista was coming." I just throw it all out there as I look at the cards in my hands, pretending that everything about what I just said is completely normal.

Kara spits her Sprite out on the table, soaking the cards. Joslyn's mouth is hanging open, and Bri keeps a straight face, unfazed, as she says, "Atta girl."

Understandably, they want details and have a million questions. I answer them as honestly as I can and apologize to them for getting so close to breaking the contract. They seem to think that Matt would never fire any of us at this point because we've created so much positive press for the tour, but I'm not convinced. He was pretty clear about the rules up front.

An hour later, we pull up to the hotel in San Diego and somehow, I'm exhausted from riding on the bus all day. I can smell the ocean as soon as I disembark, and I pull the briny scent deep into my lungs.

There are fans here holding up signs, cell phones, and stuffed animals. They're yelling, screaming, and trying their best to get the guys' attention.

This isn't unusual.

It's been like this the last couple of times we've stayed in hotels, but it's definitely getting worse.

I try to catch Noah's eye as he gets off the bus, but he has his hood pulled up over his head and his head is down, flanked by Romeo and Juan as he heads inside while people rip at his sweatshirt.

Brett stops to sign a couple of things, but even he looks pissed.

What the hell happened during that phone call Noah never returned from?

I loop my arm with Bri's. "Do the guys look pissed to you?"

She surveys Sloan and Brett, the only ones we can now see from where we are. "They don't look happy to be surrounded by all that willing pussy . . . that's strange for sure."

We ride up to the penthouses separately from the guys. Kara and Jos are lost in TikTok videos as we rise to the top floor. Their giggles make me smile, but it's short-lived.

I feel restless not knowing what's going on, so I throw my stuff down in my room and send Noah another text. Thankfully he answers immediately.

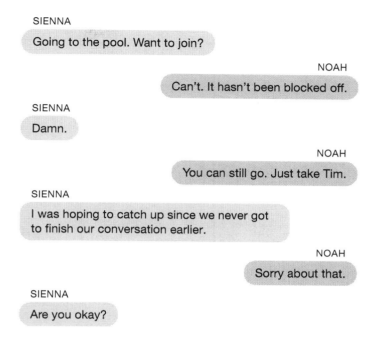

SIENNA
Going to the pool. Want to join?

NOAH
Can't. It hasn't been blocked off.

SIENNA
Damn.

NOAH
You can still go. Just take Tim.

SIENNA
I was hoping to catch up since we never got to finish our conversation earlier.

NOAH
Sorry about that.

SIENNA
Are you okay?

I ask him the same question he asks me on repeat. I'm learning it's more than just *are you okay.*

It's a plea. *Talk to me.*

It's a reminder. *I'm listening.*

It's a promise. *You're not alone.*

My phone rings a second later.

"Can you come down here?" Noah asks, causing my thighs to clench together as memories of what we did the last time we were together float around in my head.

"Yeah, let me grab a quick shower, and I'll head over."

After completing a shower in record time, I throw on my favorite pair of gray cotton shorts and a black tank top with a built -in bra. Hair still wet, I creep down the hallway, staying as quiet as possible because announcing my presence at Noah's front door to everyone on this floor just seems like a bad idea right now.

I knock gently and glance furtively around the hallway as I wait.

Sloan answers the door and of course, he's shirtless. I swear these guys can't keep their clothes on to save their lives.

"Oh, uh, hey Sloan."

"Sienna," he smirks knowingly and runs a hand across his chest, the light from the nearby lamp glinting off his dog tags. "See something you like?"

At that exact moment, Noah comes walking barefoot around the corner into the living room. His light blue t-shirt a stark contrast to the black one he was wearing earlier, and my eyes drink him in hungrily, but it's too late.

He's already seen me eyeing Sloan and his brow creases together before his features return to neutral.

I came here to put his fire of rage *out*, not stoke it, so I smile sweetly at Sloan and say loudly enough for Noah to hear, "As a matter of fact I do." I cut my eyes to Noah and point to him with a nod of my head. "It's over there," I tease with enough sincerity that if Sloan didn't know how I felt about Noah before, he definitely does now.

Noah's face brightens slightly at the same time Sloan says, "Ouch," and grabs his bare chest. "That cut deep, Sienna."

"Did it though?" I ask, mocking him because I know he's been with at least four women so far on this tour.

He chuckles and closes the door before walking through the large kitchen and into one of the other rooms in the penthouse, leaving Noah and me alone.

Noah is on me in two strides, grabbing my hand and pulling me through a doorway tucked into the corner of the suite's living room. Once we're through, he pushes the door shut and cages me in against it.

Being this close to Noah is like being sucked into a tornado. It's disorienting and dangerous and beautiful all at the same time.

His right hand slides to my hip as he dips his mouth to my ear.

"I can't stop this."

He pulls back to look at me, his request for permission written clearly on his beautiful face.

I should say no.

I should leave.

I should be the stronger one. At least until this tour is over.

But I can't.

Not when he's everything I never knew I needed in my life.

"We can't get caught," I tell him as a way of saying *yes,* while my hands trail up his sides and wrap around his back.

Giving in never felt so damn good.

"I know," he mumbles as his tongue traces my bottom lip. "Callista's on a call with Matt, and she's already been by to remind me of the schedule for tomorrow, so I don't expect her again tonight," he says, answering my unspoken question. "Which reminds me, I can't go surfing."

I figured as much, but it was a nice dream. I nod my understanding but immediately ask my next question. "What about the guys?"

"Ryan and Sloan know. I haven't had a chance to tell Brett yet, but with the other two on board, I'm hoping he won't care. It's not like we didn't try to avoid this." He dips down and gently bites my lips before kissing them. "Goddamn. Your lips have had me fucked up ever since we met, Sienna. Tell me you want this. Say it out loud," he begs, nearly unraveling me.

I expect to wake up from this blissful dream any minute.

"How about I *show* you how much I want it?" I taunt, not sure where this boldness is coming from as I stare at the face of the most beautiful man on the planet. I trace his jawline with kisses of my own before turning my attention to his soft lips. I feel his smile as I kiss the corner of his mouth.

"Sienna, you're killing me." He groans at the same time I let out a whimper of desire. His voice will be the end of me. Or maybe it's the beginning of me? All I know is, I don't want it to ever stop.

My mental mind-fucks have never been about my looks. I've always been comfortable with my face and my body – not that I ever dreamed I was in the same league as Noah Kinkaid, but I've never lacked confidence in my appearance. No, my wounds and insecurities have been of the emotional and mental varieties ever since I was old enough to feel my mother's growing resentment.

And that's what plagues me now in this emotionally and sexually charged interaction.

Being able to sense my hesitancy and read my mind, Noah cups my face. "You're not going to get anyone in trouble. No one's going to be mad if you do something for yourself, Sienna. And if they are, they'll have to deal with me. This is just between us."

The fire of passion goes out a little as my reality slams into me. Always choosing honesty, I grip Noah tighter as my legs struggle to hold me up and words come spilling out of my mouth.

"I can't do this—" I get choked up before I can finish thinking about the consequences my actions could have. Not just for me, but the girls as well, and although that weighs heavily on me, it's not the *only* thing causing me to hesitate.

Noah backs up, dropping his hand from my face to my wrist, and leads me to sit on the massive king-sized bed. He pulls the desk chair over and sits down facing me.

"Breathe, Sienna." His thumb grazes my cheek, and I shudder.

"It's hard to breathe when you're touching me like that."

"So, you *do* feel this?" he asks, a little uncertain and a little relieved.

"*This* as in the overwhelming desire to be near you constantly and feel you against me? Or *this* as in the visceral need to protect you and know you're happy and healthy? Either way, yeah, I feel *this*." I admit, staring at his knee which is in between my thighs so that his chair is as close to me as possible.

"Then what's holding you back?"

I wet my lips, and his breathing turns ragged.

"I can't do sex with no strings attached, Noah. I thought I could, for you, because *fuck me,* I want this . . . but I'm going to end up crushed. And when you've had your fill, and I have to finish this tour and pretend like it was just fun while it lasted, it'll kill me and it will affect my perform—"

"Who the fuck said I didn't want any strings attached?" he asks, almost angry, definitely bewildered.

I stare at him with wide eyes in disbelief. Is he saying he wants to *date* me?

He clenches his jaw at my response but leans forward and tucks my hair behind my ear.

"I haven't adjusted well to the fame, Sienna. You asked me about my demons earlier, but I wasn't sure how to answer because how fucked up is it that my most desired dreams and my worst nightmares are the same thing? The guys are all living their best lives, but they don't quite understand why it's different for me. Yes, we're a team, all needed for the overall success of the band, but they can choose to fade into the background when they need a break. I can't. The success is incredible, but the only time

I don't feel like I'm drowning is when I'm with you. So, no, this isn't a hook-up and then move on situation. And for the record, in case you haven't noticed, that's not really my style anyway."

I feel the exact moment my heart breaks the rest of the way for the man in front of me. Launching off the bed, I crawl into his lap, right in the desk chair, my arms around his neck, wanting to do anything to alleviate the pressure he feels and apologize for allowing my own insecurities to coerce me into making assumptions about his character I know aren't true.

It's suddenly clear how and why so many stars end up on drugs or battling alcohol or other addictions. This lifestyle can be so oppressive with no offer of escape so they try to find one any way they can.

I pull back to search his eyes.

"How are you managing your stress currently?" I ask, knowing he won't lie to me and wondering if he's been harboring dangerous secrets. We'll circle back around to he and I in a minute.

"I haven't been managing it. That's why I'm so angry all the time, and I'm not sleeping well. It's also why I'm having trouble writing new music and hearing the notes I want."

He goes on to tell me about Callista being his new boss at the record label as well as her history with the band.

"We just aren't sure if she knows it was us that cut down her demo. We tried to wrack our brains and see if there were any other interactions, negative or positive, that we could remember but we came up with nothing. Seeing no way out of our current contract, we're all just hoping the past is water under the bridge. She certainly has a lot to lose now which could make her dangerous, but luckily, we're her biggest revenue generator."

An idea strikes me, but I don't want to bring Josh up right now. That can wait.

"Noah," I start and then grow shy and quiet.

"Don't hide from me, Si. What were you going to say?"

He rubs his hand back and forth on my thigh giving me strength to finally ask, "What if this ends poorly?"

He thinks about it for a few seconds before answering. "If we decide this isn't going like we'd hoped, I'll still respect you as a performer and a member of this team. I'll keep our business private and do my best to give you space if you decide that's what you want."

Well, damn.

That was a good answer.

But it also makes me sad to think about the end when we haven't even really had the beginning.

Sensing my struggle - because apparently Noah and I operate on the same wavelength at all times - he raises my chin so my eyes meet his. "But I'm pretty sure this is going to be as good as we think it'll be."

And just like that, I'm all in.

Chapter 21

Noah

I'm not sure which part of what I said finally convinced her to let go and give this a try, but in a heartbeat, my reserved, considerate, hesitant dancer threw herself at me as if she wanted to climb into my soul and heal me from the inside out.

I grab her ass and hold her against me as I stand up and move us from the chair to the bed six inches in front of us. Her rapid, shallow breaths remind me she hasn't done this in a while, and I need to slow down.

It hasn't been a recent act for me either, but certainly more recent than three years. I splay my hand across her stomach under her shirt as she reaches for the button on my jeans, her knees on either side of my hips.

"Not yet, Sienna. I want to savor this." I pull her hands away from me in a vice grip and pin them to her sides. "I won't last more than three seconds if you touch me right now."

"Can't you savor it once you're inside me?" she asks impatiently. Now that she's made her decision, she's clawing at me like a woman possessed, no hesitancy in her movements at all.

"I won't have a single coherent thought once I'm inside you," I admit, trailing the underside of her breasts with my fingertips, quickly realizing she isn't wearing a bra as her back arches and she pushes herself into my hand.

She returns the favor and slips her free hands under my own shirt and starts to lift.

"You're so warm," she observes.

I roll us so I'm on top of her and reach behind me to pull my shirt over my head, trying to watch her eyes as they watch me.

"Fuck, that never gets old," she says, mesmerized, causing me to smile.

"I'm glad you like it."

I lean forward to inhale her vanilla scent and nuzzle her neck before trailing kisses to the neckline of her tank top, reaching down to pull it up so I can slide it over her head. I throw a quick glance over my shoulder, relieved when I see that I remembered to lock the door. I hear Sloan plucking away at the acoustic somewhere in the suite, and I feel an over-whelming sense of peace.

Flinging her tank top to the ground, I groan when she's in nothing but her shorts beneath me. Once those come off, there's no turning back, and I feel myself prepare to take a flying leap off the proverbial cliff of Sienna Kennedy.

She reaches for the button on my jeans again and this time, I don't stop her.

"Get them off," she whispers desperately, causing me to hop off the bed and yank them down in two seconds flat before returning to my perch on top of her, boxers still in place.

Slow and gentle, Kinkaid.

She pushes her hips up in to me as she arches her back once more. God, she's the most glorious thing I've ever seen. Her red hair is spilled on the pillow under her head, and it looks like she's mocking my flames of desire. My mind flashes with images of how I can bend her and twist her into positions that will drive us both wild.

She scrapes her nails down my abs and whimpers, "Noah, please."

"What do you want, baby?"

"You know what I want."

"I want to hear you say it."

Because truthfully, she could want anything, and I want to give her exactly what she wants. But then a thought occurs to me . . . maybe she doesn't know what she wants? Three years is a long time, not to mention she's only been with one guy. Who didn't even have the decency to fuck this beautiful creature against a wall.

"I want you inside me," she finally says.

Although I can take a wild guess at what she means, it's not detailed enough.

"Which part of me, Sienna? My fingers? My tongue? My cock?"

"Um, all of it," she says shyly, looking away from me.

This is going to be fun.

I've kept her thighs trapped together with my knees planted on the outsides of them, but now, I slide her shorts down her legs and throw them on the floor, nudging her legs wider and repositioning myself in between them.

Her resulting moan makes me pause and find the Bluetooth connection to the speakers in the corner of the room.

Her sounds are for my ears only.

I'd hate to have to maim my best friends for knowing what she sounds like when she comes. Because she's about to do that . . . a lot.

Once I'm satisfied that although they can guess what's happening, they can't *hear* it, I stretch my body out along hers and trail my fingers over her hip bone, across her thigh, and toward her center.

I can already tell she's fucking *soaked* because it's dripped onto the inside of her thigh.

Running my finger through it, I ask, "Is all this for me?" I can't keep the pride out of my voice because I know damn well it is.

It's not like I haven't made a woman wet before. Hell, I make thousands of them wet every night we perform, but there's a big difference when it isn't my stage presence that gets them off. It's just . . . me.

Sienna's seen more of me than anyone has since Nicole – and I regret ever sharing myself with that spiteful bitch - but I know I've chosen wisely this time.

I slip my fingers under Sienna's panties from the side and pull them down.

There is no doubt that the resulting groan that erupts from *my* throat can be heard through the walls regardless of what I have playing through the speakers.

"Holy shit, you're beautiful." I put my middle finger in my mouth and watch as her pupils dilate before I slip that same finger into her waiting pussy. She clenches down and I almost come from imagining this pressure on my swollen dick, which is currently trying his best to punch his way out of my boxers. I run a hand across it, trying to alleviate the growing pressure, but Sienna eyes the movement hungrily.

"Let me."

"Baby, I can't. Not yet." I move to her side and lay down next to her, allowing for a better angle for my working fingers.

When her face falls, I explain, forgetting that she doesn't have a ton of experience.

"I just meant, if you touch me right now, I'm going to explode, and I have other things I want to accomplish first. But we'll get there. Before this night is over, I promise you can touch me wherever you want."

Momentarily appeased, she relaxes her hands and gives in to my fingers as I push a second one inside her. She has the tightest pussy I've ever felt. I have to work hard not to push my hips forward into her side as I'm propped up on one elbow looking down at her gorgeous face. A light sheen of perspiration is coating her skin as I slowly pump my fingers in and out.

When she starts to tense, I withdraw my finger.

Her eyes flash open. "Noah!" she whines. "Put that back right now."

She's so damn sexy with those lips of hers.

"I'm going to replace it with something better."

I slide down the bed, exceedingly careful not to let my cock drag down the mattress because I swear the slightest amount of pressure and my orgasm is going to rip through me like a thousand-horse stampede.

Having her naked before me erases all other thoughts from my mind. Her eyes connect to mine, and I see the trust and awe in them.

It's fucking humbling.

More so than hearing thousands of people chant my name.

One swipe of my tongue, and I know I'm done for.

"Sienna, you taste like a fucking cupcake."

Vanilla. Just like I knew she would.

I try to go slow, but I've lost all sense of speed, direction, time, place, my name, everything. I reach over the top of her thighs to draw her down in to my face as I move my head from side to side, trying to burrow as far as I can inside her.

When I feel her hands in my hair and her muscles squeeze, I know I've found a spot she likes. Which she confirms a second later.

"Noah," she pauses, but continues when instead of stopping, I keep eating. "Noah, I'm gonna come."

That's the goal, sweetheart.

I don't dare take my mouth away to say that out loud though. Instead, I slip one finger back inside her as I continue to eat the most delicious dessert I've ever tasted.

She shatters as I curl that finger and graze her clit with my teeth at the same time, her hands holding me to her as she rides her orgasm out on my face.

I can't breathe, but I also can't think of a better way to die.

When she finally stops writhing and releases her pressure on the back of my head, I lick my lips and assess her to make sure she's okay.

"What the actual fuck was that?" she asks with her eyes closed.

I'm not sure how to answer her as my own insecurities creep in. *Was it not good?*

"I think it was an orgasm," I say, hesitantly.

After an eternity, she peeks one eye open and laughs. "No, I've had an orgasm before, Noah. *That* was something in a whole different league. It needs a different name because that was fucking life changing. Is that what it's supposed to feel like all the time? Because I've definitely never felt *that*," she rambles, sitting up on her elbows.

I can't keep the grin off my face. I guess her ex-boyfriend didn't bother to find her G-spot either.

"I'm glad you approve." The smugness in my voice is present even to my own ears.

She stretches her arms over her head, and I love how comfortable she is with her body. Reaching for me again, I see the heat in her eyes.

"My turn," she says with a wicked grin.

I open my mouth to stop her. Although I want her mouth

on me, it isn't tit-for-tat. I didn't just lose myself in her pussy solely because I want her lips around me, but she cuts me off before I can even get a word out.

"Noah James Kinkaid, if you tell me *no* right now, I'm going to walk my naked ass out into that living room and make your bandmates tie you down until you give me what I want."

Well, if she's going to put it like that . . .

Wait.

I feel the corners of my mouth tick up into a smile. "How do you know my middle name?" I ask, even though I know *exactly* how she knows.

Her cheeks flame red as she looks away from me. Grabbing her chin, I pull her face back to mine. "You Googled me, didn't you?" I tease.

"Not recently," she admits with a coy smile.

"What classifies as *not recently?*" I ask, curious to know how long she's been invested.

"Um, like two years ago? When Bri first introduced me to your music and the genre as a whole."

If it were anyone else, I'd be annoyed, but with Sienna, I find it endearing that at some point, *two years ago*, she wanted to know more about me. Putting us both out of our misery, I finally get back on track. "Where do you want me?"

"Stand up," she orders. I'm rewarded with a smile when I do so. She slides my boxers to the floor and inhales sharply, causing me to smile wider and stifle a chuckle.

Mimicking Sloan's earlier words, I smirk, "See something you like?"

"Mm hmm," she hums, never taking her eyes off my aching cock.

I'm all proud and shit until she drops to her knees and pulls me in her mouth, causing me to sway and almost lose my balance. I throw my left hand out and catch myself on the edge of the bed, and it's her turn to smile.

Squeezing me with one hand, she wraps her other around my thigh and takes me deeper down her throat.

Fuck, I'm already there.

"Sienna," her name comes out as a whisper as I try to draw away from her, but she's relentless. "Sienna," I say again, stronger this time. "I'm going to come, and I really want to be inside you for that."

She nods as I pull her to her feet, unable to keep with the slow pace. I'm fucking desperate for her. Not to mention I've been primed for what feels like an eternity, and no matter how many times I used my hand to jerk myself off to images of her in my head, it's something else entirely when it's *her* mouth, and I can't do anything to help how fast I'm going to blow this load.

Knowing I might hurt her if I'm on top, I grab her under her ass and lift her, wrapping her legs around my waist. I sit back down on the bed and pull her backwards with me until I'm sitting with my back against the headboard and she's sitting up on her knees.

"Shit, I need to grab a condom out of my bag." I grab her hips, ready to move her off me when she shakes her head.

"I know you guys have to get tested every month and thanks to Matt's contract, I'm on birth control so . . . " she trails off, after dropping the bomb she wants me to fuck her bare.

Taken aback, I choose my next words carefully. "I've never actually done that with anyone," I admit. "It sounds kind of boy-scoutish when I say it out loud, but I'm saving that for the woman I marry one day."

I watch as her face falls, unable to believe I'm actually saying no to fucking her without a condom.

"I know it seems odd," I continue, needing her to understand, "but it's the one thing I can still offer my future wife. Being celibate wasn't really in my cards, but I've always made sure I was sheathed, saving that for the woman who won't get any of my other sexual firsts."

Sienna recovers quickly while trying to hide her disappointment.

"Yeah, sure. Of course. That's really sweet of you, actually." Her words are encouraging, but her face betrays her true emotions.

"Hey," I trail kisses up her neck as I try harder to explain, begging her to understand. "It's just like the last physical piece of myself I have to give, you know? I'm not saying no forever, just for right now." I'm terrified I've ruined the moment, but honestly, I didn't expect her to want that. "This is already turning into more than I've ever felt for someone," I confess.

It's a strong statement but a true one. She can't do this with no strings attached, and now she knows I need *all* the strings attached before I can give in to her request.

She nods, wearing a small smile, and I quickly grab a condom, surprised I'm still hard after that conversational detour.

Returning to my spot on the bed, she straddles my lap, her knees bent underneath her. I place my hands on her waist to offer support, briefly forgetting I'm about to fuck an acrobat, and she doesn't need any support from me.

She slowly spreads her knees and sinks down on me causing all the air to leave my lungs. Even though I have a condom in place, I can feel how warm, tight, and wet she is right through it and my hips buck up involuntarily.

"Oh . . . *fuck* . . . *Sienna* . . . *shit.*" My words come out as an incoherent train of cusswords spoken like praises and unintelligible grunts.

And then she starts moving.

Chapter 22

Sienna

I totally respect Noah's decision to reserve something for his future wife even if it feels like a punch right to my solar plexus. I try hard to school my features and not let my disapproval show at the thought of someone other than me touching him, sharing this life with him, being the woman he greets backstage after a show with that satisfied, tired, smile.

Feelings are complicated in general, but with Noah, I know it can get messy fast. As a singer and songwriter, he mentioned before that emotions are his language. He – like most artists – seems to feel every emotion more intensely than say, those with a mind for law, accounting, or something else rooted in the factual world, and I've found it far easier to be myself and bare my soul around him than I thought I would.

His staccato moans pull me back to here and now and although it's too soon to make any more declarations, I lower myself on to him and try to show him how I feel.

Gripping the headboard for leverage, I move slowly up and down, thankful he let me be on top so I can control the angle and speed. For such a lean guy, he packs quite a punch below his belt.

I smile when I feel his fingers dig into my hips, and I add forward and backward motions to the up and down, creating a circle. It's unbelievable how natural everything feels with him. I lay back in a full saddle position with my knees still tucked under me and my back lying flat on his outstretched legs. Because this position doesn't stress me physically, I can still roll my hips to create friction, tugging on him harder inside me.

"Oh my god, Sienna. That feels so good, baby . . . and that *view . . . fuck,*" Noah rasps, his voice strained, his hands splayed over my stomach and hips, pushing me down as he pushes himself up into me.

He makes it about three minutes like that before he pulls me upright, and flips us again, this time with him on top. Rolling me over onto my stomach, he asks, "Can you reach your ankles?"

I arch back, reaching for my ankles over my head. With my knees spread wide and my pelvis pushing into the mattress, I easily grasp my ankles and point my toes as they come to rest next to my shoulders.

"Like this?"

"Oh my god. Uh, yeah . . . that's . . . uh, that's good."

I feel the mattress shift and expect to feel him enter me again but instead, I feel his tongue. I'm splayed wide open, and my guess is his past partners probably couldn't give him this kind of access. Between swipes of his tongue and nips from his teeth, he lets me know how much he likes this.

"Can we do this every day?" *Lick.* "I'll never get over this." *Lick.* "You're incredible." *Bite.* "This pussy belongs to me."

The possessiveness in his last statement gets me and I come, hard, letting go of my ankles and finally allowing my spine to flex as my body gives in to the pleasure. Once I can find my words again, I praise his skill.

"Holy shit, Noah. In case no one's mentioned it, your oral talents go far beyond your singing voice."

He ignores my compliment and rolls me onto my back. When I see his eyes, it's clear he's about to fuck the soul out of me.

"Si, I can't hold back anymore. I promise I'll last longer the second round . . . I think," he adds with a dark chuckle. "Tell me if I hurt you, okay?"

I nod, ready for whatever he wants to give me and grip his broad shoulders, holding on as he slams into me with no further warning.

"Can you put your right leg over my shoulder?" he asks, forgetting how his last question turned out.

"No problem," I smile as I effortlessly sweep my right leg out to the side before bringing it up by my head and grabbing my ankle with my right hand while dragging the nails of my left hand down his back. "How's this?"

His eyes are wide as he nods furiously. "Okay, I have to stop asking stupid questions," he says, seriously, which makes me giggle.

He swallows hard and pushes inside of me repeatedly and forcefully, driving me up toward the headboard. I feel his hand on the top of my head just in case I make it that far.

"Fuck, your pussy's tight, Sienna. I'm gonna be unconscious after this."

My breathing is shallow, and I feel him swell inside me as he keeps talking.

"I want you to come all over my dick, baby. I want you to still be able to feel me while we're on stage tomorrow. I want your pussy sore and screaming my name as loud as I'm screaming into that mic."

The only partner I've ever had didn't talk during sex. He sure as hell didn't reference my pussy. Noah's words alone could get me off.

"Come on baby, I need you with me."

No sooner do the words leave his mouth than I feel him start to jerk inside me. That's all it takes to send me plummeting after him and his name tears out of my mouth so loudly, I probably woke those three floors below us.

Noah claps a hand gently over my mouth, and I feel his chest vibrating with silent laughter.

I want to lay here forever, sated and wrapped in his arms, covered in sweat, but he kisses my cheek and whispers, "Don't move. I'll be right back."

I watch as he walks to the ensuite and cleans up before slipping his boxers back on. I arch an eyebrow at him. I know he didn't put those on for my benefit.

"I'm going to grab some water," he rasps. "Would you like anything?"

"Water sounds good."

When he slips out the door, he's greeted by a round of applause, and I cover my face with the closest pillow in embarrassment even though I'm in the room alone.

Guess I was as loud as I thought I was.

Another second goes by, and I hear voices arguing. I throw the covers off, grab a hotel robe from the bathroom and press my ear to the door.

"I can't believe you'd be that selfish," Brett says.

All the guys' voices are distinguishable. Brett's is the highest and always sounds like he has a sore throat because it's raspy, probably from the cigarettes. Ryan's is by far the deepest. Sloan's is the closest to Noah's but no one can match Noah's tone of perfection.

"B, chill out, man. When does Kinky ever broadcast his business? So he fucked her, who cares?" Sloan says, trying to be reasonable while I wince as he makes it sound like I was just a way for Noah to get off.

"I care. It's in the fucking contract, and we need them, dude. They're half our show at this point," Brett argues. "Not to mention, after the fiasco at the gas station, Callista's probably looking for any reason to fuck our shit up, and you're going to hand it to her on a silver fucking platter."

"No one's going to find out, Brett. This thing between Sienna and I is just for us. She's not going to say anything because she wants to keep her job and she's not some groupie in it for the bragging rights," Noah says, defending me, somehow still in a calm voice.

"Well, hell, if Kinkaid can do it, why don't we all fuck the dancers?" Brett fires sarcastically.

It's Sloan who points out what's really going on first. "Oh, right. You're pissed because Noah beat you to it. You've had your eye on Bri from day one."

"Yeah, and I haven't fucking touched her because it could fuck us all over!" Brett starts to shout causing Noah's temper to flare again even though his voice is eerily calm and quiet.

"Brett, tell me, how many radio interviews do you give? How many people do you interact with on that stage? How many fucking podcasts and journalists are reporting on your every move, every mistake, every choice, including the stuff you try to keep out of the press, and it just makes them discuss it more? None! Because unless you're the front man, you fade into the fucking background, able to live life how you want. You can *choose* to be in the spotlight or not, but me? They choose for me. So yeah, I did something for myself for once—"

"But that's just *it*, Noah! That *is* the role you play so

someone *is* going to find out you're banging Sienna. And fuck you for thinking the rest of us aren't as important because we don't sing the goddamn songs."

I recoil from the door. How can Brett not know the nerve he just tapped on?

Or perhaps he does, and that's why he said it.

"Guys, we need to take it down a notch before someone says something fucking stupid. We have a show in less than twelve hours, and we can't take this shit on stage," I hear Ryan say as a lump forms in the back of my throat.

I've done it again.

It's like the universe will do anything to keep me from playing the violin. I know it sounds ridiculous, but that's the way it feels, even if Noah is an adult who makes his own choices. Every time I drag the bow across the strings, someone I care deeply about gets hurt.

I've spent enough years of my life throwing a pity party, so I can at least check that box off and move on to the next phase which is a plan.

Too embarrassed to go out there now, I'll wait for Noah to come back and then tell him that we can't do this.

At least not until the tour is over.

I don't have to wait long before a door slams somewhere in the suite and I hear Ryan's deep voice once more as Noah's footsteps get closer to my door. "Noah," Ryan pauses and I realize I've never heard him call Noah by his first name. "Is she worth this?"

Noah's words take me by surprise. "Yeah, Ry. I think she is."

"Then we'll figure this out."

When the door to Noah's room opens, I don't move. I don't try to pretend like I didn't hear anything.

Clutching the robe together with one hand, I take the glass of water Noah offers with the other. His hand moves to my lower back, and I feel him guiding me back toward the bed.

While I've always prided myself on telling the truth, I've never been great at hard conversations – mostly because I'm afraid I'll hurt someone's feelings. I just want to take all the blame, ease all the tension, and move on quickly. I always start patching up the hole before allowing myself to bleed and make sure all the poison is gone. Which means whatever is left behind festers, causing infection and ruining the relationship for good.

"Noah," I start, fighting the building emotion in my voice, "I would never ask you to choose between me and the band. Making music is your passion, and you're amazing at it. Let's just put this behind us and continue the tour, okay? You guys can't be fighting like this, and Brett's right. Someone will find out."

My usual M.O. strikes again.

The look he gives shatters me as realization dawns . . . I've fallen *hard* for Noah Kinkaid.

"Is that what you want?" he asks.

I should tell him *yes* so he can focus on the band and the tour, but I'm tired of the cycle I perpetuate for myself. The same cycle I encouraged with my parents, with Josh, with Brad . . . I can't allow myself to sabotage this chance with Noah by trying to pretend it never happened and moving on, shoving all these thoughts and feelings in some imaginary storage container in my head.

This isn't just on me. This is on *us*.

"Of course not. What I *want* is to do everything we just did, repeatedly. To continue to get to know you and work with you. But I've never been fortunate enough to have my cake and eat it too, and we still have six months left. You have an obligation to the guys, and I have an obligation to the girls . . . *and* the guys."

"But what about our obligation to ourselves?" he asks, slipping his hand inside my robe to encircle my waist and draw me against himself.

Fuck that's distracting.

Before I can remember what words are, he continues, "Sienna, the only time I can draw a deep breath is when I'm near you. I'm so stressed the music has completely disappeared from my mind unless I'm around you. It's like the notes in my head have transferred themselves to you and the only way I can get them back is when we're together. Aside from the guys, you're the only person who sees *me*. I don't take that lightly because I know how easy it is to get caught up in the lights. I just like talking to you, and I feel the distance between us like a tangible thing when we're not together."

I feel the look of shock warp my features as my eyes widen and my lips part.

"All I'm saying is don't make me give you up before we have a chance to see what this is. The guys will be okay. I'll talk to Brett in the morning."

"You have two interviews and an extra meet and greet tomorrow," I remind him.

"Fuck. You're right." He blows out a heavy sigh. "Then I'd better go talk to him now. Will you stay?"

What else can I do? The walk of shame does not sound appealing, and it's not like I'll sleep if I go back to my room anyway.

I nod, and he pulls back the covers, hands me the remote to the TV and kisses my forehead. When he goes to stand up, I catch his wrist and pull him back down and give him a real kiss.

A lasting kiss. I want him to be able to taste me as he talks to Brett so he remembers I'm in his corner.

If he's willing to fight for this, then so am I.

Chapter 23

Noah

The talk with Brett didn't go as well as I'd hoped, and I got the distinct impression that something else is going on. I told him he could sleep with Bri, and we'd deal with the consequences because she's pretty obviously into him too, but it didn't appease him. He just seemed to get more pissed off. Even after I apologized for making it sound like I thought I was more important than the other guys.

I *don't* think that, it's just *different*.

But I didn't get through to him. I finally left after his fifth "fuck off", figuring I wasn't helping by forcing myself on him.

I didn't want to risk being caught with Sienna in my room, especially with Brett being so stubborn because I realized I don't trust him enough right now to not say anything. I kissed her hard and tried to reassure her and promised to check in as often as I could tomorrow. I apologized for having to bail on our surfing lessons and then said goodnight and spent the night with my arms wrapped around the pillow trying to inhale any remnant of her scent left behind.

Clutching my coffee in my hands this morning, I'm

thankful for my hoodie as the crisp San Diego air smacks me in the face just outside the hotel entrance.

I'm on my own for the interviews today since Ryan was asked to collaborate on a song with another band that happens to be based here, and is spending the morning working on that.

I didn't mind having to leave before everyone else though. With Brett acting the way he is, I know the other two feel caught in the middle, and I was glad for some space.

At least I was, until Callista tried to climb in the back seat of the Cadillac with me. I gave her a stern look and pointed out that Romeo sits in the back. I argued that I didn't want press overreacting if they caught photos of she and I getting out of the back of the vehicle together. Shockingly, instead of arguing, she moved up front, and I smiled as Romeo silently slid into the seat next to me, giving me a fist bump out of her line of sight.

"Okay, Noah, you've got twenty minutes to record the interview. They can choose to play it back on their station however they want, but we have to be across town for a podcast appearance by ten."

Most of the time, I can do podcast interviews from the house, and they just splice the screen for viewers and link the audio for the listeners so it seems like they're just listening to a phone call, but today, I'm onsite for the podcast because this guy has a crazy set up and like four million followers. Since he's local, it was decided we should just be in the same room.

I start to tune Callista out when she says, "I've gone ahead and extended the meet and greet until three to get more face-time with the local press, and we'll go straight to the arena from the hospital."

"Where's my down time?" I bark. "Good thing I don't need any energy left for the show tonight."

I hope she chokes on my sarcasm.

"This is the life of a successful musician, Noah. Get used to it," she snaps. "There's a charity event in a couple of weeks you're attending as well. All four of you. And I've blocked studio time for you to get to work on your single. From L.A., we're flying to Seattle, and then you'll have a week off."

My head is spinning.

"Seattle?" I still know enough about the tour schedule to know Seattle isn't until later.

"The response to ticket sales was overwhelming and the venue operator asked if we'd be willing to do two shows. You don't turn down money like that. So, we're playing them right before the week off, and we'll play them again at the regularly scheduled time."

"*We* aren't playing anything. The *guys and I* play the shows. And you need to run these additions by us. We didn't agree to the extra night, and I can't guarantee we can make that happen. Someone might have plans already," I argue.

"Do I need to remind you I now own your record label? Which means I own *you*, Noah. All of you. So, play by my rules, or you'll find your career over just as it's getting started," she threatens.

I fire off a text to the guys and include Matt.

NOAH

Callista is threatening us if we don't follow her every command now that she's about to be the owner of Apex.

I want a meeting with our attorney and I want it now.

RYAN

What else does she want? We're doing as much as we can.

MATT

I'm looking into it, but please don't push her until I know more.

SLOAN

This is bullshit.

BRETT

There's a lot of that going around recently.

MATT

Maxwell, your attorney won't help you.

NOAH

Why?

(Also, *middle finger* Brett)

MATT

He's in-house counsel for Apex.

NOAH

Again, conflict of ducking interest

FUCKING

MATT

Big time COI, but they get around it by having two – one for them and one for artist representation. But don't be fooled, they're fed out of the same pot.

RYAN

Can we hire someone else?

MATT

Good luck finding someone who's going to go against that media giant.

NOAH

Apex Records isn't even that big!

MATT

Not their music division, but their multimedia platform is huge. Radio, streaming services, print . . . how did you guys not know this?

I've got to run. Keep it together until LA. We'll talk more then and watch what you put into text from now on.

Brett's text message makes me want to throw my phone and scream *get over it already*. Instead, I switch gears and text Sienna just as we pull up to the radio station.

NOAH

I can't wait to see you tonight.

Thankfully, her text comes in immediately, almost as if she were holding her phone, waiting to hear from me. The thought makes me smile.

SIENNA

I'm not sure I can wait that long. Send me a selfie.

I hold my phone out and flip the camera toward myself. I'm already wearing the dopiest grin, so I just leave it in place, take the picture, and send it to her knowing it's safe. She won't sell it

. . .

I hope she doesn't think I'm being possessive and demanding. I just want to make sure I don't miss her if she's here, but she doesn't answer me.

Instead of waiting around for her text, I go off to find Brett. The tension between us is still too high.

I find him eating in the backstage lounge where we end up spending a lot of our pre-show time when the dressing rooms are no bigger than closets.

"Hey man, can we talk?" I ask, taking a seat on the loveseat adjacent to him. I don't want to crowd him for this conversation. "We need to clear the air before we get on that stage."

Brett won't meet my eyes, and he sighs heavily, but he doesn't answer me.

"Come on, man. Talk to me, what's going on? Is this just about Sienna?"

At that moment, Callista comes into the lounge. "What about Sienna? Is there something I should know?"

I see Brett shoot daggers at me with his eyes before I address Callista. "No. Now can you excuse us? We're having a discussion that doesn't involve you."

Her smile drips with poison. "It all involves me, Noah. Come on, I need you two on stage, I want to take a look at something." She turns, leaving the room, and I hold a hand out to stop Brett.

"B, we gotta fix this. I can't not have you in my corner, man. You're my best friend. What's going on?" I plead with him to open up to me.

He stops moving toward the door and gets in my face. His whisper is menacing but also laced with . . . fear? "You want to know what's going? I'm being fucking blackmailed because I gave a fan the best night of her life. *That's* what's going on," he says, shocking the piss out of me.

"*What? Who?*"

"That dumb cunt I took out that first night the girls wore those damn V outfits that had my dick hard the entire fucking show."

Well, that certainly explains his mood swings over the past few days. We all thought he just needed to get laid.

Turns out, him getting laid was the problem.

"I remember that night." It was when Sienna didn't sleep because she thought I was out with them. "What does the girl want?" I ask, although I can probably already guess.

"Me. She said she wants a chance to prove we're soul mates, and if I don't give it to her, she's crying rape. Said she's going to claim I forced her into the back of the Cadillac. It'll be her word against mine and who do you think will win?" He squeezes his eyes shut and runs a hand down his face. "I can't have that come out *now*. We're still early on in this tour. No one will come to the fucking shows if they think I'm a rapist. I mean *fuck*, why would I rape someone? I wouldn't. *I didn't!*"

And then it clicks. Why's he's been so furious with *me*.

He's dealing with this and trying to hold it together to not fuck up the tour and then I go and break the cardinal rule of our contract and fuck Sienna, *and* I accused him of having it easier than I do. I see why he thinks I'm a selfish bastard. Not to mention, he's in this hot water because instead of just sleeping with Bri, he tried to preserve the contract and now I'm flaunting the fact that I broke it right in his face.

"Brett, we have to tell Matt. Surely our PR team can handle this," I try to reassure him.

"You mean the PR team now owned by Callista? Who knows how she'll use this information?"

"Do you have the text message where this girl threatened you?" I ask, going into detective mode.

"She didn't text it. She called me." The expression on his face is pure agony. "I answered because it was a hot hookup, and I thought she was calling for a repeat. Fuck, I'm usually better at weeding out the crazy." He drops his head into his hands. I've never seen Brett this upset.

"Let's get through tonight's show. L.A.'s going to be a bitch, but at least Matt will be there. We can talk to him about all of this, and I'll come clean about Sienna. Surely, with as well as this tour is going, we can renegotiate the terms of the contract and figure out how to get this bitch . . . and that one," I nod my head toward the door that leads to the stage, indicating Callista, "off our backs."

"Yeah, okay," he says, sounding defeated.

"Hey, B. We got you. Even if it all blows up in our faces, we're family. You're not alone. Besides, it's been a helluva ride already, but I'm always waiting for the other shoe to drop anyway," I joke, trying to diffuse the tension.

"Thanks, Kinky. Sorry I got so upset about Sienna. I mean, I still think it's a little fucked up, but you do seem happier around her."

"I'm sorry for thinking my shit has been harder to deal with than everyone else's," I admit sheepishly.

He nods and takes a deep breath. "Okay, are we done now? Because I feel like all that's left is to either whip our dicks out or cry, and I'm not really down with either," he says, pulling on the hem of his black muscle tank.

"Yeah, we're done." We clap hands and pull each other in for a pat on the back – bro style. Turning serious, I add, "All the shit you don't think about when you make it big, huh?"

"Yeah. We aren't in Kansas anymore," he says, quoting Dorothy from Wizard of Oz.

"You got that right."

When we get out to the stage, I realize the girls still aren't here, and Sienna hasn't texted me back. A sinking feeling sits in the pit of my stomach as I begrudgingly turn my attention to Callista.

Chapter 24

Sienna

I can't believe I'm meeting Josh. I feel incredibly slimy for playing on his attraction to me, but I didn't know who else to call.

I came clean and told Bri and the girls about Noah and I *actually* breaking the contract this time. Not *all* the details, but enough to satisfy their wonderful whore-ish brains, and I told them about the fight with Brett. They were supportive and all agreed that if they had the chance, they would have taken it too which made me feel so much better. And of course, Bri was ready to run down the hall and fling herself into Brett's shorts when I told her that Sloan had called Brett out for wanting her.

It was only Bri I told about meeting with her brother though. She knew he was in town and agreed he might be able to help me help Noah with the Callista situation.

"Sienna, I'm so glad you changed your mind." Josh's wearing another suit, no doubt meeting me for a late lunch after schmoozing with his client.

He pulls me in tightly for a hug and a kiss on my cheek,

causing my guilt to crash into me like waves against a rocky cliff as his lips connect with my skin.

It feels all wrong.

"Josh," I start, wanting to be very clear about my intentions. "Thank you for making time for me—"

He cuts me off, the longing in his voice making me feel awkward and uncomfortable. "I'll always make time for you. Besides, I was the one who invited you first, remember? You look beautiful by the way," he says, indicating my simple black dress.

Our waitress approaches the table, and Josh orders a whiskey, neat, but I opt for water since I have a show in a few hours. He also orders the chicken parmesan which sounds delicious but is way too heavy, so I choose their seasonal summer salad.

My phone buzzes in my lap, and I see another text from Noah. I want to answer so badly, but I can't tell him where I am, and I won't lie to him, so I let it go unanswered.

"I remember," I confirm. "Look, I feel disgusting for asking, but I didn't know who else to call," I admit.

Immediately, Josh's eyes flare with concern, "Sienna, did someone hurt you? Is this about the guy you were seeing?"

"*Am* seeing," I correct him, "And no, he didn't hurt me at all. But it is about him."

As soon as Josh's drink is deposited on the table, he takes a hearty gulp.

"Well, let's hear it." If I couldn't tell he's shutting down by the tone of his voice, the way he glances at his watch and folds his arms would communicate it loud and clear.

"Well, see, the thing is . . . I'm not supposed to be seeing him."

Josh holds up a hand. "Sienna, I do corporate law with an emphasis on media and entertainment. I can't help you if your new boy toy is married," he bites out taking another sip of his drink.

"*Jesus, Josh.* No, he isn't married, and I *know* what kind of law you practice. That's why I'm asking *you* for help," I fire back angrily.

He loosens his tie and sits back in his chair, his perfectly coiffed hair pissing me off.

"You know what? I made a mistake in coming here. Sorry to have wasted your time." I push my chair back from the table and reach down to grab my purse when Josh stands and reaches across the table to catch my hand.

"Sienna, I'm sorry. Stay. Let's start over." He waves his hand at the seat behind me. I give him a hard look, and he must see I'm torn because he softens his voice and tries harder. "I'm sorry, okay? My emotions got the best of me. It won't happen again."

I slowly sit back down and let out a long exhale. It's time for another hard conversation where I let the wound bleed until it's clean.

"Josh, you've been in my life a long time. You've done things for me I will never be able to repay you for, and I love you as if you were my own brother. But I've told you *repeatedly* over the last decade I just don't see you that way. Please don't punish me because I don't return your feelings. It was never my intention to hurt you."

"I know," is all he says for a full minute, rubbing his eyes and pinching the bridge of his nose. Finally, he looks at me across the table and takes a deep breath. "Tell me what's going on."

"Do I get attorney/client privilege?" I ask.

"Christ, Sienna, is it that bad?"

I decide to let him judge for himself as I dive right in. "I'm seeing Noah Kinkaid even though when I was hired, I signed a contract saying I wouldn't . . . uh . . . *see* him."

"You mean sleep with him. You're *fucking* Noah Kinkaid."

"Shhhh!" I hiss, looking around. "Look, I know this is awkward, but that's not even the reason I'm here."

"By all means, enlighten me," he snarls.

"Not until you curb the attitude, Josh. This is hard enough as it is."

"I apologize. Continue."

He doesn't sound remorseful, but fuck it, I came here to help Noah, so I explain about Callista and her being hired with the tour company as a "favor" just before her dad got caught having an affair and was forced to hand her the company to avoid a scandal from his ex-wife. She's now double dipping and playing two major roles for Beautiful Deceit that are total conflicts of interest and the guys want nothing to do with her.

When I stop talking, he mulls over this new information before answering.

"I'll need to see the contracts in order to be sure, but if the ownership has changed with the record company, and they didn't write in a continuation-under-new-management clause, which I doubt they did since I'm guessing daddi-o didn't plan on getting busted, then Beautiful Deceit may be able to walk away."

"And if they did write that in?" I ask.

"Then it will take a little more to get out from under it. The guys could always breach the contract on purpose and nego-tiate a payout to avoid a lawsuit, but it sounds like this Callista is well aware of the bands' worth and won't go for it," he explains. "I won't really be able to offer anything concrete until I see the contract."

"Okay. Would you have time to come back to the arena with me, and I'll see if Noah has a copy on his phone?"

Annoyance flashes across Josh's face followed by him rolling his lips inward and looking up toward the ceiling like he's trying to find his patience in the space above his head.

The waitress chooses then to place our meals on the table, but she must be able to sense the tension between us because she doesn't stick around to ask how everything looks or if she can get us anything else.

"You realize you're asking me to help the one person who currently has everything I've ever wanted, right? Which, coincidentally, makes him the person I hate most in this world," he confesses on an exhale.

My eyes fall to the colorful plate before me, and I push it away. I no longer have any interest in touching its contents.

"I didn't realize that. But I guess I do now." And then I decide to hell with everyone else's feelings. Mine matter too, and it's time to make sure Josh understands that my *no* means *no*. Not now. Not ever. "But even if it wasn't Noah, Josh, it still wouldn't be you. And I know that sounds awful, but I can't change the fact I don't have feelings for you like that. Let me go. Find someone who loves you the way you love them. You deserve that. I'm asking you to help Noah and the band because it's the right thing to do but whether you do or don't help, nothing will change between us."

I'm shaking with nerves but proud of myself for finally having the hard conversations. I can't wait to tell Noah.

After what feels like an eternity, Josh sighs and rubs his temples. "I can't make any promises, but if he'll show me the contract, I'll see if I can find a loophole."

I feel my face brighten, and I clutch Josh's hand on the table. "Thank you!"

"I'm charging $800 an hour to read it though and I'm taking my time on every, single word."

I just laugh with relief. "Deal."

"Well, that went swimmingly. I don't have much of an appetite anymore. Let's just box this up, and go see your boyfriend."

Hot damn.

Noah Kinkaid is my *boyfriend,* and Josh Vorossi finally heard my *no.*

It's three-thirty p.m. when we get to the arena. San Diego's reputation has held up and the weather today was gorgeous. I'm glad I got outside the hotel for a bit. Although I would have loved to sightsee a little, it's nerve-wracking straying too far on concert days.

I know the guys are here because I saw Noah's text. I texted him in the car with Tim to let him know I was on my way, and I'm vibrating with excitement to see him.

Josh and I enter the arena to see the guys on stage with the girls which is strange because we don't really do rehearsals or placements anymore. We're all intimately familiar with the stage, as well as our positions on it at this point.

I feel Noah's eyes slide past me and land on Josh. His jaw tenses and I shake my head. *It's not what it looks like.*

But he doesn't understand. This *one* time, arguably the most *important* time, and Noah and I aren't on the same page.

Fucking great.

Callista turns around to see me and says, "Didn't I say to be in the arena by three?"

"I'm afraid that's my fault," Josh speaks up trying to spare me from Callista's wrath, but he's just made it sound like I'm late because we were on a date.

"And you are?" Callista asks.

Josh's eyes find mine before looking back at Callista. "Just a friend."

"Well, this is a closed rehearsal, so you'll have to wait outside."

"He's also my brother, and he stays," Bri pipes up as I take my time walking toward them all. I nod at Romeo and Juan as Tim joins them while I climb the stairs to the giant stage still in my dress.

"I don't believe you have the power to make that call," Callista sneers.

"Enough with the pissing match," Noah barks. "Can we just get on with it already?"

He's clenching his fists and jaw so tightly I'm surprised we can't hear his bones grinding down to nothing. I'm sure his heart rate is close to a thousand, and I wish I could just get him alone to explain. I'm regretting not telling him before I met Josh for lunch, but in case Josh refused to help – which was a big possibility – I didn't get want to get Noah's hopes up.

"Fine. The press pass holders will be seated there," Callista points to a section of floor seats to the right of the stage. "I want to switch Ryan and Noah's places on stage, so the pass holders have direct access for all their shots."

"No." Noah's voice is hard and low. "We're here for the fans, not the press. They can get their shots just fine from there."

"For crying out loud. Stop being so difficult, Noah. Here, just come right here." She reaches her hand out to grab his arm and physically move him.

I shout so loud I see everyone flinch. "Don't touch him!"

It's effective in making Callista pause her movements. "Excuse me?" Callista snarls.

I'm about to repeat myself, but it's Bri who speaks up next.

"Noah doesn't like to be touched. Everyone knows that." I hug her so hard in my head, I see her eyes bug out like a cartoon.

"Remember your place, ladies," Callista warns. "You're not his bodyguards."

Romeo steps forward from the edge of the stage. "No, but I am." It's the first time I've heard him speak.

"Is that a threat?" she asks in disbelief.

"Depends on whether or not you touch him again," Romeo responds.

"This is ridiculous. I'm trying to appease all the parties and make you available for the press who has the power to build you up or tear you down, and you all seem to not want my help."

"You can't just bulldoze your way into changing our set, our rules, our schedules, and our image, Callista," Ryan tries to reason with her while the crew mill about in the background getting set up for the show tonight, expertly pretending they can't see or hear the drama on this stage.

"I own you. That's *exactly* what I can do," her entitled ass spits out.

"Actually," Josh clears his throat and starts walking toward the stage, "That's not entirely correct."

"Why are you even in this conversation?" Noah barks.

"I'm merely trying to help," Josh responds calmly and cryptically.

"Well, you're not," Callista says.

"Okay, well, I'm a little slow, and I'm curious. Did you just tell the members of Beautiful Deceit that you *own* them?" Josh asks, and I'm wondering where he's going with this.

"Yes. Because I do," Callista says, hand on her hip, lips pursed together.

"And, um, Noah, are you okay with that? I mean, that sounds a little aggressive."

Knowing Josh is an attorney makes his line of questioning make sense, and I can only hope that Noah plays along.

"Of fucking course not. I don't know why you care so much, but if you must know, she's a fucking nightmare. And now she's using every chance she gets to threaten us into changing the set, adding more shows, and hanging our fucking record deal over our heads to keep us in line," Noah growls as he kicks an extra mic stand, shooting it off the stage on to the floor below, his hands waving wildly as he talks.

"Interesting," Josh pauses and scrunches up his nose, looking confused. I also noticed that he's ditched the tie, unbuttoned his shirt at the top and taken off his jacket. He looks very nonthreatening and much less professional. "Ma'am," he says, addressing Callista. "Doesn't that sound a lot like coercion to you?"

"Call it whatever you'd like, I'm just trying to do my job," she says, clearly ready to be done with this conversation.

I was really hoping Josh would throw down the attorney card and say something in legalese to get her to shut up, but he just holds his hands up and takes a seat in the second row and starts typing on his phone.

The time period between Callista's impromptu stage changes – which no one follows – and when backstage becomes absolute mayhem from everyone getting ready, is only about fifteen minutes. Soon, the opening acts will start showing up. Crew members will be racing around looking for lost cords, someone will lose their pick case, someone else will have moved Brett's drumsticks – even though they know better. And we'll be a microphone short.

Thankfully, our crew is awesome, and everything will be resolved like it always is before the lights go down, but right now, I'm not concerned with any of that.

I need to talk to Noah, except he just hauled off the stage like his ass was on fire. I can't just chase him down and tackle him without giving anything away, can I?

No. I cannot.

So I slip through the backstage curtain and take the long way around hoping to bump into him, when I feel a strong hand grab my biceps and spin me around.

"What the—"

Ryan is towering over me, his jaw is also clenched. "Normally, I'd say whatever you're doing with Kink isn't my business. But right now, it definitely is. Are you playing him, Sienna?" Ryan whispers.

If I wasn't so desperate to talk to Noah, I'd think it was sweet that Ryan's asking me about my intentions with his best friend.

I pull my shoulders back and look Ryan dead in the eyes. "Absolutely not, Ryan. I met with Josh because he's a lawyer, and I was hoping he'd be able to help get Callista off your backs. I didn't tell Noah because I wasn't sure Josh would help me after I turned him down. I would *never* do that to Noah. This isn't a game. I know what's on the line."

Damn, why does everyone assume the worst about me? Josh thought I was seeing a married guy. Ryan thinks I'm already sneaking around behind Noah's back. Do I give off slut-with-no-morals vibes or something?

Starting to get angry, I rip my arm out of his grasp. "Now, either help me find him or get out of my way."

He nods, and I see the ghost of a smile spread across his lips. "This way."

He starts to lead me down a deserted back hall of the arena toward huge bay doors. Out back is a small concrete courtyard with a basketball goal. It's surrounded by a high brick wall so passersby can hear the ball bouncing but they have no idea it's Noah Kinkaid doing the dribbling.

"Thanks," I whisper, because it's all that will come out.

Noah's in his regular jeans, but he has on a grey tee with the sleeves cut off, making the arm holes so big I can see his sides. His biceps flex with every shot and every shot finds its mark.

"Kink, you'll want to hear this."

When Noah turns his attention toward us, his gaze is cold until Ryan leans down and kisses my head.

"Thanks for trying to help us," he says so low only I can hear. To Noah, it probably looks like he's whispering something dirty because I look up at Ryan, feeling the heat in my cheeks, and nod. *You're welcome.*

Noah tucks the ball under his arm and walks over to me. "If Ryan's being all cozy," he says loudly and throws the ball, hitting Ryan in the back of the legs as he walks away, "then it must not be what it looked like."

Ryan holds up his middle finger as he passes back through the open bay door.

I narrow my eyes at Noah in disbelief.

"Noah, we'll discuss how you could think I could share myself with you like I did and then turn around and go out with someone else in just a second, but the *reason* I met Josh was because I'm trying to help you."

I explain about our conversation at lunch, and Josh's expensive offer to take a look at the contract for loopholes.

"I don't know why he didn't mention he's an attorney this afternoon in their standoff, but maybe he wants to collect information without her being defensive or careful?" I suggest at the end.

Noah runs a hand through his hair and looks away, his guilty conscience painting his features with remorse.

"Shit, Sienna. I'm sorry for reacting like a total asshole and not trusting you. I, uh," he rubs the back of his neck, his biceps flexing so hard I can see the veins popping out. It's distracting as fuck, and I almost miss his words. "I have more invested in this than I realized, and I already knew it was going to be serious."

"Invested in what?" I ask, still mesmerized by his arm.

It's only when he answers, "Us," that my gaze finds his face.

My lips part on a sigh that he swallows quickly as his hands cup my face. My hands fly to the holes in his shirt needing to feel his skin.

"I'm so sorry, Si," he apologizes again, peppering my face with kisses. "I promise to work on not being such a dick. Please forgive me."

"I'm not perfect, but I won't purposely hurt you, Noah," I explain. Feeling him nuzzled against me makes me feel better, but I crave physical connection to know we're okay. "How much time do we have before someone comes looking for us to get ready?" I ask as he moves his mouth to my neck and shoulder.

"Not enough," he grumbles against my skin, "but we'll make it work."

Seems like we're back on the same page, thank God.

He takes my hand and pulls me behind him, back inside the building, down a different vacant hallway and opens a door to a room that looks like storage. Empty food carts line one wall. Chairs, wet floor signs, boxes of cords, something that looks like a giant motherboard, and a bunch of other shit is scattered all around the room. There are no windows and thankfully the door has a lock on the inside.

"Do you trust me?" he asks, "Even though I was an ass?"

"Of course." My reply is instant even if he demonstrated his *lack of trust* in me. I've already decided to forgive him. I know what it looked like.

"I'll be right back. Don't move."

He slips out the door in a flash.

Chapter 25

Noah

I'm so fucking giddy, I race through the hallways like an idiot. For a brief second, I think about *skipping* and then mentally slap myself. I need to be fast and quiet.

Slowing my pace, I start to peer around corners like I'm James fucking Bond and dash from hiding place to hiding place until I reach the door that says BEAUTIFUL DECEIT in gold, capital letters. If I wasn't on a mission, I'd stop for a minute and savor seeing our name like this . . . our fame spilling out in the chosen font.

I slip inside our dressing room, surprised the guys aren't in here and grab what I need before hauling ass back to Sienna, chastising myself the whole time.

You know her, dumbass. You know she wouldn't sneak around. You're such an idiot. Make it up to her.

I plan on it.

I get back to the storage room in half the time it took me to get to the dressing room, and I notice that the voices of the crew are closer and more frequent.

Time is running out.

When I open the door, I find Sienna bent forward at the waist, standing on one leg, hands planted on the floor in front of her while her other leg is braced on the wall behind her, straight overhead. Her dress is riding high on her waist because of the position, exposing her whole ass.

Good God.

"I was just stretching," she explains, bringing her leg off the wall and straightening up.

It's 4:45. Doors open at 6:00 and show starts at 7:00. The opening act does, anyway. But we have to be mic'd and sound checked by 5:30 which means I have about fifteen minutes at best.

"Perfect. Maybe I can help with that part," I give her a wicked grin and stalk toward her causing her to smile and yelp when I slam my body into hers and push her back against the wall.

"I heard you've never been properly fucked against a wall, Ms. Kennedy," I growl in her ear.

Her whimper and the way she's pushing her hips against me tells me she's in to this, so I keep going.

I reach down and grab her wrists placing them in my left hand and hold them against the painted concrete wall above her head. I kiss her hard but keep my tongue in my own mouth, chuckling when hers darts into mine, searching. Her groan of frustration has me hard as granite.

Using my right hand, I trail my fingers up the side of her thigh, thankful she has a dress on instead of her body suit.

She thrusts her hips toward me once more.

"Noah, I swear —"

"Yeah, baby? What do you swear?" I taunt.

"If you don't fuck me, I'm not getting on that stage," she threatens. I can't hide my laugh. She reminds me of a pissed off kitten.

"Well, we can't have that. My whole stage performance would be off." I'm not kidding about that part.

"Please tell me you went to get a condom," she pants and my heart swells because she remembers everything I've told her.

I reluctantly pull my hand away from her thigh and dig in my pocket, holding up the foil packet between my index and middle fingers just in front of her face.

"Oh, hallelujah," she says in relief.

I let her wrists go so I can get my belt off, but she bats my hands away.

"I want to do that."

"Yes, ma'am." I brace my hands on the wall over her shoulders, and my head drops back as I feel her struggle to get my jeans over my erection.

"Damn, Noah, doesn't this thing get in your way on stage?" Right on cue, my dick swells even bigger with pride.

"Never had an issue with it until you started getting handsy in front of thirty thousand people." The smile on my face is almost as big as my dripping cock in her hands.

"I'll remember that," she says, making me wonder what stunt she's going to pull tonight.

Finally getting my pants down, I kick them off one leg.

With my eyes closed, I'm waiting for her to roll the condom on when I feel a different sensation entirely.

"*Shit,*" I hiss as I feel the warm wetness of her mouth engulf me. My right hand instinctively flies to the back of her head. "Oh fuck, that feels so good." And it does. But I want to be in her pussy before this show. I want to claim her. I want to know that no matter who's lusting after her in the audience, she's *mine*.

Wow, that thought was powerful . . . and new. By this point, I'm usually already trying to figure out how best to extract myself from the situation once my partner gets off, not laying claim for God's sake.

I pull my hips back causing my dick to slide from her eager mouth and set a new world record as I roll the condom into place before grabbing her elbow, helping her to stand. Just as quickly, I wrap my hands under her perfect ass and scoop her up like I've done before, her legs flying around my waist with ease as I get her positioned over my cock and slowly lower her down. Once I'm seated deeply inside her, I lean forward with all my weight to trap her against the wall and start thrusting.

"Oh shit, Noah," she cries, gripping my shoulders.

"That's it, baby."

She bounces easily, and I know this won't take long even though I could hold her like this forever.

My cell phone starts buzzing in my back pocket, and I'm positive it's the guys looking for me. We must be out of time.

I need her to come.

Her moans fill the air around me. She's still fully clothed because I couldn't wait. Her panties are shoved to the side as I pump in and out of her, creating extra friction across the ridges of my dick.

"You're so fucking sexy, Sienna. I want to hear you scream my name as I fill you up."

I know my words turn her on because I can feel her start to clench around me.

"That's it, baby. Take what you want. What you need."

"Ah!" she cries, grinding her hips into me harder and faster.

Her ankles are locked behind my back, and she's squeezing her thighs to gain leverage to move up and down. At this point, my arms are offering her no support as she rides me.

"Noah . . . I'm . . ."

"Come for me," I command as she digs her nails into my shoulders and her pussy milks my cock. Watching her chase her orgasm sends me over the edge after her, needing to brace my hands on the wall again to keep us both from falling on the floor.

"Holy shit," she whispers against my neck a few seconds later as she unwraps her legs from my torso.

"*Holy shit* is right."

I look around for something to clean us up with and say a quick prayer of thanks when my eyes land on a paper towel dispenser on one of the abandoned food carts. The condom couldn't contain it all.

I pull my phone out of my back pocket to check my texts as I hand her the towels.

"Looks like it's show time," I hold my phone up so she can see the text from Sloan.

SLOAN

> Could you wrap it up? Literally and figuratively. You're mic's up in 5.

I laugh as I shove myself back in my boxers. A sense of peace and calm pouring over me as Sienna presses a kiss to my lips.

"Let's go entertain these people, shall we?"

The look on her face is innocent . . . *too* innocent. She's planning something in that devious, brilliant, mind of hers.

My moment with Sienna was exactly what I needed to get my mind right before this show. Determined to push dealing with Callista's threats, working with Josh, and helping Brett to the back of my mind, I focus on our crowd and on Sienna. I'm so proud of how much she's grown as an artist over the past two months. And I decide to add *convince her to help on new song* to the top of my priority list. Apex Records wants a new single? Then we'll give them a new single.

I can't help but notice as we enter into another song that despite the demands on my time today, and the fact that I definitely got *peopled-out*, I enjoyed my time at the impromptu meet and greet. I was actually able to enjoy it knowing that when it was all over, I could return to Sienna. And now, I'm enjoying this crowd.

Performing.

The cheers.

The flashing lights from the cell phones.

The fans singing along to my lyrics.

The dream that has become a reality.

I grab my mic out of the stand, preferring to have something in my hands, and I walk back and forth on the stage, really looking out at the crowd. Taking in their faces. For the next chorus, I do something I've never done, and I walk around to each of the guys, having fun and just dicking around on the stage, realizing that until now, I've been too rigid. Too focused on routine and what comes next.

I bang my head in rhythm to Ryan's bass, and he mirrors my movements. Since I play guitar and know all our songs, I reach in my pocket and grab my pick, strumming a few notes while Sloan's fingers work the fretboard. I can't hear him, but I can see him laugh and shake his head. He knows what I was up to earlier and can probably correctly guess the reason for my good mood.

When I get to Brett, who has a can of extra drumsticks next to his seat, I reach over and pick one up. I know nothing about drums, but fuck it.

I belt our lyrics into the microphone and pause while Ryan blasts the bass. Brett nods his head at the high-hat, indicating which cymbal I should bring the stick down on in three . . . two . . . one.

He works the pedal on the bass drum furiously as I bang away at the cymbal before chucking the stick into the crowd. I can barely hear my thoughts over the roar of excitement.

I've been going about this the wrong way.

I've been letting Matt, Callista, Nicole, and the pressure to perform rob me of my joy of making music and being out here. I'm not a fucking victim being tossed about by the violent winds of this industry.

I am the goddamn storm.

And it's about time I started acting like it.

Watching Sienna face her demons is the absolute kick in the ass I needed. We play L.A. in two nights, and I'm going to help her banish those motherfuckers once and for all.

I accidentally get in Bri's way as I head back to the front of the stage, so I hold my hand out and twirl her once as an apology and to artistically get *out* of her way.

The crowd is going wild as I replace my mic in its stand, getting ready to belt out my favorite part of this song.

You can't stay, 'cause I need you to go.
You wasted all the secrets I needed
**   you to know.**
You betrayed my trust and caused me
**   to lie.**

You vicious fucking monster, there is no you and I.

There are about two measures before Brett goes ham on the bass drum again, and I see Sienna making her way to me. I arch a brow as I turn to face her fully and can't help the smirk painting my face. I grab my mic because I'm about to have to scream into it, and I don't want to turn my attention away from her. I can feel the crowd holding their breath in anticipation alongside me.

What is she up to?

She's supposed to be doing a move that reminds me of a boxing match with Bri on stage left . . . but instead, she's two inches from my face, turns around and drops her hands to the floor. Her ass right in my crotch.

If someone had told me a month ago that there would ever be a time I would be okay with *twerking* on my stage . . . I would have laughed in their face and called them a liar.

But now?

Now, I grab her hips and pull her into me.

I'll show her *vicious*.

I'll sink my teeth in,
Wear your soul thin,
Make you wish we'd never met,
Watch as my words still make
you wet.

The move only lasts a second because she has to be up on her silks by the time I start the next verse, but it was enough. Between her stunt and mine, the crowd is off the hook. I hear them singing even though my earpiece is in, and the speakers are aimed right at me.

By the end of the show, I feel more energized than I did at the beginning even though I gave it more than I thought I had to give.

I didn't know performing could be like this.

I hadn't realized just how much mental headspace and physical energy all my stress was taking up, hanging out in the background like open apps on an iPhone. Letting go of that tonight made this show an entirely different experience.

One I want to do again. In fact, I feel bad for the first sixteen shows we've played because I now know those crowds did not get the best of me.

Once our last song finishes, I really lay on the praise for the band and our dancers. It's definitely a pop-concert thing to do, but I don't even care. If the fans like it, then let the lines get blurred.

When the house lights come up and the guys and I are backstage, I'm unable to keep the giddiness out of my voice as I slap Sloan on the back.

"That was fucking *awesome!*"

"Dude, if getting laid before a show gives you that much energy, then I'd say stay on that regimen. Where's Sienna? I need to tell her thank you," Sloan laughs as he whips his head around, pretending to look for Si.

Callista rounds the corner at that exact moment, her eyes narrowed.

"I *knew* something was going on when you followed her onto that bus. Kinkaid, you know the rules, and *she* signed a contract. Unfortunately, you just sealed her fate. She's off the tour."

"*What?*" Sloan and I yell in unison. "Didn't you *see* that out there?" he yells, throwing his hand out in the direction of the arena. "Didn't you *hear* them? The crowd fucking loved them!" Sloan yells in my and Sienna's defense.

"You want this tour to be successful, but you're going to fire one of its core members just for the sake of your precious fucking contract? I'm calling Matt. This is ridiculous."

I storm off to find Sienna.

Good mood, *gone*.

No. I am the storm, not the victim, and I will make it rain holy fire on Callista Richardson.

Chapter 26

Sienna

The girls and I are taking our time in the dressing room, savoring the moment.

"I thought I had gotten used to being on stage with them, but tonight was a whole different beast," Joslyn says as she strips out of her costume. At this point, we've seen each other naked so many times we don't even bother using the individual dressing stalls.

"The crowd could feel it too," Kara agrees. "I kept watching this one girl up front. I don't think she blinked the entire show. She looked too starstruck to even sing along."

"It really makes me realize how fucking lucky we are," Bri says with a small amount of wonder in her voice.

"And just think," Jos adds, "one of our very own is fucking the moodiness right out of Noah Kinkaid, himself."

It still makes me giggle in disbelief. "Whose life am I even living right now?"

We move on to talk about the other guys - mostly the girls talk about them, I just listen. I only have eyes for Noah.

A knock on the door interrupts our conversation, and

before any of us can answer it, it flings open.

"Jesus! Give us a second, our boobs are out for fuck's sake," Bri says at the intruder.

Noah, rushes into the room and slams the door shut before striding over to me and kissing me hard. When he pulls back his eyes are tortured, the excitement and peace that were present during the show, long gone.

"Noah, what's wrong?" I ask, scanning his face.

"We'll just give you guys some privacy," Kara says, herding the girls toward the door even though they're all in various states of undress.

"No. Stay. You need to hear this too," Noah says. "And sorry for barging in." He shields his eyes and then turns to look at me. Since he's already seen me naked, it doesn't matter I'm standing in a bra on top and the rest of my body suit on the bottom. "Sienna, I am *so* sorry." His voice is hoarse from the show, and he needs to be on vocal rest, not straining his voice further.

Which means something must be really wrong.

"Noah, please tell me this isn't a breakup speech already. And in front of my friends."

"What? No. Definitely not." He pauses and then jerks his head back, his eyebrows pulled together. "In order for it to be a breakup speech, you'd have to be my girlfriend. Are you saying you want to be my girlfriend?" he asks, his voice softer, less urgent.

Umm, duh?

I'd already reached that conclusion, but I'm glad to know he's finally arriving there as well. I guess there is something different about seeing each other privately and taking it public but either way I'm ready to slap a label on this and call him mine.

"Noah, let's define our relationship after you tell me what's wrong," I say, trying to get him back on track so I can stop freaking out.

"Okay, but we are *definitely* coming back to that. Look, Sloan and I were so hyped up from the show, and he knows about us, and he was just relaxing and fucking with me." Noah's words are coming at me so fast I can barely understand him. "And then he told me if getting laid before the show gave me that much energy on stage, I should do it every time and he was going to tell you to keep it up, because he thinks you're good for me, and then Callista appeared out of nowhere, and she said we broke the contract and you can't dance anymore, but I'm going to fight this. I'm going to fix this."

I feel the color drain from my face.

Thank God there's a couch behind me because my knees give out and I plop down on it. Immediately afterward, Noah's on his knees in front of me, his hands on my thighs.

"Sienna, I'm so sorry. We can try denying it, but I think how I feel is pretty obvious. It's still her word against ours though and the boys will back us up. *All* of them," he says, emphatically, telling me he and Brett must have worked their shit out.

"No, Noah. We're not lying. That doesn't ever make anything better. I knew the risks when I slept with you." *And it was worth every single one of them.*

I blow out an exhale as the girls surround me. Tonight was our best show yet. Why would Callista choose to fire me and ruin what we've built just because I slept with Noah? Especially if no drama arises from it?

"Look, I'm going to tell her and Matt we'll boycott the rest of the tour if they try to fire you."

"And if you do, you'll be in breach of your contract, Kinkaid, and I will ruin you just as your career is gaining speed," Callista says, beating her dead horse from the doorway.

"Why are you being like this?" Noah fires off. "You'd think you'd encourage anything that makes more money and makes our performance better. *Sienna* makes our performance better."

"But rules are rules. Sienna, I'll have the plane ready to fly you home tomorrow. Please make sure Jayne has your wardrobe before you go." She turns on her heel and disappears without another word.

"Something is seriously wrong with that bitch," Bri says. "I'm going to find Josh. It's time to put this cum dumpster in her place."

"He's in the band's dressing room. Ryan keeps a copy of our contract in the lining of his bass case. They're going over it now," Noah offers, skipping right over Bri's atrocious nickname for Callista.

I'm still stunned. My limbs feel heavy and there's a nauseating feeling settling deep in my stomach. Oddly, the first thing that comes to mind is *great, now I'll have to tell Lana I got fired and I can't get her those tickets after all, and she'll resent me even more.*

"Hey, baby, look at me," Noah coos. He's still on the floor, balancing on one knee. His other foot is planted, his muscular thigh resting against mine. "I don't know why Callista has it out for us, this bad but we're going to find out, and you're not going anywhere. You're staying with me, because I need you."

His words melt my heart. I may be fired from dancing, but she can't take me away from Noah. If I'm not a dancer anymore then the contract isn't an issue, and I can sleep with him and see him all I want. I'm still devastated of course, but Noah makes it a soft landing.

He reaches up and wipes my tears away with his thumbs. I hadn't even been aware I'd been crying.

"So, about this whole relationship thing," he pauses, and I can hear the nervousness in his voice. "I haven't been in an actual relationship for a while, but you make me want to try again. As you can see, there's a lot of bullshit that goes along with being involved with me, but—"

"Just say it already, Kinkaid." I'm teasing, but I'm also desperate for him to not drag this out.

"Sienna, will you be my girlfriend?" he asks before breaking out into laughter. "Fuck, that sounds so juvenile."

A laugh bubbles up from my throat because he's right, but it's also perfect.

"Yes, Noah. I'd love to be your girlfriend."

He jumps up from the floor and lands on the couch next to me, pulling me to him. I clutch his black t-shirt that is still completely sweat-soaked and inhale the familiar scent of coffee and leather as he kisses me hard and makes me forget everything going on. I've forgotten Jos and Kara are still in the room until we hear clapping.

We break apart reluctantly, both wearing smiles.

"I promise we'll make it official, but let's figure out the job situation first," Noah says.

"Make it official?" I ask. He literally just asked me to be his girlfriend on one knee in front of witnesses, isn't that official?

"When pictures of us hit the tabloids, we want to make sure we control the narrative," he explains. "I've been told there's a lot of interest around my love life so when people find out I'm dating someone, it could get a little wild."

Am I ready for that kind of attention? Of course, I'd do anything to stay by Noah's side, but what if it goes south like my family's history has taught me it can? Our painful breakup will be splashed across multiple news sources. Could I handle that kind of intrusion? It hits me like a ton of bricks, the perpetual stage Noah is on. The eyes constantly on him. The fans digging into his personal life. No wonder he stays so stressed all the time.

"How do you do it?" I ask, knowing he knows what I mean.

He smiles, realizing I'm starting to understand. "It hasn't been easy. It still isn't, but you've given me a sense of calm. A safe place to shelter in the chaos. Someone who sees me beyond the fame and realizes I'm more than just a voice and a pretty face." His tone says he's joking, but his eyes tell me he's just being honest.

I know the moment is serious, and that I just lost my job and my salary, but I can't help but bring a little levity to the conversation.

"But if you *were* just a voice, that's one hell of a voice to be. I've never seen so many women go ape shit on an opening note. Singular. One note. And they lost their damn minds."

Tonight, Noah opened the show with his voice instead of his guitar. In the pitch black, he belted out one word, acapella, using one note, and the arena erupted. It was so loud, they didn't even hear him finish the line of the song. He managed to crack his voice in that sexy way some guys can, in the middle of the word, and then ended it as if it had a tail that whipped him, leaving him breathless. I'd never heard anything like it.

Villain.

I knew it was a war cry for Callista even before things took the turn they did.

He stands to straddle my knees, bracing his hands on the cushion behind me, and nuzzles my neck, driving me farther into the couch. His skin is salty as I lick his neck and he whispers roughly in my ear. "And what about you, Sienna? Did you lose your mind?"

"Consider it lost."

I'm still in my bra, offering Noah easy access to my collarbone and chest which he's inhaling and trailing his tongue across, causing my hands to fly to his hair and a moan of desperation to leave my throat.

A moment later, our door opens, and Josh comes into our dressing room, his tone clipped. "Okay, okay, we get it. You two are in to each other."

Sloan, Ryan, Brett, Bri, Jos, and Kara all come in the room after him and Noah throws himself down on top of me. I hadn't even been aware that Jos and Kara stepped out. Noah's presence is all-consuming.

"Guys! A little privacy please? My girl's half naked over here!"

Bri laughs as she comes closer and picks up a shirt to toss to me. "Relax, Kinkaid, she's half naked every night in front of all of us . . . and thirty thousand total strangers. Besides, I've seen Si's naked body as much as I've seen my own."

Brett's groan is audible. "Care to tell us more, Bri, darling?"

"I'll save that pillow talk for later," she winks at Brett.

"Gross. Brett, that's my sister. And Noah, you're currently dry humping the love of my life. Could we all get dressed and on neutral ground? I have some things we need to discuss in light of recent events," he grumbles. "I'm also charging your asses $1,200 an hour for giving me mental images I'll never unsee."

The band chuckles as they follow Josh from the room.

"Si, you know we're here for you, and we'll say and do whatever we need to in order to keep you with us, but it sounds like everyone's already on it," Jos starts. I know she and Kara have gotten close with the band that do our opening act, so I wave them away.

"Congratulate the guys from Reckless on a great show. You girls have fun. I'll fill you in later."

I pull the shirt Bri threw me on over my head and start for the door. Noah waves me on as he puts his phone up to his ear. "I'll be right there."

Chapter 27

Noah

Thankfully, he picks up on the first ring.

"Matt, we've got a problem."

"So I hear."

Shit. That means Callista beat me to it.

"Matt, Sienna's not a random hookup. The tour isn't in jeopardy because we're seeing each other. Callista's pulling the contract shit, and told Sienna she's going home tomorrow. She can't single-handedly make that decision, can she? You're still the manager of this tour, right?"

Help.

He exhales loudly. "That contract was created for a reason, Noah. *This* reason. Besides, don't you remember what I told you if you actually start dating her? Your fans will turn on her."

"Fuck them. I need her."

"You need *them.* Your fans are who give you value and negotiating power. Without fans, you're back to square one."

"Okay, fine. I'll figure out some way to appease the fans. What if we wait until the tour is over to make the announcement? People will eat our story up, and by then she won't be in

269

the limelight anymore and people can go back to their delu-
sional daydreams."

"Not sure it works like that," he says, solemnly.

"Well, it'll have to, because I'm not giving her up." My tone
stays even despite my burning rage. "Now answer me. Does
Callista have the power to fire my dancers?"

"Not on her own." His words allow me to breathe easier
until he adds, "But as the new owner of Apex Records, she is
threatening to avoid using our tour management company in
the future if we don't back her and honestly, Sienna *did* break
her contract. Unless you two are going to try and deny the
accusation against you?"

I don't always like Matt, but I trust him. I kind of have to
right now.

"Sienna doesn't want to lie. She said it only creates more
problems," I admit.

"Smart girl. Says a lot about her that she won't lie even if it
means getting kicked off the tour," Matt says with what sounds
like reverence in his voice.

"She's not going home, Matt. So help me figure a way out of
this."

He's silent for a moment and an idea slams in to me harder
than if I'd been smacked by a freight train.

"What if we offer her a different contract?" I ask, getting
more and more excited about the idea.

"Go on," Matt says hesitantly.

"What if we change her role. Okay, yes, *we* broke the last
contract - so don't put the no-sex clause in this one because
otherwise we'll just break it again. But what if we make her a
new offer as a musician? She's been helping me write a new
song on the violin. What if we offer her the chance to tour with
us as a musician instead of a dancer?" The excitement in my
voice can't be dimmed.

"Noah, are you sure about this?"

Am I? I close my eyes and think through the last three months of seeing Si every day. Of the things we've shared, of the way it's easy to be around her, of how I felt when I saw Josh enter the arena with her.

"Yes. I'm sure."

"I'll have it drawn up and emailed to you within the hour."

"Matt, thank you!"

"I can't promise I can prevent a lawsuit for her breach of current contract though, Noah. Make sure she's ready just in case."

"Yeah, okay. Do me one more favor?" I swear Sienna is my muse and the good ideas just keep coming.

"Include a sign-on bonus for whatever you think the lawsuit against Callista and LNV would cost. She's paid from the tour, right?"

"Yes, but I'd need the guys' to sign off on that," he says.

I'm pretty sure they'd go for it to help her out, but this isn't their fight. "Then write it so the extra comes out of my cut only."

"I hope you know what you're doing, Kinkaid."

"Never been so sure in my life, Matty."

I hang up the phone to see a text from Ryan.

RYAN

Get your ass out here. Josh is Facetiming us from his hotel room in ten.

Buses need to roll.

NOAH

I'll ride with Sienna.

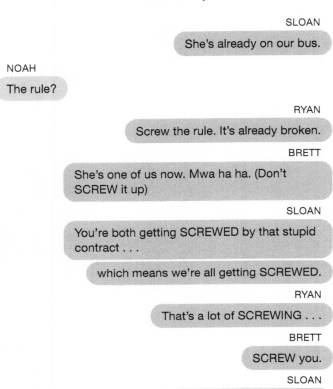

SLOAN
She's already on our bus.

NOAH
The rule?

RYAN
Screw the rule. It's already broken.

BRETT
She's one of us now. Mwa ha ha. (Don't SCREW it up)

SLOAN
You're both getting SCREWED by that stupid contract . . .

which means we're all getting SCREWED.

RYAN
That's a lot of SCREWING . . .

BRETT
SCREW you.

SLOAN
I could use a SCREWdriver.

NOAH
You all have a SCREW loose.

I laugh, feeling my chest swell with emotion over the four assholes I get to call my bandmates, brothers, and best friends. I make my way out to the buses taking one last, quick look in the arena. This was the best night of my life . . . right before it went up in flames.

As I climb the stairs, my eyes are already scanning the living area for Sienna, but I don't have to wait long to find her because she's in the first seat by the door.

"Hey," she says with a sad smile.

"Hey, yourself. It's going to be okay," I reassure her, drawing closer. "Also, why aren't you in my arms yet?"

Her sad smile turns embarrassed. "The guys said I could ride with you as long as there was no PDA," she says.

I know immediately Sloan made that comment so I turn my head toward him and narrow my eyes. "Well, since I once found one of my bandmates too drunk to remember which bedroom was his, and caught him jizzing in my sheets, I'll engage in as much PDA in front of him as I'd like for the rest of my life. Now get over here."

She jumps in my arms, my sweaty t-shirt, which is *still* wet, not bothering her at all.

Over her shoulder, I see Sloan scrub a hand down his face. "You're never going to let that go, are you?"

"Your *jizz*. My *sheets*. What do you think?" I wrap my arms tighter around Sienna, oddly happy that she gets to see more of this side of us. Relieved that this side of *me* is coming back, despite the shitshow around us.

"I bought you new sheets!" Sloan cries indignantly, as Sienna laughs in my chest, trying - but failing - to stay quiet.

"But can you scrub the image of your hand around your dick from my brain?" I fire back. I know Sloan isn't embarrassed at all despite the fact that I did, indeed, catch his money shot happening in my bed. I also know he's putting on a show to make Sienna laugh. And I love him for it.

"Alright, guys, we're getting off track," Ryan says, pulling us back to the matter at hand, but even he's grinning at the exchange.

As soon as the words leave Ryan's lips, my phone starts blaring the robotic ringtone of a Facetime call.

I keep one arm wrapped around Sienna and place the phone on the table, up against the wall of the bus.

Josh's face fills the screen, his swanky hotel room in the background.

"Gentlemen," he says in greeting, even though we just saw him like fifteen minutes ago. His eyes land on Sienna tucked into my side. "Si," he says, his voice growing husky. A growl unintentionally tears from my throat.

"Hey, Josh. Thank you for helping us," Sienna says quickly, trying to cover my noise.

Childishly, I relax a little when she says *us*.

He just nods. He's removed his suit coat, his tie is gone, the top two buttons are undone on his shirt, and the watch on his left wrist sparkles in the camera as his hand holds a glass of bourbon, whiskey, or scotch based on the color.

"Okay, so I understand you all will be a little contract shy given what's currently happening, but I need in writing that you're hiring me as an independent attorney outside of Apex Records for the purpose of autonomy from your record label due to suspicions of entrapment."

"Uh, what? We're musicians, man. Can you translate that?" Brett asks. He was the graphic design major.

I pipe up to tell Brett what he needs to know before Josh can confuse him anymore. "We already have representation under Apex Records which prevents us from hiring Josh. *Unless,* we think they're being shady in which case we're allowed to seek representation outside the big house. So that we don't get in further trouble with Callista, and so Josh doesn't get in trouble at all, we need to send him an email stating we think we aren't being represented fairly and have hired outside council."

Sienna pulls her head back to look up at me. "Where'd you learn that?"

"I went to college for business administration. My

emphasis was entertainment. Some of it stuck." *Not enough of it though since we're in this mess in the first place.*

"He's right," Josh says through the speaker. "It'll also give us attorney-client privilege which means I can't be forced to testify against you should Callista bring suit, nor can I go to the tabloids with anything that I've seen, heard, or learned." He looks at me directly when he adds, "Not that I would, mind you. But I know your trust has been broken in the past and because of our competing love interest, you have no reason to trust me now."

I nod my thanks at his acknowledgment.

"Okay," he continues, "I've emailed everyone a copy of a very basic contract. Sign them now, please."

I pull my phone back and swipe up making Josh's face small in the corner. We all open our email, open the DocuSign document and zip them back to Josh.

"Great. You've hired me. I now work for you. Everything you say can't leave me or be forced from me, and I now have the right to read and examine all documentation between you and Apex Records. If I'm looking for loopholes to get you out of this contract, I need to see everything. Your original contract, dates for singles, album royalties, studio time, how many albums or years they own you, rights and producing privileges, financials. All of it."

"I'll send you everything I have," Ryan pipes up. As the oldest and most mature, he's got nice, neat files with all that shit in it. I, on the other hand, have printed copies of a thousand pages stuffed haphazardly in a manilla folder in the safe at the house.

"I'm afraid for now, there's nothing I can do about Sienna losing her job." His eyes flash with hurt. "She was aware of the consequences when she fuc . . . *got involved* with Mr. Kinkaid, but if I come across something that could help, I'll certainly let you know as soon as possible. And Brett? Get your phone handy. I have something separate I need to discuss with you."

"Josh!" Sienna blurts before we disconnect.

"Yeah?" he asks, defeated and hopeful at the same time.

"Thank you . . . for helping me every time I've needed it."

She gets choked up on the last two words, and I remember her telling me Josh and Bri helped her after things blew up with her parents and he helped them secure their apartment for a fraction of the rent it was worth.

"Always," he answers and then hangs up without another word.

My email pings, and I see Matt's name and the subject *New Contract.*

I feel my face break out in a smile, and I turn my attention back to the guys - minus Brett who's headed down the hall - and Sienna and I tell them about my conversation with Matt before getting on the bus and my grand plan to keep Sienna with us until she can get back on the silks with the girls.

I'm fueled by excitement at the possibility – not to mention getting to work with Sienna on new music – and my eyes rove around the group. The looks on the guys' faces and a couple of head nods tell me they're into it. When I get to Sienna's face though, my excitement is met with a look of sheer terror.

Chapter 28

Sienna

My ears are ringing.

My heart flutters at the kindness behind Noah's offer and my throat burns from holding back tears of panic. My body tenses from the inability to choose which emotion to follow and which reaction to give.

"Sienna?"

I hear my name being called, but I can't move, not even to blink.

"*Sienna.*" Noah's pulling me onto his lap, peppering kisses to the side of my face.

I take a deep breath trying to pull air deep into my lungs to recover.

Feeling my heart rate come down slowly, and the ringing in my ears subside, I turn my head to look around at the guys who all have no clue as to what in the hell is wrong with me.

"Sienna, talk to me. Talk to *us.*"

"Noah, I'm so grateful for the offer, but you know I can't play the violin on that stage. Especially not in L.A."

Sloan and Ryan look on, still lost as ever, so I give Noah

permission to tell my story. After all, they're sticking their necks out for me so the least I can do is let them know why I can't accept this proposition.

I tune most of the story out, already intimately familiar with the details, but I check back in just as I hear Noah say, "But you guys heard her play that small part on the bus. She's fucking amazing."

"What if she stayed behind the curtain and no one knew it was her?" Sloan asks.

"People will think we piped it in and that won't work. Especially if we're playing something new," Ryan explains patiently.

"Sienna, I think you need to be on that stage," Noah urges. When I bristle, he pushes my hair away from my face, "Just hear me out."

I don't nod, but I relax and stop trying to move out of his arms, so he continues.

"I think you need to reclaim that passion and talent you have for playing the violin. Don't give your parents the ability to rob you of that joy one more day. I've seen you play. I've *heard* it. That's not just someone dabbling in music, Si. You're an artist. You're an amazing dancer, but that skill was taught, trained. The music that flows inside you is already there. Your talent is a *gift*, Si. Not a punishment like you've been led to believe."

"But L.A.? You know my mom will be in that crowd," I argue, interested in the idea that perhaps with Noah by my side I could overcome this, but still scared shitless.

"Seems like the perfect time to shine. To prove you're stronger than her bitter resentment. To make a statement and free yourself from the chains she's convinced you you'll never escape."

I can't help but chuckle sadly and look at the guys. "Are

you guys writing this down because I swear those were grade A song lyrics."

"Sienna, focus," Noah says seriously.

"I am, Noah, but this is a lot. I just picked a violin back up for the first time in seven years, what? A couple weeks ago?"

"Yeah, and you blew me the fuck apart. We need you, Si," he begs.

I feel myself slowly giving in. Not for him but for myself. Part of me knows he's right.

Sensing I'm close to agreeing, Noah says, "You won't be up there alone. We'll be with you. All of us. And the girls. Bri will be on that stage, and I can make sure she's right next to you. Whatever you need."

I can't believe I'm about to do this, but I also can't believe I've allowed this to fester and eat away at me for so long. I've accepted this treatment and allowed Lana to continue to control me even in her absence long enough. It's time to make some changes.

"Okay," I whisper, my eyes downcast.

"You don't sound sold, Si. I don't want you to feel forced into doing this. I want you to want to free yourself," Noah says, raising my chin to look at him.

I nod, my voice stronger this time. "I want to do this."

"Hot damn!" Sloan barks.

Noah immediately gets down to business discussing songs, what we should start with and where they should be played in the set. Two days isn't enough for a new song so he wants me to play his violin part, and add in a couple of interludes and such.

God, what have I agreed to?

I'm not worried about messing up, he could tell me to think of something on the fly and as long as he told me what key he wanted it in, I could come up with something on the spot. I'm also pretty sure I could play every Beautiful Deceit song on the violin right this second if I had to.

Ten minutes later, I've signed the contract with a shaking hand and have called Bri and the girls to both apologize for the hundredth time and to tell them the new plan.

"Callista is going to flip her fucking shit when she sees your ass on that stage," Bri says excitedly on the other end of the line.

"God, I hope so. I hate that bitch," Jos says in the background, making me laugh.

When I get off the phone with the girls, Noah tosses a pair of his boxers and a t-shirt at me.

"Will this work? The guys told me they kind of hustled you out of the arena and there wasn't enough time to swing by your bus for any of your stuff."

"This is perfect."

Sleeping in clothes that smell like Noah . . . while *next* to him? Yes, please. If anything can distract me from my current mental state, it's *that*.

In the silence that follows, I hear Brett's low voice in the back of the bus. I hope Josh is taking it easy on him. His big brother routine can be just as ugly as his jealous-love-interest routine.

Sloan looks back and forth between me and Noah. "Okay you two, no hanky panky. The bus is too small for that. Hence, having the rule in the first place." He turns his gaze to Noah and teases, "If I get woken up by moans and groans, I can't guarantee there won't be another jizz-fest in your future."

Noah laughs and punches Sloan in the shoulder. "No need to worry. You think I want my girl's moans up in your head for all eternity? Na, man. We're just going to sleep."

Sloan ducks into the small bathroom, and Noah leads me back to the kitchen table which transforms into a double bed. *Didn't know they did that.*

He pulls the black privacy plexiglass shade that separates us from the drivers up front just as Ryan strips his shirt over his head and strolls into the small bathroom once Sloan comes out. *Christ, he is huge.*

"How does he fit in there?" I ask, trying to imagine Ryan's massive frame in the small, moving bathroom.

"Bathroom's bigger than you think. We have a full-sized stand-up shower so he doesn't have to stoop so low," Noah responds.

Exactly four minutes later, Ryan comes out, one towel around his waist, one drying his hair. "Kinky, you're up."

Noah turns to me. "We all get four minutes to make sure everyone gets some hot water. Do you want to go next? It's basically just enough for a quick shampoo and a rinse, but it's better than nothing. You can have my spot."

"I'll go last. I don't want to put you guys out."

He shrugs a shoulder and kisses my cheek before heading for the bathroom. "You're not putting us out. We want you here. If we didn't, the guys would never have brought you onboard." He reaches his hand out. "Come on, we'll share. Save time and water by washing each other." He wags his eyebrows and leads me into the bathroom.

"Whoa! This is gigantic!" Our buses have the same kind of layout, but theirs definitely has some upgrades over ours. This bathroom being one of them. I swear it has to be at least thirty square feet.

Noah chuckles. "Not the first time you've said that," he teases.

I love the light dancing in his eyes. They're still dark, but instead of being swallowed up by the shadows, there's a small window near his pupil where the shadows have been cast out. Even with everything going on, he seems to laugh easier and joke more.

I smile and shake my head as he turns on the water and strips out of his clothes like he does this in front of me all the time. The familiar question pops into my head as if it were a broken record: *Will I ever get used to this?*

The more crushing thought is *if this ends, how would I ever go back to before?*

"Hey, it's going to be okay," he says, bringing me back to the present as he pulls my shirt over my head. He correctly guessed I was retreating into my own head, but incorrectly guessed over what.

Both naked, we step into the shower, and he starts to lather his hands immediately. "Time is of the essence," he says, chuckling again. It's music to my ears *and* my heart.

When he places his hands on me to wash away the stage dirt, grime, and sweat, I feel my knees buckle and my shoulders finally relax. A loud groan escapes from my throat. He puts his mouth to my ear, "Shh, I meant what I said. Your noises are only for me."

"I'm not sure I can help it if you keep touching me like that," I admit, my voice thick with lust.

"Here," he spins me around to face him and rubs the soap in my hands. "You wash me, and every time you want to make a noise, just rub harder."

Right, because washing Noah's gorgeous, hard, wet body while his sinful, decadent voice whispers in my ear is sure to prevent me from making noises.

Our four minutes feel like twenty seconds. Noah got the washing part out of the way quickly, and has his hand between my legs when Brett starts pounding on the door.

"You don't get eight minutes just because there's two of you," he barks.

"*Chill.* We're done," Noah yells back.

"He sounds legitimately upset," I observe, feeling bad

because I'm already causing a rift.

"He's, uh, dealing with some shit," Noah says but doesn't elaborate. He wraps a towel around me and opens the door. Butt-ass naked.

"Nice," Brett says flatly as he's greeted with a face-full of Noah's dick. Since the bathroom is actually up two small stairs, Noah's dick is almost eye-level with Brett.

"Only one towel left. I saved it for you. You're welcome," Noah says sweetly, before jabbing his hips in Brett's direction.

"Hey man, keep that thing away from me," Brett cracks a smile and jumps back. "I swear, between you and Sloan, it's a meat party all the time."

"Says the man who's junk I saw the first time I ever boarded the Meat Express," I say, jumping to Noah's defense.

"Noah, tell your girlfriend she's not allowed to team up with you against us."

"Noah, tell your boyfriend that although millions of women want to see his man meat, I am not one of them, and he should be grateful you saved him a towel." Brett's face falls at my joke, and he storms past us into the bathroom without another word.

"Shit, what did I say? I was just messing with him. I'm not *that* repulsed by his junk. God, is he that sensitive?" I ramble, upset that I've offended him somehow.

"First of all," Noah says as he reaches for a drawer across from the kitchen galley that contains his clothes. "Don't reference Brett's junk ever again. Forget you ever saw it. Second of all," he lowers his voice and slips on his boxers, "Brett's being blackmailed by a fan he stuck said junk in and now we're dealing with that on top of everything else."

"Oh my god! Who would *do* that?" I ask, truly horrified at people's cruel nature.

"Some girl he took out the night you thought I went with them," Noah says, pulling the t-shirt he threw me earlier over my head so I can hold on to the towel. It sounds like Ryan and Sloan are in the back playing video games, but they could easily poke their heads out at any time.

"The one he was tongue fucking in the parking lot?" I ask.

"Uh, yeah, I guess so."

Now fully clothed, I reach for my phone and text Bri.

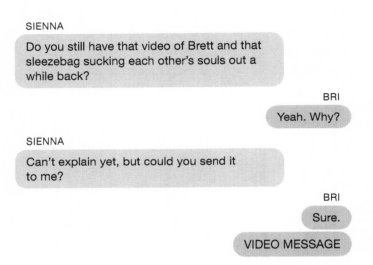

I hold my phone out to Noah.

"This bitch?" I ask with venom in my voice. These guys have become my family and anyone who messes with them, get the girls and I as well.

"I'm not sure, but we can ask Brett."

When his four minutes are up, Brett comes out of the bathroom, towel low on his waist. Really low. So low it almost isn't worth wearing. His flat stomach is fully on display and his happy trail is visible all the way to the manicured lawn below. He has ink all over his torso and shoulders. It's well done, but I appreciate that I can see the majority of Noah's skin when he's shirtless.

"Sienna, I'm sorry for—"

I jump up and shove my phone in his face. "Is this the girl that's claiming she was forced into that car?"

He jerks his head back to try and focus on the screen, but I'm shaking so he grabs my wrist to steady the camera.

"Yeah, it is. Where the hell did you get this?" he asks.

"Oh. Uh, shit . . . " I don't want to throw Bri under the bus, but also, she and Brett have been dancing around each other for months, so, fuck it. "Bri took it. She was so pissed that night that she slept with one of the guys outside of our bus to get back at you but then didn't even tell you, and I've never known her to be so indirect. But I'm pretty sure she has it bad for you and took this video to judge your poor taste in women and shame you at a time of her choosing."

"Give me her number," he says, rolling his eyes as a huge grin breaks out on his face.

I rattle it off and he kisses my cheek.

"Watch it," Noah growls.

"Jealous?" Brett asks, before he grabs the back of Noah's neck and plants a kiss on his cheek as well. "Better?" We watch as he goes to the back of the bus and says, "Out fuckers. I need to make some calls."

"Well, that was interesting," I muse.

"I think Bri just saved his ass," Noah says.

"God help us when those two finally hook up. They're likely to start an earthquake." My smile threatens to tear my face in half.

"Come on, baby, let's go to bed. Tomorrow we'll start working on your musical debut."

I can't tell if I want to cry, throw up, or laugh so I decide to burrow into Noah's chest and deal with it tomorrow. The steady beat of his heart almost has me asleep twenty minutes later, until I hear him humming.

"Noah?" I ask quietly but get no response.

He's humming a new song in his sleep.

Chapter 29

Noah

I know why he's here, and I'm incredibly thankful Josh has come to our rescue even if it's only for Sienna, but I still feel the need to have my hands on her when he's near. Thankfully, she doesn't seem to mind the contact as she leans into me, as desperate to claim me as I am her.

We're all seated around the conference room table at the hotel: me, the guys, Sienna, the dancers, Josh, and Matt. We arrived in L.A. sometime a little after four this morning.

It's now seven a.m. and there is not enough coffee in this building for the conversation we're about to have.

This is our whole fucking future.

"I'm going to start at the beginning," Josh says, flipping on a tape recorder. "This conversation is being recorded. Please state your name and your consent to be recorded. By consenting, you're also agreeing you are under no duress or pressure to be here."

We all go around the room and do as he asks.

"I was hired by the members of Beautiful Deceit to review their contracts with Apex Records as well as LNV Entertainment, their record label and tour management companies respectively. Upon examination of all documents provided, I have discovered a serious lapse in fiduciary responsibility on the part of Apex Records to pay the members of Beautiful Deceit according to their contract in the amount of one hundred thirty-eight thousand, seven hundred and sixteen dollars and twenty-nine cents." He flips the switch on the recorder and addresses the guys *off* the record. "Apparently, Cal was skimming from his artists to fund his secret getaways with his mistress."

"What the fuck?" I wasn't expecting that, although maybe I should have.

Josh holds up a hand, flips the recorder back on and continues.

"I've also discovered that the previous contract was signed specifically with Cal Richardson *before* Apex Records' music label was filed as a corporation. It started as a separate entity which was smart on Cal's part. If the label failed, it wouldn't affect the parts of the company that he'd successfully built."

"What does that mean for us?" I ask.

"It means that once the transfer to Callista is complete, your current contract will be null and void. Cal never had your contract rewritten so your obligation was technically only to Cal. Not Apex Records. While he was in contol of the majority shares and still CEO, it wasn't a big deal because Cal and Apex Records were one and the same. Now, they are not, and your contract ends when Cal walks away."

I had completely forgotten that Cal had just split from his larger record label and was branching out on his own when he signed us. He took a chance on us, but we took a chance on him as well as he was just building his studio.

"Furthermore," Josh says, flipping through a folder in his hands.

"Jesus, there's *more?*" Ryan says, echoing my own thoughts.

"I found evidence suggesting why Cal Richardson broke off to form his own label rather than staying with the prominent one he was already with. Anyone want to take any guesses?"

"Embezzlement," I answer, immediately. All the pieces are starting to slide into place.

Josh nods his head. "Finally, the daughter of Cal Richardson, one Callista Richardson, has violated her responsibility to protect her clients. I discovered this morning she's leaked the news about Noah Kinkaid and Sienna Kennedy on the band's social media page, violating her own NDA with you, although I doubt she's aware of that. She cleverly posted that the band was in full support of the union but decided that it was too much to have Sienna remain on as a dancer, so Sienna would be stepping down."

"You have got to be fucking kidding me!" I yell, slamming my fist down on the table.

Josh calmly holds his hand up again and points at the tape recorder.

I'm going to murder her.

Sienna, reaches over and grabs my fist in her small hand, prying my fingers open to lace ours together. She leans in and whispers in my ear, "It's okay. We'll be rid of her soon enough."

Callista fucking orchestrated it to make it look like she didn't fire Sienna, and she just spread our business without our knowledge or consent. This news is going to catapult Sienna right into the spotlight.

This is bullshit. This is the part of fame I could live my whole life without.

"I'll be contacting Callista at the conclusion of this meeting to see how she wants to proceed. I spoke with their in-house attorney this morning who admitted it's a shit show and the record label is collapsing. Cal Richardson didn't own Apex

Records outright. He had a board of trustees and a handful of investors who were taking a chance on his name by allowing him to control the label under the Apex Media umbrella. Since that backfired, they're able to pull out without consequence because Mr. Richardson broke the law and therefore, nullified his own contract."

Holy shit.

I blow out a harsh exhale.

"If Apex Records collapses, what happen to us and the tour?" I ask.

Matt starts to speak, drawing my attention to him. He's pale, and he's rubbing his eyes but his voice is strong.

"LNV will foot the up-front costs for the remainder of the tour if you guys agree to reimburse those costs and continue to stick to the original contract agreement. You're in a good position to be picked up by another record label, and I doubt it will take long, but for God's sake, vet them, do your homework, and negotiate a better contract. Leave yourself loopholes because you won't get this lucky a second time."

"*Lucky?*" I ask in disbelief.

"He's right," Josh says, "You're too big for Apex Records anyway and your contract basically handed them everything you create on a silver platter. Them stealing from you and Callista taking over is the best thing that could have happened to you guys."

"Go figure," Sloan mutters from the other end of the table.

"So where do we go from here?" I ask.

"If you want, I'm happy to stay on as your attorney. I can review all your contracts, discuss negotiating points and help you optimize your terms. Sounds like Matt here can help with getting you an actual agent who can seek out those contracts and deal with interested labels while you guys continue to tour.

As for Callista, I'll let you all know what she decides after I speak with her."

"Sounds good. And complicated. And over my head, so if you guys have got this, I'm going to go work on some music," Sloan says, pushing back from the table.

"Ditto," Ryan mumbles as he follows Sloan.

Brett looks at Josh who shakes his head. Brett sighs and slides his chair back. "Those two can't do anything without a beat. Catch you later."

The girls cast a look at each other before also politely leaving the room. All except for Sienna, who is still firmly clutching my hand.

Matt is the next to stand. "If you're done with me, I'll get to work as well."

Josh nods, and Matt turns to me as he stands to go. "Noah, I owe you an apology. There wasn't anything I could have done to prevent Callista from joining us on tour, but I'm sorry about it nonetheless."

"Yeah, thanks."

I find that I'm not mad at Matt. At Callista? Yes. At the situation? Yes. At Apex Records? Yes. And there was a time not so long ago my temper would have derailed my mood for the entire day, and anyone I encountered would feel my anger. But now, it doesn't feel so much like the world is ending, and I know it's because Sienna's by my side.

The need for control isn't as strong as it has been. Her presence in my life has shed light on how great of a team I have with me, and I need to trust them more. Hell, I already do.

"And Sienna," Matt continues. "Well, the rules are there for a reason, but in this case, I'm glad they were broken. You're a sweet girl, and I look forward to hearing you play tomorrow night."

Once Matt exits the room, Josh turns to Sienna. She's got

both of her hands wrapped around my biceps now, and she's pressing herself into my side. I lean over and kiss the top of her head as Josh addresses her.

"Off the record, your life is about to change, Si. The entertainment world is about to blow up with news of you and Noah. You'll be as famous as he is just because you're together."

I don't like him trying to warn her away from me, so I interrupt and lay the truth down myself, as I start talking into her hair.

"Some people, true fans who care about our music, will be happy for us. There will be plenty of others, *mostly women*, who will be pissed that someone finally took me off the market, and they'll attack you. Online of course. I don't think your life will be in danger, but we'll up your security just in case."

She leans away from me and the loss of contact punches a hole in my chest. *Damn I've got it bad.*

"God, I hadn't thought about any of that," she says to me with wide eyes. "I just want to be with you, Noah, not *Noah Kinkaid, mysterious, untouchable lead singer of Beautiful Deceit.*"

I crack a smile. "I'm afraid they're one and the same, baby."

"It's not too late if you're having second thoughts, Si," Josh chokes out, his eyes boring into Sienna, careful to avoid mine.

I feel my jaw clench, but I keep my mouth shut.

She needs to answer this on her own. And as much as I don't like it, Josh is right. She can still back out if she wants. I don't know how to help her process the fact that when we get home, her whole life will change. She can't stay in the apartment with Bri anymore because there isn't enough security. She won't be able to just pop into her favorite resturants anymore because she'll be spotted and harassed. Shopping without security won't happen anymore. Trolls on her social media will be ever-present. And those are just a few of the things that will change for her daily routine. I should warn her about all of that, but I don't. We'll cross those bridges when we get there.

She pauses briefly, and I watch as a smile begins to spread across her face, reaching her eyes, which are holding mine even as she speaks to Josh.

"Bring on the masses. With Noah is where I'm meant to be."

She says it with such conviction in her voice, I think I might implode from the surge of happiness coursing through me. I slide my hand up to her cheek and swipe my thumb across her smooth skin. "Are you ready to make your musical debut *and* announce to the world that you're mine?" I ask, assessing her reaction to my words.

She smiles as she says, "Sort of for the first one and *absolutely* for the second one."

I kiss her hard and hear a door close softly in the background.

When we break apart, I study her face. It feels like I've searched her eyes a thousand times.

"Nothing like trial by fire, huh?" I ask, making a joke, but not joking about our rough start.

"I'd willingly walk right into the furnace if it meant getting to be with you, Noah."

"Right back at you, baby."

Most of the day is spent in a whirlwind of phone calls, text messages, and general pandemonium. Matt is working on securing an agent and keeping the tour afloat.

Josh is meeting with Callista to tear her world down, and I'm also hoping he can get some answers as to why she was so aggressive with us from the start. Something is off with her. I know she's young, but she was just handed not one, but *two* opportunities of a lifetime. Surely, she understands that nothing about the way she behaved was good for business? The guys and the rest of the dancers are all in our suite – thank God for back-to-back shows in L.A. so we can get off the bus.

"Maybe she wants to have your babies," Bri says to me in regards to Callista. "There seems to be a lot of that going around." She eyes Brett and gives him a sarcastic smile.

He fires right back, "That's why you'll be signing another NDA *and* a consent form before I let you under me, woman."

"*Let* me under you?" Bri bristles. Based on the smirk on Brett's face he's pushing her buttons on purpose. "It'll be the highlight of your fucking life if I ever *let you* touch me."

"Oh, you'll let me. In fact, I bet I can make you beg for it," he says so confidently that my money is on him.

"Is that so?" Bri asks, but her voice betrays her. She's losing steam in this argument already.

"There are four bedrooms in this suite. Pick any of them. Please, we beg you, just go bang each other so we don't have to hear about it anymore," Kara says, drawing laughs from all of us except the two in question.

"I think I'll wait. I find the chase to be quite fun. You know, make it so you can't stand it anymore. Wait until you're ready to drop to your knees in front –"

"We get it!" we all shout in unison.

Bri stays uncharacteristically quiet for the next several minutes. The poor girl won't win this fight. Brett has excellent swagger and the confidence to back it up. I don't know anything about his bedroom skills, but I've never heard a woman leave his room with a complaint.

All at once, four phones buzz. A group text to me and the guys.

JOSH

> Callista has wisely chosen to release your contract instead of fighting over semantics in court.

> She is not happy about it.

> Be on your guard.

> I've alerted all security details

"Do you guys remember when all we had to worry about was earning enough money for a McDonald's run so we didn't have to ask our parents?" Ryan says from across the room.

"Oh, the good old days," Sloan jokes.

We don't see or hear from Callista for the next twenty-four hours, which is almost worse than her presence. Her unknown location has us all on edge despite our security team working around the clock.

Before we know it, it's almost time to start the meet and greets at the arena. Sienna was unusually quiet the entire afternoon, but I'm positive her nerves have more to do with seeing her

mother than they do with playing the violin or the drama with
Callista.

Jayne was able to locate a beautiful black dress with cap
sleeves that Sienna loves, and the sweet woman spent all
morning sewing little silver "V"s into the fabric in honor of the
headlining album. I can't wait to see it on Sienna's incredible
body.

Callista knows Sienna is still here because the jet was
unavailable to fly her back to the east coast this morning, but
she *doesn't* know Sienna is going to take her rightful place on
that stage, and I can't fucking wait to see her face. I hope
someone grabs a picture . . . if she even shows up. But something in my gut tells me she'll be here.

I knock on the girls' dressing room door when it's time to
head to the VIP lounge and have the wind knocked out of me
when Sienna follows the other girls into the hall.

"Sienna, *wow*."

"Thanks," she swallows hard. "I'm afraid my hands are so
sweaty I won't be able to hold on to the bow," she says.

Before anything else is said, Kara ducks back inside and
returns with something that looks like an old school ice pack
like my grandmother used to have and pats it on Sienna's
palms. A cloud of white dust goes into the air.

Chalk.

Sienna forces a smile. "Thanks, Kara."

"I'll leave it on stage next to Sloan's amp, okay?" she says.
"You're going to do great."

I appreciate the support these women have for one another.
They remind me of my guys.

Grabbing Sienna's chalky hand, I kiss her cheek.

"Are you ready?" I ask, knowing she knows I mean to see
her mother.

"You bet your ass we are," Bri says, coming up behind us.

"We're ready to stick it to all these bitches aren't we, Si? To Callista, to Lana-fucking-Mariano, to Noah's shady ex, to that bitch trying to ruin Brett . . . to *All. Those. Bitches.*" She claps as she says each of her last three words drawing a smile out of Sienna.

"I'm ready," Sienna confirms, and I lead my beautiful, talented girlfriend down the hall.

Chapter 30

Sienna

I t isn't until I hear the words come out of my own mouth that I know they're true. Flanked by my boyfriend on one side and my unwavering best friend on the other, I am finally ready to be face-to-face with Lana Mariano for the first time since my college graduation two years ago.

Noah places his hand at the small of my back to guide me down the hall. Bri takes a sharp right at an intersection in the hallway to get ready backstage. The dancers don't ever accompany the guys to the meet and greets. No one cares who we are.

I guess the same can't be said about Noah Kinkaid's girl-friend, though. We pick up the other band members farther down the hall and then turn the corner where the fans are lined up, winding back and forth through a roped off lane.

As soon as the people in the front see the guys, they start screaming, which tips everyone else off that the guys are here. I watch in awe as the band gives humble smiles and throws hands up in a wave to the room.

Girls are clutching each other's arms and bouncing up and down. Guys look like they're really trying to act cool but are holding up their cell phones trying to capture themselves in the same frame with the band members in the background. A couple girls are actually crying and one guy close to the front keeps repeating, "Oh my god, Noah Kinkaid is *right there.*"

"This is intense." I lean into Noah's side as we approach the table we'll be sitting behind, acutely aware of how everyone's eyes follow my movement, and then his as he wraps his arm around my waist.

"When you've had enough, just let Romeo know, he'll walk you backstage to the girls."

"And leave you unattended in front of the masses?" I whisper, looking out at the all the females in the crowd. "I don't think so."

"Jealous?" he whispers in my ear, squeezing my thigh as we take our seats.

"Protective," I clarify. "Now sign some shit so we can get this over with."

"Yes, ma'am," he chuckles. "You probably won't have to sign anything, but people may talk to you. Engage as much or as little as you'd like. Remember, people are going to pick you apart no matter what you do, so just be yourself and be honest if you need a break, okay?"

I nod and then continue scanning the crowd for my mother. It occurs me that it would be just like her to not show up. I've been stressed ever since she sent me the text about this show, and Lana could have easily decided she'd rather get her nails done instead.

Fans begin stepping up to the table once the guys are settled. Noah is seated last in the row – except for me who is on the very end. It's a whirlwind of fans bumbling about, trying to find their words in the presence of the guys. I remember when that was me.

They're given all kinds of gifts, so I'm not entirely surprised when one woman presents her underwear to Noah.

"I was going to throw it on stage but then I won these passes and figured I'd just hand them to you myself," she says in a seductive tone.

I shift in my seat next to Noah who doesn't bat an eyelash as he leans back and stretches out his left arm over the back of my chair.

"I'm going to have to respectfully decline seeing as it's disrespectful to my girlfriend for me to accept that, but I'm pretty sure I heard Sloan recently mention his stash is low."

The woman's eyes flare to me, her judgements clear in her expression.

She's wondering why Noah chose me, and she's not even trying to be discreet about it. I'm too soft for this. Why can't people just be nice? Sensing my hurt feelings, Noah ignores the woman and leans into me and whispers in my ear, dropping his voice to a lower pitch, "It's not personal. They just wish they were you. Don't let them ruin your night, baby. I'm yours, remember that."

I turn my head toward him to nod, and he kisses me square on the mouth. Tongue and everything.

Giving a cocky half smile he says, "Let them post that shit."

Sure enough, people are videoing us.

This is fucking weird.

"Well, that was certainly unexpected," a voice I'd recognize anywhere sounds from down the table.

"*Shit.* Here we go," I mutter to Noah as my mother makes her way toward our end of the table.

Noah pulls me into his side so hard I'm halfway on his seat. Almost in his lap.

"Sienna," my mother says, as a tall gentleman trails behind her. A young girl is still at the beginning of the table taking her time with Brett before moving on to Sloan with stars in her eyes.

"Mother," I reply just as coldly. As of tonight, she doesn't control me anymore. In fact, she looks older, frailer. Like all her years of jealousy, resentment, and bitterness have finally caught up to her.

"Thank you for the tickets and the backstage passes, Sienna. It means a lot to me and my daughter. I'm Greg, it's a pleasure to finally meet you," my mother's boyfriend says as he extends his hand. He sounds so decent. So normal and kind. *How did he end up with her?*

"You're welcome." My words get stuck in my throat like those of the fans that have come through the line. Noah takes the silence as his opening and he reaches forward, first to Greg, then to my mother.

"Greg, Lana," he says as they look on, shocked that he's addressing them. "I'm Noah Kinkaid, Sienna's boyfriend."

"What?" my mother asks, shocked.

"Wait," comes the voice of the teenager who has finally caught up with my mother and her father at our end of the table. "Do you mean to tell me that my stepsister is *dating* Noah Kinkaid?"

Stepsister?

"You got married?" I ask my mom in disbelief before addressing the lanky teen.

She shrugs, "Six months ago. Small destination wedding. Didn't think you'd be interested."

"Would've been nice to have been given the option to decide for myself," I bite back.

"Okay, my turn," the teen says as she pushes her way in front of her . . . *our?* . . . parents and addresses me next. "Hi! I'm Sylvie. I'm fifteen, and I'm in love with your boyfriend. But also, I love your dress. Your mom said you dance in the show. Is

301

that how you two met? I follow all the sites and I *just* found out *you*," she says, turning her attention to Noah and sighing loudly, "have a girlfriend. Who I *now* find out is my stepsister! Can you sign this? Oh my gosh, I can't believe Noah Kinkaid is signing my shirt. And this definitely doesn't mean we're related, Noah. So, you know, if things don't work out, I'm still available."

The girl is talking a mile a minute unable to let anyone get a word in edgewise. It's kind of charming actually. I suppress a giggle as I see Greg wipe a hand down his face at her last statement.

"I think he's a little old for you, Syl," Greg says, looking at Noah and I apologetically.

"Dad! Do *not* embarrass me in front of my people," she says emphatically.

She looks like she's on the tail end of her awkward years. Her hair is still a little bushy like she hasn't discovered a straightening iron yet and her teeth are straight but still clad in braces.

Noah chuckles as he signs the t-shirt she's holding out for him. "It's nice to meet you, Sylvie."

"You have the most *amazing* voice," she whiny high-pitched tone only teenage girls can achieve.

"You've got that right, sister," I say seriously as I agree with the enthusiastic teen. Suddenly, a thought occurs to me as I see the line of impatiently waiting fans.

"Tell you what, Sylvie, take this pass," I pull my *crew* badge off my neck and hand it to her. "It'll get you backstage after the show. I'll meet you here, and we can get to know each other a little better." It's not *her* fault my mom's an egotistical asshole. Besides, Sylvie seems to be a genuine fan.

"Oh my gosh, really?" Her eyes light up like I just gave her a million dollars just as my mother's eyes narrow.

Lana's smile drips with poison as she says, "Trying to lure her away from me too? Always had to have all the attention, didn't you? Some things never change."

She might as well have just slapped me across the face. It's the first time she's ever mentioned that night, and of course she would do it here.

Unable to speak and feeling the tears pool in my eyes, I turn my head toward Noah so my tears aren't seen by Lana or Greg. I faintly hear Greg say something to my mother but his voice is drowned out when Noah stands so abruptly, his chair scrapes the floor before falling over backward. Ryan jumps up next to him ready to intervene. Not knowing what's going on, but knowing something is wrong, Sloan and Brett abandon their chairs and come to flank me on either side.

Leaning forward with his hands on the table and a smile plastered to his face, he says so only our small group can hear, "Sienna is the most kind, talented, driven person I've ever met. Tonight, she'll play the violin on our stage as an honored guest, and we couldn't be luckier to have her. Whatever issues you have with her are due to your own shitty self-esteem and inability to make your own dreams come true. Your failed marriage is *not* her fault, and your bitter attitude is *not* her problem. Enjoy the show."

He snaps his fingers indicating my mother and her family's time is up, and security falls in behind them to usher them on to their seats. Noah doesn't even give them a chance to speak.

Before Sylvie follows the adults, she turns to Noah and holds up her hand for a high-five.

"Hell yeah," she says enthusiastically as he smacks his hand against hers. I think I like my stepsister. "Thanks again," she says to me, holding up the badge. "See you after the show."

When the guys are finished signing, it's time to get mic'd up.

"Thank you," I manage even though I'm still reeling from the whole encounter with my mother as well as seeing what the guys deal with before every performance.

"Let's show them the music," Noah says as he kisses my hand before turning his back to Tasha who clips his mic in and turns him to the right channel, checking for feedback.

"Here, baby girl," she says to me, "you get one, too, tonight."

Seeing the panic on my face because I didn't realize I was expected to say anything, she says, "You won't have the mic part, but you need the earpiece and receiver box so when Noah talks into his, you can hear him. That way if he gives instructions on the fly, he can talk to you without the crowd hearing him."

Oh. I wondered how the guys always seemed to know when Noah was feeling a song and wanted them to do an extra verse or something.

"Okay."

She clips me up, and Noah grabs his violin out of the case that's laid open backstage on an amplifier.

This is really happening.

With my nerves fraying, Bri and the girls encircle me. "We'll miss you up there, but you're going to be incredible," Joslyn says squeezing my side.

Shit. They're going to make my makeup run.

"And I heard Noah reamed your mom out," Bri says excitedly. "I can't wait to hear the whole story." When I flash her a look asking how she found out already, she shrugs and gives me a coy smile. "Brett," she says by way of explanation.

"Okay, baby. We're doing the song with your prelude first so you can get it out of the way and just relax for the second one, okay?" Noah asks, coming to stand behind me.

I simply nod. I've got this.

"Good luck, girls." I choke out as I grab the bow and follow

Noah on stage to the deafening roar of the crowd. All the guys pat my shoulder as they file on stage.

Brett starts the song with eight measures of a drum solo before Ryan and Sloan strike their first chords. As soon as those chords are struck, the lights go up and then it's just me playing Noah's haunting melody.

I raise the violin and tuck it under my chin like I've done a thousand times. Noah's voice fills my ear.

"You've got this, Sienna. Show them all."

I put the bow to the strings and pull the first note across. Hearing it ring out in the speakers, I gain confidence and continue on. The crowd seems mesmerized as I play and I'm struck by how *right* it feels. At some point, I close my eyes, getting lost in the piece I've played for only two days. I'm nearing the end, but I don't want it to be over.

Noah's voice sounds in my ear piece, "Sienna, if you can, follow along in the song and slowly fade out after the first chorus. The crowd is eating that sound up so let's give them more."

A hush has fallen over the crowd as they watch me play. Cheering isn't right for this part of the song, but there aren't any boos, shouts, or other disruptions to the prelude, making me believe they like it and are as mesmerized hearing it, as I am playing it.

I bow slightly toward Noah indicating I understand since I can't nod my head.

When Ryan and Sloan come in with a note that reverberates through my chest and lights the crowd on fire, I pick up my pace and play a song I know so well.

Victorious.

With every note I coax from the instrument, I feel my demons lose more and more power. Not just slinking into the shadows but disappearing altogether.

When Noah's voice fills the speakers, I open my eyes again and continue playing as I scan the crowd for Sylvie. I find her on the front row, singing along and banging her head in time to the music. Greg is watching his daughter but catches my eye and sends me a thumbs up and a huge smile. I remember when my own dad looked at me like that while I was playing the violin.

When I see my mother, she's standing with her arms folded across her chest looking every bit like the ice queen she is. Her jaw is tight, and I see the hatred in her eyes as she sneers at my violin.

She was right, some things never change.

The second time I come out on stage, my eyes find Noah and stay there a while before finding the girls whirling and twirling overhead. I eat this up like it's my last meal. I miss being on the silks but having a violin back in my hands feels better than anything . . . except maybe Noah's hands on me and his voice whispering across my skin.

After the show, I experience both a new level of exhaustion and a new level of euphoria when Noah calls me back out on stage, takes me hand and encourages me to bow.

Unexpectedly, he takes my face in his hands when I stand and kisses me deeply. In front of thirty-eight thousand people.

I guess people definitely know we're together then.

And I couldn't be happier.

Chapter 31

Noah

I couldn't be prouder of Sienna tonight if my life depended on it. I am so excited to see what we can create together as we both move forward away from the psychological burdens that held us back.

Sienna's additions on the violin were received so well by the crowd that I couldn't help but claim her in front of everyone. I wanted to share my joy with that audience. Selfishly, I also wanted to make sure everyone knows she isn't available. I've never had a famous girlfriend before and if I'm honest, it's going to take a little while for me to get used to it. Everyone's eyes on her. Men obsessing over her, trying to get her attention or close enough to touch her. Yeah, it's going to take some time to adjust.

After the show, Sienna wanted catch up with her stepsister so I left Romeo to watch over her while I went in search of the rest of the girls to tell them what an amazing job they did, and then on to my boys.

I'm finally ready to fucking celebrate.

Before I can reach our dressing room though, Callista flies into me from one of the side hallways with pure rage on her face. She's caught me alone because I left Romeo with Si.

"What the *fuck* was that, Kinkaid?" she demands.

"That was us taking control over our tour, Callista," I reply using her angry tone of voice right back at her.

"You had no right to make that addition without consulting me!"

"And you had no right to leak the news about Sienna and me," I fire back calmly this time. Callista isn't worth my emotions anymore. "Besides, I know you're releasing our contract, so I no longer have to ask your permission for anything."

The pure hatred in her features has me on high alert. It's not like Beautiful Deceit is the only band on her roster. Why isn't she at the record label comforting her other artists and assuring them everything is under control?

"Callista?" I ask, softening my voice. "Why are you so angry with us? Why did you want to be on this tour so badly? And why do you seem to hate *me* in particular?" I ask, genuinely curious what in the hell I did to earn this reaction from her from the very beginning.

She loses some of her fight as the truth spills out. "You don't remember a young girl named Reneé, do you?" she asks.

"Doesn't ring a bell. Where would I know her from?"

"Your first tour. No one was there," she laughs bitterly. "But Reneé was at every show, granted there were only eight of them back then. Desperate for a chance to gain your attention, she worked your merchandise table, made sure you always had water, sang your praises to all the patrons." She has a faraway gaze in her eyes like she's watching a movie screen only visible to her.

I make circles with my pointer finger asking her to get on with it.

Her eyes snap back to mine. "She believed in you when no one else did and three years ago she convinced her father to take a chance on you." She hands me a business card as she continues talking.

Callista Reneé Richardson, Apex Records

Oh shit, *she's* Reneé.

This hits hard because we had never been told how we'd been discovered. I certainly didn't know it was by Cal's daughter. The same daughter I raked over the coals for her lack of musical talent.

"My dad had just separated from his record label and was embarking on his own, but the dumb bastard had to sell my horses and our farm to make up for what he stole from his previous employer. To make it up to me, he let me pick the first band he signed. I picked you guys because I loved your music before anyone else had even heard it. But nothing's changed, you didn't give me the time of day back then, and you still don't."

"Callista, I barely even remember our first tour." At least not outside of the exhausting drives, the parking lots we overnighted in, and how little money we had. "We'd only been together as a band for two years at that point. We weren't in a place to take on collaborations or additional members," I argue, assuming that's what she means by not giving her the time of day.

Her laugh makes the hair on the back of my neck stand up.

"I never wanted to permanently be in your band, you pompous ass. I wanted to learn. I wanted to create. I wanted to make my own music, but you took my best opportunity away from me. Even after I gave you yours. Music is in my blood, Kinkaid. It's all I know, and I've never forgiven you for telling my father my voice was *flat and lacking inspiration.*" She uses air quotes around the last part.

Okay, so I guess she was told it was us who reviewed her demo. *Fucking thanks, Cal, you dense, heartless bastard.*

"I sang my heart out on that recording, and you called it flat," she says, starting to get angrier.

"So, what? You got your dad to give you a job so you could plan all this out for revenge? Wouldn't your time have been better spent working with a voice coach?" I ask in disbelief.

"No, of course I didn't," she clarifies, sounding offended. It's not lost on me she doesn't answer the comment about the voice coaching. "When it came time for me to find a job, I saw you were going on tour, and I asked my dad to help me get hired, that's all. This industry is all about who you know, after all. But it cut deep when you didn't even recognize me. I've been in the studio almost every time you have." She looks away briefly and her eyes fall to the floor. "My father never gave me another chance at making my own music, and he wouldn't allow me to take studio time away from paying artists." She clenches her teeth and adds, "And now no one else will either because of my last name."

I want to say *no, no one else will because you're fucking psycho, and you can't sing worth a damn,* but I hold my tongue.

I also don't point out she had the opportunity to turn her name into something good and respectable, but she let her immaturity and anger get in the way.

Instead, I opt for a different truth.

"When we're in the studio, all I see are the guys and that microphone. Ignoring you . . . it wasn't personal. Nor was our review of your music." I try to explain.

"Either way, I couldn't have known my stupid father would get his ass caught with Megs *again* and land me with the label. For a brief second, I owned you, and I wanted to take this opportunity away from you. The only problem was I didn't know how to ruin this for you because you're now the biggest fucking band on my label. I couldn't destroy you without hurting myself. But then you got hearts in your eyes for Sienna. So, I went after her instead. But it all fell apart quickly."

At least she has the decency to admit it.

She seems calmer now, and I know to keep my distance, but it doesn't stop me from wanting to offer her comfort. I had no idea she was so wrapped up in us. Or that anything I ever said impacted her life so much.

She's staring down at the floor, and I don't want to touch her to get her attention, so I bend at the hips and lower my torso to get her to look at me as I offer one final apology.

"Callista –"

"You're still the same amazing musician I remember, Noah, but you've grown up." I don't like the way she's eyeing my chest as she begins a slow circle around me and interrupts my attempted apology. "You aren't the soft, naïve boy I remember so well." She drags her eyes down my torso causing a shudder to rip through me. "It's so fucking unfair."

In a flash, she springs forward, knocking her body into mine, her hands are every where and I think she's about to start kissing me until I feel her fist land square against my cheek, snapping my head back.

She's out for blood. I don't retaliate partly because I don't want to go to prison and partly because I'm too stunned to move. Callista's unhinged eyes are mere inches from my face. My cheek is throbbing as I listen to the words she's spitting at me.

"You got the looks. You got the voice. You got the record deal because of *me,* and all I got was a life ruined by my selfish father and a career ruined by you! And for the record, it wasn't

Nicole who leaked those photos of you two years ago. It was me. Right after you told my father my demo was trash."

What? Shit. I owe Nicole a massive apology. Like, a galaxy-sized apology, but that'll have to wait.

"What the fuck is wrong with you?" I shout at Callista.

"Oh please, it was over between you two anyway. I just wanted you to suffer. I just wanted the golden boy to fall, even if it was only a couple of rungs down the ladder I helped him climb in the first place."

I think briefly about all the work the guys and I have put in over the years. We climbed that ladder ourselves. "Fuck you, Callista. You wouldn't have made it even if I'd lied about your demo. For the record, it wasn't just me who thought it sucked."

With that sentence, the lid barely containing her anger flies off, and Callista kicks me in the stomach, sending me backward, stumbling, unable to regain my balance. My arms are flailing by my sides to try and stop myself from falling, which means they *aren't* pushing her off me as she follows me down, throwing punch after punch. I land flat on my back and smash my head against the concrete floor. The breath leaves my lungs as Callista climbs on top of me, her fists pummeling my face and chest. I may be bigger than her, but her anger is larger than me.

I'm dazed and dizzy, and I don't have any perception of time so I'm not sure how long she stays like that, knocking the breath out of me with each blow, before she's hauled off me.

I hear a mix of voices moving around me, but I still haven't caught my breath enough to sit up and figure out what's going on, not to mention all I see are dark, blurry, ambiguous shapes, and I feel the warm trickle of blood behind my head and running from my nose into my mouth.

The next thing I know, Sienna is on her knees next to me. I know it's her based on the scent of vanilla that hits my busted nose. She cups the back of my head and I wince, "Ow, *fuck*," I hiss as her fingers graze the cut back there.

"Noah, are you okay? Can you hear me? Shit, he's bleeding, and I can't get his eyes to focus," she says to someone behind her.

I try to sit up for a second, but the room starts spinning so violently it causes my stomach to roil, so I immediately lay back down.

"I think he has a concussion," Sienna says to someone. "Go get medical. And get *her* the fuck out of my sight before there are two assault charges to file."

"She jumped on me," I try to explain, but I'm not sure my words are coming out. "I couldn't catch my balance." The effort it takes to speak is exhausting, and I'm out of breath all over again. *Damn, how hard did I hit my head?*

"Shh, it's okay. I've got you," Sienna coos next to me, my head now cradled in her lap.

Her lips brushing mine are the last thing I remember before I black out.

"Try to keep him awake as best you can for the next two to three hours. Unfortunately, I don't think he should perform tomorrow night."

I recognize the words, but I don't recognize the voice as I struggle to open my eyes. *Fuck, it's bright in here.* My eyelids slam shut immediately.

"No problem."

Matt.

"Come on, Noah. I need you to stay with me. Open your eyes, baby."

Sienna.

I blink behind my closed eyelids and slowly pry them open. My head feels like it's splitting in two. I open my mouth to speak but my throat is too dry, and nothing comes out but a strangled rasp.

"Matt, hand me his water," Sienna instructs from the side of my bed. Helping me sit up, she puts the straw in my mouth, and I feel like an absolute invalid.

"Do you remember what happened?" Sienna asks, concern marring her beautiful features.

"Yeah," I'm relieved to hear my voice come back fully after a few sips. "Callista fucking mauled me in the hallway backstage, and I fell backward and smashed my head on the floor," I recall.

"It's good he has no memory loss. And he didn't get sick, which is also in his favor. Keep the ice pack on his head and the ibuprofen handy. He should be fine in a couple of days."

I'm assuming the man is a doctor even though he doesn't introduce himself to me.

"Where's Callista?" I ask anyone who will answer.

"She's gone. Unless you want to press charges, I don't think you'll hear from her again, but I'm having a restraining order drawn up since she didn't seem to get the message the first time," Matt says. "Also, your first week of vacation starts now. You've all more than earned it. We'll reschedule the second L.A. show for later in the tour, and I cancelled the additional Seattle show as well. Your next concert will be in ten days."

I look around the room and realize I'm back in my bedroom of the penthouse suite of our hotel in L.A.

"Where are the guys?" I ask as the doctor packs up his things and heads for the door.

"They're in the living room," Sienna says, before immediately yelling, "Guys!"

In an instant, Brett, Ryan, and Sloan fill the doorway. The worry on their faces makes my heart warm.

"Jesus, Kinky, work on your balance, would you? We're all out there having a panic orgy," Sloan says, slumping against the wall when he sees me sitting up.

God, I love him.

"What the fuck is a panic orgy?" I ask, my smile making my head hurt worse, but I don't even care.

"You know, it's where we're all so worried about you that we sit around naked, dicks in hand, and discuss who's going to be our next lead singer," Brett says with a shit-eating grin on his face.

"Fuck you. Don't you have a dancer to bang?" I tease.

Matt wipes a hand down his face. "No more banging the dancers! Christ, what did I do, pick the four women on the planet you assholes can't resist? Stop sticking it in my employees!"

"For the record," Ryan's rational voice fills the space, "none of the recent drama was directly caused by Kinky and Sienna sleeping together. It was from your company doling out favors and hiring people without our consent. I'd just like to point that out."

"You know what? Fine," Matt says, resigned to losing this argument. "Everybody pick a dancer. Maybe if you all pair off with a fuck buddy you'll leave the groupies alone too, which *is* a direct cause of recent drama."

"Any word on that front?" I ask Brett, trying to stoically ignore the pounding in my head.

"Yeah," Brett gives a genuine smile. "Josh was able to match the girl from Bri's phone to videos at the club that showed her hands all over me." His face turns a nice shade of red so I probe, knowing there's more.

"And?"

He clears his embarrassment out of his throat, "The, uh, hallway by the exit door had cameras, which I should have known were there but was too drunk to think about, and they caught her giving me a blow job. I didn't even touch her except when she grabbed my hand and put it on the back of her head which was right before she stood up and pulled me into the bathroom, so . . ." he trails off.

I blow out a harsh breath.

"So, all that shit's over, then?" I ask, hopeful.

"For now," Matt says. "Guys, this is your life. The more famous you become, the more people will come after you. All of you," he says, looking at the guys and landing on Sienna. "I think we need to restructure your contracts with additional safety precautions and when you choose a new label – which will need to happen soon because the interest is very high – be sure you include provisions for NDAs, consent forms, protocols for dates and hook ups. You need to work on private social media accounts if you want to be on them at all outside of the band account. You need cell phone numbers listed under an ambiguous LLC and you need to make sure you don't give those numbers to anyone outside your circle. We can talk about the rest later. For now, focus on your plans for the next ten days off. I need details about where you want to go within the next two hours so I can get everything booked and the proper level of security in place. This tour has turned into a thing all its own, and if you thought you were famous two months ago, it's absolutely nothing compared to the demand there is for you now."

Matt leaves the room, but none of us speak.

That's a lot to process.

Sienna must sense the somber mood of the room because she stands up and yells loudly, "Congratulations, mother-fuckers!"

We all snicker as we give her our undivided attention.

"In the last eight weeks, you've kicked off the most amazing tour of the year, grown your fan base exponentially, escaped a shit contract, put multiple crazy people in your rearview mirror, *and* survived all of Matt's horrendous wardrobe choices." Growing slightly more serious, she adds, "People love you. Your *fans* love you. Not everyone is crazy but maybe we should act like they are. Your music is reaching people, and I am so damn proud of you guys, but this shit has gotten insane, and I won't handle it well if this," she points to me, lying in bed with a bruised cheek and a concussion, "is a common occurrence."

I can tell the guys are humbled by her speech as they all thank her and nod their heads in agreement.

"Okay, assholes, get out so I can have a moment with my woman." The words haven't even left my mouth when Sienna jumps back off the bed.

"I don't think so, Mr. Kinkaid. You heard the doctor. You have to take it easy for the next couple of days," she warns.

"Sienna, if you think I'm going to let a slight concussion stop me from being inside you in the next sixty seconds, you've got another thing coming. Callista was the last person who had her hands on me, and that's not okay."

"Bye!" Brett says, making a beeline for the door.

"I'm out," Ryan says as he follows.

"I've got nothing else going on," Sloan jokes, pretending to take a seat in the chair as Ryan yanks him by the arm toward the door.

"Then I'll help you shower. Slowly. Celibately," Sienna says, pulling back my covers.

I know I'm going to win the argument though when she

strips my shirt off and her pupils dilate. Her hands are shaking as she reaches for my pants.

"You okay, baby?" I tease.

"Jesus, Noah. That sight never gets old," she repeats her previous words to me, and I hope like hell that she always feels this way.

"It's all for you, Sienna. Only you."

Chapter 32

Sienna

I can keep Noah's hands off me for approximately zero seconds. I'm not complaining, but I don't want him to overdo it with a concussion, so I make him a deal.

"Put your hands here," I place one on the little grab bar in the shower, "And here." I place his other hand on the top of my head and then drop to my knees in the shower - after I wash every trace of Callista off my man's skin, of course. "Your only jobs are to coat my throat and not black out, Kinkaid."

"You drive a tough bargain, woman, but I'll do my best," he says with that tired smile I love.

I take my time. The doctor said to keep him awake for another two to three hours anyway, so I savor the flavor of his skin. The muscles of his stomach tighten beneath my fingers and my tongue. I can still smell *him* even through the soap.

I let the water pool as it runs down his glorious body and into my waiting mouth. Feeling his fingertips flex into my wet, tangled hair, I look up. His eyelids grow heavy with desire as he watches me on my knees for him.

"Sienna," he groans, and I know it's a request to hurry up.

His swollen cock bobs in front of my face, making an argument for itself.

I grab on to his thick shaft and feel him sway.

"Noah, do *not* fall down in this shower." The last thing I need is for him to knock his concussed brain out on the faucet.

"I make no promises," he teases.

I secure my right arm around his thighs to support him while my left gets to work matching the rhythm of my mouth.

"Fuck, Sienna."

Knowing he likes the vibrations, I hum the song I heard him singing in his sleep on the bus. Suddenly, I feel him tense up.

I pull back to look at him.

"How do you know that song?" he asks.

"You were humming it in your sleep."

"How does it end?" he asks.

I slip him back in my mouth and finish humming the song as I think it should go. When I carry out the last note, I feel him finally let go. He tries to pull back right before he comes, but I clutch him to me, wanting to drink him in.

When I look back up at him, he has his face in the water stream, and I'm not positive, but I think he's trying to hide a few tears.

"Noah, talk to me," I whisper.

He reaches behind him, turns the water off, then leads me out of the shower and wraps me in a towel. Dripping water all over the floor himself, he pulls me to him and kisses my forehead.

I feel the emotions swirling around him, but I can't place them. I'm not even sure he knows what he's feeling until he holds me at arms' length and inhales deeply.

"Fuck," he says, clearly nervous about something, making

me think he's about to tell me he made a mistake, or he doesn't want my help with the violin pieces anymore.

He must be able to sense the turmoil in my eyes and finally finds the strength to finish his thought.

"I'm in love with you, Sienna."

Well, I honestly didn't think that's where he was going, but I'm elated that he did. Because the truth is, "I love you too, Noah."

"I've never loved anyone like this before," he says, and I hear the slight tremble of fear in his voice.

"Me either, so, we'll just take it slowly, okay? Just promise you'll always talk to me and be honest with me," I beg, terrified of how fragile relationships created in the spotlight seem to be.

"Always." Reading me like only Noah can, he adds, "We're not everyone else, Si. We're you and me. And only we get to write our story."

I drop the towel and encircle my arms around him and hold on tightly.

I never loved Brad. I was always living in fear he would grow to resent me for one thing or another, and I could never let my guard down. Obviously, my relationships with my parents were full of the same tension. Yes, Josh claims to have been in love with me but even he couldn't put me at ease, always making me feel like I needed him to be the hero who saves the day instead of helping me realize I can be the source of my own strength. Bri loves me unconditionally, but she swore off relationships a long time ago and can't understand why I can't be physical with a partner without an underlying connection.

But Noah? Noah understands it all.

"Will you play that song for me?" he asks.

"Anytime you want."

We slip the hotel robes on, and I lead him to the living room where I deposited his violin when we came in tonight, but all the guys are hunched over the coffee table looking at something and their excited voices catch our attention.

"What are you guys looking at?" Noah asks.

"Are you supposed to be out of bed?" Ryan returns, ever the parental figure.

"Why would you *want* to be out of bed?" Sloan says, giving me an exaggerated once over in my robe, trying to goad Noah.

"I think it's okay for brief periods. I feel better after drinking water and taking a shower," Noah answers Ryan. But just in case, I still have my hand bunched in the back of his robe. "And Sloan, you'd better watch it. Check Sienna out like that again, and I'm taking your eyes out. You play by ear anyway."

Sloan laughs and waves him over. "Glad you're back, man. Come look at this."

On the coffee table is a map of a resort.

"What is this?" Noah asks.

"We were thinking Costa Rica for our week off. You guys in?"

The invitation catches me off guard. "Wait, you mean to tell me that you guys have spent every day together for the last three months, and you want to spend your week of freedom together, too?"

I mean, I like the girls and all, but I wasn't going to plan my vacation with them . . . okay, maybe Bri.

"Three months?" Brett asks, laughing. "Try five years. Don't forget we live together too."

Right.

"Don't your families want to see you?" I ask, wondering how normal families interact. I knew I wouldn't be spending any time with mine, but I figured the guys might want to see theirs, but now I'm realizing, they *are* each other's family.

"You'll get to meet some of them over the course of the tour, but you'll meet everyone right before our last show at home. They know what this lifestyle means. We see them when we can," Noah says, a sympathetic smile playing on his lips.

I'm momentarily stunned by his voice. Again. I didn't even know that someone's physical voice could bring me to my knees. The man could recite the alphabet, and I'd end up in a puddle in the middle of the floor.

It takes me far too long to realize Noah, as well as the rest of the guys, are looking at me, waiting for an answer.

"Oh, uh, yeah, Costa Rica. Sounds great." I say, momentarily stunned by my reality.

"Don't worry," Brett says, "We'll make sure you and Kinky have your own bungalow away from all of us. Bri said just make sure you save some time for her and the beach."

"Bri's coming?" I ask, startled by how excited that makes me.

"Yeah, we asked the other girls, too, but I guess they already made other plans," Brett explains with a dopey grin on his face.

"It'll be a contest to see who can still walk at the end," Sloan teases.

"Oh, Bri will be able to walk," Brett says, "because I'm not going to fuck her until she begs for it, and I can see her stubborn streak from a mile away." The wicked grin on his face tells me he's going to have fun wreaking havoc on my best friend and torturing her in the best kind of way.

It's also painfully obvious even after being cleared, Brett's a little gun-shy about getting back in the sack, and who could blame him? That shit will decimate your peace of mind.

A laugh tears from my throat at how right Brett is about Bri, just as Noah tugs me toward his violin case.

"Okay, sounds good, just give us the details. We're going to work on a song," Noah says impatiently.

Back in his room, he yanks open the belt to my robe and

moans against my mouth before swallowing my exhale. His hands are picking up speed as he pushes against me.

"Noah, slow down. You really do need to take it easy," I warn. "Get back in bed. I'll play. You sing." I grab the little notepad and pen every hotel room keeps on the bedside table and hand it to him. "Write down whatever comes to you."

He leans against the headboard and closes his eyes. He draws a deep breath, and I can't help but notice how peaceful he looks. A stark contrast to the stressed out, anxious, tightly wound man I met three months ago.

Standing naked in our hotel suite, I pull the bow across the strings and conjure up the melody I heard him sing in his sleep. I hear it in my bones, and now that I've been released from my own invisible burdens and feel freedom in playing again, I know exactly where to take this song. Based on the way his pen is moving furiously across the notepad, Noah hears it too.

His music has returned.

Epilogue

Six months later

Noah
Last Night of the Tour: Washington, D.C.

"I can't believe this is it. Where have the last eight months gone?" I muse out loud, savoring the last few minutes before our families arrive for the final meet and greet of the tour. We'll hang out with them for an hour before the doors open for the fans, and we play the finale of our North American tour.

Sienna and Bri are staples in our dressing room at this point, and Sienna has her legs stretched across my lap, her fingers flying as she types on her phone.

"Vorossi, if that's your brother blowing her up, I'm going to burn her phone," I tell Bri, only half kidding. Sienna is so into her message she doesn't even hear me.

"Doubtful," Bri said. "Josh is finally moving on. He started seeing someone a few weeks back. Finally got it through his head he couldn't compete with a rockstar of your caliber, Kinkaid," she teases.

"Don't stroke his ego, Bri," Brett says from across the room.

"I wouldn't have to if you'd let me stroke something else." I see Brett's nostrils flare from here.

"Not until you beg," he says, his voice dropping an octave, and I realize he's dead ass serious.

"Never gonna happen, drummer boy. I don't beg for *any* dick," she responds in a bored tone, picking at her nails.

Brett swears up and down he and Bri haven't slept together yet. I'm not sure I believe him, but he seems to be having fun pushing her buttons and trying to make her break after some bet they made six months ago on our trip to Costa Rica. In return, I think she's left him with blue balls more than he cares to admit. At this point, I'm not sure who will break first, but Sienna was right. God help us when they finally collide.

Sienna's phone pings again, and her perfect lips spread into a wide smile, her top teeth gently digging in to her bottom lip.

"What's got you so happy?" I ask.

"Other than Noah's dick, of course," Bri shoots from the table where she's working on her makeup. Maybe it should bother me that my girlfriend's best friend references my dick so often, but honestly, that's just Bri. She talks about dick constantly, and she's entirely unapologetic for the things she says, and I love that about her. It's exactly what Brett needs.

"Of course," I deadpan, causing her to chuckle.

"Sylvie just got here."

Sienna has stayed in touch with her younger stepsister since our show in L.A. The girls have formed quite the bond even though Sienna's mother couldn't bother to put forth more of an effort. Sienna paid to fly Sylvie to our last show tonight and arranged the whole thing with Greg, never speaking to her mother once. It just goes to show, family can look a lot of different ways.

A knock on our door followed by Matt's voice tells us our families are arriving and my heart hammers in my chest. My parents know about Sienna by now. Hell, the whole world knows about us, but this is their first time meeting her in person. Although they've Facetimed several times, it's always different when you're physically face-to-face.

"Are you ready, baby?" I ask, tapping her thighs.

"Ready."

Sienna began missing her silks routine more than either of us anticipated and she didn't like watching from backstage. She was born to perform. It took some restructuring, but we managed to give her a dual role. She's on her silks for four songs and plays violin for five songs and the combination suits her beautifully. Just like the deep purple and gold bodysuit she's currently wearing.

We walk down the hallway hand in hand and turn the corner into the large room, my eye catching Josh first. Bri runs right to him. I notice the brunette with stars in her eyes on his arm. Still holding Sienna's hand, we address them first since they're closest to us.

I hold my free hand out to Josh. "Vorossi, nice to see you again. I'm glad you could make it." Josh remains our attorney and has been vital in helping us negotiate the terms of our new record deal. Since Sienna and I have been together, he's backed off, giving her space which is the only reason he's both employed and still sporting all his teeth.

"Kinkaid," he says with a head nod. "Sienna," he says, his eyes swinging to my girlfriend. The appreciation is still there, but the lust has dimmed. "This is my girlfriend, Jessa."

"It's so nice to meet you!" Sienna gushes, pulling the girl in for a hug. "I'm Sienna, and this is my boyfriend, Noah."

Boyfriend.

It sounds so temporary. So indecisive. It's not enough.

Good thing I'm going to change that tonight. Is it fast? Not really. I've been waiting my whole life for Sienna. Besides, the bond we have is only coming around once. I'd be a fool to pass this opportunity up because of some preconceived notion that we're too young or haven't been together long enough.

I know what I want, and she's standing right next to me.

Jessa looks frozen in the moment, so I hold out a hand to shake hers. "Jessa, nice to meet you." My voice is a little raspier than usual because of the shows we've done the last two nights.

"Did you know your voice is *perfect*?" she asks shyly.

Sienna laughs beside me, and I place a kiss on her temple, a dopey grin on my face. "I've been told once or twice, but thank you."

Just then I hear my dad's voice above the others.

"Noah James, get your ass over here, son!"

"Please excuse us," I tell Josh and Jessa, leading Sienna toward the boisterous voice of my father.

I'm a grown ass man with a face that's recognized all over the world, and Jim Kinkaid doesn't give a *shit*. My father is still bigger than me and he lifts me up and twirls me around like a ragdoll. "Oh, it's good to see you, son."

"You, too, Dad. Hi, Mom," I say around my dad's shoulder as he sets me down.

"Hello, sweetheart." My mom kisses my cheek and wraps me in another hug as her eyes move past me to Sienna. She quickly abandons me for my girlfriend, her arms outstretched. "Sienna! You're even more gorgeous in person, honey, come here," she says pulling Sienna into an embrace. "I'm Gina but of course you already know that," my mother rambles. It dawns on me she's nervous. How cute.

"Mr. and Mrs. Kinkaid, it's so nice to finally meet you both in person," Sienna says.

"Oh, please, call us Jim and Gina," my dad replies, pulling Sienna away from my mom for a hug of his own.

It's a whirlwind of meeting, catching up, joking, family updates, and trying to say everything we've wanted to say since we left for tour eight months ago in the span of five minutes.

Sienna is eventually pulled away by Bri's parents and as my parents are catching up with Brett, I notice Ryan, hunkered in a corner talking to Emma, Brett's sister.

He towers over her even though she's almost 5'8". Her stance is shy but also playful, and I can't help but notice she's touching him every few seconds. He looks happy but also like he can't see anyone else in this room, including his bandmate who has now latched on to where the pair are standing.

I make my way over to the couple in the corner and pull Emma in for a side hug.

"Hey, Emmie. Congratulations on Stanford."

Brett's baby sister is a genius. Literally. She was just accepted into grad school at Stanford even though she isn't even twenty. She graduated high school with enough credits to start college as a junior and is hellbent on getting in and out of it as quickly as possible. Now that I'm watching her interact with Ryan, I'm wondering if he's some kind of driving force for that motivation. She's always portrayed herself as older and wiser than her actual age.

"Thanks, Noah." Her eyes wander to Sienna and Sylvie who are catching up on one of the couches. "Congratulations on the girlfriend. I'm glad to know *someone* knows it's possible to manage a band *and* have a life." She smiles at me sweetly, but something tells me the venom in her statement is aimed at Ryan.

"Uh, thanks?" I say awkwardly. I hadn't anticipated she'd

be so open about her attraction to Ry considering their age gap and Ryan's role in Brett's life, but it looks like I was wrong. I reach out and clasp Ry's hand and pull him in for a hug so I can deliver my message privately. "Just a head's up, Brett's noticed your cozy corner, so I'd change conversation partners sometime soon."

He lets out a heavy sigh, "Yeah, Kink. Thanks."

I make the rounds catching up with the rest of the band's families. Sloan is from the largest family of the group with two brothers and an older sister. It looks like a couple of his army buddies made it, too. He doesn't talk about his time in the army often and just like with Brett, I don't pry. He'll share what he wants when he wants to.

Being surrounded by everyone I love on the last night of this tour has me overwhelmed, and I'm so glad it isn't over yet.

I feel her in my space before I see her as she slips her arms around my waist and whispers in my ear, "Let's make this the show of a lifetime and then go home."

Home.

The guys and I get to go home tonight.

And Sienna is coming with me.

Sienna

I've never felt so many emotions at once.

Stepping through the front door of the guys' house, I can't decide if I want to drink a bottle of champagne, fall asleep immediately, spend the next three hours running my tongue along every inch of Noah's skin, or just sit and absorb.

"Fuuuuuuck, it feels good to be home," Sloan says dramatically, dropping his bag unceremoniously inside the door.

"Damn, I missed this place," Brett agrees, walking straight to the kitchen.

"I'm going to bed. If I'm not awake by Thursday, someone come get me up." Ryan trudges toward the stairs before pausing and turning back to face the living room and entryway. "I love you fuckers, and that was the most incredible eight months of my life." Before anyone can respond, he turns and disappears up the steps.

Brett comes back in the room raising a beer in Ryan's direction, "You too, man," he says, even though Ryan can't hear him.

"Come on, Si. Let's go to bed."

Noah grabs my bag off my shoulder and pulls me along behind him.

"Goodnight, guys!" I yell, elated to still be with them. The relationship of this band is nothing like I've ever experienced or expected. They've all become some odd mix of friends, brothers, and protectors.

"Shower first?" Noah asks. The fatigue of the tour clear in his unsteady voice.

"Please."

I had expected a communal bathroom, but it seems they each have their own. Either that or Noah has the master bedroom.

I start reluctantly peeling off the sweatpants I have on but Noah gently bats my hands away. "Let me."

"Baby, you're so cold your hands are shaking. Here, I can do it. You get the hot water going," I say as I try to undress myself. "Why the hell is your a/c on blast?" I yell to Noah in the bathroom. It's November in D.C. and cold as shit outside.

I'm taking my hair down and the long waves cascade over my shoulders. I didn't have it cut once while we were on the road, and it hangs down over my breasts, reminding me of the Starbucks logo.

When Noah turns back around, his face is pale and his jaw is trembling.

"Noah? What's wrong?"

"Fuck this," he grumbles under his breath but still loud enough for me to hear. He pulls my naked body from the bathroom and brings me to stand in front of his dresser. He slides one of his sweatshirts over my head and helps me into another pair of sweatpants before donning himself in similar attire.

"Noah, what the hell?" I ask alarmed, but it's like he doesn't even hear me. He rummages around the bottom of the bag he had on tour and puts something in his pocket. I can't see what though because his back is to me.

His eyes are shining when he turns to face me.

"Come with me." Opening his bedroom door, he yells loudly for Ryan and Sloan. "Meet me in the living room!"

"Baby, they're probably asleep already. Everyone's exhausted."

"They'll get over it," he says with a smile on his face which makes me relax a little.

When we get to the living room, Brett has another – or maybe the same, I'm not sure – beer in his hand and a coy smile on his face. "You couldn't wait, could you?"

"Fuck no," Noah replies with a smile, and I've never been more lost in my life.

"I knew I should have made you bet money on it."

"Wait for what?" I ask as Ryan and Sloan slip into the room and take seats on the couch looking adorable in sweatpants and socks with no shirts. Ryan looks half asleep, but this is how the guys operate. One calls, they all come running.

God, I love them. All of them. But I'm hopelessly *in love* with Noah James Kinkaid.

My heart rate kicks up as I try to figure out what's going on just as Noah drops to one knee.

What the actual fuck?

"Damn, I wanted to hold out and do this with a better back drop and a better plan, but I won't sleep until I know the answer. Sienna, you were the most unexpected thing about this tour. Somewhere along the way you burrowed deep in my heart and soul, and I can't imagine what would happen to me if you left. I want to make music and chase our dreams together for the rest of our lives. I want to walk off stage every time and know you're waiting for me just like I want to be in the wings at every performance of yours. Sienna Marie Kennedy, will you marry me?"

I can't see him clearly through my tears, but that voice will always lead me home. I nod fervently until I can manage to choke out a whisper.

"Hell yes."

He lunges off the ground and wraps his arms around me before impatiently shoving his ring on my finger like he can't claim me fast enough.

Two seconds after that, there are three more massive bodies enveloping us, and I hear a champagne cork pop right before cold liquid splashes me in the face.

Wait, if the guys are all wrapped around Noah and I, who's spraying the champagne?

"Congratulations, bitch!" Bri's voice rings out.

I squeal as the guys slowly back away and my best friend in the whole world is standing in the doorway to the kitchen. I throw myself at her and squeal, "What are you doing here? When did you get here? It's two in the morning!"

"Brett called me. He said he knew Noah wouldn't be able to hold out for three more days like he'd planned and asked if I wanted to be here."

"But what if I *had* held out?" Noah says indignantly.

"Then I was going to take the opportunity to make her

pussy scream for me until sunrise," Brett says without cracking a smile.

"Maybe we could do that anyway," Bri says, a little breathless.

"Does that mean you're ready to beg for it?"

"Beg? Still no. Ask politely and make it worth your while? Absolutely," she responds.

"Okay, well while you two are figuring it out, I'm going to go make love to my fiancée," Noah laughs.

His words from a lifetime ago flash through my brain. *I'm saving that for the woman I marry one day.*

"Noah?" I whisper in his ear as he leads me up the stairs.

"Yeah?"

"Does this mean I get to feel you tonight? *All* of you? With nothing between us?"

"Damn right it does. I've been saving it just for you."

It doesn't matter that it's two a.m. It doesn't matter we're both tired enough to sleep for a week straight. Along the course of the tour, we helped each other banish our demons and finally broke the surface, freeing ourselves of the current of invisible burdens that threatened to pull us under. Now, nothing can stop us from living our lives on our terms.

Acknowledgments

Every book baby is precious, but this one stole my heart. I wrote this book in six weeks but then spent three months editing, proofreading, perfecting, because Noah and Sienna deserved the best.

I gave them everything I had.

A huge thank you to my beta readers: Kelsey, Raven, and Emilie. Their feedback and recommendations are critical to helping me make the story the best it can be for my readers!

I would also like to thank my ARC readers. My hype team. The ones who decide if my book is worth reading and spreading the word about. I appreciate all of you sharing your time with the characters who live in my head and for creating amazing posts I can add to my Instagram stories since technology and I do not get along at all!

A major shoutout to my editor, Stephanie. Hers was not an easy job since I have NO CLUE how to use a comma, and I love to italicize things unnecessarily. I appreciate your attention to detail!

As always and forever, thank you to my husband, who never fusses when I become a recluse for hours at a time to write and who encourages me to make sure I get a few words in everyday to keep the "mojo" alive. I'll never be able to repay you for all you've done for me. Just know, I love you with all my heart! You are my person. My best friend. And I'm so lucky you have a personality that matches every one of mine.

Lastly, the hugest thank you to of all to my readers. Without you, I couldn't do this. I understand your time is precious and your most valuable asset. Thank you for sharing your time with the characters in my stories. I hope you gained encouragement from Noah and Sienna to face whatever threatens to bring you down.

Contemporary Stand Alone Romance Books:

What Are You To Me – Forbidden Romance, Step-Siblings

From Purgatory to Paradise – Childhood Best Friends, Sibling Rivalry

All My Choices Led Me Here – Workplace Romance, Medical Romance, Surgeon/Therapist

Break My Rules – Workplace Romance, Sworn-off Relationships, Pilot/Flight Attendant

Series:

Nothing Lasts Forever Series:
Submit
Defy
Reign

Beautiful Deceit Series
Invisible Burdens - Noah & Sienna
Brett and Bri's Book Coming Soon
Book 3 - Coming Summer 2024
Book 4 - Coming Fall 2024

A Note From the Author

Let's Connect! Find me on Instagram @Jillian_wray_author

Don't forget to leave a review! Loved it? Hated it? DNF'd it? Let me know, just remember: constructive feedback is always welcome . . . being an asshole is not.

XOXO,
Jillian D. Wray

About the Author

Jillian lives in North Carolina with her incredibly supportive husband and three awesome stepkids. After over ten years in the healthcare industry, it was time to pursue a new passion. An avid reader her whole life, she sat down one night and let the words begin to flow. Four hours and ten thousand words later, a love of writing was discovered.

She writes fast-paced, spicy, bingeable reads that encourage self-discovery and come with all the angst and excitement of a new relationship.

When she isn't reading or writing, you can either find her in her vegetable garden, at CrossFit™, or on a plane headed toward her next adventure.